the day we met

the day we met

a novel

rowan coleman

ballantine books

new york

A Ballantine Books Trade Paperback Original

Copyright © 2014 by Rowan Coleman

Reading group guide copyright © 2015 by Penguin Random House LLC

Published in the United States by Ballantine Books, an imprint of Random House, a division of Penguin Random House LLC, New York.

BALLANTINE and the HOUSE colophon are registered trademarks of Penguin Random House LLC.
RANDOM HOUSE READER'S CIRCLE & Design is a registered trademark of Penguin Random House LLC.

Originally published in the United Kingdom as *The Memory Book* by Ebury Publishing, a division of Random House Group, London.

Grateful acknowledgment is made to Farrar, Straus and Giroux, LLC, for permission to reprint "An Arundel Tomb" from *The Complete Poems of Philip Larkin* by Philip Larkin, edited by Archie Burnett, copyright © 2012 by The Estate of Philip Larkin, Introduction copyright © 2012 by Archie Burnett. Reprinted by permission of Farrar, Straus & Giroux, LLC.

Library of Congress Cataloging-in-Publication Data
Coleman, Rowan.
The day we met : a novel / Rowan Coleman.
pages cm
ISBN 978-0-553-39412-2   eBook ISBN 978-0-553-39413-9
1. Dementia—Fiction. 2. Domestic fiction. I. Title.
PR6103.O4426D39 2015
823'.92—dc23   2014045330

Printed in the United States of America on acid-free paper

www.randomhousereaderscircle.com

2 4 6 8 9 7 5 3 1

Book design by Elizabeth A. D. Eno

For my mum, Dawn

Time has transfigured them into
Untruth. The stone fidelity
They hardly meant has come to be
Their final blazon, and to prove
Our almost-instinct almost true:
What will survive of us is love.

—"An Arundel Tomb," Philip Larkin

the day we met

prologue

Greg is looking at me; he thinks I don't know it. I've been chopping onions at the kitchen counter for almost five minutes, and I can see his reflection—inside out, convex and stretched—in the chrome kettle we got as a wedding present. He's sitting at the kitchen table, checking me out.

The first time I noticed him looking at me like this I thought I must have had something stuck in my teeth, or a cobweb in my hair, or something, because I couldn't think of any reason my sexy young builder would be looking at me. Especially not on that day, when I was dressed in old jeans and a T-shirt, with my hair scraped back into a bun, ready to paint my brand-new attic room—the room that marked the beginning of everything.

It was the end of his last day; he'd been working at the house for just over a month. It was still really hot, especially up there, even with my new Velux windows open. Covered in sweat, he climbed down the newly installed pull-down ladder. I gave him a pint glass of lemonade rattling with ice cubes, which he drank in one go, the muscles in his throat moving as he swallowed. I think I must have sighed out loud at his sheer gloriousness because he looked curiously at me. I laughed and shrugged, and he smiled and then looked at his boots. I poured him another glass of lemonade and went back to my last box—Caitlin's things—yet another box of stuff I couldn't bring myself to throw out and that I knew I'd be clogging up the garage with instead. It was then that I sensed him looking at me. I touched my hair, expecting to find something there, and ran my tongue over my teeth.

"Everything okay?" I asked him, wondering if he was trying to work out how to tell me that my bill had doubled.

"Fine," he said, nodding. He was—is—a man of few words.

"Good, and are you finished?" I asked, still prepared for bad news.

"Yep, all done," he said. "So . . ."

"Oh God, you want paying. I'm so sorry." I felt myself blush as I rooted around in the kitchen drawer for my checkbook, which wasn't there—it was never where it was supposed to be. Flustered, I looked around, feeling his gaze on me as I tried to remember where I'd last had it. "It's around here somewhere. . . ."

"There's no hurry," he said.

"I had it when I was paying some bills, so . . ." I just kept wittering on, desperate, if I'm honest, for him to be gone and for me to be able to breathe out and drink the half bottle of grigio that was waiting for me in the fridge.

"You can pay me another time," he said. "Like maybe when you come out with me for a drink."

"Pardon?" I said, stopping halfway through searching a drawer that seemed to be full only of rubber bands. I must have mishcard.

"Come out with me for a drink?" he asked tentatively. "I don't normally ask my clients out, but . . . you're not normal."

I laughed and it was his turn to blush.

"That didn't quite come out the way I thought it," he said, folding his arms across his chest.

"You're asking me on a date?" I said, just to confirm it, because the whole thing seemed so absurd that I had to say it out loud to test I'd got it right. "Me?"

"Yes, you coming?"

"Okay," I said. It had all seemed so perfectly plausible to him: him and me, ten years between us, going out on a date. "Why not?"

That was the first time I noticed him looking at me, looking at me with this sort of mingled heat and joy that I instantly felt mirrored inside me, like my body was answering his call in a way that my conscious mind had no control over. Yes, ever since then I've felt his looks long before I've seen them. I feel the hairs standing up on the back of my neck, and a sense of anticipation washing over me in one long delicious shudder, because I know that soon after he looks at me, he will be touching me, kissing me.

Now I feel his hand on my shoulder and I lean my cheek against his fingers.

"You're crying," he says.

"I'm chopping onions," I say, putting down the knife and turning round to face him. "You know that all Esther will eat is Mummy's homemade lasagna? Here, you should watch me make it, so you know the recipe. First, chop the onions . . ."

"Claire . . ." Greg stops me from picking up the knife again, and turns me toward him. "Claire, we have to talk about it, don't we?"

He looks so uncertain, so lost and so reluctant, that I want to say no—no, we don't have to talk about it, we can just pretend that today is like yesterday, and all the days before that when we didn't know any better. We can pretend not to know, and who knows how long we might be able to go on like this, so happy, so perfect?

"She likes a lot of tomato purée in the sauce," I say. "And also a really big slug of ketchup . . ."

"I don't know what to do or say," Greg says, his voice breaking on an inward breath. "I'm not sure how to be."

"And then, just at the end, add a teaspoon of Marmite."

"Claire," he says with a sob, and draws me into his arms. And I stand there in his embrace with my eyes closed, breathing in his scent, my arms at my side, feeling my heart pounding in my chest. "Claire, how are we going to tell the children?"

friday, march 13, 1992

caitlin is born

This is the bracelet they gave you in the hospital—pink because you are a girl. It says: "Baby Armstrong." They put it on your ankle, and it kept slipping off because you were so tiny, a whole month early, to the day. You were supposed to be an April baby. I had imagined daffodils and blue skies and April showers, but you decided to be born one month early on a cold wet Friday, Friday the thirteenth, no less, not that we were worried about that. If anyone was ever born to overcome bad omens it was you, and you knew it, greeting the world with an almighty shout— not a cry or a wail, but a roar of intent, I thought. A declaration of war.

There wasn't anybody there with us for a long time. Because you were early, and Gran lived far away. So for about the first six hours it was just you and me. You smelled sweet, like a cake, and you felt so warm and . . . exactly right. We were at the end of the ward and we kept the curtain closed around us. I could hear the other mums talking, visitors coming and going, babies crying and fussing, but I didn't want to be part of it. I didn't want to be part of anything ever again except for you and me. I held you, so tiny and scrunched up like a new bud waiting to flower, and I just looked at you, slumbering against my breast, a deep frown on your tiny face, and I told you it was all going to be fine, because you and I were together: we were the whole universe, and that was all that mattered.

I

claire

I've just got to get away from my mother: she is driving me mad, which would be funny if I wasn't already that way inclined. No, I'm not mad, that's not right. Although I feel pretty angry.

It was the look on her face when we came out of the hospital appointment; the look she had all the way home. Stoical, stalwart, strong but bleak. She didn't say the words, but I could hear them buzzing around in her head: "This is so typically Claire. To ruin everything just when it's getting good."

"I'll move in," she says, even though she blatantly already has, silently secreting herself in the spare bedroom, like I wouldn't notice her, arranging her personal items on the shelf in the bathroom. I knew she would come when she found out. I knew she would and I wanted her to, I suppose; but I wanted to ask her, or for her to ask me. Instead she simply arrived, all hushed tones and sorrowful glances. "I'll move into the spare room."

"No, you won't." I turn to look at her as she drives. She is a very careful driver, slow and exacting. I am not allowed to drive anymore, not since I killed that postbox, which carried a far more expensive fine than you would perhaps imagine, because it belongs to Her Majesty. It must be the same if you run over a corgi: if you run over a corgi, you probably get sent to the Tower. My mother is such a careful driver, and yet she never looks in the rearview mirror when she's reversing. It's like she feels that, in this one aspect, it's safer simply to close her eyes and hope for the best. I used to love driving; I loved the freedom and the independence and knowing that, if I felt like it, I could go anywhere I fancied. I don't like that my car keys have disappeared, gone without me being allowed even to kiss them goodbye, hidden away in a place where I will never find them. I know because I've tried. I could still drive, I think. As long as no one put anything in my way.

"It's not come to you moving in yet," I insist, although we both know she has already moved in. "There's still lots of time left when I won't need any help at all. I mean, listen to me. I can still talk and think about . . ." I wave my arm, causing her to duck and look under my hand, which I tuck apologetically back in my lap. "Things."

"Claire, this isn't something you can stick your head in the sand about. Trust me, I know."

Of course she knows: she's lived through this before, and now, thanks to me, or strictly speaking thanks to my father and his rogue DNA, she has to live through it again. And it's not as if I'll do anything sensible like dying nice and neatly with all my faculties intact, holding her hand and thanking her, with a serene look on my face as I impart words of wisdom to live by to my children. No, my annoyingly quite young, reasonably fit body will linger on long after I've checked out of my mushy little brain, right up until the moment when I forget how to breathe in and out and in again. I know that's what she is thinking. I know the last thing in the world she wants is to watch her daughter fade away and shrivel up, just like her husband did. I know it's breaking her heart and that she's doing her best to be brave, and stand by me, and yet ... It makes me so angry. Her goodness makes me angry. All my life I've been trying to prove that I can grow up enough to not need her to rescue me all the time. All my life I've been wrong.

"Actually, Mum, I *am* the one who can stick my head in the sand," I say, staring out of the window. "I *am* the one who can completely ignore what is happening to me, because most of the time I won't even notice."

It's funny: I say the words out loud, and feel the fear, there in the pit of my stomach, but it's like it isn't part of me. It really is like it's happening to someone else, this terror.

"You don't mean that, Claire," Mum says crossly, as if she really thinks that I mean I don't care, and not that I'm just saying it to annoy her. "What about your daughters?"

I say nothing because my mouth is suddenly thick with words that won't form properly or mean anything like what I need them to mean. So I stay quiet, looking out of the window, at the houses slipping past, one by one. It's almost dark already; living room lamps are switched on, TVs flicker behind curtains. Of course I care. Of course I'll miss it, this life. Steam-filled kitchens on winter evenings, cooking for my daughters, watching them grow: these are the things I will never experience. I'll never know whether Esther will always eat her peas one by one, or if she will always be blond. If Caitlin will travel across Central America, like she plans to, or whether she'll do something completely different that she hasn't even dreamed of yet. I won't ever know what that undreamed wish will be. They'll never lie to me about where they are going, or come to me with their problems. These are the things I'll miss, because I'll be somewhere else and I won't even know what I'm missing. Of course I bloody care.

"I suppose they'll have Greg." My mum sounds skeptical as she ploughs on, determined to discuss what the world will be like after I'm no longer in it, even though it shows a quite spectacular lack of tact. "That's if he can hold it together."

"He will," I say. "He will. He's a brilliant father."

I am not sure if that is true, though. I'm not sure if he can take what is happening, and I don't know how to help him. He is such a good man, and a kind one. But lately, ever since the diagnosis, he is becoming a stranger to me day by day. Every time I look at him he is standing further away. It's not his fault. I can tell he wants to be there, to be stalwart and strong for me, but I think perhaps the enormity of it all, of all this happening when really we've only just started out on our life together, is chipping away at him. Soon I won't recognize him at all; I know I already find it hard to recognize the way I feel about him. I know he is the last great love of my life, but I don't feel it anymore. Somehow Greg is the first thing I am losing. I remember it, our love affair, but it's as though I've dreamed it, like Alice through the looking glass.

"You, of all people." Mum cannot help lecturing me, telling me off for being in possession of the family's dark secret, like I brought it on myself by being so damned naughty. "You, who knew what it was like to grow up without a father. We need to make plans for them, Claire. Your girls are losing their mother and you need to make sure they will be okay when you aren't capable of looking after them anymore!"

She brakes suddenly at a zebra crossing, causing a chorus of horns to sound behind her, as a little girl who looks far too young to be out on her own hurries across the road, huddled against the rain. In the glare of Mum's headlights I can see she's carrying a thin blue plastic bag with what looks like four pints of milk inside, bumping against her skinny legs. I hear the break in Mum's voice, hovering just below the frustration and anger. I hear the hurt.

"I do know that," I say, suddenly exhausted. "I do know that I have to make plans, but I was waiting, I was hoping. Hoping I might get to enjoy being married to Greg and grow old with him, hoping that the drugs might slow things down for me. Now I know that . . . well, now that I know there is no hope, I'll get a lot more organized, I promise. Make a wall chart, keep a rota."

"You can't hide from this, Claire." She insists on repeating herself.

"Don't you think I know that?" I shout. Why does she always do that? Why does she always push me until I shout at her, as if she isn't satisfied I'm really listening until she has made me lose my temper? It's always been that way between us: love and anger mixed up in almost every moment we have together. "Do you think I don't know what I have done, giving them this shitty life?"

Mum pulls into the drive in front of a house—my house, I realize a second too late—and I feel the tears coming against my will. Slamming out of the car, I don't go into the house, but instead walk into the rain, dragging the edges of my cardigan around me, heading defiantly up the street.

"Claire!" Mum shouts after me. "You can't do this anymore!"

"Watch me," I say, but not to her, just into the rain, feeling the tiny droplets on my lips and tongue.

"Claire, please!" I just about hear her, but I keep walking. I'll show her; I'll show them all, especially the people that won't let me drive. I can still walk; I can still bloody walk! I haven't forgotten how to do that yet. I'll just go to the end of the road, where the other one crosses over it, and then turn back. I'll be like Hansel following a trail of breadcrumbs. I won't go far. I just need to do this one thing. Go to the end of the road, turn around and come back. Although it is getting darker now, and the houses round here all look the same: neat, squat 1930s semis. And the end of the road isn't as near as I thought it was.

I stop for a moment, feeling the rain driving into my head, tiny cold needles of icy water. I turn around. My mum isn't behind me: she hasn't followed me. I thought she might, but she hasn't. The street is empty. Did I reach the end of the road and turn around already? I am not sure. Which direction was I walking in? Am I going to or from, and to where? The houses on either side of the road look exactly the same. I stand very still. I left my home less than two minutes ago, and now I am not sure where it is. A car drives past me, spraying freezing water onto my legs. I didn't bring my phone, and anyway I can't always remember how to use it anymore. I've lost numbers. Although I look at them and know they are numbers, I've forgotten which ones are which, and which order they come in. But I can still walk, so I begin to walk in the direction that the car that soaked me was going. Perhaps it's a sign. I will know my house when I see it because the curtains are bright-red silk and the light shining through them makes them glow. Remember that: I have red glowing curtains at the front of my house that one of my neighbors said made me look "loose." I will remember the red glowing curtains. I'll be home really soon. Everything will be fine.

The appointment at the hospital hadn't exactly gone well. Greg had wanted to come but I told him to go and finish the conservatory he was building. I told him that nothing the doctor said would make our mortgage need to be paid any the less, or mean that we don't have to keep feeding the children. It hurt him that I hadn't wanted him there, but he didn't realize that I couldn't cope with trying to guess what the look on his face meant at the same time as guessing what I felt myself. I knew if I took Mum she would just say everything in her head, which is better. It's better than hearing really terrible news and wondering if your husband is sorry that he ever set eyes on you, that of all the people in the world he could have chosen, he chose you. So I wasn't in the best frame of mind—pun intended—when the doctor sat me down to go through the next round of test results. The tests they had given me because everything was happening much faster than they'd thought it would.

I can't remember the doctor's name because it's very long with a great many syllables, which I think is funny. I mentioned this as Mum and I sat there waiting for him to finish looking at the notes on his screen and deliver the bad news, but no one else was amused. There's a time and a place for gallows humor, it seems.

The rain is driving down faster now, and heavier; I wished I'd flounced off with my coat. After a while all the roads round here start to look the same: 1930s semis, in row after row, either side of the street. I'm looking for curtains, aren't I? What color?

I turn a corner and see a little row of shops, and I stop. I've come out for a coffee, then? This is where I come on a Saturday morning with Greg and Esther for a pain au chocolat and a coffee. It's dark, though, and cold and wet. And I don't seem to have a coat on, and I check my hand, which is empty of Esther's, and for a moment I hold on tight to my chest, worrying that I've forgotten her. But I didn't have her when I started. If I'd had her when I started, I'd be carrying her monkey, which she always insists on taking out but never wants to carry herself. So I've come here for coffee. I'm having some me time. That's nice.

I head across the road, grateful for the rush of warm air that greets me as I enter the café. People look up at me as I walk in through the door. I suppose I must look quite a sight with my hair plastered to my face.

I wait at the counter, belatedly realizing that I am shivering. I must have forgotten my coat. I wish I could remember why I came out for coffee. Am I meeting someone? Is it Greg? I come here sometimes with Greg and Esther for a pain au chocolat.

"You all right, love?" the girl, who's about Caitlin's age, asks me. She is smiling, so perhaps I know her. Or perhaps she is just being friendly. A woman sitting with her toddler buggy, just to my left, pushes it a little further away from me. I must look strange, like a lady recently emerged from a lake. Haven't they ever seen a wet person before?

"Coffee, please," I say. I feel the weight of change in my jeans pocket, and produce it in my fist. I can't remember how much the coffee is here, and when I look at the board over the counter where I know the information is displayed, I am lost. I hold out the coins in the palm of my hand and offer them up.

The girl wrinkles her nose, as if money I've touched might somehow be tainted, and I feel very cold now and very lonely. I want to tell her why I am hesitating, but the words won't come—not the right ones, anyway. It's harder to say things out loud than think them in my head. It makes me scared to say anything to anyone I don't know, in case I say something so ludicrous they just cart me away and lock me up, and by that time I've forgotten my name and . . .

I glance toward the door. Where is this café? I went to the hospital with Mum, we saw the consultant, Mr. Thingy, I couldn't remember his name, I thought that was quite funny, and now I am here. But I can't think why I am here, or even where here is. I shudder, taking the coffee and the brown coins that the girl has left on the counter; and then I go and sit down, very still. I feel like if I move suddenly, I might trip some hidden trap, and that something will harm me or I might fall off something. I feel like I might fall very far. I sit still and concentrate hard on how come I am here and how on earth I will leave. And where I will go. Little pieces come back to me—fragments rushing forward with pieces of information that I must somehow decode. The world is shattered all around me.

I'm not responding to the treatment, that much I know. It was always likely. The odds of the drugs doing anything for me were just the same as flipping a coin and calling heads: fifty-fifty. But everyone hoped that, for me, the treatment would make all the difference. Because I am so young, because I have two daughters, and one of them is only three and one will be left to pick up the pieces. They all hoped it would work for me, and work better than anyone—even the doctor with the long and difficult name—ever thought possible. And I too hoped for the groundbreaking miracle that would change everything. It seemed right that fate or God should allow me, of all people, some special dispensation because of my extenuating circumstances. But fate or God has not done that: whichever one it is that is having a good laugh at my expense has done the opposite. Or perhaps it's nothing so personal. Perhaps it's just genealogical accidents stretching back millennia that have brought me to this moment in time when I am the one chosen to bear the consequences. I am deteriorating much faster than anyone thought I would. It's to do with these little emboli. I can remember that word perfectly well, but I have no idea what the metal stirring thing that came with my coffee is called. But the word "emboli" is quite beautiful, musical almost, poetic. Tiny little blood clots exploding in my brain. It's a new feature, not something the experts expected. It makes me almost unique in the world, and everyone at the hospital is very excited about it, even though they try to pretend they are not. All I know is that every time one pops up, some more of me is gone for good—another memory, a face or a word, just lost, like me. I look around me, feeling colder now than before, and realize I feel afraid. I have no idea how to get home. I'm here, and I feel sane, but leaving this place seems impossible.

There are Christmas decorations hanging from the ceiling, which is odd. I don't remember it being Christmas; I am sure it is not Christmas. But what if I've been here for weeks? What if I left home and just walked and walked and didn't stop, and now I'm miles from anywhere and months have gone by and they all think I am dead? I should call Mum. She'll be angry with me for running off. She tells me that if I want her to treat me like an adult, I need to behave like an adult. She says it's all about trust. And I say, well, don't go through my things, then, bitch. I don't say the bitch bit out loud.

I'd text her, but she doesn't have a phone. I keep telling her, this is the twentieth century, Mum, get with the program. But she doesn't like them. She doesn't like the fiddly buttons, she reckons. But I wish Mum were here; I wish she were here to take me home, because I am not sure where I am. I look intently around the café. What if she's here and I have forgotten what she looks like?

Wait, I am ill. I am not a girl anymore. I am ill and I have come out for a coffee and I can't remember why. My curtains are a color, and they glow. Orange, maybe. Orange rings a bell.

"Hello." I look up. There's a man. I am not supposed to talk to strangers so I look back down at the table. Perhaps he will go away. He does not. "Are you okay?"

"I'm fine," I say. "Well, I'm cold."

"Would you mind if I sit here? There's nowhere else." I look around, and the café is busy, although I can see other empty chairs. He looks okay, even nice. I like his eyes. I nod. I wonder if I'll have enough words to be able to talk to him.

"So you came out without a coat?" he asks, gesturing at me.

"Looks like it!" I say carefully. I smile, so as not to scare him. He smiles in return. I could tell him I am ill. He might help me. But I don't want to. He has nice eyes. He is talking to me like I'm not about to drop down dead at any second. He doesn't know anything about me. Neither do I, but that's beside the point.

"So what happened?" He chuckles, looking bemused, amused. I find I want to lean toward him, which I suppose makes him magnetic.

"I only popped out for a pint of milk," I tell him, smiling. "And locked myself out. I share a flat with three girls and my . . ." I stop short of saying my baby. For two reasons. First, because I know that this is now, and that it was years ago when I shared a flat with three girls, and back then I didn't even have a baby. Secondly, because I don't want him to know that I've got a baby, a baby who is not a baby anymore. Caitlin, I have Caitlin, who is not a baby. She will be twenty-one next year, and my curtains are ruby-red and glow. I remind myself that I am not in a position to flirt: I'm a married mother of two.

"Can I buy you another coffee?" He signals to the woman behind the counter, who smiles at him as if she knows him. I find it reassuring that the café woman likes him too. I'm losing the ability to judge people by their expressions, and by those little nuances that let you know what a person is thinking and feeling. He might be looking at me like I am a nutter. All I have to go on is his nice eyes.

"Thank you." He is kind and he is talking to me just like I'm a person. No, not that; I *am* a person. I am still a person. I mean he's talking to me like I'm me, and I like it. It's warming me through, and I feel oddly happy. I miss feeling happy—just happy, without feeling that every moment of joy I experience now must also be tinged with sadness.

"So, you're locked out. Is someone going to ring you when they get back, or bring you a key?"

I hesitate. "There will be someone in, in a bit." I have no idea if that's a lie. "I'll wait a while and then go back." That *is* a lie. I don't know where I am or how to get to back, wherever that is.

He chuckles, and I look at him sharply. "Sorry." He smiles. "It's just that you do actually look like a drowned rat, and a very pretty one, if you don't mind my saying so."

"I don't mind you saying so," I say. "Say more like that!"

He laughs again.

"I'm a fool," I say, warming to my new not-ill status. It feels good to be just me, and not me with the disease, the thing that now defines me. I've found a moment of peace and normality in this maelstrom of uncertainty, and it is such a relief. I could kiss him with gratitude. Instead I talk too much. I'm famous for talking too much; it used to be a thing about me that people enjoyed. "I always have been. If something can go wrong, it happens to me. I don't know why, but it's like I'm a magnet for mishap. Ha, 'mishap.' There's a word you don't hear often enough." I rattle on and I don't really care what I am saying out loud, conscious only that here I am, a girl talking to a boy.

"I'm a bit like that too," he says. "Sometimes I wonder if I will ever grow up."

"I know that I won't," I say. "I know it for sure."

"Here." He hands me his paper napkin. "You look a little bit like you've escaped the apocalypse. Just."

"A paper napkin?" I take it and laugh, dabbing it on my hair, face, wiping it under my eyes. When I take it away, there is black stuff on it, which means I put some black stuff on my eyes at some point today, a fact I find comforting: black stuff on my lashes means my eyes will look better, I will look better, even if I look like a better panda. "Better than nothing, I suppose."

"There's a hand dryer in the toilet," he says, pointing at a door behind him. "You could give yourself a quick blast under that. Take the edge off."

"I'm fine," I say, patting my damp knees as if to make a point. I do not want to leave this table, this seat, this coffee, and go anywhere else. Here it feels like I am almost safe, like I'm clinging on to a ledge, and as long as I don't move I will be fine and I won't fall. The longer I can sit here, without having to think about where I am and how to get home, the better. I push away the surge of fear and panic, and concentrate on now. On feeling happy.

"How long have you been married?" He nods at the ring on my finger, which I notice with mild surprise. It feels right there, as if it has bedded into its place on my person, yet somehow it doesn't seem to have anything to do with me.

"It's my father's," I say, the words coming from a long ago moment in the past, another time when I said them to another boy. "When he died my mum gave me his ring to wear. I wear it always. One day I'll give it to the man I love."

There is a moment of silence, awkwardness, I suppose. Once again, present and past converge, and I'm lost. I am so very lost that really all there is in this world is this moment, this table, this person speaking kindly to me, those very nice eyes.

"Perhaps I could take you for another coffee, then?" he says, sounding hesitant, cautious. "When you are dry and not stuck in the middle of a disaster. I could meet you here or anywhere you like." He reaches over to the counter and picks up a stumpy writing thing that is not a pen and scrawls on my folded napkin. "The rain has stopped, shall I walk you home?"

"No," I say. "You might be a maniac."

He smiles. "So ring me, then? For a coffee?"

"I won't ring you," I say, apologetically. "I'm very busy. Chances are I won't remember to."

He looks at me and laughs. "Well, if somehow you find the time or the impulse, then ring me. And don't worry; you'll get back into your flat. One of your flatmates will turn up any second, I'm certain."

"My name is Claire," I tell him in a rush as he gets up. "You don't know my name."

"Claire." He smiles at me. "You look like a Claire."

"What's that supposed to mean?" I laugh. "And you, what's your name?"

"Ryan," he says. "I should have written it on the napkin."

"Goodbye, Ryan," I say, knowing that very soon he won't even be a memory. "Thank you."

"For what?" He looks perplexed.

"That napkin!" I say, holding up the scrunched-up sodden piece of tissue.

I watch him leave the café, chuckling to himself, and disappear into the dark night. I say his name over and over again. Perhaps if I say his name enough times, it will stick. I will be able to pin it down. A woman at the next table is watching him leave. She is frowning, and her frown is disconcerting. It makes me wonder if everything I thought just happened really did—if it was a nice happy moment or if something bad happened that I hadn't seen, because I've stopped being able to tell the difference. I'm not ready for that to happen yet. I don't want that to be true yet. It's dark outside now, except for a slash of pink sky cutting through the clouds as the sun sets. The woman is still frowning, and I am stuck on this chair.

"Claire?" A woman leans over me. "Are you okay? What's wrong?"

I look at her, her smooth oval face, long straight brown hair. The frown is concern, I think, and I think she knows me.

"I am not exactly sure how to get home," I confide in her, for want of any better solution.

She looks toward the door and then obviously thinks better of what she was about to say. Instead she turns back to me, with the frown again. "You don't remember me, do you? It's fine, I know about your ... problem. My name is Leslie, and our daughters are friends. My daughter is Cassie, with the pink hair and the nose piercing? And the awful taste in men? There was a time about four years ago when our girls were inseparable."

"I've got Alzheimer's," I say. It comes back to me, like the last rays of sun piercing the clouds, and I'm relieved. "I forget things. They come and go. And sometimes just go."

"I know, Cassie told me. She and Caitlin met up a few days ago, caught up. I have your Caity's number here, from that time they were supposedly sleeping over at each other's houses, and attempted to go clubbing in London. Remember? You and I waited all night for every single London train that came in, until they finally got home at about two. They hadn't even managed to get into the club. A drunk man had propositioned them on the tube, and they were crying so much we let them off the hook in the end."

"They sound like a right pair," I say. The woman frowns again, and this time I decide it's concern rather than anger.

"Will you remember Caitlin," the woman asks me, "if she comes?"

"Oh yes," I say. "Caitlin, yes, I remember what she looks like. Dark hair and eyes like rock pools under moonlight, black and deep."

She smiles. "I forgot you were a writer."

"I'm not a writer," I say. "I do have a writing room, though. I tried it, writing, but it didn't work, and so now I have an empty writing room right at the top of the house. There's nothing in it but a desk and a chair, and a lamp. I was so sure I was going to fill it to the brim with ideas, but instead it just got emptier." The woman frowns again, and her shoulders stiffen. I'm talking too much and it's making her uncomfortable. "The thing I'm scared about the most is losing words."

I've upset her. I should stop saying things. I'm never that sure what I am saying anymore. I have to really think. And wait. Talking too much is not a fun or sweet thing about me anymore. I close my lips firmly.

"I'll sit with you, shall I? Until she gets here."

"Oh . . ." I begin to protest, but it peters out. "Thank you."

I listen to her make a call to Caitlin. After exchanging a few words, she gets up and goes outside the café. As I watch her through the window, in the glow of the streetlights, I can see her still talking on the phone. She nods, her free hand gesturing. And then the call ends and she takes a deep breath of cold damp air before she comes back in and sits at my table.

"She'll be here in a few minutes," she tells me. She seems so nice; I don't have the heart to ask her who she is talking about.

2

caitlin

I open the front door for Mum, and then step back, secreting my key in my pocket. Mum doesn't have a key anymore, which is one of the things she really doesn't like about this new world order. Her hair hangs down her back—its bright, fiery auburn now a dark ruby-red. She is soaked through and shuddering. When Gran told me Mum had just marched off into the night, I wanted to ask her why she'd let her go, why she didn't try to stop her, but there wasn't time. I was out looking for her when I got the call from Cassie's mum.

Now we are back and, for Mum's sake, I am struggling to not be furious. What would have happened if I hadn't been here to go after her? Would Gran have stubbornly refused to stop Mum, determined to stand her ground and make a point, still somehow believing that Mum was showing off and should be ignored? I'm supposed to not be here soon. In the next few days, actually, I was supposed to be returning to London for my final year of university. What then? What would have happened then? Mum would have been lost out there in the rain, and who knows when or even if she would have got home.

Perhaps it is a good thing after all that I am not going back—not that any of them know that yet. Perhaps I can just tell them that this is why I have decided not to go back—because Mum needs me.

Gran is in the hallway waiting, one hand clasped in the other, her lips pressed into a thin line. She's anxious and angry and upset. Mum is instantly on edge the moment she sees her. I watch the pair of them look at each other, angry, uncertain, resentful, and I don't know what to do. I don't know how to make this better, especially not when I know that when the truth comes out, I will have made everything much worse.

I feel that now familiar sickening feeling, the surge of nausea that hits me when I think about what I've done, and I push it away. I have to: I don't have a choice. My mum is sick, really sick, and our family is falling apart around her. I don't have time for my own problems, not yet. I'm waiting, waiting for it to be the right time. But the right time might never come, and then . . . It might be better for everyone if I just left.

"Mummy!" Esther, my little sister, charges at Mum, bowling into her. Mum picks her up and attempts to hug her hard, but she is cold and wet, and Esther quickly squirms out of her arms. "You're icky! I hungry, I tired, I poorly."

It's Esther's new mantra whenever things aren't going exactly the way she wants them to. Her sad little face, her querulous bottom lip—it's a winning act every time, and Esther knows it. She does it because she knows it works so well on all of us.

"Want some biscuits before bed?" I ask her, offering the

naughtiest thing I can think of, just to see her smile. She nods and jumps up and down, happily.

"Go on, then." I nod in the direction of the living room. "I'll put some on a plate for you." Mum lets go of her hand, releasing her back into the living room, her fingers hovering in the air for just a moment, perhaps regretting letting Esther go.

"What were you thinking?" Gran asks Mum furiously.

"Look," I say, handing Mum a towel that I grab from the downstairs loo. She stares at it, and after a moment I take it and rub her hair for her. "There's no point going over this now, is there? There's no point having a go at her. I mean, if we are going to get into the whole blame thing, we might be wondering what she was doing heading off like that in the first place, mightn't we?" I look pointedly at Gran, but it rolls off her.

"I was worried sick," Gran says accusingly. "You have to understand, Claire, you have to realize that you can't just . . ."

"Gran," I say, taking a step between her and Mum. "Gran, Mum knows that."

I don't understand why Gran is so angry. I can see why she would be sad, and at a loss, unable to deal with this all happening again, but the anger I don't get. The anger makes no sense.

"Well, I just went out for a walk and . . ." Mum waves at the door. "And I forgot the color of the curtains."

"Mum, why don't you have a hot bath, I'll run it for you." I gesture toward the stairs, but she doesn't move.

"I can run my own bath still," she says. "And anyway, I don't want one."

"I know, but, you know . . . I'll run it for you. You can relax, warm up a bit."

Just as I think she is about to agree, Greg comes in through the kitchen, back from work. He's carrying a bag. "Hey, babe," he says. "You're soaked through."

"Winning awards for stating the obvious!" Mum looks uncomfortable, self-conscious, as soon as she sees him. "I'm just going to have a bath actually, so . . ." She looks at me, hoping I'll whisk her straight upstairs and out of the path of her husband. But I don't. If there was just a way to make her see him again, feel good around him again . . . If I knew she at least felt safe, then, then I could talk to her. I could tell her about me, like I used to, like I always have. A sudden surge of loss threatens so I turn my face away from Mum's silent but obvious pleas and I look at her husband.

"What's in the bag, Greg?"

He smiles, pleased with whatever it is. "I just wanted to give you this." He reaches into the brown paper bag he's carrying and brings out what I recognize at once as a notebook. It's large, A4 size, with a smooth, shiny, deep-red leather cover.

Greg has chosen the perfect notebook for Mum, because red is her favorite color. She wears it all the time, even though she is a redhead and it's not supposed to work: red hair, red dress, red lips and nails, even to school, the most glamorous teacher in the county, possibly the world. When I was little, I used to wish Mum would be less obvious when she came to pick me up after school; I used to wish she'd wear a parka and jeans like everyone else's mum. But now the fact that she always dresses up for everything seems like something precious, something special. Mum will always be Mum as long as she is dressed right up to the nines. Once, when I'd complained about how she always stuck out like a sore thumb, she told me that red was her warrior princess color, and red lipstick was her war paint. She felt braver when she wore it, and I understood that. I understood needing to feel brave; it was just a shock to me that it didn't come naturally to her. I'm not sure how old I was then, maybe around ten, but I remember it because I remember feeling like I knew something that made me a little bit more grown up. And the older I got, the more it made sense, the more I understood. Mum's been fighting for something for as long as I can remember.

This is the first battle she's ever engaged in that she knows she cannot win.

"It's a memory book." Greg holds out the notebook to her. "For you—for all of us—to write in. Remember how Diane said it would help you?"

I had not been there when Mum first met her counselor, Diane, or heard about Diane's idea for her to write down everything that seemed important to her—everything that had ever meant anything. The idea of a book of memories had intrigued Mum, who'd joked at the time: "I wish I'd thought about doing that before I lost the plot."

"Yes, I remember the memory book to help me remember," Mum says now, smiling carefully.

It's her polite smile, her meeting bank managers, greeting parents at parents' evening smile. It's not real. I wonder if Greg notices that too, and I think he does. I used to be the only person in the world who really knew Mum, and she used to be the only person in the world who really got me. There was always Gran, of course, the third musketeer, and we all love one another fiercely. But somehow Gran has always seemed a little out of step. Everything she says and does rubs Mum up the wrong way, and everything Mum says or does seems to disappoint Gran, ever so slightly. I've gotten used to it over the years, the constant bickering between the two of them; it's only recently I've come to wonder why they don't really get on. But anyway, I was the one who really knew Mum—I was the one she truly belonged to—until there was Greg. And when he showed up on the scene

I was fifteen, not a little kid, and yet still I was jealous and angry, and I didn't want him around even though I knew well enough that wasn't fair of me. It wasn't until I realized that he got her, exactly the same way I did, that I finally understood: Greg wasn't going anywhere, and Mum belonged to both of us now.

She reaches out and takes the book from him.

"It's a very fine notebook, beautifully made, thank you," she says politely.

The three of us follow her as she walks into the kitchen and puts it down on the table. "I always wanted to write a book, you know. I always thought the attic would make a good room to write books in."

The three of us do not look at one another. The times when we exchanged glances over Mum's head when she did or said something a little off stopped a few weeks ago, when we realized that those moments were going to happen every day now. It is amazing to me how quickly something that had been so extraordinary and so alien has become normal, part of our little world, the world that Mum has always ruled. The stomach-clench of sadness still accompanies those moments, but the looks and the disbelief have gone.

"You *have* written a book," I remind her. "Remember your novel?"

It sits in the drawer of her empty, abandoned desk in the attic, all 317 pages of it, held together by a long, thin, red rubber band stretched to its maximum capacity. Mum insisted on printing it out because she said it wasn't a book until it had pages, and I remember her reading it through up there in a day, then putting it in the drawer and climbing down the ladder. And as far as I know, she never went back up there again. She never did anything with the book, never asked anyone else to read it, never sent it off to a book agent or a publisher, never even talked about it again. She said that when your business was literature—teaching it, reading it, knowing it, loving it—you ought to at least have a crack at producing some of it yourself. So she had done, and that was that.

When Esther was about six months and I was deemed sensible enough not to accidentally kill her if I looked after her, Mum and Greg went away for a night in a hotel, just up the road, just to be alone together. The moment Esther was asleep in her cot, I pulled down the ladder and went up into the attic room. It smelled musty and damp, old, and . . . empty. I was going to pull the book out of the drawer and read it. I'd been planning to do so for a long time, and this was my chance. I wanted to know what the book was about, what it was like, if it was any good, and part of me, a part I am not very proud of, sort of hoped that it wasn't. Mum has always been so good at everything—even her falling in love, when it finally happened, happened like something out of a movie—and sometimes it feels like she is an impossible act to follow, even now that she has started getting everything wrong. But as soon as I put my hand on the handle of the desk drawer, I changed my mind. I didn't even open it. For the first time in my life I understood that everyone needs secrets, and sometimes those secrets should never be uncovered. Everyone needs something that is completely private. I got the feeling that if I read the book, it might change things, and I didn't want things to change. I suppose wanting that isn't enough to make it happen, though.

"That's not really a book," Mum says, sitting down at the kitchen table, and opening the notebook at a random empty page. The book is full of thick, undulating pages of milky paper, the kind that is slightly textured with tiny ridges that almost chime against the tip of a pen: the kind of paper that Mum most likes to write on. Greg and I know that. The paper is stiff against her fingers; it resists just slightly as she turns the pages. We watch as she leans her cheek into it, laying her face down on the pillow of pages, and it's such a Mum thing to do, something she would always have done, I think, that I feel comforted. Funny how the odd things, the mad things, are also the reassuring things.

"That whole book business was more of a download," she says, lifting her head from the pages and smoothing her hand over the paper. "I guess I had to get it out of my system. Maybe the Alzheimer's is the reason why. Maybe I was already going through the process of emptying my head. Empty head, empty attic. It fits."

She smiles up at Greg, the same polite parents'-evening smile. "It's a lovely book. Perfect. Thank you."

Greg touches her on the shoulder and she does not move away. It's painful to see how relieved he is.

"That's mine book," Esther says, appearing at the table, probably looking for her long-promised biscuit. Her nose fits just over its edge. "It's mine book for drawings, isn't it, Mummy?"

I wonder if Esther has any sense of how important she has become to us all, how we rely on her to make us laugh. I look at her and wonder how it happens, how a person so complete and unique emerges from another one. A person who is so small but so essential to all of us: she is our collective smile.

"Please may it be mines, Mummy?" Esther asks her sweetly. "Yes?"

We have all learned that since Esther turned three, it's generally best not to openly disagree with her, else the famous Armstrong temper will makes its presence felt and she'll throw something, or hit someone, or lie down on the floor and wail like the true drama queen she is. None of us minds very much— well, not Mum or I, anyway. We both have the Armstrong temper too, and when we see it in Esther, we know she is truly one of us. Instead, Mum manages her, agrees with her or changes the subject, and makes it so that although the little madam doesn't get her way all the time, she doesn't know that she doesn't. Mum has been brilliant at managing Esther: mothering her, I suppose the right word is. I watch her all the time now. I try to note it all down. The things she does, her smile, her jokes, her phrases. All the things she used to do for me when I was three years old, I suppose, but back then I didn't notice, either. Now I need to notice—I need to know everything she does—so that when the time comes, I can look after Esther in exactly the same way Mum would have. That is the thing I can do, which makes everything else, the stupid, stupid mess I've made of my life, all the worse. Other people get to make mistakes at my age, but not me. I can't; I don't have time. I have to be here for Esther; I have to give her the same life that Mum would have given her.

"Oh yes, you can draw in it," Mum says, picking up a pen and handing it to Esther straight away. I see Greg wince, but Mum reaches out and takes his hand. Her touch instantly melts away all the tension in his body. "This isn't just a book for *me* to write in, is it?" she says, smiling up at him, the teacher smile replaced—for now, at least—by one that means everything. It reminds me of my favorite wedding photo of the two of them: she's gazing up at him, and he's standing behind her laughing like a loon, looking so happy. "This is a book for you all to write in too. It's for my memories, but yours as well. It's a book for all of us. And Esther can start it off."

Greg pulls out a chair and sits down next to Mum as Esther climbs onto her lap, the tip of her tongue poking out as, earnestly, she begins to carve lines into the paper with the Biro Mum hands her. I watch her as she draws two circles—one big, one small—then fills each with two dots for eyes, one for a nose, and then a big grinning smile. Finally, she draws sticks straight out of the circles, representing arms and legs. Two of the arms touch, and Esther scribbles where they join, a small tangled spiral to show they are holding hands.

"That's me and you, Mummy," she says, totally satisfied with her work.

Mum holds her a little tighter and kisses the top of her head. "The perfect way to start the book," she says. Greg puts his arm around Mum, and I see her shoulders stiffen, just for a moment, before they relax. She looks at him. "Will you write the date underneath?"

Greg writes: "Mummy and Me by Esther," and the date.

"There." Mum smiles, and I watch her profile. She looks content for a moment, at ease. "The first ever entry in the memory book."

our wedding

This is a tiny piece of the duchess satin my wedding dress was made from. I cut it from the hem, where it will never be missed. I half hope that perhaps one of my girls might like to wear this dress on her own wedding day. . . .

I had my dress made in scarlet because it seemed more appropriate than white or ivory, and anyway red is my favorite color. It's not like I was a spring chicken when I married Greg: it was two weeks before I turned forty, although we don't talk about that. And I certainly wasn't anywhere close to being virginal. I felt more beautiful on that day than I have ever done—more beautiful and more alive, with every single person present that I have ever loved, or will ever love.

It was an August wedding, held by the sea at Highcliffe Castle in Dorset. I wanted a big, blinging wedding; I wanted everything to be shiny and covered in glitter, just like my crystal-encrusted shoes. I knew that the six-tier cake, the trays of tiny canapés, the endless glasses of champagne didn't matter as much as the man I was marrying, who was marrying me and my family against all the odds. But that's just me; it's always been me. I wanted the air to be full of the scent of lilies, and the laughter and chatter of my guests; I wanted the sea to sparkle bright blue in the sunlight, and every emerald-green blade of grass to stand proudly to attention under a smiley-faced sun, just like one of Esther's drawings.

Caitlin walked me down the aisle, which meant a lot to me because even on our wedding day she still couldn't quite believe that Greg genuinely did love me. When I first told her I was seeing our sexy young builder, she was appalled. She said, "It's some kind of scam, Mum. He's probably trying to rip you off for money. He's using you for sex, Mum, because he knows you are desperate." And when, after only almost a year of being with Greg, I told her I was pregnant: "He'll leave you in the lurch, Mum." That's my girl, always says it how it is, never pretends for the sake of it.

As we walked down the aisle, Caitlin and I held hands like a couple of little girls. She looked stunning, of course, although she was still sulking over the fact that I hadn't let her wear the little black cocktail dress she'd had her eye on. She was dressed in ivory organza—it floated around her ankles as she walked—and her hair, the dark tumultuous curls she got from her father, fell in soft tresses around her heart-shaped face.

The ceremony took place in a room with a full-length window of diamond-paned glass that looked out across the ocean, which was just as blue and as sparkly as I wanted it to be. I could see tiny white sails on the horizon, little boats far out at sea, bobbing away completely oblivious to this, the happiest moment in my life. But even so, I felt like those tiny boats, miles and miles away, were part of my wedding too. And so was the sun, and the stars beyond it, which sounds a bit over the top and a little crazy. But that was how I felt: like the center of all existence.

Neither one of us fancied the pressure of writing our own vows, so we stuck to the traditional ceremony. I was just looking at Greg, feeling the love and goodwill of all the people in the room, hearing Esther, who was swathed in organza with orange blossom in her hair, shouting baby babble at the top of her voice, when I caught my friend Julia's eye and she mouthed "You lucky bitch" at me clearly enough for the registrar to raise an eyebrow. Caitlin read Philip Larkin's "An Arundel Tomb." I remember those things and for me they were the vows. Those things, and the way Greg looked at me, made me realize I was getting married to the love of my life. I have been happy before, and my girls make me so happy all the time, but that day was the happiest I've ever been all in one go.

I got very drunk, of course. I insisted on making a speech after Greg's, which went on for at least ten more minutes than it should have done, but everybody laughed and cheered and put up with me showing off, as my mum would put it, because everyone there wanted the best for me. Afterwards, during the dancing, Esther spun round and round and round so that her skirt floated upwards like the petals of a flower opening outwards, and then fell asleep on my mum's chest as she sat in the quiet room next door to the party, pretending she wasn't actually a little tipsy and hadn't really flirted with Greg's Irish uncle, Mort. Julia had taken off her shoes and was dancing with everybody's husband, whether they liked it or not, terrifying one of the young waiters into slow dancing with her.

Greg and I danced all night long, spinning and shimmying, doing high kicks and jazz hands. We never stopped dancing. We never stopped laughing, not until he finally picked me up and carried me up the stairs to bed, calling me "Ms. Armstrong," teasing me because I'd asked him before the wedding if he'd mind very much if I kept my maiden name. It had been my name for so long, and it was Caitlin's and Esther's too, that it just didn't feel right to change it. Of course, he hadn't minded—he liked it, he'd told me. He liked being married to a Ms. and as he carried me into the bridal suite he whispered in Ms. Armstrong's ear how much he loved her, whatever she was called. Finally, when I did go to sleep, the last thing I remember thinking was that this was it. This was the time that my life finally began.

3

caitlin

I thought about waiting in the car for her, but then I realized it was entirely possible that I would be here all day. Mum doesn't have much of a sense of time anymore: hours seem like seconds to her, and vice versa. I don't want to get out of the safety of her confiscated cherry-red Fiat Panda and run through the rain, which is weighted like lead pellets, into the school, but I know that I have to. I have to go and collect her from her last ever day as a teacher, a day that I know is breaking her heart. And somehow, on the way home, before we are back in the middle of Gran and Esther, I have to tell her what I have done, because time is running out.

The receptionist, Linda, whom I've met a few times but mainly know through Mum's vivid and comic tales of school life, sits behind bulletproof glass, making it look like the school is in downtown L.A. rather than Guildford.

"Hi, Linda!" I grin fiercely, which I find is the only way to get through these sorts of conversations—the sympathy conversations that always seem to have this quiet undertone of glee.

"Oh, hello, love." The corners of Linda's mouth pull down in an automatic, so-sad little pout.

After her diagnosis, Mum hadn't wanted people to know right away: she had wanted to keep going for as long as possible, and everybody—even Mr. Rajapaske, her hospital consultant—thought that was feasible. "You're a bright woman, Ms. Armstrong," he told her. "Studies show that high intelligence often means diagnosis is delayed because clever people find ways to compensate and strategize. You should disclose your condition to your employer, but, on the whole, if the drugs have the desired effect, then there's no reason your life should have to change drastically any time soon."

We'd all been so reassured, so grateful, for what felt like a reprieve, giving us time to adjust and get our heads round what was happening; and then Mum drove her lovely little Fiat Panda—the first new car she'd ever owned—into a postbox. And to cap it all, this happened right outside the school gates. If it had been during the school run, the chances are she would almost certainly have run down a child. It wasn't that Mum had stopped concentrating—it wasn't that. She was concentrating very hard on remembering what the steering wheel was for when it happened.

"Hello, darling." Linda repeats herself in a singsong whine. "Here to collect your poor mum?"

"Yes." I smile ever so brightly, because I know Linda is being nice, and it's not her fault that the sound of her voice makes me want to break down the door of her bulletproof cubicle and pour that cup of cold tea over her head. "How did it go, do you know?"

"It's been lovely, dear. They did an assembly about Alzheimer's awareness. All the Year Sevens have made a friend at Hightrees Retirement Home, in mem—in honor of your mum."

"That's nice," I say, as she lets herself out of her cubicle with the jangle of an ostentatious bunch of keys, and buzzes us through into the inner sanctum of Albury Comp: Mum's school, as I and many other people have thought about it for the last few years, especially since she got her promotion to head of English. Mum made this school what it is. "And they had special tea and cake—you know how your mum likes cake. And I think she seemed really happy, you know, taking it all in. Smiling."

I bite my tongue, stopping myself from telling her that she is a silly cow, and that Mum is still Mum and not some brain-dead vegetable all of a sudden. That the diagnosis doesn't make her any less human. I want to say this to her, but I don't, because I don't think Mum would want me to insult the school secretary on her very last day here. Actually, I take that back: I think Mum would love it. But I hold it in anyway. Mum thinking something is a good idea is sometimes a good reason not to do it.

"She's not actually so different from how she was six months ago," I say carefully, as I follow Linda, keys swaying on her hip. "A year ago, even. She's still Mum. She's still the same person." I want to add that she's still the same woman that told you to get over yourself when you tried to call the police to escort Danny Harvey's mum out of reception the day she got so sick of the bullying that she came to school to sort out the bullies herself. Mum had been in the staff room when she'd heard the shouting. She'd come out to see Mrs. Harvey, and taken her into the staff room, where she tactfully pointed out that the last thing a twelve-year-old boy needed was for his mum to pile in and beat up the bullies. Mum had got involved then, even though she hadn't even taught Danny at all. Mum had it sorted within a week. Mrs. Harvey nominated her for the South Surrey Teacher of the Year award. Mum won it. She isn't some empty shell of a woman yet. Mum is still fighting, and this is her last stand.

Linda opens the door to the staff room, where I find Mum sitting with her best teaching friend, Julia Lewis. Before Mum met Greg, Julia was her pulling buddy—that's what she used to call her. Most of the time, I tried to pretend that I didn't know what they got up to, and when Mum got together with Greg, the one thing I was relieved about was that I didn't have to think about my mother having a mysterious sex life anymore. Not that she let me see her getting dressed up to the nines and going out dancing and drinking cocktails, flirting and whatever else I didn't know about. And Mum never brought men home when I was there, not once, not until Greg. He was the very first man she had wanted me to meet, and I really hadn't wanted to meet him. It's no wonder their romance all came as a bit of a shock to me. But I know there have been men, and I know a few of them must have happened when she and Julia were "letting their hair down" and "blowing off steam." Once, she said to me that we never had to talk about our love lives unless we really wanted to, and we never have. Not even when I met Seb—not even when I fell so much in love with him that it hurt me to breathe whenever I wasn't with him. I never talked to her about him, or my feelings. Perhaps I should have, because if anyone could have understood, it would have been Mum. If I had, then telling her everything that has happened since Seb, because of Seb, would be so much easier. Now, I'm afraid that the moment when I can confide in her and she can, well, just be my mum, has already passed. I'm afraid that soon when I walk into a room where she is waiting, she won't recognize me, or she will forget what I'm for, like she did with the steering wheel.

But Mum smiles at me now as I walk into the staff room.

She is clutching a large bunch of supermarket flowers. "Look!" She wields them at me, cheerfully. "Smell-nice things! Aren't they pretty?"

I wonder if she's noticed that she's lost the word "flowers," but I don't mention it. Gran always corrects her, and it seems to make Mum cross, so I never do. I do wonder if "flowers" is one of the words that have gone for good, though, or if it will come back. I've observed that sometimes the words come and go, and sometimes they're gone for good. But Mum doesn't notice, so I don't tell her.

"They are lovely." I smile at Julia, who's grinning broadly, determined to keep things light.

"It's been ages since a man sent me flowers," Mum says, burying her face in the petals. "Julia, we need to go out on the razz again, get some hot man action."

"You've got the hot man action," Julia says, not missing a beat. "You're already married to the fittest man in Surrey, darling!"

"I know," Mum says into the flowers. Although I'm not entirely sure she does—at least for a second or two, anyway. Until very recently, Greg made her so happy that he lit her up like one of those Chinese paper lanterns Mum had the guests set free at their wedding. Back then, she would glow from the inside out, floating above the world. And yet now, Greg, their love, their happiness, their marriage, comes and goes in her mind, and one day I suppose it too will be gone for good.

"Shall we be off, then?" I say, nodding toward the door. There isn't really a reason to go right away, except that I can't bear to prolong this final moment of the job Mum loved so much. When she walks out of here, she'll be leaving behind something that defined her. And the longer she stays, the harder it will be.

I also know that today, or tomorrow, or the day after, Greg and Gran, or maybe even Mum, will notice that I still haven't gone back to uni, and then it will all come out. And everyone will have an opinion and something to say. And I don't want that. I don't want all the secrets and mistakes that I have so carefully managed to keep close for so long to suddenly just spill out everywhere, in one big bloody mess, because then it will be real and I am not ready for it to be real. It's really terrible but the truth is, when Mum got her diagnosis, just as I'd returned for the summer break, I was relieved—relieved to have a reason not to tell. And that's the thing, that's the thing that's doing my head in. I mean, I am almost twenty-one years old, but I am still so stupid, so immature and selfish, that I actually saw a plus side to my mother being told she had early-onset Alzheimer's. That is the kind of person I am, and I don't know, I just don't know how I can be better. Suddenly I've got to grow up quick and decide what is to be done, and I don't want to. I want to dive under the duvet and bury myself in a book just like I used to do not that long ago.

I am not ready for this, not for any of it.

Part of me wants to tell Mum now, about everything that's going on with me, before everyone else gets to jump in with an opinion. And yet I worry: should I tell her at all? I am not sure whether she will even understand or be able to remember what I say for more than a few hours. If I tell her now, does that mean that, in the weeks to come, I will have to tell her again and again and again about how I have so comprehensively ruined my life, and see the shock and disappointed look on her face again and again?

But she's my mum, and I need to tell her. Even if it's just for now.

"Mum, are you ready?" I prompt her again.

Mum doesn't move. She sits on the rough, brown, horrible school chair and suddenly her eyes fill with tears. I feel the strength drain away from my legs, and I sit down next to her, putting my arm around her.

"I love my job," she says. "I love teaching, and I'm so good at it. I get the kids really interested, really caring about Shakespeare and Austen and . . . This is my vocation. I don't want to go, I don't want to." She turns to Julia. "They can't make me, can they? Isn't there something we can do? They're being prejudiced against Alzheimer's." Her voice begins to rise with indignation and something like panic. "Isn't there some sort of court we could go to, and make them see my human rights? Because they can't make me go, Julia!"

Julia smiles as though it's all absolutely fine, crouches down in front of her friend and puts her hands on Mum's shoulders, grounding her, grinning just like she always does. Like it's all a joke. I feel the tears begin to sting my eyes. They come so easily, these days.

"Mate . . ." She looks into Mum's eyes. "You are the best teacher, drinker, dancer, and friend that there has ever been. But darling, although the rule about teachers not driving cars into postboxes outside of schools might be a stupid one, it still stands. But don't cry, okay? Chin up, walk out of here like you don't give a damn. Be free." Julia pauses to press a kiss on Mum's mouth. "Go now, out there, and be free for me, and be brilliant like you always have been. All of the time. Be brilliant you and stuff this bunch of ungrateful bastards. Because you know what, doll, now is *the* time to have the time of your life. You can do what you like, sweetie, and you'll get away with it."

"I don't want to go," Mum says, getting up and hugging the flowers to her chest so hard that some of the petals are crushed and fall to her feet.

"Think about the marking," Julia says. "The admin, keeping it a secret that Jessica Stains is having an affair with Tony James, and that we all know they secretly liaise in the English Department stationery cupboard when no one is looking. And the politics, and that bastard government doing its best to ruin our perfectly good school with bullshit policies. Think about all that crap and go out there and be free, okay? And be as crazy and as adventurous as you can be, for me."

"Okay," Mum says, hugging Julia. "Although my adventures will have to be really local now I'm not allowed to drive anymore."

"That's my girl." Julia hugs her back. "I'll ring you in a couple of days, and we'll arrange a night out, yes?"

"Yes," Mum says. She turns around, looking at the room.

"Goodbye, life," she says.

We walk back to the car, and I find I'm almost trying to act as if it isn't there, so that maybe Mum won't notice that I am driving her lovely red car, complete with a shiny new wing. She stops at the passenger door as I climb into the driver's seat and put the key in the ignition. I wait for her to open the door, but she doesn't, so I reach across and open it for her. As she slides into the seat, she twists and retrieves the seat belt, which she clicks into place. This morning I had to do it for her, which means this is one of the things that went and then came back again. A small victory.

"So, back to the real world, tomorrow!" Mum smiles at me, out of the blue, suddenly very present. "Are you packed? You don't seem to have produced a mountain of washing like normal. Don't tell me you've finally started to do your own! Oh, now wait, I bet Gran has done it for you, hasn't she? The thing about Gran, Caitlin, is that she'll do your washing, but you will pay for it, maybe for the next four to five years."

Mum laughs, and I catch my breath. She's back, she's here: it's Mum, all of her. It's only in these moments that I realize how much I miss her when she goes away.

"Back to the world of hopes and dreams and futures, Caitlin," she says happily, her departure from school forgotten. "A few months from now, you'll be a graduate. Imagine! I can't wait to see you in your cap and gown. I promise to keep sane enough, for long enough, to not think that you're Batman and I'm Catwoman. Although I quite like the idea of wearing a leather catsuit to your graduation ceremony."

I smile. How on earth do I tell her?

"I feel like I should be making a speech," Mum says, pressing her palm flat against the window as if she's only just discovered glass. "Telling you what to do with your life; giving you some intensive mothering before it's too late. But I know that I don't have to. I know that all I have to do is trust you and you'll do the right thing. I know I go on about what a wretched child you are, and how I wish you'd tidy your room and stop listening to whatever the bloody awful dirge is that you insist on listening to, but I am awfully proud of you, Caitlin. There, I said it."

I keep my eyes on the road, concentrating on the traffic, the people on the pavement, the speed camera coming up. Suddenly, I know exactly how it happened that she just forgot how to drive in the middle of driving. Sometimes I feel like the weight of everything I'm not saying out loud might push everything I think I know right out of my head too. I concentrate hard on driving, the miles running out, the car eating up this time we have together. If ever there was a time to be brave, to be grown-up and strong, this is it. Mum is here; we are alone. But I can't. I can't.

"Ethan Grave cried," Mum says suddenly, and her face falls a little as she remembers her last day again. "When I went to say goodbye to my class, the girls had made me a card. Oh . . ." She twists around in her seat. "I've left the card."

"I'll call Julia," I say. "She'll pick it up."

"The girls had made me a card, and did a dance routine. It was so *girls,* you know? Like they'd written a musical called 'We're Gonna Miss You, Miss.' And I loved it. I should thank God they hadn't penned a song called 'Alzheimer's Ain't No Joke,' or something, and got Miss Coop to play along to it on that old out-of-tune piano in the hall. Anyway, then Ethan Grave came up, to say goodbye, I suppose, and just started crying. Right there, in front of everyone. Poor kid, he'll really pay for that with the other boys next week, when I'm a distant memory and they are all trying to look down that busty supply teacher's top."

"He won't," I say, and I mean it. "They all love you. Even the ones that pretended they didn't, even they love you."

"Do you think they will remember me?" Mum asks. "When they are old and grown, do you think they'll look back and remember my name?"

"Yes!" I say. Two more roads and we will be home. "Yes, of course."

"Esther won't remember me, will she?" Mum says so suddenly that I have to stop myself slamming down hard on the brake. It's like my body thinks we're heading for a collision.

"She will. Of course she will," I say.

Mum shakes her head. "I don't remember being three," she says. "Do you?"

I think about it for a moment. I remember sunshine, sitting up in my buggy that I was really far too big for, and eating a bread roll. I might have been three, or two or five. I have no idea. "Yes," I say. "I remember everything. I remember you."

"She won't," Mum says. "She might just catch glimpses of me now and then, but she won't remember me, or how much I loved her. You'll have to tell her for me, Caitlin. Don't let Gran be in charge of telling her about me. That won't do at all. Gran thinks I'm an idiot, she always has done. You have to tell Esther that I was funny, and clever and beautiful, and that I loved her and you more than . . . Just tell her, okay?"

"She will remember you," I say. "No one can forget you, even if they tried. And anyway, you're not going anywhere— you're not dying any time soon. You'll be in her life for years and years." I say it, although we both know for sure now that it is not likely.

At first, just after diagnosis, Mr. Rajapaske told us that there are basically three stages to Alzheimer's, but that it was impossible to know which stage Mum was at yet, because she has a high IQ, and may have been hiding the deterioration from everyone, including herself. Mum might have been deteriorating for a year, or years, he said, sitting in his neat little office lined with family photos and certificates. She might be at the end of the time when any part of the world makes sense to her. There was no way of telling, and I for one thought that was better than knowing for sure: it was the next best thing to hope. But the night she ran away in the rain, the night Greg gave her the memory book, Gran filled us in on the latest test results. It was the worst possible news—a complication that no one had expected, and that was virtually unprecedented. The disease was progressing more quickly than anyone had anticipated. Gran had taken notes, determined to deliver all of the information to us, as best she could. But I didn't hear any of the details, the rationale, the results of the brain scans, the schedule for several more. All I could do was picture Mum walking blindly toward a cliff, knowing that at any moment she might just plummet into the darkness. None of us knows when that will happen, least of all her. I glance over at her. I have to talk now.

"Mum," I say. "I want to tell you something."

"You can have my shoes," she says. "All of them, but especially those red heels you've always liked. And I want you to go and see your father."

This time I do stop. We're just moments away from our house, but I pull over onto a double yellow line, and turn off the engine. I wait for a second, for my heart to still, for my breathing to even out.

"What are you talking about?" I turn and look at her, unexpected anger surging through my veins like adrenaline. "Why the hell would you want me to do that?"

Mum does not react to my anger, although she sees it. She sits calmly, her hands folded passively in her lap. "Because I won't be here soon and you need—"

"I don't," I say, cutting across her, "I don't need a replacement parent for you, Mum, and besides, that's not how it works. He never wanted me, did he? I was a mistake, an error that he wasn't ready to face, that he wanted rubbed out in an instant. Wasn't I? Wasn't I?"

"They used to be your gran's, you know, those red shoes, before she gave up a life of dropping LSD to become a miserable old bat—"

"Mum!" I find myself slamming the heels of my hands down on the steering wheel. She knows I don't want to hear about him; she knows that the thought of him, this person who has never been anything in my life, makes me pulsate with anger—all the more because I hate the fact that I care enough about the man who didn't want me to even feel so much fury now. "Don't tell me to go and see him. Don't!"

"Caitlin, you and me, we were always so close when it was just the two of us. Three, if you include Gran. And I always thought that was enough, and I would still think that if it weren't for . . ."

"No!" I am adamant, the tears springing into my eyes. "No, this doesn't make any difference."

"It does make a difference. The difference is that it's made me see I was wrong to think you could do without knowing about him, and wrong to bring you up without your ever knowing, and . . . and, look, the thing is, I have to tell you something. Something you won't like."

Mum stops midsentence—not to think or to pause; she just stops—and after several moments, I realize that whatever she was going to say has been lost over the cliff edge. She sits there quietly, oblivious to the rage grasping at my chest, the anxiety and confusion; she smiles serenely, waiting patiently for something to happen. And then I just can't hold it in anymore, and the tears come, lots of them. I rest my head against the center of the steering wheel, gripping on to it as tightly as I can. I feel my whole body shudder and shake, and I hear myself repeating, over and over again, "I'm sorry, I'm sorry."

I cannot imagine a time when this sobbing will stop and I will be able to turn the engine on again. It feels like we might stay here forever, just like this, and then I hear Mum release the seat belt and I feel her lean over, putting her arms around my neck.

"It's okay," she coos softly in my ear. "Who's my big brave girl, hey? It was a shock, that's all, but you'll see in the morning that you'll have a bruise to be proud of. My big brave girl. I love you, chicken."

I fall into her arms and let her comfort me, because whatever day it is, whichever moment of our lives she is reliving right now, I just wish I could be there with her, back there in the time when a kiss and a hug made everything okay.

When I finally pull into the drive, and open the front door for Mum, I realize I still haven't told her my secret. And there is something else: she still hasn't told me hers.

claire

This is a letter from Caitlin's father.

He wrote the date at the top of the letter, in his bold black spirally handwriting that soared and sloped across the page. His handwriting alone showed me that he was artistic, unconventional, dangerous, and fascinating . . . and he had written me a letter.

Letters weren't such a rarity then: I wrote to my mum from uni, and to my uni friends in the holidays. But I'd never had a letter from a boy before, and even if it isn't exactly a love letter, that is why I kept it. I think I expected it to be the first of many, but there was only one.

I read it now, and I can see what I didn't see then. It's a snare, a trap. A carefully constructed ruse to lure me in—to make me feel clever, and as if I must be something special to be so worthy of his attention. This wasn't in the words he wrote—it

was the letter itself that was supposed to show me he was woo-
ing me. The words were almost inconsequential.

It arrived at some point during the night. I slept on the
ground floor, in what had once been a front room but was now
an extra bedroom in our shared house. It was my damp little
hovel, strewn with clothes, posters lining the walls. It smelled
of washing that's been left in the machine too long. Whenever
I smell that, I'm right back there in that room, staring at the gas
fire on the wall, waiting for life to really begin.

That morning, the morning the letter came, when I pulled
back my curtains I could see something that shouldn't have been
there, shrouded by the mist of the nets that were slick with con-
densation from the inside of the window. Once I'd peeled the
graying lace curtains back from the damp glass, I could see it
more clearly: a long, thick, cream-colored envelope taped to the
other side of the window, my name written on the front.

It was cold still—spring had yet to set in—but I danced
outside in my bare feet to retrieve it anyway, diving under the
covers for warmth when I came back in. This was the most exciting thing that had ever happened to me, and my first instinct
was to tear it open, but I didn't. I sat very still and looked at it
for a long time. For the first time in my life, I got that feeling—
the one when you know something momentous, something life
changing, is going to happen. I wasn't wrong.

You can see how he didn't bother with my name. No
"Dear Claire." "I enjoyed our conversation on Saturday night,"
was his opening line. Our conversation. I thrilled at his turn of
phrase. He'd sought me out at a party; I remember the moment
exactly. I'd noticed him as soon as we'd walked in. He was taller
than most of the other boys, and he had this self-assurance, like
he was at ease in his long, skinny body. There was nothing about
him that a girl would instantly be attracted to—nothing except

that he had that rare quality among young men: he looked like he knew what he was doing. We'd been there a couple of hours when I noticed him looking at me, and I remember glancing behind me, in case I was mistaken. When I checked again, he was still watching me. He smiled and held up a bottle of wine, summoning me to his side with a jerk of his head. Of course, I went. I didn't think twice about it. He poured me red wine in a real wine glass, and questioned me extensively about my taste in art, literature, and music. I lied about everything I could in the hope that it would impress him. He knew I was lying. I think he liked that about me. Everyone, including all of my friends, had left by the time the party finally wound down. I told him I'd better get back, and should call a minicab home, to be on the safe side. I wasn't even sure where the party was: we'd arrived in a miasma of cheap wine and a cadged lift, laughing and talking too much for any of us to take note of where we were going, only there on the say-so of a friend of a friend. It was then he revealed that this was *his* house, and asked me to stay the night. Not for sex or anything—he was very clear about that—just because it would be safer than taking a cab home alone. Hadn't I heard about that girl who'd gotten into a local cab last week, then passed out and had woken up in the middle of nowhere with the driver masturbating over her?

Of course, for all I knew, I was exchanging one danger for another, but I didn't think about it that way. I thought he was chivalrous, protective, mature. In retrospect, I think he was trying reverse psychology on me, convinced that if he denied me access to his manhood, I'd be clawing off his boxers in desperation before dawn broke. Only I wasn't that kind of girl. There had been a boy, one boy only, whom I'd had sex with before then. I hadn't told him I was a virgin. It didn't seem a very cool thing to confess, because I was eighteen, which seemed so old. It had

been a one-time thing, awkward and embarrassing. I'd decided
to pretend it hadn't happened at all, except now at least I'd got
"it" out of the way, and knew what to expect the next time,
which wasn't very much.

For all the brash confidence I put on display, I was very
inexperienced. I let him lead me upstairs to his room. He had
a single bed. I lay down on it, and after a few minutes standing
awkwardly in front of the electric bar heater, he lay down beside
me, pressing my body against the length of the cold wall. We
talked for a long time, lying side by side, fully clothed. We talked
and laughed, and at some point he laced his fingers in mine. I
can remember even now the quiet thrill his touch gave me—the
promise, the anticipation. The sun was up when he kissed me.
We kissed and talked for a few more hours after that, each kiss
growing ever bolder on his part. I think he was surprised when I
got up, exhausted and still lost, and said I had to go. I didn't have
to go, but I wanted to. I wanted the opportunity to miss him.

There were only two occasions in what was to be our relationship that I did the right thing, played the right move, and
this was one of them . . . a move made before I even guessed that
we were involved in a game. I left before he wanted me to, and
that made him want me more.

"I haven't stopped thinking about you." The second line
of the letter. A standard line, I suppose, but one that made me
swoon back onto my bed, collapsing into the pillow, clutching
the piece of paper to my chest. He was so funny, so clever, so important in our little world, and he couldn't stop thinking about
me! "Something about the sun on the carpet this morning made
me think about the smell of your hair." I had thought this line
impossibly romantic and clever. Much later, I found out he'd
used it more than once: it was a line from a love poem that he'd
given to several girls during the term. "I would like to see you

again. I will be in the Literature section of the library today, from midday until about six. Come and find me there if you want."

I looked at my watch. He'd been there an hour already. If I'd been thinking straight, if I'd been older, wiser, more cynical, and less in love with his handwriting, I'd have gone—but not until after five. But I wasn't any of those things. I carefully folded his letter inside my copy of Eagleton and, after dressing hastily, I went to find him at once.

He was not surprised to see me. He smiled, but it was restrained.

"I got your letter," I whispered, sitting down next to him.

"Evidently," he replied.

"What shall we do?" I asked him, preparing to be whisked away on a romantic whirlwind.

"I've got about another hour to spend on this essay, then the pub?" he said, waiting for my nod of approval before he turned back to his books. Slowly, I pulled my own books from my bag, and made a show of beginning to read them. But I didn't see the words; I just sat there, trying hard to look clever, fascinating, and beautiful, waiting for him to be ready. I should have got up; I should have left. I should have kissed him on the cheek and said, "Ciao." But I didn't, and from that moment on, I was his, right up until the moment that I wasn't anymore. And that was the second thing I did right in our relationship.

4

claire

I've known about the Alzheimer's, or the AD as we in the know call it—a nifty little nickname for those of us in the special club—for a long time. I think I've secretly known about it for years. There was this nagging little suspicion nibbling away at my edges. Words would drift away just out of reach when I called for them; promises that I made to do something were broken because I simply forgot them. I put it down to my lifestyle, which had become so very full in the last few years, what with Greg and Esther and my promotion at work. I told myself that it was because my head was so very full of thinking and feeling that I frequently felt like I'd sprung a leak, like parts of me were seeping away. At the back of my mind, though, I'd always have that last image of my dad, so old and empty and utterly lost to me. I worried and wondered, but I'd tell myself I was too young, and that just because it happened to him, it didn't mean it would happen to me. After all, it hadn't happened to his sister, my aunt Hattie. She'd died of a heart attack, with all her marbles intact. So I told myself not to be so melodramatic, and to stop worrying. And I felt like that for years before, one day, I really knew that I couldn't hide from it anymore.

It was the day I forgot which shoe belonged to which foot, had two breakfasts, and forgot my daughter's name.

I came downstairs carrying my shoes, and went into the kitchen for breakfast. Caitlin was already home from uni, looking tired and thinner. Wrung out from living life, I supposed, although her habitual black outfits and black-rimmed eyes didn't do a lot to flatter her obvious exhaustion. I asked her once why she liked dressing like a Goth so much, and she grabbed a handful of her mass of jet-black hair and said, really, what other choice did she have? School hadn't broken up, and she was taking Esther out for the day—because the childminder was sick—which was good of her. She looked like she really just wanted to stay in bed all day, and part of me wanted to put her there—tuck her up, like I used to when she was little, brush the hair off her forehead, and bring her soup.

They were already up when I came into the kitchen. Esther had dragged her big sister out of bed and down the stairs, and was ensconced on her lap talking babble and demanding to be fed like a baby. I walked into the kitchen, still carrying my shoes, and I looked at them, my two daughters, seventeen years between them, and I felt this little bubble of happiness that even with all of the life I had lived between giving birth to each of them, they still were so close and so bonded. I'd gone to call Esther over for a cuddle when it happened. There was just this wall of gray, this dense fog between me and her name. No, no, it wasn't even a wall: it was . . . a void. A vacuum where something had been before, perhaps just moments before, and now it was obliterated. I panicked, and the harder I tried to think, the thicker the fog became. And this wasn't a meeting at work I'd forgotten to attend, or that woman from the book club I went to about three times, whom I sometimes have to avoid in supermarkets because I can't remember her name. This wasn't "someone off the telly, who used to be in that thing." This was my little girl, the apple of my eye. My treasure, my delight, my sweetheart. The child I'd named.

I knew it then, in that instant, that the same thing that had come to claim my father had come for me too. I knew it, even as I tried with all my heart and head combined not to know it. You are stressed and tired, I told myself. Just relax, take a breath and it will come.

I filled a bowl with muesli, which tasted like cardboard in my mouth, and afterwards I went to brush my teeth. Keep the routine, do what you know, and it will come. I came back and filled a bowl with muesli, and Caitlin asked me if I was extra hungry, and I realized that actually I wasn't hungry at all. Then I noticed my first empty bowl, still sitting on the table, and realized why. But still, I told her I was, and forced down a few more mouthfuls, making a joke about starting the diet tomorrow instead. Caitlin just rolled her eyes, in that way she had perfected over the years. "Oh, Mum."

Trying to press the panic down, I looked under the table and stared and stared at my shoes. Low, black, kitten heels with a long pointed toe that I loved. I wore them because they didn't hurt, even after a long day teaching, and they looked purposeful and just sexy enough to get away with. But that morning, the more I looked at them, the more of a mystery they became to me. I simply couldn't decipher which shoe went on which foot. The angle of the toe; the buckle on the side—none of it made sense to me anymore.

I left the shoes under the kitchen table, and went and pulled on my boots. That day, the whole day at work, simply went by: I remembered which classes to go to, what I was teaching, characters and quotes from the books we were studying . . . they were all there. But not my daughter's name. I waited and I waited for Esther's name to come back to me. But it was gone, along with which shoe was left, and which was right. And it only returned that evening when Greg called Esther by her name. I was relieved and so frightened at the same time that I cried. I had to tell Greg: there was no hiding anymore. The next day I went to see my GP, and the testing began—test after test, all aiming to try to tell with as much certainty as possible what I already knew.

And now I live with Mum again, and increasingly my husband feels like a man I barely know; and even though Esther's name hasn't slipped out of my tightly clenched grip ever since, other things do, every day. I open my eyes each morning and tell myself who I am, who my children are, and what is wrong with me. And I live with my mum again, even though no one ever asked me if that was what I wanted.

And there's something else, something important I have to say to Caitlin before she goes back to uni. But whatever it is, it's standing just out of reach behind the fog.

"Do you want to set the table?" Mum asks me, holding a bouquet of shiny metal in her fist. She is eyeing me skeptically, as though I might somehow do her in with a blunt butter knife. What she is wondering is: am I capable of remembering which implement is which, and what it is for? And what really pisses me off is that I am wondering the same thing. At this exact second, I know precisely everything I need to know about setting the table, and I will do right up until the moment she hands me the objects that require placing in a particular order. And then . . . will the fog roll in, and will that piece of information be gone? Not knowing what I don't know stops me from wanting to do anything. Everything I attempt is fraught with the possibility of failure. And yet I am still *me,* at the moment. My mind is still me. When will the day come that I am not me anymore?

"No," I say, like a sullen teenager. I am decorating my memory book. I keep finding little things, little items that aren't quite whole memories, that wouldn't fill a page or even a line in the book, but which make up parts of a life, my life, like pieces of a mosaic. And so I decided to cover the book with the things I find. I tape on a fifty-cent piece, a remnant from my trip to New York, next to a ticket to a Queen concert that I ran away from home to watch when I was only twelve. I'm trying to think of a way to attach a hedgehog charm that my dad gave me for my birthday before he became sick; I'm wondering if I can somehow sew it onto the thick cover of the book. It's small work, in a small world, in a place I know, and it absorbs and comforts me in the way that Diane the counselor said it would. But that's not why I don't set the table: I don't set the table because I don't want to not remember how to set the table.

"Did you show Caitlin the letter?" Mum takes a seat opposite me, reaching across the table to lay out the objects that make a frame for a plate to sit within. "Did you talk to her?"

For several long moments, I turn the small silver hedgehog over and over in the palm of my hand, rubbing it with the tip of my finger. I remember how delighted I was with it, how even when it was attached to my bracelet I played with it, making it walk over the carpet and hibernate under cushions. I lost it once for a full day, and didn't stop crying until Mum had found it secreted at the bottom of a box of tissues: I'd forgotten where I'd put it to bed. I can remember all of that in perfect, crystal-clear detail.

"I don't know," I tell her, embarrassed, ashamed. "I think I said something. I'm not sure what I've said."

"She's upset," Mum tells me. "When she came in, she'd been crying. Her face was red; her eyes were swollen. You should show her the letter."

"I don't know," I say. I have always hated it when my mother has decided it's time to force the issue, to box me into a corner and make me act. But now, instead of feeling like I've got my back against the wall, it's as though I am lost in a maze, and I'm not sure of the way out. "There's a lot she isn't saying, and I don't know if I can, if I should, force the issue. Not now, not after all this time."

"Whatever else, she does deserve the truth, doesn't she? That girl, she's so angry a lot of the time. So unsure of herself, so . . . closed in. Haven't you ever wondered whether half of it's because she feels like she was abandoned by her father before she was ever born?"

I say nothing. This doesn't feel fair to me, the new crusade that Mum is on, determined to get me to set my house in order. I don't want to set my house in order; I want to glue things into my book. I raise the tiny hedgehog up to eye level, and begin to make a loop for it out of a length of cotton.

"Ignoring me won't make it go away," Mum says, but a little less sternly this time. "You know how I feel about it."

"Yes, Mother," I say. "I know what you feel about it because you've been telling me more or less nonstop since the day Caitlin was born. But it wasn't your choice to make, was it?"

"Was it yours?" she says, which is what she always says, and I realize there are some things I am quite looking forward to forgetting.

"Nothing would be any different from the way it is now," I tell her, going back to my book.

"You can't possibly know that," she says. "You made assumptions, and Caitlin's life is based on them. She's a child that has always felt abandoned, and lost. Even if she never says it, you only have to look at her to know she doesn't feel like she fits in."

"This from the woman who used to always wear a full-length kaftan and flowers in her hair?" I say. "You've heard of personal expression, right? Why does it have to mean more when it's Caitlin?"

"Because it *does* mean more because it is Caitlin." Mum struggles to find the words, turning over a peeler in her hand as she thinks. "When she was little, she never stopped singing, always grinning like a loon. Shouting, making herself the center of attention, just like you. I just ... I just feel like she's not ... reaching out enough. I mean, where are the jazz hands and the high kicks? What happened to that little girl? And don't say she grew out of them. You never did."

"Mum, what do I have to do for you to give me a break? I mean, if a degenerative brain disease won't do it, what will? Would you let me off if I had breast cancer, maybe?" The words come in quick angry bursts, low and strained—because I know Caitlin is upstairs, curled in upon herself, furled around all the words she feels she cannot say; and because I know that Mum is right, and Mum being right is the hardest thing to stand. Picking at this same old wound with my mother won't help Caitlin, so I force myself to back down, finding the imprint of the tiny hedgehog driven into the palm of my hand as I unclench my fist. "Caitlin might not have had a traditional upbringing, but she has always had me, and you, and now she has Greg and Esther. Why isn't that enough?"

Mum turns her back on me to boil orange vegetables, probably to mushy oblivion, and I watch her: her shoulders are tense, the tilt of her head set in repressed disapproval, perhaps grief. She is very angry with me—it feels like she always has been, although I know for a fact that is not true. Now more than ever, the times when she was not angry shine like polished silver in a sunny sitting room, and those memories positively dazzle. Sometimes I try to pinpoint the exact moment things changed between us, but it always shifts. Was it the day Dad died, or the day he became ill? The day I didn't choose the same dreams that she had always had for me? Perhaps, though, perhaps it began with this one choice, made a long time ago—this choice that somehow became a lie, and the worst kind of lie. A lie I didn't exactly tell Caitlin, but one I let her believe.

Caitlin was six when she first actively noticed that she was the odd one out at school. Even the kids whose parents were no longer together had dads somewhere on the horizon, and even if they rarely saw them, they knew of their existence. They knew, at least approximately, where they were in the world. There was a vague connection to them, a tenuous sense of identity. Caitlin, though, had none of that, which is perhaps the reason that, one day, on our usual walk home from school, as she plucked the tulips and the daffodils that strayed between garden fences so she could make me a stolen bouquet, she asked me if she was a test-tube baby. The question, the phrase, so awkward and unnatural, so obviously implanted in her mouth by another, shocked me. I told her that she wasn't a test-tube baby, and that she'd been made in the same way most other babies were. Hurrying on before she could ask me exactly how that was, I told her that the moment I'd known about her, I'd wanted her, and I'd known that together we could be a brilliant little family and as happy as could be, which we were. I hoped that would be enough, and that she'd run ahead like she usually did, and hop and jump in an effort to pull sprigs of blossom off the cherry trees that lined the road. But instead she remained thoughtful and quiet. And so

I told her that if she wanted me to, I'd tell her all about the man who'd helped make her, and help her to meet him. She thought about it for a long time.

"But why don't I know him already?" she asked, her hand slipping into mine, leaving a trail of fallen petals behind. "John Watson, he knows his dad, even though he lives on an oil rig and he only sees him twice a year. He always brings him loads and loads of presents." Her tone was wistful, and I wasn't sure if it was because of the visits or the presents.

"Well . . ." No words came. I was ill-prepared for this moment, although I should have seen it coming; I should have practiced and rehearsed and been ready. And so I told the truth that somehow became a lie. "When I found out that you were in my tummy, I was very young. And so was your father. He just wasn't ready to be a dad."

"But you were ready to be my mummy?" Caitlin had looked puzzled. "It's not very hard, is it?"

"No," I said, squeezing her warm sticky fingers gently. "No, being your mummy is the easiest thing in the world."

"I don't want to know about him, then," Caitlin had said, quite determinedly. "I'm going to tell everyone at school that I *am* a test-tube baby."

Then, with an unexpected bound, she did run ahead, leaping up at a low-hanging branch laden with blossoms, creating a fall of pink confetti all around us as I walked under the tree. We laughed, tipping our faces up as the petals floated down, all thoughts of dads forgotten. I had thought that the time would come again when she'd want to talk more, and next time she'd be older and I'd be better prepared, but it never did.

That was the only conversation in which he was ever mentioned to her, and it was all she ever asked. And yet I had the uneasy feeling that Mum had always been right about this, and that the quietness, the uncertainty in Caitlin, the shyness she hides so well behind the black eyeliner and hair, and the always-black clothes that she wears like a shield ... it might all have come from that one ill-thought-out conversation. It might all be my fault. And that idea, the thought that the one thing I always thought I could be proud of—being her mother—might be untrue, fills me with horror. I'm going soon; I'm going and I need to make things right.

So this afternoon I pulled out a dust-filmed shoebox and found this letter, which I pasted into the book. It was folded around a photo of him holding my hand. Taken on a sunny day, we were both laughing, sitting on swings in the park, our fingers outstretched to claim the other's, leaning toward each other in a concerted effort to remain connected, no matter how gravity and kinetic energy might try to pull us apart. I must have been just pregnant with Caitlin by then, not that I'd known it. Strange how quickly that determination to touch dissolved so absolutely, so quickly, into nothing. I tucked the letter and photo into the back of the book, and I waited for Caitlin to come down to dinner. That would be the right time, I decided. With everyone here who cares about her: Esther to make her smile, and Greg to offer her support. That would be the best time to set things right.

"Well, she can't just turn up on his doorstep and find out that way, if that's what you are thinking. Imagine it!" Mum raises a brow as she sets out a trio of objects around my memory book. I slide it off the table and hold it to my chest, feeling the chill of the fifty-cent coin against my skin.

"Of course I don't think that," I say softly, suddenly exhausted.

Mum stirs something, a sauce she's made to go with the

meat that's in the oven. "I mean, think about her," Mum says. "Think about what she is facing now. A dad might come in handy."

This time, I don't answer. Instead, I find myself resting my head against the book, laying my cheek on its uneven surface. I've run out of effort.

The front door opens, and I am grateful to see Esther running in, clutching a bright-pink teddy bear, which must be a present from her other granny. Greg has been to his mother's. She rarely comes here. She did not approve of her son's aged wife even before I officially became a burden, and now she is distraught at his predicament. The sight of me does actually move her to tears. Greg did offer to take me along as well, and for a while it was a close thing: an afternoon with my mother, or his. . . . But in the end I chose my own. Better the devil you know.

"Look!" Esther shows me her bear, proudly. "I'm going to call him Pink Bear from Granny Pat."

"How lovely," I say, smiling over her head at Greg, and for a second we share a familiar joke. Esther's literal soft–toy animal names are legendary. Lined up on her bed right now are, among others, Ginger-Colored Dog with One Eye, and Blue Rabbit That Smells a Bit Funny.

"I don't know why it has to be a pink bear," Mum says, regarding the creature scathingly as if it were Granny Pat herself. "Why is it that just because she is a little girl, she must have pink foisted upon her?"

"Pink is my favorite color!" Esther tells my mum, eyeing the food that Mum is putting into serving dishes. "It's much nicer than blue or green, or yellow or purple, or something. Actually, I do like purple, and that really bright green, like grass. I like Granny Pat, but I don't like broccoli or meat."

"You are just like your mother." Mum doesn't mean it as a compliment, but Esther takes it as one, and beams.

"How was school?" Greg asks me, sitting down. He reaches out to touch me, and then, seeing how uncomfortable I am, withdraws his hand. I just can't hide it, even though I try to because I know that he's my husband, Esther's dad, and that I have loved him very much. I've seen the wedding photos, the video. I remember the way I felt about him—I feel the memories still, like an echo, but they are in the past now. In the present, I am numb. I see him, and I know him, but he feels like a stranger. It hurts him—the awkward small talk, the polite chitchat we make. Like two people stuck in a waiting room forced to discuss the weather.

"Sad," I say, like I am apologizing. "I still don't know why I can't teach. I mean, I can't drive, fine, but why can't I teach? It's so ..." I lose the words. They fall away from me, cruelly answering my own question. "And then I tried to talk to Caitlin about her father, but I don't think it went very well, so I thought I'd try again when we were all together."

"Daddy is Daddy," Esther says helpfully, as Mum puts a dish of orange on the table. "I don't like carrots."

"Oh." Greg is taken aback. "What, now?" Greg never asked me about Caitlin's father, and it was one of the things I do remember I loved about him. Caitlin was just my daughter, the person who came with me, no negotiation, and he accepted that right away. It took him a long time to make friends with Caitlin: years of inch-by-inch dedication that slowly allowed her to relent and accept him in her life, long after she'd accepted Esther, who was instantly just one of us, an Armstrong girl, from the moment she was born. "Will she be okay with that?"

"She doesn't know," Caitlin says, arriving in the living room. "She doesn't like the sound of it, though, whatever it is."

"It's carrots and them other vegibles," Esther commiserates.

"You look refreshed," I say, and smile. Her black eyes, along with the cascades of dark hair and her strong chin, stopped being reminders of her father when she was only a few months old: she owned them from the very beginning. Now, though, with Paul's photo tucked in the back of the memory book, I see him in Caitlin's eyes, which are watching me, warily.

"But you've got my eyebrows," I say out loud.

"If only that were a good thing," Caitlin jokes.

"Darling, I want to talk to you a bit more about your father. . . ."

"I know." She seems calm, thoughtful. Whatever it was that made her lock herself in her room for the afternoon seems to have subsided a little. "I know you do, Mum, and I know why you want to do it. I get it. But you don't need to, you see? You don't need to tell me, because it won't make any difference, except to maybe make things even more complicated than they already are, and none of us needs that, trust me. . . ." She hesitates, watching me closely, and her face, which I used to be able to read like an open book, is a mystery. "I thought about it, because it's what you want. I thought about seeing him, but I don't want to. Why would I give a stranger a chance to reject me again? Because I'm pretty sure he doesn't care at all that he's had a child in the world all this time. If he were bothered, if he cared, then we wouldn't be having this conversation, would we? I'd have his number on speed dial."

Mum puts the gravy jug down on the table with a thud.

"Guess what my bear's name is?" Esther asks Caitlin, sensing the tension spilling over like the gravy.

"Tarquin," Caitlin says. Esther finds that hilarious. "Marmaduke? Othello?"

Esther giggles.

"The thing is . . ." I start again. "What you need to remember is . . ."

"Just tell her," Mum says, thumping the meat down on the table as though she is intent on murdering it twice.

"Gran, Mum's told me she'd tell me about him when I wanted to know," Caitlin says sharply, protective of me. "Please, can we just drop it? I've got stuff I need to talk about too, before I . . . before tomorrow."

Mum looks at me expectantly, and I wait to know what to say, but nothing comes.

"What?" Caitlin says. "Come on, Gran, say what you're thinking. I'm sure we'd all like to know."

"It's not for me to say," she says.

"What's not for you to say?" Caitlin asks her, exasperated, rolling her eyes at me.

"Claire?" Greg prompts me with a frown—the frown I can't read anymore.

I close my eyes and force out the words. "Your dad. Paul," I say. "He didn't walk out on me, or abandon you. I mean, if I'd known that's what you were thinking all these years, I'd have told you sooner. I said I'd tell you when you were ready, but you never asked again. . . ."

"What do you mean?" Caitlin rises from her chair. "What are you saying—that you sent him away?"

I shake my head. "No . . . I never told him I was pregnant," I tell her. "He doesn't know you exist. He never has."

Caitlin sits down again, ever so slowly, and Mum joins her, the righteous wind blown right out of her battleship sails.

"I found out that I was pregnant, with you," I continue slowly, choosing words I know won't fail me, so that I won't say anything wrong. "And I knew what I had to do, for me, for you, for him. I knew I wanted to keep you, and I knew that I didn't want to be with him. So I didn't tell him I was pregnant. I just left. I left university, and I left him. I didn't return his calls or letters. And after quite a short time he stopped trying to get in touch. So he didn't abandon you: he never knew about you, Caitlin."

Caitlin is still for a moment. Her voice is quiet. "What I've always thought," she says, looking at me, "is that you had a choice to make that would change your life forever, and you chose me."

"That was true," I say. "I still chose you."

"But for all these years, you've let me think that he *didn't* choose me. When he never had a choice. And now . . ." She stops talking. "What do I do now, Mum? What do I do now? In my head I thought he'd be waiting for me to arrive one day, expecting me. That maybe he might even find out about you, and maybe even come and find me!"

"But . . ."

"And now . . . what do I do now?"

There is silence in the room; the family I thought would be supportive seem remote and distant. I've forgotten how to touch them, reach out to them—even Esther, who's crept onto Greg's lap with her bear.

"Whatever you want to do," I say calmly, carefully. I think hard before trying to speak any word; I check and double-check that I am not making a mistake. I can't afford to make a mistake now. "If you want me to, I'll contact him, tell him about you. We can do it together, if you like—whatever you want, Caitlin. I understand why you are angry with me, but it's because you don't know everything. You can't possibly understand why I did what I did. Let me try to . . . make you see. And don't worry, because there is time, all the time in the world for you to make everything exactly how you want it to be. I promise. I'll help you do whatever you want."

All color drains from Caitlin's face, and she places an arm on the table, steadying herself.

"Are you okay?" Greg asks her.

"I'm not okay," Caitlin says matter-of-factly. She looks at me, her chin set just like it always is whenever she is doing her best not to cry. "I don't think I'll stay for dinner. I think I'll go back to London tonight."

"Caitlin, please," I say, reaching out for her, but she withdraws her hand from under mine.

"I just need some time," she says. She won't look at me, but I know her well enough to know what she is thinking, and why her eyes are glazed with unshed tears. She can't be angry with her poor diseased mother, and it's not fair. "I just . . . I need to work out what to do. Away from you . . . all."

It's such a simple sentence, but the way she says it, her gaze turned away from me . . .

"Caitlin, don't go now," her gran says. "Have dinner at least. Things will seem better when you've eaten."

Caitlin looks at the food, cooling rapidly on the table.

"I'm going back tonight. I'll call a taxi to take me to the station."

"I'll take you to the station," Greg says, rising from his chair.

"No, thank you," Caitlin says very formally. "You'd better stay here with Mum. I just . . . I think I just need to go."

"She just didn't want to talk about it," Greg says, as he watches me untangling my hair with the hedgehog-looking thing. I don't like him watching me. It makes it harder somehow, more difficult to concentrate, like trying to clasp a necklace when you are looking in the mirror: everything is going backwards. And I am annoyed that I can remember that a hedgehog is a spiky little mammal indigenous to the British Isles, yet not what the name of the spiky-backed thing is. I'm sure Greg watching me makes it worse.

"You've tried," he goes on, standing close to me with the sort of easy familiarity that I simply don't feel. He's wearing only his boxers. I don't know where to look, so I turn my face from him and look at the wall. "You owned up, and that took guts. Caitlin will get that, eventually."

"I owned up?" I say, concentrating on the smooth, empty wall. "I suppose I did. Sometimes, it's never the right time to say something, do you know what I mean? I've hurt her, and she's holding it all in because I'm sick. Thing is, I'd feel so much better if she'd only shout and scream, and tell me how I've cocked up her whole life. I could take it."

"You haven't cocked up her whole life." Greg sits down next to me on the bed, and I tense, concentrating hard on not showing that the thought of his bare thigh so close to mine makes me want to bolt for the door. This is my husband; this is the man that I should never want to stop looking at. I know that, and yet he feels like a stranger. A total stranger who somehow has access to my family and my bedroom. He feels like an impostor.

"Caitlin is a sensible girl, a lovely girl, she's just shocked," the stranger says now. "Give her some space. A few days and you'll get it straightened out."

I sit awkwardly on the edge of the bed, waiting for him to go clean his teeth so that I can undress, put on my nightshirt, and wriggle under the covers. After a moment—I know he is debating whether or not to touch me—he gets up and goes into the bathroom. Changing quickly, I dive under the duvet, tucking the cover around me and under my legs and arms, creating a sort of pocket, so that when he climbs into bed, his body won't actually touch mine—and even if he puts his arms around me, they won't touch my skin. It's easier than having to explain to him that he frightens me, and that getting into bed with him feels alien and disjointed. I can't remember how to touch him, or how to react when he touches me. And so I wrap up my body, buffering it from his. Not just to protect me, but also to protect him from being hurt by me any more than I know he is every day. He seems like such a nice man. What did he ever do to deserve me? As I lie there waiting for him to return, his breath smelling of peppermint, I think that the saddest thing about this disease is that it makes me feel like a less nice person. I always used to feel like I was pretty nice. This time, I will be the first one to talk, I decide.

"What I'm worried about is that we don't make it up in time. I worry that in a few days' time, I'll think my name is Su-zanne, and I'll bark like a dog," I say, smiling shyly at him as he climbs into bed. He doesn't laugh, because he can't: he doesn't find AD even the slightest bit funny, and it's not really fair of me to expect him to, just because black humor makes it more bear-able for me. He thought he was going to have one kind of life, and look what he's been lumbered with: a wife that likes him increasingly less and soon will mostly just drool.

He rolls over and puts an arm across my insulated body. It feels heavy. "A couple of days and it will have all blown over," he says, kissing me on the ear, making me shudder. "She'll be back at uni with her friends, in the swing of it all, getting some perspective, and it will be fine. You'll see. I mean, it's like you say, there was never going to be a good time to tell her that, but you did it. You told her."

"I hope you're right," I say. There is something off with Caitlin—something more than her thinness, her exhaustion, her quiet sadness—that I have, of course, put down to my diagnosis, because it's all about me, right? A few months ago, I would have been able to decipher it, but now that time is gone. Decoding the subtleties of people's expressions is lost to me: I have to guess, or hope they will say something really obvious. There is something else, though—something that Caitlin is hiding to protect me—something more.

Greg stretches over me and presses something that makes the room go dark. I feel his hand snake its way under the covers, breaching my defenses and resting on my belly. There is nothing sexual in it. We haven't . . . not for ages. The last time was on the day of the diagnosis, before we'd told anyone. And even then it had more to do with grief than passion—we just clung to each other, willing everything to be different. Greg is still wishing it, and willing it. I always thought I'd fight it until my last breath, but sometimes I wonder if I've given up already.

"I love you, Claire," he says, ever so quietly.

I want to ask him how that is even possible when I am so broken, but I don't. "I do know that I've loved you," I say instead. "I do know that."

Greg's arm pinions me for a few moments more, and then he rolls over onto his side, and I feel cold. He doesn't understand that from the moment the disease became a reality, I started to withdraw from him. And I don't know if it's the disease that is driving this wedge between us, or if it is me, the real me, trying to save us both from the pain of separation. But whatever the reason is, it comes from me. I close my eyes, and see the lights contorting behind my lids. I remember the love I had for him; I remember how it feels. But when I look back on those times, it's as if it happened to another person. If I chase him away now, then perhaps in the long run all this will hurt less.

greg takes me out for a drink

This is the parking ticket I got for parking on a double yellow line the first evening I went out for a drink with Greg. I was late, of course. I'd spent a stupid amount of time, perhaps the most time ever before a date, working out what to wear, and even whether I should I go. He'd asked me earlier that day, a blazing hot day, and I'd said yes more because I didn't know how to say no than because I wanted to go. I took everything out of my wardrobe, and tried it on. And everything I had made me look fat and old—or at least that's what I thought. And then I found this chiffon tea dress, and I thought it showed too much cleavage; and then I put on this tie-dyed maxi sundress, and I thought that made me look my age; and then I went into Caitlin's room, where she was lying on her bed pretending to read, and asked her what to wear on a date, and she picked out an outfit that made me look like a librarian—a librarian who is also a part-time nun. So I went back to my bedroom and found a pair of jeans and a white T-shirt, which made me look like I should be in some sort of skincare advert, but at that point it was all I had. I turned around and around, looking at myself in the jeans, wondering if I could really carry them off, sitting down to check for folds of fat surging up over the waistband, wondering about the little apron of loose skin that had never bounced back after Caitlin was born, wondering if Greg knew he was asking a woman with stretch marks out for a drink.

"It's just a drink." That's what I told my reflection. It was just a drink, but as I ran a red light in order to get to the pub on time, bringing the car to a screeching halt on a set of double yellows, my heart was racing, my skin tingling in a way I'd never felt before, or at least not for a long time.

He'd said he would be in the garden, at the back. I walked through the pub feeling like everyone was looking at me, a woman in her midthirties wearing jeans and a white T-shirt. All around me there were younger women dressed in skimpy tops and tiny shorts, boasting their summer wardrobe with the kind of certain beauty that youth and firmness gives you. I felt so old, so much older than almost thirty-six, so foolish for agreeing to meet Greg, more foolish still for allowing myself even to think it was a date. I was sure that, after a little stilted conversation, he'd bring the topic round to how he could do some more work on the house, make some more money out of me. Or perhaps it would be like those stories you hear about on TV, or read in a magazine, in which some poor woman falls for a con artist and he takes away all of her money. I didn't really have any money, but as I spotted Greg, sitting right at the back of the garden under a tree, I thought that perhaps I'd give him the key to my house in exchange for five minutes to simply look at him.

As I approached, Greg rose from the bench, still straddling it like a cowboy. That's what I thought when I saw him there: he's like a cowboy. A cowboy builder.

"I got you a glass of white," he said, nodding at the perspiring glass on the table. "I didn't know if it was right, but you have a lot of empty bottles of white wine in your recycling, so . . . It's pinot grigio. I don't know much about wine, but there were three available by the glass and this was the most expensive."

I laughed, he blushed; I blushed, he laughed. There were moments of not looking at each other, not knowing whether to kiss or touch in some way, and so after some awkward bobbing, left to right, missing each other every time, we did neither.

I couldn't decide whether to sit opposite him, on the other side of the table, or on the same bench, the one he was straddling like a cowboy. In the end, I circled round the edge of the table to sit on the other side, in the full glare of sunshine. It was evening but the heat was still intense, and almost immediately, as a bead of sweat formed at the base of my neck and trickled down my spine, I wished I'd joined him in the shade. But by then it was too late to move.

I don't remember what we talked about, because I remember everything else: the sense of him being near me; the heat on the back of my neck, and feeling the backs of my arms beginning to burn and my cheeks glaze with perspiration; the longing for another drink and a visit to the ladies', but feeling unable to get up again so soon after I had arrived.

"You look hot," Greg said.

"Oh, thank you," I said, lowering my eyes, feeling a sudden frisson at the unexpectedly frank compliment.

"No, I mean you look hot, from the sun."

For a moment I just stared at him, mortified, horrified,

and then I laughed. And then he laughed. I buried my face in my hands, feeling the blood rushing to the surface of my skin all over my body.

Then Greg suggested we have another drink inside, out of the sun. He offered me his hand to help me up from the bench, but I declined and he waited for me as I somehow got my leg stuck under the picnic table, eventually staggering to my feet and falling against him. He held the tops of my arms to steady me, and then let me go. As we walked inside, I felt that every pair of eyes was upon us, wondering what he could be doing with me. He looked like the sort of man who'd feature on a calendar, whose usual date would be a twentysomething like him with a taut body and bright blond hair. What was he doing with me?

We stood inside at the bar, and I remember the first moment he touched me on purpose. I remember it exactly—the thrill, the jolt, the longing when he ran his forefinger along the back of my hand as it rested on the bar. We looked at each other, and didn't say anything about it: we just kept on talking, his fingers coming to rest on the back of my hand.

The sun was finally going down when he walked me back to the car and I found my parking ticket. Greg apologized, and I told him it wasn't his fault. He peeled it off the windscreen for me, and I folded it into my purse.

"Goodbye," I said.

"But I can call you?" he asked, brushing aside goodbyes.

"Of course," I said, half of me still wondering if he was touting for more work.

"Tomorrow, then. I'll phone you tomorrow."

"Greg . . ." I paused for ages, not knowing how to say what I needed to say. "Fine," I said at last. I stood there awkwardly, with my hand on the car door, feeling uncertain exactly how to make my exit. Greg opened the door for me and waited until I got in. He waited while I turned on the ignition and pulled out into the traffic. It was only when I'd gone through a set of lights and turned right that he disappeared from my rearview mirror.

And in the days that followed, I forgot about my parking ticket, folded neatly in the bottom of my bag. I had far too much else to think about. No, that's not true: I could only think about one thing. I could only think about Greg.

5

claire

"I'm sorry, the number you are calling is currently unavailable," the polite female voice tells me again. I look at the thing, the shiny black slab in my hand, and give it back to Greg. The device for making calls. I know what it does, but I've lost what it is called and how to make it work. It's the same with numbers: I know what they do, but I don't know how. "Try again?"

He nods stoically, even though I suspect he thinks I am wasting his time, stopping him leaving to go to work. I don't know what he's thinking, though, because since the night Caitlin left, we've more or less stopped talking altogether. Once, we were like a tangle, two threads so intricately entwined they could never be separated ... until the disease began to unravel me, to extricate me from my connection to him. Something I did or said has made him stop trying to make things the same as they were. I can't remember what it was, but I find that I am grateful he is avoiding me.

I watch him perform some mysterious ritual with the calling thing, his thumb sliding across its glassy surface, as he tries to reach Caitlin again. He listens to it for a moment, and the female voice comes again, from a distance this time: "I'm sorry, the number you are calling is currently unavailable."

"It's been a long time with no contact, hasn't it?" I say, sitting on the floor of Caitlin's bedroom. I came in here as soon as I woke up, to look for something that might tell me where she is, and knowing that, however long it has been, it is too long. Fear racks me from the second I wake, until I come into her room and begin to look for clues again. I say "again" because before I asked him to try and connect to her, on the talking thing, Greg told me that I have been doing exactly this for several days in a row. Perhaps I have, but the fear is intense, and new. It's the fear that twenty years have gone by while I was asleep. The fear that Caitlin's grown up and gone away, and I haven't noticed. The fear that I imagined her, and that she has never been real.

I look around. This is real—Caitlin is real—and it's been too long.

I'm still wearing my gray cotton pajamas and bed socks, and I feel uncomfortable being in the same room as Greg without a bra on. I don't want him to look at me, so I pull my knees up to my chin, wrap my arms around my legs, and fold myself in. But it's okay because he hardly ever looks directly at me since the night Caitlin left, however long ago that was.

"It's not *that* long," he says, laying the thing down on the cover of Caitlin's neatly made bed, and I wonder if I can trust him. "She's a grown woman, don't forget. She said she wanted some space. Some time to think."

I used to have a number that connected to a place, an actual building instead of the device Caitlin keeps glued to the palm of her hand. When she came home in the summer, she had brought all of her belongings with her for the first time in two years, because in her final year she was going to be living somewhere else. Greg had gone to pick her up in the van, and I'd sat and watched while they unloaded it and she carried armfuls and armfuls of her life back up the stairs to her bedroom. She'd said they were all getting a better place close to campus, but she never gave us the address. I'd gotten so used to always being able to reach her that I suppose I thought we were somehow permanently connected, and could always be in touch within moments. But that was when I was still able to use the object that I don't know the name for anymore—and when she used to compulsively respond to it.

Something is wrong—more wrong than hurt feelings and anger.

"It feels like too long a time." I dig my feet into the carpet. I don't know exactly how long it has been. One of the fears I have when I wake up every day is that time might have vanished while I wasn't concentrating. She might have been gone a day, a week, a year, or a decade. Have I lost years in the fog? Is she older now with her own children, and I've missed a lifetime, lying unconscious in my own sleepy hollow?

"Two weeks and a bit," he says, staring at his hands clasped between his knees. "It's not that long, really."

"It's not long at all when you are twenty and living it up at university." My mum appears, standing in the doorway, her arms folded. She looks like she is on the point of telling me to tidy up after myself, even though this is Caitlin's room. "Remember when you went InterRailing or whatever it was with that girl? What was her name?"

"Laura Bolsover," I say, at once picturing Laura's face, round and shiny, dimples in her cheeks, her left eyebrow pierced several times. Names from the distant past come freakishly easily, because quite often I feel as though I am there, and this *here,* this *now,* is simply an intermission from reality. I met her at a party when I was seventeen. We instantly became inseparable friends and remained so for about a year, until our lives took us in separate directions, and the promises we'd made to always stay in touch were forgotten within days, possibly hours.

"Yes." Mum nods. "That was her. Cocky little thing, she was, always grinning like she was in on some joke. Anyway, you went off with her, across Europe, and for the best part of three months I never heard from you. Every day I was worried sick about you, but what could I do? I had to trust that you would turn up again, and you did. Like a bad penny."

"Well, that was before . . ." I gesture at the thing, lying maddeningly dormant on the bed. "It was harder then to be in touch. Now there's calling and emails." I remember emails. I smile, feeling quite proud of the way I've remembered emailing, and spoken about it. I've tried that too—or had Mum and Greg do it for me, at least, standing over the word book, telling them what to say. Still no reply.

Mum looks around at Caitlin's room, the tiny-pink-rosebud paper all but obliterated by posters of depressed-looking rock bands. "Two weeks isn't that long."

"Two weeks and a bit," I say, trying to highlight that piece of information in my mind, to stick it down somewhere so it will stay. "That is long for Caitlin. She's never done this before. We always talk, every few days."

"Her life has never been like *this* before," Mum says. "She's facing all this too, your . . ." She gestures in a way that I am assuming is meant to mean Alzheimer's Disease, because she doesn't like to say the words out loud. "And she's just found out she was fathered by a man who never knew of her existence. It's no wonder she feels like she needs to escape."

"Yes, but I am not *you,*" I hear myself say. "Caitlin doesn't feel the need to try and escape from *me.*"

Mum stands in the doorway for a moment longer, and then turns on her heel. I have been cruel again. I suppose everybody knows that the reason I am cruel is because the AD makes me stop knowing what and how to say things, and also because a lot of the time I feel scared. I suppose everyone knows that, but it doesn't stop them being hurt by me—and beginning to be wary of me, and I think perhaps even to resent me—and why should it? And it must be harder when I am almost like me, but not quite me. At the moment I am enough like me for Esther not to know the difference. It will be easier for them when more of me is gone.

"I'll Hoover downstairs," Mum calls out from the safety of the landing.

"There was no need for that," Greg admonishes me. "Ruth's trying her best to help. To be here for you, for all of us. You keep acting like she's deliberately trying to make your life worse, not better." I shrug and I know it maddens him. "I have to go out to work, Claire. Someone's got to be here to . . . take care of things . . . and we're lucky Ruth is willing to be that person. Try to remember that."

It's such an inappropriate thing to say to me, of all people, that I want to laugh. I *would* laugh if I weren't so afraid for Caitlin.

"Something's wrong, I know it." I clamber to my feet, hunching my shoulders to hide my breasts. "Whatever else is gone, I still know my daughter. I still know that this is about more than just telling her about her father. If it were just that, she'd have had it out with me. There would have been screaming and shouting and crying, but not this. Not silence." I pull open her drawers, looking for something amidst the bundle of dark clothes, screwed up and thrown in without thought of a system or order. "I know when something is wrong with my daughter."

"Claire." Greg says my name, but nothing else for a while as I pull open Caitlin's wardrobe doors. Something about her wardrobe—packed full of hanger after hanger of dark garments—is wrong. But I can't place what it is. "Claire, I understand you are frightened and angry, but I miss you, Claire. I miss you so much. Please . . . I don't know what to do. . . . Can't you just come back to me, for a little while? Please. Before it's too late."

I turn around slowly and look at him. I see his face, which looks faded somehow, worn away, and his shoulders have dropped.

"The trouble is," I tell him in a very quiet voice, "I don't remember how to."

Greg gets up very slowly, tilting his face away from me. "I've got to go to work."

"It's okay to be angry with me," I tell him. "Shout at me, tell me I'm a bitch and a cow. I'd prefer it, honestly I would."

But he doesn't answer me. I hear him go down the stairs, and I wait for a few beats longer until the front door shuts behind him, and then suddenly I am alone in Caitlin's room, the drone of the Hoover drifting up from downstairs. I close her door and breathe in the heated air, dust motes circling in the stream of morning sunlight that warms the bedclothes, and I wonder what time of year it is. Caitlin went back to college, so it has to be October. Or February. Or May.

I look around for a clue, anything to tell me why she isn't answering my calls. There is no secret diary, no stash of letters. I go and sit down at her desk, and slowly open the top part of her word book. There is something about it being there that unsettles me: sitting so neatly on the desk, it looks like a relic. I look at the buttons, and run my fingers over them, feeling them dip and click beneath my touch. My hands used to fly over these buttons, reeling out words quicker than I could think them, sometimes. Not now, though. Now, if I try to type, it's clunky and slow, and wrong. I know the letters in my head, but my fingers won't make them. Greg spent a lot of money getting me voice-recognition software for the computer downstairs, because I can still think far better than I can articulate in words. But I haven't used it yet. The bright-pink, blue-ink fountain pen that Esther gave me for my last birthday still works well, connecting what is left of my mind to my fingers, and the words come out okay in the memory book. I want to keep writing with my hands for as long as I can, until I forget what my fingers are for, anyway.

I close the word book and run a finger along the row of books that Caitlin has lined up on her windowsill, looking for something, perhaps a slip of paper acting as a page marker, something that will tell me what is wrong. But even the books sitting dormant on her windowsill seem wrong to me, although I don't know why. I sit there for a long time, looking at her things all around me, and then I notice that her waste bin, tucked quietly under the desk, is still full of paper, tissues, and makeup-remover wipes, smeared in black. I'm amazed Mum hasn't been here already to empty it out—she seems to clean the house on a perpetual loop, going around and around and around with a duster, keeping herself busy while pretending that she's not just making sure I don't let myself out of the front door or accidentally burn the house down. I don't seem to go out much anymore; I don't seem to want to very much. The outside world is full of clues I can't decipher. The only person who is pleased about my house arrest is Esther, who always complained that I didn't spend enough time with her. "You're not workings," she'd tell me, as I tried to leave for school. "You stay in and you play with me, yes, yes, I think so?"

She still asks me, if I go upstairs, or to the bathroom: "You're not workings, are you, Mummy?" And now I can always say that I am not. Instead, I let her draw me into her imaginary worlds—of tiny creatures with tiny voices, tea parties, deep-sea adventures, road races, and hospital, where I am always the patient and she is always making me completely and totally better with a bandage made out of toilet roll. At least I still make Esther happy. I may even make her happier the way I am now than I did before, and that's something.

I pick up the waste bin and empty it onto the floor, bracing myself to find something I don't particularly want to know about, but at first glance it looks innocuous, apart from a still mostly full packet of cigarettes, which surprises me because I don't think Caitlin smokes. And if she does, why would she throw them away? I begin to gather up rubbish again, and then I see it: a long white plastic thing. I pick it up and look at it. I know that, once, I would have known what it is, but now I don't. I only know that it tells me something very, very important, because my heart has responded to it with sickening speed.

"Mum!" I call down the stairs, but there is no answer, just the drone of the Hoover. Standing at the top of the stairs, I look at the thing again. I stare hard at it, trying to discern its mysteries. The bathroom door opens and Greg is there, and at once I hide it behind my back. I don't know why, but I feel like it's a secret.

"I thought you'd gone," I say.

"I had, but then I came back," he says. "I forgot something."

"Story of my life." I smile weakly but he doesn't smile back.

"What's that?" he asks me, nodding at the arm folded behind my back.

"I don't know." After a moment's hesitation, I hold it out for him to look at. His eyes widen when he sees it, and gingerly he takes it from my hand.

"What is it?" I ask him, resisting the impulse to grab it back.

"It's a pregnancy-test kit," Greg tells me. "It's Caitlin's?"

"It was in her room—is it used?"

Greg nods. "Yes."

"Well, what does it say?" I exclaim, frustrated.

"Nothing." He shakes his head. "The results don't stay forever."

His smile is warm, his face sweet, and just for a second I recognize him, and it's wonderful. Like seeing a lover at the end of a very long station platform, emerging from the steam. For one second, I am so happy, so full of lost love, and I am going to run to him, when all the ill-fitting, scrambled-up mosaic pieces that make up the world around me fall into place and I see everything. That's what's wrong with Caitlin's wardrobes: they are still stuffed full of clothes. The mainly black clothes she loves to wear—she's left them all behind and taken only a few things with her. Her textbooks are sitting on the windowsill; her word book is still folded neatly on her desk. Wherever Caitlin went that night, two weeks ago, it wasn't back to university. She didn't take anything with her.

"I need to go and find her," I say, stumbling down the stairs in my urgency to be with her. I hurry to the table by the door where the keys to my car are normally kept in a cranberry-colored glass bowl. Greg trots down the stairs behind me.

"Where are my car keys?" I ask him, loud enough for my mother to switch off the vacuum cleaner and come into the hallway. "I need my car keys." I hold my hand out while Greg and my mother just look at me.

"Claire, dear." Mum is talking to me cautiously, like I might be a bomb about to go off. "Where do you want to go? I'll drive you. . . ."

"I don't need you to drive me." I feel my voice rising. Esther appears in the doorway under my mother's arm. They don't realize that now, right at this moment, I know everything, just like I did before, and I need to go now before the fog rolls in again. I need to go now, while I can see and think. "I can drive. I know what the steering wheel is for, and the difference between the brake and the accelerator, and I need to go and find Caitlin. She might be pregnant!"

No one answers; no one comes to my aid, fetches my keys, or sees how serious I am. Even Esther just stares at me, bemused. Am I saying the words I think I am out loud, or are they hearing something else entirely?

"Why are you doing this to me?" I shout, finding my face suddenly wet with tears. "Why are you trying to keep me prisoner in here? Do you hate me so much? Caitlin needs me, don't you understand? And I need to go to her. Give me my car keys!"

"Babe, look . . . just take a breath, let's think this through. . . ." Greg touches my arm.

"She needs me," I tell him. "I let her down. She thinks I can't be her mum anymore, and maybe she's going through this huge thing, this thing I know about, but all she can think about is how I did it wrong. And she can't think like that because I do know, and I know exactly what she is going through, and she needs me now, before . . . it all goes again. Greg, *please, please,* I do love you. I'm here; I'm here now. I love you so much, and you know that. Please, please don't keep me from her!"

"I don't understand what's happening," Mum says, as I keep looking into Greg's eyes, willing him to see that it's me—

that I am here now. Me, the *me* he knows. Willing him to see before I go again.

"Caitlin is pregnant," I tell her. "Of course she is. I don't know how I missed it. She looks so tired all the time, and so worried. And she hasn't taken anything with her, nothing that she usually takes back to a new term at university. Why didn't I remember that? She's barely packed a bag. She's just gone, and she's not answering her phone or emails, she's not on . . . Twitter or the other thing. Where has she gone? Mum, I need to go to her. You have to let me. You can't keep me from my daughter!"

"But you don't know where to look," Mum says, and it is she who steps forward, who hooks an arm around my waist and talks to me, her voice low and soft, guiding me into the living room. Greg does not move. I look at him over my shoulder, and his whole body is clenched like a fist.

"I know, why don't you sit down and we can call the university and find out where she is living. I don't know why we didn't think of that before."

"I don't want to sit down," I say. "I want to go to my daughter."

"Come on, now." Mum soothes me like I have a cut knee. "Come and sit in the kitchen, and we'll have a think."

"I have to go," Greg says from the hallway. "I'm already late for the job. Look, Claire, you don't need to worry. We don't even know the test result. Sit tight. Ruth and I will find out what's going on."

I say nothing, and he leaves without ever seeing that it's me, that I am here. And I'm not sure if I can forgive him for that.

Esther climbs onto my lap, holding on to the hem of my pajama top.

"Is that show on that you like?" I whisper to Esther, as

Mum fills the kettle in the kitchen. "The one with the talking vegetables?"

"I want telly on, I want telly on, I want telly on!" Esther wails at once. Mum turns round, tuts, and rolls her eyes as she heads to the living room, Esther trotting behind her.

"In my day, we read books," she says, forgetting that Esther has yet to learn to read.

Seizing my moment, I go to the back door and pull on the only coat that is there: it's Greg's, and it's big, thick, and warm, spattered in mud from working on-site. There is a pair of boots I think are my mother's; I put them on. They are a little too small, but I don't have any socks on, so it's not too bad. I'll need money, so I take her handbag from the kitchen worktop and I let myself out of the back door, down the path, out of the gate. I stop. I remember everything I've just learned. I remind myself again, and it's all still there. Right now, at this moment in time, I am me— I am me, and I know everything. I start walking toward the town center and the train station. I have broken free.

ruth

This is the four-leaf-clover bookmark I gave to Claire on the day she left home, again, to start her life again. Caitlin was a little over one, and for the whole of that first year of Caitlin's life, they had lived with me. It was one of the happiest years of my life.

When Claire came to me, all those months earlier, and told me she was leaving university to have a baby, I didn't fight her or try to change her mind. I knew there was no point. Claire has always been like me: she makes up her mind to do something, and she does it, no matter what anyone else thinks. Like the day I decided to marry a much older man who had never even heard of the Beatles and the Stones. A man who the outside world could never see fitting perfectly with me. But I knew he did, and that was all I ever needed to know, right up until the day he died. And so I didn't try to change Claire's mind or prepare her for parenthood: I just took her back in, and let her build a wall around herself, cutting herself off from her old life and friends, waiting to be a mother. I thought—I hoped—that perhaps it had a little bit to do with me, her determination to bring a child into the world. We used to be very close.

One day my strident, brazen, and brave daughter was conquering the English Department at Leeds with the confidence of Boudicca, and the next she was undone. Just like the heroines of the novels she was studying. She'd succumbed to what she'd thought was love, and got lost in the middle of the whirlwind. When it was over, and the storm had set her down, somewhere very far from anything she recognized, Caitlin was already there, secreted away inside her, a tiny black pearl of life waiting to bloom into existence. Those early days, the days when she first came home, we stayed up all hours talking, about love and life, and ambition and the future, and about how sometimes what you planned for just isn't what happens, or even what you want to happen. Claire got a part-time job in the library, and I remember it as a happy time—reading books, swapping them, talking about them. Painting the spare bedroom for the baby, trying to put together a cot one evening. We nearly killed each other, but we laughed a lot too.

When Caitlin arrived, I couldn't have been more proud of Claire: she was hardly more than a child herself, but instantly she was in love with her baby. I suppose that, back then, at that moment in time when it was just the two of them, Caitlin's father didn't seem very important at all. I should have told her then that one day he would matter, but I didn't. I saw the two of them cocooned together, and I wanted to keep them safe and pure. That first year flew by, Claire sitting in the kitchen singing to Caitlin while we talked and laughed.

I knew they wouldn't be there forever, and I was right. Claire is not a person to just sit and wait for life to happen to her:

she goes and finds it, grabs on to it with all of her might. Just like the father she barely got to know.

The day she left home again was for her first job, the only job she could get without a completed degree and no work experience: a receptionist at a science park on the campus of the local further education college. She said she liked being with the other students, who were around her age, and although the job was dull, and she wasn't very good at it, she liked the boss.

She'd found a bedsit for Caitlin and herself, over a chip shop near the campus. I didn't want her to move there. I wanted her to stay at home with me, in the safe and the warm, where I could continue to protect them, but she was determined to get back to life. Even if it wasn't the life she'd planned, or I'd hoped for—her glittering career as a member of the literati, prize-winning novelist, famous wit, and raconteur. She wasn't bitter about it. About the abrupt halt that Caitlin's arrival brought to her life. If anything, I think she was relieved. Now she only had to worry about taking care of her; she didn't have to worry about fulfilling promises, or failing. There were no more great expectations. And sometimes I think it was only then, when she didn't have to burden herself with the responsibility of trying to be successful, that she started to do things right.

On the day she left, I watched her pack the last of her things into her backpack while I held Caitlin in my arms.

"You'll phone?" I asked.

"Mum, I'm down the road. Like, five minutes away."

"You don't look like you've got enough in that one bag. Why don't you let me drive you? You can take more stuff. Not that I mind you having things here. I'd like you to leave all your things here and let me look after you both."

"I've just got to do this, Mum," she said. "I've got be a grown-up."

That was when I gave her the laminated bookmark, with the four-leaf clover pressed flat beneath the plastic, one leaf slightly separated from the other three. Underneath it, in italic print, are the words: "For each leaf of this clover, this brings a wish your way. Good luck, good health and happiness for today and every day."

She must have thought I'd gone mad, because she looked puzzled when I gave it to her, an object so far removed from our lives that it seemed like it might have appeared from another universe entirely. When I'd gone out to get milk that morning from the corner shop, I'd seen it on a stand, and it had just seemed right, somehow.

"It's to remind you of all the books we've read together," I explained. "I know it's silly, it's just a token."

"I love it, actually." She grinned. "I love you, Mum."

"It sort of spoke to me," I told her. I remember putting my arms around Caitlin, the backpack, and Claire all in one go, and kissing them both on each cheek before I could let them go.

"Gran's hearing voices again!" Claire said to Caitlin.

She tucked the bookmark inside a copy of *Like Water for Chocolate* that was resting on top of her bag, and she's kept it ever since, giving it back to me when it was my turn to write in her memory book, and asking me to remember the day I gave it to her and to write about what it means.

I don't think I knew what this silly little token meant until I saw it again twenty years later, but now I think I do. I believe in luck and good fortune; I believe in fate and that nothing is arbitrary or random. I find that comforting now, because I am sure that everything happens for a reason, even losing, more than once, the people you love—even that. And I know Claire better than anyone, and I know that she will burn brighter than any star in the sky for as long as she can: she will shine, no matter what. And I know that soon, very soon, I'll need to stop being so angry and just tell her that I love her too.

6

claire

I go to the bottom of my street, where the main road is and where the buses come along. I get there, and I could wait for a bus, but I never take a bus. I'm not really a bus sort of person, at least not since I saw the other side of thirty. It is a matter of principle: I might not have access to a car right now, but I have, or at least had not so long ago, the means to own a brand-new one. Also, I don't want to be that person on the bus in her night-clothes, the one other people pretend not to see, and that makes me think how awful it must be for people who really are mad. It's bad enough feeling so low, and lost, or hearing voices in your head, without the rest of the world refusing to notice you. Of course, soon you would start to wonder if you were real at all, wouldn't you? I would. I'd start to wonder if I was real. So, no thank you, I don't want to be that invisible person, because I am certain that at the moment everything is present and correct in my head, and that I am not some poor demented woman wandering the streets but a rational, clear-headed warrior queen, making a break for freedom so that she can save the day. That's what this is . . . isn't it?

I can't stop to think about it—if I dither, I will lose the moment—so I decide to walk. March purposefully, so that everyone can see I know where I am going. It's not far, where I'm going. It's an easy walk, but I will admit I'm cold, even with this massive coat on. And I wish I'd run away with a bra on: there is something far less assertive about running away knowing that your breasts are bobbing up and down and completely out of control, flapping around like a pair of kippers. But there you go. When you are forced to break out of prison, you don't always have time to consider your underwear options. I clutch Mum's bag to my side, and scrunch my toes up in the ends of her boots. At the end of the road, I turn left—that's the hand I don't write with—and then follow this big wide road all the way until I get to the train station. I'll get to the station in the end if I keep walking along the big wide road. It's like that hotel lobby somewhere or other, where if you sit in it for long enough you will meet everyone you ever knew.

I'm not going to a hotel, though.

No one is looking at me, which is a good thing. I thought I might look like a mental-home escapee, but I suppose my gray cotton PJ bottoms, while not ideal in this biting weather, aren't stand-out conspicuous; and thanks to this fat coat, only I know that I am out in the world commando style. I giggle to myself, and for a second I forget what I am doing and why, and then I wonder whether people aren't looking at me because they can't see me.

Head up, chin up, shoulders back, remember the warrior

queen. I'm outside, I have taken myself out, and I am my own person again. Mistress of my own destiny. It's exciting. Thrilling. The sense of freedom is immense. No one knows me—I could be anyone—and if it wasn't for the fact that I have to keep a low profile, I'd sing, or skip or something, or run. I'd love to run if I were appropriately attired, but instead I content myself with marching and knowing that I could just be any normal woman out for a walk in her mother's boots and no bra.

"Hello there?" I hear a vaguely familiar voice, and I march a little more quickly. If it is someone I know, then I can't take the chance they might try to stop me—might try to take me back.

"Hey, Claire? It's Ryan, do you remember me from the café?"

I stop and look at him. Ryan. For a moment I am blank: what café, when? I take a couple of steps back from him.

"Do you remember? It rained a lot, and you were wet through. I said you looked like a very pretty drowned rat?"

And then I remember that curious collection of words, and the moment that came with them. It had been a happy moment, a moment when I'd felt like me. Ryan, the man from the café. And here I was out and about without a bra.

"Um . . . hello," I say, suddenly also aware that I didn't tidy my hair, or wash my face, or clean my teeth this morning. I turn my face from him, because I don't want him to look at me. "I'm just . . . going for a quick walk."

"I was hoping I'd bump into you again," he says. He has a nice voice: it's gentle, kind, kind enough for me to wonder if perhaps it doesn't matter that my hair is a tangle of snakes, and my eyes are naked. "Thought you might call."

"Sorry," I say airily. "I've just been really busy."

This is a lie. I have not been really busy. I have been lying on the carpet in the living room being bandaged in toilet paper by Esther, writing in my book and worrying about Caitlin. *Caitlin.* "Actually, I have to go somewhere. . . ."

"Where are you off to?" he asks me, falling into step next to me. I thrust my hands into the pocket of the coat, and find a packet of those round mints in there. Greg's been sucking mints. What does that mean? Does that mean he's planning to kiss someone, perhaps—someone other than me? I remembered him today, or at least my heart did, but it was too late. He didn't see me; he'd stopped caring and he left me. I stop my fingers circling round the mints as I think of the time when I won't be anything to my husband anymore—other than a memory of a difficult time.

"Where did you say you were going?" Ryan repeats the question, nudging me into responding.

"To the . . ." I stop talking. I feel hurt, and sad, and I don't know why. The sky is bright and golden, the air crisp and pure, but still the fog has rolled in and I am lost again. "I'm just going for a walk."

"Can I walk with you?" he asks me.

"I don't really know where I'm going," I warn him. "Just wandering around aimlessly!" There's a hint of anxiety in my voice. I know I came out for Caitlin, but why? Where am I meeting her? Am I picking her up from something? Is it school? I picked her up from school late, once, and when I got there, her face was pinched and white, her eyes swollen with tears. The bus had been late, that was why. I am not a bus person anymore. If I'm late, she'll be scared; I don't want her to be scared.

"I have to find my daughter," I say.

"You've got a daughter?" he asks me, and I realize I didn't mention her last time.

"Yes, she's at university." I listen to the words form in my mouth, and double-check them. Yes, Caitlin is at university; she's not waiting for me in a school playground somewhere. She's twenty years old and safe at university.

"You don't look old enough to have a daughter in college," he says, and I can't help grinning.

"It is a modern miracle, isn't it?" I push my web of hair off my face, and smile at him.

"Can I suggest we turn around," he says pleasantly. "That way is just the town center and shops and traffic. If we walk the other way, we might even get to hear a bird singing."

We walk in silence for a few minutes, and as we do, I steal sideways looks at him. The man I remember meeting in the café is younger in my head, but then again I thought I was younger too. For all I know, that meeting might have been ten or twenty years ago, except that the way he talks to me, shyly, hesitantly, suggests that we are recent and vague acquaintances. He must have liked me, though: if he hadn't liked me, he wouldn't have stopped to talk to me in the street.

Now I look at him, I see he is around my age, and nicely dressed in a suit and tie. He looks like the sort of man I should have married; the sort of man who would have a pension plan and probably Bupa health insurance. I bet it's better being demented on Bupa. Like NHS dementia, but with nicer food and Sky TV, probably.

"Did we really just bump into each other?" I ask him, feeling suddenly a little wary. "Or are you stalking me?"

He laughs. "No, I'm not stalking you. I will admit I have hoped that we would get to talk again. No, I am a lonely, sad man who saw you in a café a few weeks ago and thought that you looked . . . lovely, and like you needed taking care of, and . . .

Well, look, I hope you don't mind my pointing it out, but you're outside now, and you're still in your PJs, so I just thought . . . maybe you might like a friend?"

"So you're lonely and sad," I say, liking the fact that he's noticed my outfit (why am I out in my PJs?) yet he's not instantly marching me off to the asylum. "And obviously not a marketing professional. Tell me something about yourself, like why you are lonely and sad?"

"If you tell me why you don't bother getting dressed for walks," he says.

"I . . ." I am about to tell him, but I stop. I'm not quite ready yet. "I am a free spirit," I say, and he laughs. "Now it's your turn."

He doesn't know that he can tell me what he likes, and I will probably forget it any minute now; although I didn't forget him, or our first meeting, not from the moment he said the words "pretty drowned rat." I mean, I hadn't thought about him until then, but as soon as I heard those words, I knew him, and that's something to hold on to, something good. And I remember . . . I remember his eyes. He doesn't know what he can and can't tell me, and I am amazed and, yes, touched as he tells me, well, everything.

"I'm a pathetic case," he admits. "My wife . . . she just stopped loving me and she left me. And I'm heartbroken. I miss her like crazy. And some days I don't see the point of going on, but then I remember that I have to, because people depend on me. I used to like being the strong one, but not now. Now, I don't know how I will ever be happy again, and it terrifies me."

"Wow, that really is sad and pathetic," I say, but I understand. He feels lost just like me, just like I am, both literally and figuratively. I reach out and pick up his hand. He is surprised for a second, and then pleased, I think. He doesn't pull away from me, anyway.

"Glad you find my pain amusing." He smiles, and glances sideways at me.

"I'm not laughing at you," I say. "I'm just laughing at us. Look at us, lost souls out for a walk on the streets of Guildford. We need a heath, really, or a forest. We need a landscape with some proper metaphor in it. Lampposts and bus stops don't really cut it." I am pleased with myself: I'm pretty sure I was just clever and funny all in one go. The people back at home, they think I'm already a write-off. I wonder if they are looking for me—whether they are freaking out? I must have been gone a while, now. Mum has surely discovered that I have absconded in her boots. That's right, I ran away. But I can't remember why, and when I'm holding hands with Ryan, it seems less pressing.

"We'll have to make do with leafy suburbia," he says as we climb the hill, which is lined along each side with houses, 1930s semis that all look almost exactly the same. Once, these houses were paradise, Utopia. Now they seem like they were built specifically to trick me: a cruel joke, a maze with only dead ends and double bluffs, and no way out. I know I live in one of them, but I have no idea which one. There is something to do with curtains, but I forget what, and anyway I don't want to go back to where they will be waiting to lock me in.

"What about you?" he asks me, as we turn from one identical avenue into another. "Tell me your story."

"I'm not well, Ryan," I confess regretfully. "I didn't want to tell you, because I think when you know, you won't look at me the same way, or talk to me in the same way. There are only two people in the whole world who don't treat me any differently now I am sick, and you are one of them. The other is my little girl, my second daughter, Esther. She is only three and a half. I've been married to her father for a year and a bit. He's a very good man, a decent man. He deserves so much better than this."

Ryan falls silent for a moment or two, taking it all in. "Can we just assume," he says at last, "that as I'm very happy to walk hand in hand with a married woman who is wearing her pajamas in public, I won't change the way I see you, or talk to you, if you tell me what your illness is?"

"I . . ." I don't know how to tell him the truth without frightening him away, so I tell him a version of it. "Let's just say, I don't have very long left."

Ryan's slow, steady pace falters, and I feel sorry for him. I keep forgetting how frightening any serious illness is for other people. It's as if Death has just tapped them on the shoulder, and reminded them it's coming for them one day too.

"It's not fair," he says quietly, taking in the news.

"No." I can only agree. "This part is the worst part. The part when I know what I am losing. This part hurts me. More than I know how to say, to anyone. Not that I've ever tried to explain it to anyone . . . except you. This is the part I never want to end, and the part I want over now."

Ryan looks, what? Mortified, I think. Horrified. His face is white as a sheet.

"Sorry," I say. "I don't know why I've picked on you to confess my inner thoughts to. Look, it's okay. Don't feel obliged to talk to me. I'll be fine from here."

I look around me, and realize I have no idea where I am, or even when. I don't want to let go of his hand, but I tell myself that if he loosens his grip on my fingers, even a little, then I must.

"Do you love your husband?" he asks me. I look down and see he is still holding my hand, firmly. I look at it, my hand in his, my wedding ring shimmering in the morning sun.

"Sometimes I remember what it felt like," I say. "And I know that I was so lucky to have it, even for a little while."

Chewing my lip as we walk on, I wonder what I'm doing, and why. Why am I telling this perfect stranger, who quite possibly has more mental health issues than I do, the secrets I can't tell my family? By now, I should have scared him off he should be making his polite excuses, and finding a way to leave—but he is still walking next to me, still holding my hand. And it doesn't feel wrong, my hand in his. It feels . . . comforting.

"Love is a funny thing," he says, breaking the silence. "Sometimes, I'd like to be better with words, so that I could talk about it more. It seems so wrong to me that there is this condition that affects all of us, more than anything else in our lives ever will, and only the poets and song writers get to talk about it with any sort of authority."

"You can talk about it to me," I say. "It doesn't matter what words you use."

"I suppose I think it's more than just words and sentiment," he says. "I suppose that, actually, I'd really like to be your friend, if you feel you need one, even though I'm missing my wife, who I still love, and even though you are so ill. And even though we can't be friends forever, I'd like us to be friends now. If you don't mind?"

"But why?" I ask him. "Why would you want to have anything to do with me?"

"Our paths crossed at exactly the right time, don't you think?" He draws to a stop, turning to face me. "When I think about love, I suppose I think it's something outside of us. Something that's about more than just sex or romance. I suppose I think that when we are gone, all that will be left of us is love."

"That reminds me of something," I say. "I can't think what."

I try to push back the fold of fog in my memory as I glance

around, spotting a house with red curtains at the window. It's my house; somehow we have stopped outside my house.

"I live here," I say, surprised. "You've brought me home."

"More likely that you just knew the way, and led us here because you weren't thinking about it too much," he says, looking a little sad, perhaps because our walk is over. "Either that or I'm your guardian angel."

"I hope not," I say. "I've always thought guardian angels sound like right party poopers."

Something moves in my peripheral vision, probably my mum releasing the curtains, which means she's heading for the door. I don't want to have to explain Ryan to Mum—or worse, to Greg—so I guide him back a step or two behind our neighbor's stupidly tall privet hedge.

"I think my mum might ground me," I whisper to Ryan, smiling ruefully.

"Oh, shall I . . . ?" But before he can offer to say hello to my mother, I stop him.

"No, it's fine," I say. "Thank you for the walk. Thank you for bringing me back. I'd better go."

"Do you still have my number?" he asks me, catching my wrist.

"Yes," I say. But the truth is, I don't know.

"If you need me," he says, "if you need a friend who doesn't care what you are wearing, then you can reach me. Promise."

"And you too," I say. "You reach me too, when you are missing your wife more than you want to."

"Remember me," he says.

"I will," I say, and I don't know why, but I know that it's true.

"I'm sorry," Mum says, as soon as I walk in the door, my head tipped back, preparing to be grounded.

I turn around slowly and look at her. "Pardon?"

"I'm not doing a very good job of seeing what this is like for you," she says, wringing her hands over and over. "I just want to look after you—that's all I want to do. And sometimes I think I try too hard, or not hard enough, to understand how frustrating this all is, for you. I suppose I'm not listening to you enough. I was worried sick, and Greg's out looking for you. I'd better ring him."

Greg doesn't answer, and Mum leaves a message. Her voice is trembling, and I realize I've scared her. It seems so stupid to me that, just by going out of the door, I frighten my mother so much. It seems so stupid that this is my life now.

"I'm sorry," I say. "I don't do things to frighten you. I do things because I honestly think it's fine. . . . This is all happening too fast for me to keep up with, that's the trouble."

Mum nods, and letting go of the hem of her sweater, which she was holding on to for dear life, she comes toward me and puts her arms around me. It's an awkward embrace, all elbows and shoulders. At first we are out of practice, but then I remember sitting on her lap. I let myself be hugged by her, and we stand in the hallway holding each other. I am glad to be home.

"Look," Mum says gently when we finally part. "While Greg was out looking for you, I was thinking about what to do about Caitlin. . . ."

It comes back in a rush of worry—the reason I went out; the reason I escaped. I have to be with her. "Where are my car keys?" I ask her.

"Greg's coming home," she says, holding up the thing that messages come on. "He's glad you are back. He's coming home to look after Esther."

"I need my car keys," I say, lost in the mosaic of information.

"When Greg gets here, we can go, you and me."

The pieces slide and reassemble, and then I realize exactly what she is saying.

"You and me." She smiles. "We're going to London together, to find Caitlin."

thursday, november 19, 1981

claire

This is a photo of my dad in his army uniform. It was taken long before he met Mum, maybe even before she was born. He is just eighteen in this photo, so handsome, and even in this posed, formal image, I always think there is a little twinkle in his eye: a sense of a life beginning. This is how I like to remember him. He served in the last two years of the Second World War, and he never talked about it, not once; but whatever happened to him in France changed him. The only times I ever saw that twinkle in his eye was in this photo and on the day he died, when he thought I was his sister.

I wasn't allowed to see him much at the end; if I'm honest, I didn't really want to. He'd always been something of a stranger to me anyway, an old-school sort of dad who usually came home after work when I was already in bed. I remember the earliest parts of my childhood as playing all day with Mum, and then at night trying to stay awake until I heard the click of the front door, hoping that tonight would be one of the rare nights that Dad came into my room and kissed me on the forehead. He only ever did that, though, if he thought I was properly asleep. The merest twitch of an eyelash, and he would not enter the room. As I grew up, I resented that. I thought he was very cold, very remote. It took me years to realize that was just the way he was. He was all about the stiff upper lip, a pat on the back; no hugs or kisses, he wasn't that sort of father. He was the sort of dad who might make polite enquiries as to how my day had been at school. Like we were acquaintances who'd met in the street and discussed the weather. I loved him, and I am sure that he loved me, but I didn't really know him, especially not by the age of ten, which is how old I was when he died. I remember quite a lot about being ten, but very little about my dad. I wonder whether, had he lived longer, he would have meant more to me as a person. Would I remember him for the things he meant to me, instead of the things he didn't? I worry so much about how Esther will remember me, or whether she will remember me at all.

I only have two really clear memories of my dad, and one is of the last time I saw him before he died, when he thought I was his sister, Hattie.

Mum was in the kitchen, talking to the doctor, and I was in the hallway, sitting on the stairs. I spent a lot of Dad's last days on the stairs, trying to hear what was happening. Dad was in bed in what used to be the dining room. I could hear him calling. I listened to him calling for a long time, sitting on the stairs, reluctant to go in, waiting for Mum to respond to him like she always did, shutting the door behind her, and her soft voice, murmuring, soothing. But Mum was still talking to the doctor in the kitchen, and Dad sounded upset, so I went in. I didn't like to hear him sounding scared: it scared me too. He was weak, then, with advanced pneumonia, so he couldn't sit up. I went over to him, right up to the bed so that he could see me.

"Oh, it's you," he said. "Tell Mother it wasn't me. Tell her it wasn't me who broke your stupid doll, stinkers."

I didn't understand, so I leaned closer. "What do you mean, Dad? What doll?"

"You're such a crybaby, Hattie," he said. "Just a tattletale crybaby."

He pulled my hair, really hard, gripping on to it and yanking it down, so that for a moment my head was pinned to the bed, inhaling the scent of sweat and urine, and I couldn't move or breathe. Then he let me go, and I stumbled back from the bed, rubbing my sore scalp, horrified. There were tears, although I hated to cry and prided myself on not doing it. Hot tears flowed down my face. He looked at me from the bed, those pale blue eyes that had once sparkled now looking at some other time, some other world, some other girl.

"Sorry, kid," he said, his voice gentle now. "I didn't mean to make you blub. Tell you what, after lunch we'll go down to the stream and paddle till our toes turn blue, okay? I'll help you catch some tadpoles; we'll keep 'em in a bucket until they grow legs."

My mum came in then, and seeing me crying, ushered me out of the room, closing the door behind me, and then all I could hear was her voice, soft and soothing as she comforted him. Dad died sometime later that afternoon.

7

claire

The tube train rattles from side to side with a *tick, tick,* marking the passing of time as it bumps and judders along the tracks. I have been concentrating very hard on the map that's positioned above the seats opposite me—so that I don't lose myself, not only in this huge sprawling labyrinth but also in time. I need to remember what I am doing; I need to remember why. Whatever else happens, I must not forget those two things.

I'm in London; I'm looking for Caitlin.

I've thought about it, since my walk—my expedition to rescue Caitlin that didn't make it past the zebra crossing. I'm like a learner driver: I need to keep my eye on exactly where I am going, at any given moment. Any lapse in concentration will result in me veering off, lost in some off-roading adventure that I don't have the skill to navigate. I'm attempting to relearn basic life skills quicker than I am losing them. It's a bit like walking up the down escalator, which I'll take; if working hard at concentrating keeps me in the same place, that's good enough for me. It's better than going down.

Only two more stops to go. I am pleased with myself for knowing that. And yet, looking at my reflection, in the window opposite, hollow and translucent, I see a woman disappearing. It would help if I looked like that in real life—if the more the disease advanced, the more "see-through" I became until, eventually, I would be just a wisp of a ghost. How much more convenient it would be, how much easier for everyone, including me, if my body just melted away along with my mind. Then we'd all know where we were, literally and metaphysically. I have no idea if that thought makes sense, but I like that I remember the word "metaphysical."

Mum sits on one side of my ghostly reflection, reading a paper, her arm aligned carefully with mine, thus maintaining contact while appearing not to. On my other side sits a girl with multiple piercings just above her top lip. I turn and look directly at her, and see that there are five of them, jeweled metal studs piercing her white skin, echoing her perfect cupid's bow. She is wearing a white, fake-fur jacket over a deep-red shirt that is unbuttoned to reveal a scar in the center of her chest, perhaps from heart surgery. In each little dimple that once represented a stitch, she has placed a tiny sparkling jewel. It makes me smile.

If she can feel me looking at her, she ignores it, and I see she has earphones plugged in while she reads a battered-looking copy of *The Great Gatsby*. The train rattles on—*tick, tick, tick*. I can't stop looking at her, wondering why she decided to make what was beautiful, ugly, and what might have been ugly, beautiful. Perhaps it is her own version of a balancing act.

Mum smacks me rather smartly on the knee. "For God's sake, stop staring at the poor girl, you'll give her a complex," she stage-whispers.

"She doesn't mind," I say, gesturing at the girl, who catches my eye for a second. "Look, she wants to be looked at. I think it's rather wonderful."

"Perhaps, but not like an animal in a zoo," Mum hisses, although the train is noisy and the girl is listening to something very loud and heavy on bass in her earphones. Maybe she likes the same bands as Caitlin. Maybe she knows Caitlin.

"Who are you listening to?" I tap her on the wrist and she takes out her earphones.

"I'm sorry," Mum says, but she stops short of giving my diagnosis.

"It's fine." The girl smiles. "I don't mind. I'm listening to Dark Matter. Do you know them?"

"I don't think so," I say. "When was your surgery?"

I reach out and, just for one heartbeat, place a finger on the topmost jeweled stud.

"Claire!" My mum reaches across me, perhaps in a bid to physically restrain me, or maybe just to stop me talking. I shake her off.

The girl smiles again. "Four years ago now."

"I like the jewels on your scar," I tell her. "I don't like the studs on your lips, though. You are so pretty, they spoil you."

She nods. "That's what my mum says."

"I'm so sorry," Mum says again. "We're getting off at the next stop."

"It's fine." The girl chuckles and looks at me. "This isn't a phase I'm going through. This is my face and my body, and this is my statement about my life and the way I want to live it, for the rest of my life."

"You think that," I say, nodding at Mum. "But see that woman there? She used to be a hippie, dancing around naked in fields taking LSD. Now she wears support tights and listens to *The Archers*."

The girl's eyes widen and she laughs behind her book.

"And she's got early-onset Alzheimer's," Mum retorts, which, let's face it, is something of a trump card. The train slows to a halt at our station, and Mum grabs my wrist like I'm a naughty child, pulling me off the train. I wave at the girl as the train departs, and she waves back, the studs above her top lip sparkling. I'd like to be able to put jewels on my scars. But my scars are all in my head. Perhaps I can have that put in my will: after they've sliced me up, maybe they could pop in some diamantés along with the formaldehyde.

Mum knows the way, or at least she has the map. Apparently it's not far from the tube station, so I let her tuck my hand in hers, and follow her like a little girl on the way to school, the fine rain misting our skin, gently soaking us through as we approach what Mum tells me is the University College London English Department office near Gower Street.

"When we get inside, let me do the talking," she says, which makes me laugh.

"I do still possess the power of speech," I tell her.

"I know you do, but you don't possess the power of filtering out what you are thinking from what you are actually saying." She arches an eyebrow. "Then again, I suppose you never did."

"Thank you for being here," I say. "For letting me do this."

"I think sometimes you forget that I'd do anything for you." Mum's smile softens as she reaches out and touches the back of my cheek with her cold hand. "You are still my baby, you know."

"I don't know about that, although you may be feeding me mashed-up food with a spoon before we know it," I reply, before I really think about what I'm saying. Mum tucks her hand back in her pocket, her face closing again, and I follow her into the building. Guilt crawls over me. Mum lost years of her life nursing one person she loved into an early grave because of this disease, and now she is set to do it again. I want to tell her not to bother; I want to tell that I will be fine in some sort of home, cared for by strangers. But I don't, because she is my mum, and I want her. And I know I will want her, even when I don't know that I do.

The sight of us approaching does not ruffle the substantial-looking woman behind the front desk; if anything, she seems to puff herself up a little more, like a hen preening her feathers. In a brilliant tactical move, she drops her gaze from us and begins to stare intently at her computer screen, as though she is doing something terribly important.

"Hello," I say politely, repeating the word again when she doesn't look up. "Hello?"

I am greeted with a single raised finger as the woman presses something on the keyboard, waits for two more beats, then finally graces me with her attention. A lot of the time lately, I don't know if the way I feel about things is the way I really feel about them, or the way the disease is making me feel about them. But on this rarest of occasions I am sure that I—the me that still remains despite the disease—do not like this woman, and for that reason alone, I also rather like her.

"How can I help you?" she asks, looking distinctly put out that she is being required to do her job.

"My daughter is a third-year student here, and I need her address," I say pleasantly. "It's a family emergency."

"We don't give out personal information." The woman

smiles benignly. "I mean, you say you are someone's mother, but for all I know you could be the queen."

"Well, no, if I were the queen, I'm almost certain that you would know I was me," I say. "And the thing is, while I completely agree with your policy, I don't know her address and I need to contact her urgently. I mean it's really urgent: she needs me."

The woman sniffs. "You say you are this person's mother, and yet you don't know where she is?"

"Yes," I say. "Yes, I am a shit mother."

The woman prepares to look offended, but before she has time, my mother steps in. "Please excuse my daughter," she says. "She has early-onset Alzheimer's."

I know exactly what my mother's tactic is: she is planning to blindside the receptionist with my disease, go straight for the sympathy card and circumnavigate time-wasting tactics from my new nemesis. But still it smarts. I wanted to outwit her with my wits, not my lack of them.

The woman's plump little mouth forms a silent pink O, but no sound comes out.

"It's quite simple, you see," Mum continues. "All we need you to do is contact Caitlin, wherever she is on campus, and tell her that her mother and grandmother . . . just tell her we are here. It's a family emergency."

"Caitlin?" The woman sits up a little. "Caitlin who?"

"Armstrong," I say. "Do you know her?"

"Caitlin Armstrong is this poor lady's daughter?" The receptionist has stopped looking at or talking to me directly. "Well, she's not a student here anymore. She dropped out at the end of the summer term." She lowers her voice, and all but raises a hand to stop me reading her lips and seeing what she says. "Maybe the lady forgot," she whispers.

Mum and I exchange shocked looks, which I can tell are thrilling my little receptionist friend.

"Dropped out? Are you sure?" I lean over the desk with a hint of menace, on the basis that as an AD sufferer, it's fine to have no idea about personal boundaries. "My Caitlin? She's tall, like me, but with big black eyes, long hair all over the place ... She's a ... She's a ... words student. She's studying words. My Caitlin?"

"Sorry, dear." The receptionist slides on her wheeled seat. She smiles at my mother. "Are you her carer? Does she get very confused? Must be hard for you."

"I'm not confused," I tell her, although she is still looking at my mother.

"You're sure it's the same girl?" my mum asks. She takes my hand under the desk, out of sight of the receptionist, and squeezes my fingers. She is telling me again to let her do the talking.

"Quite sure." The woman nods, pressing her lips together to form an expression that is a mixture of empathy and quiet glee at being the bearer of bad news. "I remember because I was here when she came in to see the head of department. Never seen a girl cry so much. She failed her end-of-term exams. Probably something to do with a boy, I think—it usually is. She came in to talk about retakes. But as she didn't enroll for them, I assumed she'd gone home to lick her wounds, make a withdrawal from the bank of Mum and Dad. I can see why she didn't want to tell you." Her voice drops to a whisper again. *"No need to upset her any more."*

"I am standing here, and I still have ears," I say. "Which aren't deaf."

The woman looks at me fleetingly, but still doesn't address me directly, and for a second I wonder if I have turned into that other ghostly woman on the tube train—the one that no one looks in the eye anymore. The one that might not be real.

"You could try her best friend," she says, with a flash of inspiration. "Caitlin was with her every time she came here last term. Becky Firth, her name is. I can't give you her address, though. Like I said, that's against our data protection policy. But she's supposed to be on campus today. If you go to the canteen, ask around, you'll probably find her. Nice looking girl, blond, ponytailed, pretty."

"Thank you," Mum says, still gripping my hand.

I turn and look at the receptionist for one last moment, and I know this is absolutely the right time for me to come out with a witty and stinging one-liner that will make her see I am not a pitiable person, and not just a disease. But nothing comes to mind, which reminds me, only too clearly, that I am both.

It turns out that there are a lot of pretty, blond, ponytailed girls in the canteen, so many that I wonder if we might be politely escorted from the premises as we approach one after another.

Fortunately, this is one of the rare occasions when being female and over forty is actually a plus, because no one expects us to be there for nefarious purposes, although it takes several baffled, bored, and disdainful "no"s until we finally find a blond, ponytailed girl who knows who—and, crucially, where—Becky Firth is.

"She's not in today," the girl who reveals herself as Emma tells us. "Literary Crit lecture. No one comes to that one, if they can help it. She might be at home, though."

"Do you know where home is?" I ask her, relieved that Emma is clearly not remotely concerned about Becky's privacy, since she happily writes Becky's address and number down for us.

I snatch it from her hand and I feel purposeful: I am *doing* something, for me, and for Caitlin. I'm finding her, rescuing her, bringing her home. I am being her mother. I feel strong and free for a little while—seconds, even, perhaps as many as ten. And then I realize that I have absolutely no idea where I am going.

Fortunately, Becky is in when we arrive, after a fraught bus journey, which I undertake begrudgingly, for the greater good, since I am clearly not the maddest person on the bus. The afternoon has grown steadily darker and wetter; water glazes the streets, turning them into a grimy mirror, reflecting the world back, perhaps as it truly is, with colors bleeding into one another— a fluid place, always on the brink of being washed away. That's how I feel now: like I am on the other side of that grimy mirror, trying to wipe away the smear to see more clearly and be able to understand.

"Filthy weather," Mum says, and I try to remember a time when it has not been raining. Becky answers the door wearing a T-shirt, underwear, and little else. I want to tell her to put a sweater on. She looks freezing, and her long bare toes, curled on the tiled floor, are enough to make me shudder.

"I'm not religious," she says, looking from my mum to me.

"Me neither," I tell her. "Or at least, if I do believe in God, right now I'd quite like to have some mostly four-letter words with him that have got nothing to do with spreading the Gospel."

Becky begins to close the door.

"It's about Caitlin. You know her, don't you?" My mum jams her foot in the door with the sort of hard-core determination to get results that I thought only East End cops and door-to-door salesmen have. Becky looks at Mum's sensibly clad foot and warily opens the door again.

"I'm Caitlin's gran," Mum says. "Please, if she is staying with you, if you know where she is, please tell us. We know that she's not at university anymore, and we know she's pregnant."

"What the f—" Becky's eyes widen as she bites her lip hard to stop the swear word, clearly still enough of a good girl not to want to swear in front of somebody's mum and gran. Becky did not know Caitlin was pregnant. Perhaps that means she isn't. "Oh my God, I thought she'd got a . . ."

"Got a what? Morning-after pill? Condom? Education on safe sex?" I ask.

"You're a fine one to talk," Mum says. "We think she might be pregnant, but we don't know for sure. That's what I should have said. She's not at home, and we're worried about her. Please, Becky, we don't want her to be alone, not at the moment."

Becky nods and opens the door wider, her freezing bare feet taking steps back. "Come in out of the rain."

Her house smells of curry and wet washing. We stand in the hallway, and in the living room I can see Caitlin's wash bag on a squat little table. My heart leaps and I close my eyes, waiting for the threat of tears to pass. I didn't know what I'd been thinking might have happened to her.

And then I feel angry. Surely there is nothing so bad that she would be happy to let us all worry about her so much?

"She's here," I say, turning to look at Becky. "Her stuff is here."

"No, I mean yeah, she is staying here. But she's at work at the moment." Becky looks uneasy; she grabs a hoody from the banister and slips it on, hugging it around her. "She said she just needed a place to stay, to think until she got herself straight, got a place, and stuff. She said there's been some . . . trouble. She hasn't really talked to me much, or at all. She's been working all the time, so . . ." Becky peers into the front room, in which I can see a sleeping bag and some clothes strewn across the carpet. "She's not said anything about being pregnant to me, and, well, she's been here two weeks. . . . She tells me everything."

"Where is work?" I ask her, guessing from the way she is talking to me and not my mother that Caitlin doesn't tell her everything at all.

"Oh." Becky's shoulders slump and it's obvious this is one piece of information she truly doesn't want to divulge to her friend's mother and grandmother. "Um, well, it's in this . . ."

She says the last two words so quietly that I'm not sure I've heard them correctly until my mother repeats them.

"A strip club?"

claire

This is the program from Caitlin's first ever school play that she had a part in when she was eight. Caitlin was the Red Queen in the school's production of *Alice Through the Looking-Glass*. I remember very clearly the day I picked her up from school and she came bouncing out of the classroom to tell me she had a part, and lines to learn, and a song to sing all by herself. Instantly I felt my stomach knot with fear. Caitlin had always been a happy-go-lucky, cheerful little girl—in situations that she was comfortable or familiar with. But as soon as you put her in a place she didn't know, or in front of unfamiliar faces, she'd close up, turning her face away from conversations, hiding in my skirts, behind my legs. She told me she didn't like people looking at her if she didn't know who they were. Think who they might be, she'd told me, her eyes big and fearful. It took me too long to realize she was afraid of seeing her father and not knowing who he was.

Her first few weeks at school had been a nightmare: she'd wept with such genuine grief every morning as I dragged her into the playground that I'd wanted to, almost had, taken her out of school completely. "I don't know anyone here," she'd sob. "I'm going to be so lonely. Why can't you come with me?"

It had taken a good many dreadful days like that, but gradually Caitlin had made friends, with the other children and her teachers. She'd slowly come out of herself to be the funny, cheeky, popular little girl that I knew she could be. But nothing had changed in the last few years; she'd even had the same class teacher. And although she'd made a charming donkey, and then sheep, in the two previous nativities, no one had made her stand alone on a stage and remember lines, or sing. I *knew* she would fail, I was certain of it, and I knew how upset she would be because of it. My only thought was to rescue her from experiencing this crushing disappointment at such a young age. I had to protect her. The next day when I picked her up, I had a word with her teacher while Caitlin ran off to chat with some of her friends before they left for home. I watched her skip and twirl, laugh and hop as I talked.

"I don't think she's up to this," I told Miss Grayson. "You remember how she was at first? I think this is too much for her. Can't you maybe think of a reason to change her role?"

"She's so happy and proud about it, though," Miss Grayson said to me. "And she's doing really well in the rehearsals!"

"Yes, but that's not real, is it? That's not like seeing all those strange faces looking at you."

"I think you underestimate her," Miss Grayson said. And she said it with a smile and warm tone to her voice, but I knew she was criticizing me for not having enough faith in Caitlin. I didn't ask her again to take Caitlin out of the play, and I remember thinking, she'll see. When Caitlin freezes with terror or runs off the stage in floods of tears, she'll see.

Costumes for school plays, I think, were invented and put on this earth to test mothers. I hated putting together school costumes, so Mum came over and we made the costume together, all three of us. Mum was bossy and controlling, Caitlin was honing her diva skills, and I kept sewing the wrong bits of material together. But it was a happy time, a laughing time. Caitlin rehearsed her lines and sang for us while we fitted her into her little red shift dress and painted her cardboard crown.

I wanted that time, the preparation time, to go on forever. I didn't want the play to ever come, and I started to hope that maybe Caitlin would get a cold, or lose her voice. That something would happen to save her.

I turned up half an hour before the play was due to start so that I could claim a seat at the front, and be there for her when she rushed into my arms. I still had to fight for my front row seat, mind you. The other mothers—the real ones that had husbands, and parkas, and who baked cakes for the fairs—had already put cardigans on chairs, claiming all of the front row seats in advance. Most of them disliked me anyway. I was an unknown quantity, turning up at the school gate in high heels and lipstick; with no obvious husband on the scene, I was viewed as a threat. I would stand there on my own at chucking-out time, pretending to be reading a book while we waited for the bell to go, the other mums all standing around in little huddles, and—in my head, at least—bitching about me. So it took quite a lot of nerve for me to pick up one of the reservation cardigans and put it on the second row behind me, but all I could think about was being there for Caitlin, right in front of her eyes when she needed me, ready to scoop her up in my arms and protect her.

"You can't sit there," one of the mums told me, a cake-baking PTA mafia mum—the sort that organizes tombolas and sells raffle tickets door-to-door to old ladies who really need the money for food.

"I think you'll find that I can," I told her, crossing my arms, settling my large bottom onto the tiny chair and giving her a look that said: "You can try and mess with me, bitch, but if you do, I'm taking both your arms and that bloody stupid bob hairdo with me."

Scandalized, she marched away and left me in my prime seat. I could hear her shrilling to the other mums about what a terrible monster I was, and that it just "wasn't the done thing," right up until the lights went down and Miss Grayson struck up a tune on the piano. I clenched my fists, my fingernails biting into the palms of my hands.

My poor Caitlin.

For the first few scenes, she wasn't on stage. In any case, these were dominated by coughs and shuffles in the audience, and small children whispering to each other, or waving to their mothers, when they should have been delivering lines. I tried to relax, to tell myself that this was what school plays were all about, but I couldn't. I knew Caitlin and I knew how bitterly disappointed she would be, and how crushed, and how much it would take for her to come back from this failure.

And then she walked on stage, in her little red shift dress and her cardboard crown, and she was . . . brilliant.

I sat open-mouthed while she delivered her lines with such imperious queenliness, making the crowd laugh at every punch-line, and boo when she demanded someone's head must come off. She outshone every other child on the stage, which I know I would think, because she was my Caitlin, but it was true. My little girl had found her element, and she was completely at ease in it. Yes, when she came to sing her solo, her voice trembled; and instead of the loud, booming, queenlike voice she'd been using to deliver her lines, out came the small melodic voice of an eight-year-old girl. But nevertheless she sang, without faltering once. And when, as she finished, the audience burst into spontaneous applause, she beamed with such pride, right at me in the front row, and I knew then that Miss Grayson had been right, and I had been wrong.

I learned something about both Caitlin and myself that night. I learned that she was and is a work in progress—a human being evolving in the world—and that no one, least of all me, should try to guess what her limits are. Being a mother is about protecting your children from every conceivable thing that might cause them hurt, but it's also about trusting them to live the best way for them, the best way they can; and trusting that even when you are not there to hold their hand, they can succeed.

8

caitlin

The girl spins slowly, languorously, around the pole, sliding down it so that she hangs upside down; her acrylic nails graze the grimy stage as she performs inverted arabesques, her thighs holding her in place until somehow she's folded back on herself. Her arms wrapped around the pole, she kicks her legs out behind her, scissoring through the air as she circumnavigates the stage. At her feet, three or four men watch her slight frame contort and stretch. All eyes are fixed on her, on her meager breasts, barely there at all, her ribs straining against her taut, pale skin, her flat, boyish behind and her bored, vacant expression. At least this girl keeps her thong on.

I am glad I don't work in a club where everything comes off, although I know that does happen in the private room. A lot goes on in there that I'm not supposed to know about, and so I do my best not to notice the other money-making opportunities available for the dancers if they want them, which most of them do now and then, treating it as casually as they might an extra nightshift stacking shelves at Tesco. I suppose that was what shocked me the most when I first took this job in the spring: the way that selling yourself for sex, one way or another, is so ... doable for the dancers. In this club there are none of those well-bred, educated girls that you read about in Sunday supplements who decided to strip to be postmodern or pay their way through university. Here, every single dancer is a woman without choices, without a future that extends beyond the next dance. I saw them, saw their faces, and I got that. I feel the same: a girl without a future. No college degree, no boyfriend, and a fifty percent chance of carrying the gene that could give me a degenerative brain disease before I've even really worked out what I want from life. Mum did not know she had the gene, and neither do I yet. But now I know that I could find out whether or not I do have it, I don't know if I want to. Because there is one choice I don't want to make based on what might happen; there's one choice I know I need to make based on the kind of person I am now.

And that's the choice I made: to keep the baby.

Mum raised me on Austen and Brontë, and the notion of romantic love and sex as one—a pure, sacred thing. I grew up believing in true love, and that improbable coincidences would always save the day. Even in our little, uniquely female world, where there was no father or grandfather, no brothers or uncles, I still thought that when my hero came, he would be infallible: he would be my key to being happy. Like when Greg came into Mum's life, and she just ... relaxed. Like he was her missing piece, which she didn't even know she was constantly searching for, but had now found.

Until Greg, though, Mum had always been careful to keep her private life private. There had never been any boyfriends sleeping over, or staying for tea—not that I knew of, anyway. No parade of men making halfhearted attempts to get to know me as I grew up. I wonder if it might have been better if she'd let me see that relationships come and go, that people can use you and hurt you, tell you one thing and then just change their minds in the blink of an eye. Maybe, maybe it would have helped if I didn't believe so much in the idea of falling in love. For years as a little girl, I used to dream that the reason Mum chose to be alone was because she was still so in love with my father—that ultimate shadowy hero—who I felt certain would come back one day and reclaim us both. But he didn't come back, and, if he's thought about Mum at all during the last twenty years, I know now that not for a single moment of his life has he ever been preoccupied by me—because, for him, I don't exist. All this time I've been worried I might somehow bump into him; but even if I had, it wouldn't have mattered. It would only have mattered if, for all of these years, he'd been worried about somehow bumping into me too.

Of course I was hurt and angry when Mum told me the truth, but I don't know why the news was quite so hard to take. I don't know why it drove me out of the house, away from Mum and Esther, when they both really need me, and back here to this place that I had hoped I'd seen the last of. But I couldn't stay there. Knowing that he'd never once worried about bumping into me, knowing that I didn't exist for him, I couldn't be at home and not be angry with her. And I can't be angry with her.

Not when I have also carelessly lost the father of my own baby.

I look at my watch. It's just after three in the afternoon. The club is dead at this time of day during the week, except for the regulars or the occasional table of suited business guys— maybe a stray all-day-drinking stag or birthday do. Another twenty minutes and I'll be ejected once again into the real world of car fumes, bus lanes, twenty-four-hour supermarkets, the very real and pressing need to work out what to do . . . I want to go to Mum—I want to ask her for help—but I can't. I can't let her know what a mess I'm in.

The old man who comes in every pension day arrives at the bar, and I pump cheap imitation draft Coke into a shot of watered-down whisky for him, just the way he likes it. He turns on his bar stool and licks his lips as he watches the girl finish her act. It comes to something when being in here is a better prospect than being out there.

The dancer finishes, scoops up the scrap of material that constitutes her bikini off the floor, and walks off stage, tottering awkwardly in her high platforms. There is a lull between performances, and briefly the room is filled with coughs and sniffs. Even the smell of sweat and stale beer seems more acute in the silence. Ten more minutes and my shift will be over, and then what? Is today going to be the day I call home and tell them what I've done? Tell them not to worry, that I'm fine?

I know they will be worried sick, but I don't know if I'm ready to see them yet. Especially not Mum. Mum always thinks I can do anything at all I set my mind to, and be brilliant at it, and I know she won't judge me for what's happened, but I also know she will be disappointed. And I don't want the last thing she remembers feeling about me to be disappointment.

The first morning after I arrived back in London, I went to see Sebastian, just to make sure he hadn't changed his mind about us. I know that is pathetic; I know how it sounds. If it were Becky saying the words to me, I'd be handing her a giant bar of Dairy Milk and a bottle of wine and telling her to forget about the loser. Easier said than done, though, isn't it? To be grown up and rational. To know when something is really over—especially if it's not really over for you. It seemed to me that someone couldn't just appear to feel so much for you one minute, and then for that all to be gone the next. That just didn't seem possible, or even proper. Love isn't something that comes and goes, is it? Isn't it something that, when you boil it right down to its essence, always has to be true? That's what I always thought falling in love would be like, and then I went and did it and it was crap.

It had been easy enough to find Sebastian's new house-share. All I'd had to do was to wander onto campus, ask around a bit. The same people I'd sat in lectures with until recently all smiled, nodded, and stopped to catch up, never guessing that I wasn't meant to be there. My departure obviously wasn't news. No one knew yet that I'd failed my exams—no one knew I'd dropped out—and although they all knew that Seb and I weren't together anymore, none of them knew I was pregnant. Not even Seb, to be fair. Which was another reason I couldn't stay at home and be angry with Mum. I couldn't be angry with her for having done something I was thinking about doing myself right now. Her choice back then made me furious and hurt me, and it had certainly been the wrong thing to do, but it was a choice I now understood, all the better after seeing Seb again.

The thing I had most wanted from him was a hug, but from the moment he opened the door, he was pissed off that I was there.

"What do you want, Caitlin?" he asked wearily, rolling his eyes.

"I don't know," I said. I tried not to cry, but I did, just like that. Stupid, red-faced, noisy snotty sobs that went from naught to hysterical in under six seconds. "I wanted to see you. I miss you."

"Don't miss me," Seb said irritably. "I'm not worth missing."

"Can I come in?" I pleaded, like some bloody girl. "After everything that's happened, I just need to talk, and you are the only one I can talk to about it."

Seb sighed heavily, looking back over his shoulder toward where the pounding sound of some shoot 'em up video game was coming from.

"There's nothing else really to talk about, is there?" he said, allowing me into the hallway. He did not shut the front door. "We had a thing, and it's over now." He pursed his lips, unable to look directly at me. "I'm sorry about the . . . you know. It must have been shit for you. But . . . it's time to let it go, babe, okay? We've both got to get on with our lives now."

"Don't you care at all?" I sobbed, so stupidly. Like I wasn't even me, I grabbed hold of him, grabbed his T-shirt in my fists, wailing, hoping that he'd fold me in his arms and kiss my snot-soaked face. Like that was ever going to happen.

The reason I'd gone to see him—the other reason apart from hoping he did still love me—was to tell him that I didn't go through with the termination: the termination that he hadn't come along to with me, because he'd had an important university rugby match. Which, by the way, I'd said I was fine about, when what I should have said was, "You are an unbelievable dick, Sebastian." But I couldn't make myself, because I still thought that maybe, maybe, he might change his mind and want me back again. I make myself sick. If I were a guest on *The Jeremy Kyle Show,* or something, I'd throw a shoe at my head.

When the day came, I just couldn't do it. I got up, had a shower, got dressed, picked up my bag, and then . . . I looked at myself in the mirror and I thought, this is the dress that you will have worn to the termination of your pregnancy. And just knowing that meant I couldn't go through with it. Which surprised me. I believe in the right for women to choose, but it never occurred to me that if I were in that situation, I would choose life—even though, actually, when you think about it, it's completely obvious: Mum chose me. Instead, I curled up into a small ball in my bed, folding myself up as tightly as possible. I closed my eyes and stayed very still, as though somehow I might be able to wish myself out of time and stay just like that forever, with the tiny essence of life inside me, and pretend I hadn't just found out that Mum was desperately ill, or that there was a fifty percent chance I might have a gene that would make me more likely to develop early-onset Alzheimer's too, and that if I did, there was also a fifty percent chance of passing it on to my child. I did my best to un-know those things, because facing the future was hard enough, and I wanted my choice to be made by the person I am now, and not the person I might be one day. It wasn't that simple, though, and I just wanted one other person to tell me I was doing the right thing.

I was going to tell Sebastian all of that, thinking he might suddenly feel the same, and we might have this baby together. When I looked at his face, though, I knew that the last thing he wanted to know was that I was still pregnant. Was that the look Mum had seen on my father's face when she broke up with him?

"What does it matter if I care or not?" Seb said, glancing back over his shoulder again, toward where the fun was. "What point is there going over and over it? Really, Cat, pull yourself together. You're not doing yourself any favors."

And that last look he gave me . . . It was such a cold look; it was the look of a boy who was entirely detached from me and us, and everything we might have been. I couldn't stop crying, the tears rolling down my face while he just stood there and looked at me.

"Christ." Seb shook his head, closing the door two inches. "You are too much, don't you see that? I did like you, at first, but you ... you killed it. And I'm sorry about everything else, but that's not my fault, Cat. You're the one who didn't revise.... I passed my exams."

He slammed the door shut.

I stood there for a moment or two more, until I'd stopped crying and the bitter wind had dried the tears on my face, and I thought, right, that's it, then, I am not going to waste another single second on him—even though I knew I would do, but thinking it was a start. And then I went to work, back to my job behind the bar at a strip club, the job I had got just before the end of the spring term, and the job I got back easily when I dropped in to see my boss with my new, slightly improved, bigger bust. He's a total pervert, but I can handle him.

I look at my watch again. The next shift should be here any minute now, and then it's back to Becky's, where she will stay in her bedroom all evening with her boyfriend, and I'll sit in the living room alone, wondering why I'm not at home, why I haven't told my mum any of this, and why I always mess everything up.

I look up as the beaded curtain at the entrance jangles, expecting to see Mandy lumber her way into view. But it's not Mandy, in her faux-fur coat and thick fake eyelashes, who tumbles into the room so dramatically and noticeably that even the dancer on the stage turns to look. It's my mother, and right behind her is Gran.

I turn around and head for the office behind the bar, hoping that somehow I might be able to hide from them, maybe even squeeze out of the tiny window in the truly grim unisex staff toilet. But they follow me into the small dingy office a few moments later, and find me standing in the corner, just standing there like an idiot.

Gran looks me up and down, sees the Venus logo on my too-tight T-shirt, and breathes a sigh of relief. "Well, at least she's got her top on," she says.

I want to laugh out loud. They've come down here to find me—my mum and gran, working together as a team, like some grizzly old cop about to retire for good when she's paired up against her will with a maverick upstart to work one last case together. Seeing my mum and my gran, both looking worried and cross, but here together, is somehow sort of wonderful and funny.

Mum is looking at me, and she looks just like Mum. Like she knows me. I want to hug her, but I don't want to break this moment.

"Nice place," Mum says, looking around. There is no window in the office, just an extractor fan filmed with thick dust. An ashtray full of cigarette butts sits on the desk, because laws on smoking in the workplace don't count for very much here.

"I'm sorry," I say uneasily. "I know I should have told you what happened, where I was, and everything. I know I should have told you about failing my exams and . . . and that I am pregnant by this boy I'm not going out with anymore, and who . . . who doesn't know that I am keeping the baby."

I say it like a challenge. I say it like it should be followed by the phrase: "And what are you going to do about it?"

"Oh God, you silly goose," Mum says. "And me spilling the beans about what a stupid cow I was over your parentage, that just tipped you over the edge, didn't it? I'm so sorry, darling, come here. . . ."

She holds out her arms and I go into them without hesitation. Twenty years old and I still need a hug from my mum. I expect I'll be hugging my own baby and still need a hug from my mum.

"You don't have to explain," Mum says. I close my eyes and rest my head on her chest. "I'm guessing it hasn't ever quite seemed like the right time to tell your increasingly senile mother that you were up the duff and had no prospects."

I smile at her blunt assessment of the situation, but I don't say anything; I don't feel like I need to.

Gran is still standing in the doorway, staring up the corridor as though she's expecting a raid. "Hey, Caitlin," she says. "Your bosses—are they Mafia? Armenians?"

"No, he's Greek, I think," I tell her. "His mum owns a taverna up the road."

"It must have been so hard for you," Mum says into my hair. "I do understand. You have no idea what the future is going to hold, not mine or yours, not the baby's. And then realizing that your dad didn't ever know about you . . . I don't blame you for wanting to run away."

"You're being too nice," I say. "I left you. I didn't have to. I didn't have anywhere to go, just . . . here."

"Yes." Mum looks around her. "I must say that the fact you ran away to here is a bit insulting. And I was so worried about you, Caitlin. For you to not let us know you were okay . . . it was too hard. I think I get it but . . . every day I've wondered if I've lost you forever. I know I'm not really the best mother material, at the moment, but come home, Caitlin. Please. Let me look after you."

"Shhh," Gran hisses urgently from the doorway, flattening herself against the fake-wood-effect wallpaper. "I think someone is coming!"

I find laughter gurgling in my stomach.

"What's so funny?" Mum asks me, grinning.

"You two," I say. "It's like some decrepit Scooby-Doo adventure."

"Oh no," Mum says. "This isn't Scooby-Doo. In your gran's head this is *The Untouchables*, and we are Eliot Ness."

I've missed Mum.

"Remember when you were little, how you used to sit on my knee to read a book or watch a film? We were always together, weren't we? I miss that, Caitlin. Come home. I'll probably be a burden, and Gran will most likely attempt to smother you with carbohydrates as a substitute for love, but the fact remains that we do love you."

"I finish my shift soon," I say, winking at Mum. "If my boss catches you two here, he won't like it. There's a chance you might end up wearing concrete boots and sleeping with the fishes. There's a café over the road. Wait for me there. I'll be five minutes."

But Mum doesn't move; she just stands there, looking at me. "You were a lovely queen," she says. "So regal, it was like you were born to royalty."

Just at that second my boss, Pete, arrives, unwittingly barging my gran out of the way so that she clatters against a filing cabinet—not because he is a thug, but because he didn't expect to find an old lady casing his office. He looks at my mother, who is clutching her hand to her chest and doing a passable impression of being frail, and then at me.

"What the bloody hell is going on in here?" Pete says, looking at me. "What is this, some kind of raid? Listen, I've dealt with you religious types before. No one round here needs saving, thanks very much, except from bitter old spinsters who don't like anyone having fun."

"What is it about me that makes me look so pious?" Mum asks me. "Honestly, I'm going to have to review my wardrobe. I'm clearly losing my scarlet woman status."

"Who the bloody hell are you?" Pete asks, before looking at me again. "And what are *you* doing? The bar's not manned, and there's a bloody queue."

"There are only two people out there," Mum says. "And one of them is asleep."

"Oh, fuck off." He spits the words at her, and I watch open-mouthed as Mum draws herself up to her full height and grabs Pete by his grubby T-shirt, slamming him into the side of the filing cabinet—where Gran was standing a moment ago— with a metallic thud. He is stunned. I want to laugh, but I'm too surprised.

"You do not speak to me like that," she says. "Now, I am taking my daughter, and we are leaving. And you, you vile little stain on humanity, if you don't want me to rip the last remaining hairs off your head and stuff them up your arse, you can shut it."

She lets go of him and marches out of the office. I grab Gran by the arm, my bag and coat off the peg, and I follow her through the bar, past the dancer, the bouncer, the girl on the door, and out into the chill of the dark afternoon.

Mum stands on the street, her face tipped up to the rain, letting it drench her face. She is laughing, her hands upstretched toward the sky, her fingers playing with the droplets of water.

"Mum!" I put my arms around her, laughing. "You were going to stuff his hair up his arse—that is the most hilarious threat of menace I have ever heard."

"Well, it worked, didn't it? He was menaced, wasn't he?" She grins at Gran and me, and I feel a rush of relief that they are here, almost like my heart just started beating again. I remember that I am part of a family, and I always was. I am such an idiot.

"Are you coming home now?" she asks me, pressing her cold wet cheek against mine.

"Aren't you angry with me?" I ask her.

"Aren't you angry with *me*?" she replies.

"How can I be?" I say.

"Because of the AD?" she asks me.

"I understand now why you did what you did," I say. "And I know that I'm going to do things differently. Maybe not just yet, because I'm still at the stage where I'm not sure if I want to kiss Sebastian all over or beat him to death with a blunt instrument, but at some point I will tell him about my baby, because then, whatever else happens after that, at least he will know.

"I'm sorry," Mum says again.

"Mum," I ask her. "Was my dad a terrible dickhead?"

She laughs, and takes my hand. "No darling, he was just very, very young and not half as clever as me."

"I never liked him," Gran says. "I only met him once, but he brought me a box of chocolates when I was on a diet."

"Come home, Caitlin," Mum says, placing her hand gently over my tummy. "And come home, baby, and you and I will figure this out together, just like the old days when you used to sit on my knee for a story."

I tuck my arm under hers and, as we start back toward the bus stop, I realize it's been a long time since I've felt so certain.

"What story would you like?" Mum asks me. "How about Pippi Longstocking? She's always been your favorite."

As we walk into the rain, Mum asks me if I want a hot chocolate before bed, just this once, as long as I promise to brush my teeth—and I know that, for now at least, I am around ten years old to her, and it doesn't matter, not now. Because I feel safe.

friday, july 11, 2008

greg

This is the scan photo of Esther in the womb, at just six weeks. It's the photo Claire gave me on the day she told me we were having a baby, and until now I've always kept it in my wallet.

We hadn't been together for very long when Esther was conceived—less than a year. But I already knew that I loved Claire more than I'd ever expected to love anyone. Even though, most of the time, she didn't believe it. She still thought the age difference was too big, or that I wasn't serious about her. Nothing I could do or say would change that. That's why I think she was so scared to tell me about Esther.

It was a very warm day. I had been working on-site, out in the sun all day, and I should have gone back to my flat to get a shower before seeing Claire, but there was just something pulling me to her. I'd been thinking about her all day, about the way she'd looked when I woke up that morning, so pissed off that I'd woken her up at six A.M. and the sun was fully up, which meant she couldn't get back to sleep. There was last night's makeup around her eyes, her hair was tangled and she'd scowled at me when I went to kiss her goodbye.

"I love you," I'd said.

"Yeah, right," she'd said. And then, just as I'd been about to go out of the bedroom door, she called my name. I'd stopped, but she'd just smiled at me and said, "I love you too, worse luck."

After work, I arrived at her house, our house now, covered in muck and grime. She opened the door and told me I wasn't coming in like that, so I stripped off on her doorstep—my boots, and my work trousers, even my shirt—looking her right in the eye the whole time. Claire leaned against the doorframe and watched me, with her arms crossed under her breasts, laughing, frowning, and flushing this gorgeous shade of pink all at once.

I stood before her on her doorstep in my boxers, the sun on my back.

"Good job. Mrs. Macksey's privet hedge is so damned high," she said, looking me up and down. "She'd have a stroke if she could see you right now."

She led me into the kitchen, which wasn't exactly the room I expected to be taken to, but I followed, my hand in hers. We stood there on the tiles and she went to her handbag. I could tell she was bracing herself to tell me something, and suddenly I was certain she was going to end things. I remember thinking, what sort of person lets a man strip down to his knickers to tell him it's over? And that's when she finally came out with it.

I was standing there in just my underwear when she told me I was going to be a father.

"I went to the doctor's today," she said. She looked so edgy and nervous that it worried me. I thought it might be something serious.

"Are you okay?" I asked her. I remember how she nodded, pressing the palm of her hand onto my bare chest. She closed her eyes for a moment, then presented me with this thin slip of paper.

"I was a bit worried, because I'd been bleeding a little bit, just a few spots when I shouldn't have been. And I read somewhere it could be serious, so I went to get it checked out."

"Oh, babe." I was instantly worried.

"But it's fine," she said. "Sort of. Look at it."

I stared at it, this odd grainy image, and I couldn't make sense of it for a few seconds. I wasn't sure what she was showing me.

I must have looked confused, because she laughed.

"Gregory," she said. "I am having your baby."

I remember my knees going, and hearing myself gasp as I sank onto them, right there on the kitchen tiles, which I try not to bring up too much—it's kind of embarrassing. And I remember the look on Claire's face as she watched me. She thought I wasn't pleased.

"I know it wasn't planned or expected," she said. "And it's fine, you don't have to worry. You can be as much or as little a part of the baby's life as you want. After all, I know you weren't exactly thinking of settling down and having a family with an older woman, so . . ."

"Yes," I said, grabbing her hand and pulling her to me. "Yes, that is exactly what I was thinking about, Claire. All day today, I was thinking about you. You, and that having you in my life has changed me, for the better. Before I met you I was just a . . . bloke. But you love me and I feel . . . beautiful."

It was maybe the most stupid thing any grown man has ever said to any woman, especially when he is wearing just his underwear and kneeling on her kitchen floor, but it was the way I felt, so I thought I'd say it out loud and see how that went. I expected Claire to do the usual thing she did when I told her I loved her, and laugh it off as if it were a joke, but she didn't. She just stood there, in the kitchen, holding my hand, and I realized she was trembling.

"You *are* beautiful," she said, reaching out and touching my face. "I should know, you are in my kitchen in your pants."

We stayed there for a moment, looking at each other, and then we laughed. Without having to think about it for a second more, I put my arms around her middle, and gently pressed my face against her stomach.

"Claire, we are going to get married," I told her.

"Because I'm up the duff?" she asked me.

"Because I love you, and our baby. And this is the best and happiest moment of my life."

And amazingly enough, she agreed.

Whenever I look at this picture, of Esther in the womb, I remember that day, and I think it was then that I really became a man.

9

claire

I watch Caitlin's profile as she is driving. I am taking her shopping—we decided it last night, during an impromptu sleepover. Caitlin didn't want to go back to Becky's house to get her things, not even her iPod. She didn't want to see Becky, at least not for the time being, and I understood that: Becky was part of her old life, and Caitlin is getting ready to embark on a new one. Even so, Mum called Becky to tell her that Caitlin was coming home, and asked her to pop a few things in the post.

So even though she barely took anything with her to London when she ran away, and I am taking her shopping, it's still a tenuous excuse to leave the house, but I'll take it. I am allowed out if Caitlin is with me, and it's the next best thing to being alone. Things have been a bit better between Mum and me since I went for a walk with Ryan, and she took me to London to find Caitlin. It's not that we suddenly understand each other, or that everything is now okay between us, simply because we got a train and fronted up to a strip club owner, but it's the first time in a long while that we've had a shared experience that I still remember. We've got something to talk about apart from the articles she cuts out for me from the *Daily Mail*. And we are trying to be kind to each other. She is trying her best not to be quite so in charge of me. I have even been allowed my credit card, and I know my PIN—it is the year of my birth, 1971. I am unlikely to forget the year I was born, which is why I chose it a few years ago, way before I was diagnosed, because I'd forgotten the standard issue one so many times that I was getting my card retained and cut up on almost a monthly basis. We used to laugh about it, Caitlin and I. We used to laugh about how ditzy and silly I was. How cute, I suppose. Silly Claire, never can remember her PIN, her head is so full of thoughts. Now it's hard not to wonder if, even then, little chinks of darkness were breaking through the light, claiming little bits of me.

Caitlin yawns, just as she used to when she was a baby, her whole face stretching into a wide circle.

"Are you tired?" I ask her, unnecessarily, and she nods.

"I've been exhausted almost since it happened, I suppose," she says.

I do remember that we got home after nine last night, but Esther was still up, engaged in a game of hide-and-seek with Greg. I felt odd seeing her with him: she looked so happy, so smiley, and yet I felt like he shouldn't be looking after her. Almost like I'd left her with a stranger. Although I know he is her father and my husband, I didn't like the fact that she had been with him. The sense of unease and disquiet I feel, whenever I see him, grows. I read what I have written, what he has written, in the memory book, and it's such a beautiful story. But that is exactly what it feels like to me: it feels like a story. It's such a shame that the heroine has checked out already. Like Anna Karenina throwing herself on the railway tracks at around chapter three, or Cathy dying before Heathcliff even arrives.

Esther was overjoyed to see Caitlin, and she fell asleep in her big sister's arms within a matter of minutes. Caitlin had carried Esther upstairs, but I'd steered Caitlin into my room and tucked her up in my bed, Esther still in her arms. Then I got in too.

"Remember when we used to have sleepovers, you and me?" I said.

"You must be the only mum in the world that wakes their child up so they can come and sleep in bed with them." Caitlin smiled.

"I missed you," I said. "I never got enough time with you when you were little. I was working or studying so much. There isn't a rule book that says you can't have a little midnight chat with your children!"

She settled down into the bed, and we put on the TV, keeping the volume low so as not to wake Esther. We didn't talk about the pregnancy, or the boy, or the exams, or the secrets, or my illness—we only watched some terrible film until finally Caitlin drifted off too. For a long time after that, I watched my daughters sleeping—the colors from the screen playing out across their faces—feeling very calm, very peaceful.

At some point, I heard Greg stop outside the bedroom door, probably thinking about coming in, and my heart raced and every muscle in my body clenched, because I didn't want him to. The idea of this man that I know increasingly less coming into my bedroom unnerves me. Perhaps he sensed it because, after a moment, the shadow of his feet at the bottom of the door moved away. I stayed awake a lot longer after that, though, listening, waiting. Anxious that he might come back.

When I announced that I was taking Caitlin shopping, I could see that Mum thought this was a bad idea—the woman with dementia going out alone with her fragile daughter—but still she let us go, watching Caitlin pull my car out of the drive, standing with Esther on her hip, my younger daughter still protesting loudly about being left behind.

"How are you feeling?" I ask Caitlin.

"You mean, aside from tired?" Caitlin says. "Sort of better, now that it's all out. Relieved, I suppose."

"Gran's making you appointments," I tell her, even though I am fairly sure she knows it already. I tell people things more than once, so that I can also remind myself. Load and reload my short-term memory, like constantly filling up a bucket with holes in it. The opposite of bailing out my brain. "GP tomorrow, hospital, and then . . ."

I stop talking, and Caitlin keeps her eyes straight ahead as she pulls into the shopping center car park. She doesn't want to talk about the pregnancy; even though she's decided to keep the baby, she doesn't want to discuss it. Perhaps it's because she thinks it's insensitive to talk about the future, when that word has so little meaning for me. Or perhaps it is because she is so uncertain about what the future will mean to her. We have never talked about it, about the possibility that this affliction might be lying in wait for her and her children. That alone would be enough to make anyone hesitant about what may come.

"Where shall we start?" I ask her, determined to be cheerful, as we head into the first store. "Dreary Black Goth Clothes 'R' Us? Or maybe something with a bit of color?"

Caitlin looks around us, at rail after rail of garments, all of which I could have worn and probably did in the late 1980s— me and Rosie Simpkins, who was my best friend back then. Every Saturday we would try to buy an outfit for under a fiver.

We did it nearly every week, as well, going out that night feeling like the bee's knees, with our bits of lace tied round our wrists, trying to look like Madonna, circa "Like a Prayer." Everything in this shop could have come from that era.

Funny how things change, and yet nothing changes. I look around for Rosie, wanting to show her a leopard-print shoulder-pad dress I've found in the sale, when I remember that Rosie Simpkins is married now, and fat and round and happy as a clam, with about a hundred kids. Caitlin looks up at me, over her arm a seemingly endless array of leggings and large T-shirts, all of them black, everything almost identical to what is already in her wardrobe, except slightly bigger and made with Lycra.

"I know what it's like," I say to her, as she adds another T-shirt to the bundle. "I have been there, remember, with you? Maybe this is the time, you know? To give up the Goth rock-chick look and just be what you are naturally, which is exceptionally pretty. You know, as you are about to become a mother?"

She stops and looks at me for a moment, and then, taking a deep breath, walks on.

"Okay, then, fine. I'll go there. Please, buy a nice dress for your mother, who is seriously ill. You made me say that, and you're making me say I just want to see you in something pretty just once before I die. It's your fault!"

I expect Caitlin to laugh, or at least smile in that way she does when I crack a joke that she knows is funny but doesn't want to admit it. Nothing.

"I'm not you," she says, pausing by a rack of peach ra-ra skirts. "Or then again, maybe I am you, and that makes it worse. Not because I don't want to be you, just because . . ."

I follow her as she stops in front of a mirror and looks her reflection in the eye, refusing to dwell on her abdomen. Her breasts look a little bigger, but her stomach is still pretty flat;

perhaps there might be a little bump there, but if so, it's barely visible, and yet she doesn't want to look at it.

"Are you afraid of coping, on your own?" I ask her. I had my mum, of course. Most of the time, I didn't want her—most of the time, I thought she fussed too much and was controlling or cross, or sometimes just crazy—but she was always there, and I was always grateful. My mum has always been my constant fallback position, and she has never once shirked from that. Not even now, when it's costing my mum her happy little life, her operatic society, her bridge club, that nice chap who plays piano at the am dram and takes her out every Wednesday when it's two-for-one at the cinema. The films they've seen this last year, Mum and her gentleman friend. She's become quite an expert on Tarantino. I'm sure they don't care what they see: it's just an excuse to hold hands in the dark. Now, though, all of that, all of the life she has built for herself away from me, is on hold, perhaps forever. And yet still she came.

"I'm afraid of everything," Caitlin says suddenly. "This . . ." She gestures at her middle. "This has happened at the worst time, hasn't it? It feels like I shouldn't be happy about this now, but I am. I know I am, but it's like my heart won't tell my head that I am. My head is still freaking out about it."

"Of course it is," I say. "And it will take you a while to adjust to that little person. But you can be a great mum and still do whatever you want to. This isn't the end of your life, Caitlin, it's just the beginning. . . ."

"Or maybe the middle, if I get sick like you." Caitlin looks at me, and for a moment she is Rosie Simpkins again, and I have to look very hard at the little mole on her left earlobe, the one she's had since she was born, and pull myself back into the present moment. It's like hauling myself through mud, but I make it.

"Mum, you are ill. You are so ill and . . . Esther will need me. She will need looking after, and so will Greg. And Gran can't do it all on her own—she can't bring up a three-year-old—she's too old for that now. They will need me to be someone that I'm not. I'm just not. I can't even take an exam, or get dumped by a boy, without cocking up my entire life. How can I do anything for them, or for you, or this baby? How will I ever be good enough in time?"

A sob catches in her throat, and she turns away from me, walking quickly out of the shop, still carrying the clothes, setting off peals of alarms. I go after her, and get to her just as the security guard catches up with her.

"Sorry," I say, and take the bundle of clothes from Caitlin's arms, standing between her and the guard. "My fault. I've got early-onset Alzheimer's. It means I make so many stupid mistakes, but we're not shoplifters. We are going to buy all of this, so if we can just go back to the . . . thingy where the money goes, and I'll pay for all of them."

The security guard looks at me, certain that I am lying. And who can blame him? First of all, it was clearly Caitlin holding the clothes when she went out of the door; secondly, I am hardly a little old lady in a nightie. At least, I don't think I'm wearing a nightie. I look down to check. No, I am fully dressed and not looking the least bit like a mentalist.

"I know," I say. "It's really tragic, isn't it?"

"And I'm pregnant." Caitlin sobs out of the blue, tears rolling down her cheeks. "And I don't even like any of these clothes. I don't want to wear leggings. Leggings are for people who've given up on life!"

I stifle a giggle as the poor baffled young man takes the bundle of clothes from my arms. "Just be more careful," he says. "Okay? Maybe don't go out without a . . ."

"Grown-up?" I nod solemnly, and Caitlin sobs onto my shoulder in gratitude.

"So you don't want this, no?" I look at Caitlin, who mutely shakes her head against my shoulder, and watch the guard go back into the store, scratching his head.

"We should take up shoplifting for a living. There's never been a better combination of hustlers in the history of retail fraud," I say to Caitlin, who lifts her head from my shoulder, suddenly dry-eyed and smiling.

My little Red Queen has still got it.

We walk through the shops, arm in arm, without talking. I look at the people going past. They seem to be walking, talking, breathing, thinking, much faster than me, as if the world has speeded up around me, leaving me half a frame behind. We stop at a coffee shop in the middle of the floor, and Caitlin orders us drinks while I sit at a table. She glances over at me from time to time, probably to make sure I haven't wandered off, and I try not to think about Rosie Simpkins—because every time I do, I'm tempted to find a phone box and dial her old number, which I suddenly know off by heart, and ask her if she's coming down the rec to look for boys to hang out with. I know where I am, and whom I am with, but I have to work hard to pin myself into this moment of time—to cling on, and make sure I stay here. I have an idea that this concentration works, but it's probably a lie I'm telling myself. I don't have any control, no idea where the fog will reach next, or when it will next blow in, always obliterating something forever.

Caitlin puts a milky coffee down in front of me, and I sip it gratefully. I don't like milky coffees, but every coffee I seem to get these days is exactly that. When I was younger, I only drank Mellow Birds. I wonder where you can get Mellow Birds from now? I drank it until I went to university and met Paul, and he drank espresso in tiny cups the way he liked it, and that's when I changed, to seem more grown up. But now I just get endless pints of warm coffee-flavored milk, which I find pointless.

"Your dad is called Paul Sumner," I say. "He's forty-two, he's married, has been for about ten years, he's got two daughters, you have two half sisters. He lectures in English literature and philosophy at University of Manchester, which isn't quite the world-changing poet that he said he wanted to be, but it's not bad. The university page on the word book says when and where his lectures are. He'd be really easy to stalk."

"When did you find all that out?" she asks me.

"When you were missing," I said. "Greg did it, actually." I've forgotten how to use the word book thingy. "He found it all out and wrote it down for me. He's got a file of info for you at home. You need to go and see Paul Sumner."

"No," she says adamantly. "I thought about it a lot, after I stormed off. I thought to myself, is it really worth putting all of us, including him, through some forced reunion? I'm nonexistent to him, and what will I get if I turn up on his doorstep and crowbar my way into his life? He won't want me there, and I've got enough on my plate. I don't need to see him."

"You do," I say, determined. "He's waited long enough, even if he doesn't know it. And so have you. You are so young, Caitlin. You need someone."

"I don't," she insists, a flash of defiance in her eyes. "You never had anyone."

"Oh, that is such a lie," I say. "I had your gran, and I had you. You might have been the little one, but I relied on you as much as anyone."

"Until Greg." She looks at me carefully. "When I first met Greg, I thought he was a dick, but then I watched you two together, and it was so . . . happy. The way you just cared for each other. It was almost like you must have always been looking for each other, right up until the moment you met, because you were just so pleased when you got together that it was like a . . . a reunion. Sickening, but in a sweet way."

I dip my head and stare into the pallid white coffee. I want to remember how that felt, the things she describes. I can see them, I can picture them as though they are on a screen, but I don't understand them anymore.

"Can't you be nicer to him, Mum?" she asks me. "He loves you so much. I hate to see him so sad."

"You don't understand," I say, looking back up at her. "I feel like I don't know him. It frightens me, having this stranger in our house."

"But we all know him," Caitlin says. "He's Greg."

"Is he, though?" I ask her. "Is that who he is?"

I see her face change, and I suppose she is puzzled and frightened by something that seems completely real and rational to me. This is the essence of the disease and what it does—the widening gulf between my reality and that of the people in my life. I try, every day, to reach back across it, but there comes a point when I can't, and they can't either, and then they don't even try, because my world is the one that is wrong.

"You need to go and see Paul," I say again. "You'll need him, a parent, another grandparent for the baby. A bigger family. Don't make me play the Alzheimer's card twice in one day."

"I can't think about it like that," she says. "I do better if I just think about one day at a time."

"You know how you need to live your life?" I tell her. "As though everything is completely fine. Make your choices that way. That's the way I want you to live your life, Caitlin. The way you want to, not the way that circumstances dictate."

"But you *are* ill," she says. "And maybe I am too. And

maybe I could pass the gene on to my child. And it could do the same. It's not the same as you, aged twenty, deciding to keep a baby, Mum. You had no idea about the hereditary gene; you were making a decision just based on one thing. But I do know, and I have to think about more than just will I be able to cope or get a job or get an education. I know that I can do all of those things, because I've seen you do all of those things and still be a brilliant, brilliant mum. It's not that. It's will I be leaving my child alone before it's properly grown up? Will I be turning him or her into a carer? Will I be giving them this disease that is . . . I've decided what I'm doing, and it feels right. But it's still so . . ."

She doesn't finish her sentence—she doesn't need to. If I had known then, on the day I discovered I was pregnant with Caitlin, if I had known, on the periphery of that sunny day, that the fog was already gathering, and slowly, slowly beginning to roll in to claim me and perhaps my unborn child too, would I have gone through with the pregnancy? Would I still be sitting here opposite this wonderful young woman? I look at her now, her black lashes sweeping her cheeks, the cupid's bow of her lip, that mole on her ear, and of course I say with my whole heart: yes, yes. I'd never miss a second of my life with her, or her life with me, because I know how golden and how shining it has been. But then, at that moment, when the line on the stick turned pink, if I had known then? And I realize I don't know the answer.

"You can take the test," I say. "You can find out for sure about the gene, if you think it will help. And it doesn't have to follow that you have it. Aunt Hattie had all her marbles, right up until she dropped dead of a heart attack. You don't have to wonder; you can find out."

"I don't know if I want to know," she says. "And knowing that I *can* know makes it so much harder to put it out of my head. So, what's better, for me to know for sure, or not know for sure?"

"I know the answer," I say. "I know what you have to do."

Caitlin looks skeptical.

"You have to decide as if it's not even a possibility, you have to decide to live your life the way you would, whatever else is happening. And do you know how I know that?"

She raises a brow.

"I know because that's what I did. I gave birth to you, and brought you up and turned down a million lovers, and married the very last one because I believed that I had all the time in the world. And I'm glad I've lived my life that way; I wouldn't have changed anything. Not a thing."

"Not even Greg?" she asks me. "Would you have waited all of those years for the love of your life if you'd known that almost as soon as you had him, you'd lose all the feelings you had for him?"

"Let me buy you that dress," I say, nodding at a little floral frock in the nearby shop window, cream cotton covered in pink roses. "It's so pretty, and if you team it with some nice red shoes, and nails and lipstick, imagine what a delight you will be!"

"I hate colors," Caitlin says, "but as you've played the AD card . . ."

She lets me pull her up from the table and into the shop to try on the dress, which suits her so perfectly and allows for some bump room too. Happily, I take her to the money counter and get out my card. It's then I realize that I've forgotten my PIN. It seems I can forget the year I was born after all.

thursday, october 25, 2007

caitlin

This is the cover of the CD that Greg brought me on the first day I met him as Mum's official boyfriend. I'd met him before, of course: he'd been around the house for a while. But then he was just the builder, listening to Radio One like he thought it was cool. I hadn't really noticed him. Then, after he'd finished the loft, that was when Mum started seeing him, and I thought, how could she be so stupid? I mean, he's a lot younger than her, a lot. And although Mum is sexy and funny and pretty, I couldn't see why a man would ever seriously want a woman so much older than him. I thought he was taking advantage of her, playing her. And Mum said she thought that might be the case too, except she'd already given him all of her money when he converted the loft into her writing room. And anyway, she said, if it was just a fling, it didn't matter. It wasn't a fling, though. We both knew that when she invited him to have dinner with us. And he brought me this CD of the Black Eyed Peas, because he thought they were cool. But I hate the Black Eyed Peas, and it was a CD, and no one had a CD player by then, not even Gran.

He gave it to me and I looked at it and chucked it on the side, which I knew was really bad-mannered. I knew I was being a textbook-rude potential stepkid, but for me it didn't seem like a cliché. What did this man want with my mother? I mean, I was fifteen—if he was going to take an interest in either of us, it should have been me. Even though that was wrong in a different way! Not that I was jealous—don't get me wrong. If I think of Greg in that way, I feel a bit like I want to puke. No, I never fancied him, even before he was my stepdad, and now . . . well, now he's just my stepdad. But I didn't want him to like me and not Mum. It was just that I couldn't make sense of it. Which shows that I was pretty small-minded back then, all of five years ago.

Greg sat at the table. Mum had gone to town making a paella. Seriously, she'd seen it on some cookery program and went out and bought a special pan, and saffron, and all these prawns with legs and heads, which made me want to vomit, and she spent all day on it, without bothering to inquire if the builder ate seafood. Well, I thought that he certainly wouldn't: he would eat bacon sandwiches and maybe hunks of cheese. And I was right—about the not eating seafood part, at least. Greg is actually severely allergic to seafood, and it took him ages to say anything. He just sat there, staring at the prawns, which were staring right back at him, seriously considering risking anaphylactic shock just so he wouldn't let my mum down or look stupid in front of me. I asked him, quite rudely, what his problem was with the food that Mum had made. Which was when he went bright red and confessed he might die if he ate it. Mum was mortified. She tipped the whole thing in the outside bin, like somehow even a prawn eyeballing Greg might set him off, and that pissed me off because I'd only just decided to like paella.

Mum ordered Chinese, which on that night I decided I didn't like, and I pushed some special fried rice around my plate and made it very clear that I was missing the prawns. Greg kept saying he was sorry, and I kept blanking him. And then he went to the loo, and Mum leaned over and pointed her finger right in my face and said, "You do realize that you are playing the role of nasty spoilt brat to perfection, don't you, Caitlin?"

I shrugged. "I'm sorry," I said. "Someone has got to protect you, and there is only me."

"I don't want you to protect me," she said. She sat back a little bit and looked at me, and she looked surprised, which hurt me. "You are old enough to know that I don't want protecting from feeling this excited or giddy about the way he looks at me, or when he touches me. I want to feel those things, and be happy, even if it's just for a little while, and even if it all goes wrong. That's what life is about, Caitlin—taking chances to try and be happy."

"Why do I have to meet him, though?" I said. "I've never met any of your other men."

Of course, I said it at the exact moment Greg came back into the room, and I made it sound like he was only the latest in a very long line of conquests. Of course I did. But Greg didn't go red or flinch away from it, like he had the prawns.

"I asked your mum to let me meet you," he said, "because I want to be part of her life, and that means being part of your life too. And even if you don't like me, your mum does. So how about you go back to being just this really funny, clever girl that your mum tells me you are, and we can decide from that point on if we can stand to be in the same room as each other? I'd like us to get on, but just so you know . . . if we don't, there is no way I am giving Claire up."

I stopped playing the brat after that, because it did seem like such a terrible cliché, and I could see he and Mum were serious about each other. But I did still think he was a dickhead. Right up until the day Esther was born. That day, he became my hero.

10

caitlin

We get back from shopping and I think Mum is happy. She is singing as she goes into the house, taking up to her room the bags full of clothes that were meant for me and trying them on. She's talking about going out later with someone called Rosie, down the pub, to see who's about, maybe get a snog. I thought I'd get used to the way she fades in and out of our lives, but I don't. Each fade-in is a little shorter; each fade-out is a little longer. I stand at the bottom of the stairs for a moment, wondering what I should do to try to bring her back, but she is singing and she seems so happy.

Gran is in the living room with Esther, making her watch a program about elephants that is narrated by David Attenborough.

"Look, sweetheart, look, aren't the elephants lovely," I hear her say.

"I want *Dora the Explorer* or *Octonauts* or *Peppa Pig*," Esther insists. Gran isn't like Mum, though, who has always given Esther her way with everything, cheerfully stating that she has her in training for a career as a despotic dictator. Gran tries really hard to make things *better:* she likes to improve things. And now she's trying to improve Esther by making her watch something educational, which is funny. I love Gran, and I love Esther, and I'll love my baby, the same way Mum and Gran have loved us. Perhaps not exactly the same way: similar, but better.

I feel better, having spent a morning with Mum, and after what she said to me. Before she decided she wanted to go out on the pull with Rosie, it was all making sense. It sort of feels like she's given me back my future.

I go and sit down on the sofa, and Esther brings me the remote control.

"I want *Dora* or *Peppa Pig*," she whispers, as if Gran will not notice.

Gran despairs, and rolls her eyes, and I switch channels. I know all of Esther's favorite channels by heart.

"Was it okay?" Gran asks me, and I nod, because it was okay.

"I'm taking you to the hospital tomorrow. The appointment's at ten," Gran informs me. "They'll check you over, give you a scan."

I nod, and shift in my seat. Esther has climbed onto my lap, and weighs heavily on my abdomen. I can feel the resistance there now, the pocket of life expanding into my body. I move Esther to one side and wrap my arms about myself, realizing it's an unconscious gesture to protect that unknown universe that's spiraling inside of me. Does that mean I'm becoming a mother already?

"I cut this out for you," Gran says, and offers me a flimsy bit of newsprint. "It was in the *Daily Mail* about getting back into further education after having kids."

"Thanks," I say, taking it and folding it up before tucking it into my pocket.

For as long as I can remember, Gran has always sent us pieces of paper she has cut out from newspapers. Articles about diets or parenting, or about books on how to be a teacher ... Everything that Mum already did, Gran would persist in sending her clippings from papers with advice about how to do those things better—which I took to mean that she thought Mum didn't do them very well in the first place. Once, I asked Mum why Gran did it, and Mum said she was trying to be helpful, even if she was coming across as batty and controlling. And then Gran sent her a clipping about diets to control yeast infections, and Mum sent it back with the words I DO NOT HAVE A THRUSH PROBLEM written in red marker pen across it.

After that, the clippings escalated into some kind of crazy war of attrition, with Gran sending Mum ever more bizarre articles about sex addiction, weight loss, body dysmorphia, all kinds of cancer—and Mum sending them all back again, sometimes with a red-penned message, sometimes torn into little bits. It was like a constant joke they each played on the other, but a joke that annoyed them all the same. Gran still cuts things out of the paper, but she keeps them in a drawer in her spare room now. I know this because I saw her secretly filing one away the other day. The headline read: THE ALZHEIMER'S EPIDEMIC.

Now that Esther is engrossed in the TV, I get up and go find Greg in the kitchen. He's bent over the memory book, writing. Greg has taken to writing in the book almost as much as Mum. I wonder if he's read my bit yet. I wrote it for him, really, more than for Mum. I know it's supposed to be her book, but I want him to remember that he is part of this family too, and that we all love him. Even me. I love him too, now.

I sit down next to him, and he looks up at me. There are tears in his eyes. Greg was always a bit soppy, a bit poetic. Mum used to tease him about it, this big burly man with a poet's heart. He said she brought it out in him.

"It's hard for you, isn't it?" I say. "You're losing her first."

"I keep thinking, if I can just remind her, somehow, then it will all come back. She'll remember me again, like she used to. Then we'll have each other again."

"What are you writing?" I ask him, but he closes the book. It's thick now, bursting with memories, and mementos—objects and photographs peep out from the pages. Mum's tried to stick literally everything in there over the last few weeks. On one page there is a half-sucked boiled sweet that she swears blind was partially eaten by Nik Kershaw at her first ever gig. The book has become part of Mum, and part of the family: it's always around, always being added to or read. But the pages will run out soon, and that frightens me. As Mum puts more and more of her head into the book, I'm scared that when she runs out of space, her head will be empty and she will be gone. Before I went to London, I was trying to think of ways to add more pages to it—maybe tape some in the back, or staple them. But as I pick up the closed book, I can see that it isn't just its contents that have bulked it out—there are several new pages in the back too. The quality of the paper is the same, and I can only see they are new because the alignment isn't exactly perfect. Opening the book, I examine them closer and see that someone has painstakingly glued a strip of material to the inside spine, and then stitched on the pages by hand. I look at Greg, and he shrugs.

"I don't want it to end." He goes to the fridge and gets out a beer. "Are you okay?"

"Everyone keeps asking me that," I say. "I don't know. I'm stuck in a sort of limbo. I think we all are, don't you?"

"Maybe," Greg says. "I'd like to be. I'd like to be stuck in one perfect day where everything is just the way you have always wanted it to be. I've had a lot of days like that with Claire and Esther and you. I always thought there'd be so many more. It turns out there weren't nearly enough. Nothing can ever stay the same, not even if you want it to, *so* much." He stops, waiting for the emotion to fade out of his voice. "Life is moving on around you, Caitlin, and in you. You need to make sure you keep up with it."

"What do you mean?" I ask him, although I think I know what he is going to say next.

"Go and see your dad," Greg says. "Go and see this Paul Sumner bloke. I know it's scary and you've got a lot on your plate already. But something like that, reaching out to a person who is so much part of you . . . it's not something you should put off, not for anything."

"I've never had a dad before," I say. "Well, not before you."

"Don't be silly," he says, looking at his feet. "You think I'm a dork."

"Oh God, dork is such a dorky word!" I laugh, and he smiles. "But seriously, though, you are my sort of dad—a kind of one and, well, you know. Thanks for that."

Greg laughs again. "That's the most underwhelming endorsement of fatherhood I have ever heard!"

"You know what I mean," I say, and the thought of him not being around inspires a surge of panic. "Please, Greg, don't disappear, will you, please . . . afterwards. Don't take Esther and go, please. Because . . . it's not just Esther, it's you too. You are my family now. I mean, you won't just go and leave me, will you?"

It's not until I've stopped talking that I realize there are tears on my cheeks and I'm holding on tight to my own wrists, clenching them hard.

"Caitlin." Greg says my name, looking anxious, surprised . . . "I'd never do that, love. I'd never split you and Esther up, not for anything. And . . . we are a family. We always will be. Nothing will change that. I'm your dad, and you're stuck with me."

"Good," I say, nodding. "This Paul Sumner . . . I don't know anything about him. But you two . . . I can't do without you two."

Greg rests his hand on top of the book. There's a thump from upstairs where Mum is in the bedroom, and we both look up. We both will ourselves to stay where we are, and not go and check on her. Mum hates it when we check on her, especially at home. She hates that her life is never private anymore.

"Look," Greg says. "Go and see your father. You need to. You need to look the other person who made you in the eye and declare yourself. I don't see how you could possibly know yourself completely until you've done that."

I shake my head. "There's Mum, and Esther and . . ."

"The baby," Greg finishes for me, choosing his words carefully. "If you like, I could take a couple of days off, drive you up there?"

"No," I say, and suddenly the decision is made, and it feels freeing. "No. You know what? Gran is taking me to the hospital tomorrow for a checkup, and then I think I'll just go. And stay in a hotel up there. I mean, if you and Mum will sub me some cash . . ." I give him a hopeful smile, and he nods.

"But you'll be okay, up there on your own, in your . . . ?"

"My condition?" I laugh. "I have to decide what to do, and

I have to decide now, don't I? Mum would never wait around, like I have been ... dithering. She would never wait for life to happen to her—stick her head in the sand, hide away from her past or her future. She's never done that, has she? She has always been brave. Look at what happened when she met you! She was brave, and took a chance. And look at what happened when Esther was born! She never gave up, not ever. And even this thing that she cannot fight ... even now she isn't giving up. So yes, fine, I'll go and introduce myself to my biological father. It's something to do, isn't it? It's something that I *can* do. And maybe it will help Mum too."

Greg is about to say something when a fat plop of water lands on the kitchen table. For a second, Greg and I stare at it, and then up at the ceiling ... where a damp dark circle gives birth to a second droplet.

"Oh," I say, standing. "She said something about going to run a bath...."

"Wait here," Greg says. "I'll go."

But I follow him anyway, thinking about what Mum said in the shopping center. Greg might be the very last person she wants to see.

He gets to the top of the stairs in three easy strides, skipping stairs as he goes. At once we see the water seeping out from under the bathroom door, and soaking into the landing carpet, a small tidal wave adding to the damp patch as Greg opens the bathroom door and we are enveloped in steam. Stepping into the water in his socked feet, he hisses in a sharp breath: it must be boiling hot. Fighting the wave of heat, he turns off the hot tap and throws down what towels he can find before returning to the landing, where I am standing. Mum has let the bath overflow. It's a simple enough thing, and an easy mistake to make, for anyone, not just her. So why does it feel so ominous?

There's another bang and the door to Mum and Greg's bedroom opens, slamming against the wall. Which is when we notice a pile of clothes on the landing. A shoe, Greg's, ricochets off the doorframe and lands at his feet.

"Claire?" He approaches the room hesitantly. I am just behind him.

"How dare you!" Mum scrambles over the bed to confront him, her eyes full of fire. "You must think I'm an idiot. I've read about men like you. Well, you've met your match in me, mister. I'm not some poor little old lady who you can con out of her cash. Take all your stuff and get out of my home!"

"Claire." Greg says her name again. "Babe, please . . ."

"I know your game," Mum says, pushing hard against the center of his chest. "You thought because I was older and single and lonely that you could fool me into thinking you were interested in me, then move in, take my house, my money, everything. But you can't! I'm not about to be hoodwinked by you. You don't frighten me. I want you to go now, or I'm calling the police."

Her face is white with fury, her eyes hot and dry, and there is something else: she is frightened.

"Mum." I step in front of Greg. "It's fine. It's okay. Greg is a friend."

It doesn't seem anything like an adequate enough word to describe him—what he is, who he's been to my mother—and I know that hearing it must hurt him, even if he understands why I've used the most neutral word I can think of.

"Claire." Greg says her name once more, softly, as gently as he can. "It's me, darling. We're married. Look, there's a photo of us on our wedding day. . . ."

"How dare you!" Mum shouts at him, grabbing me by the wrist and pulling me away from Greg. "Don't you dare pretend you're their father! Why are you here, in my house? What do you want from me? Caitlin, can't you see what he's doing? Get out! Get out!"

"Mummy!" Esther, attracted by the noise, arrives at the top of the stairs, followed by Gran, who stands one stair down, peering anxiously at the scene.

"What's all this racket?" she asks. "Claire, what on earth are you playing at?"

Something in Gran's voice calms Mum, who loosens her grip on my wrist. Her eyes are still wide with fear as she stands there, breathing very hard.

"I was . . . I was running a . . . a bath . . . and then there was all this stuff in my bedroom. And it's not mine!"

"Mummy!" Esther shakes Gran's hands off her shoulders and runs to Mum, who scoops her up and hugs her hard. "They are Daddy's things, Mummy. You are very silly, Mummy-forget-me-not."

With Esther in her arms, Mum sinks down onto the carpet. The air is still damp with hot steam, and the smell of wet carpet rises in the air.

"I forgot," she told Greg, unable to look at him.

"Mummy, get up!" Esther commands, taking Mum's cheeks in her hands and pressing them together between her little palms, twisting Mum's face out of shape. "Get up now, Mummy. It's time for tea."

We stand back, the three of us, and watch as Esther tugs at Mum's hand until she finally climbs to her feet.

"What do you want for tea?" Mum asks her, not looking at any of us, as she carries Esther down the stairs.

"Lasagna!" Esther says.

"Or beans on toast?" I hear Mum say, as her voice recedes into the kitchen.

"Lasagna!" Esther repeats.

And then there is silence.

"I'll get the camp bed," Greg says. "Sleep on the floor in Esther's room."

"No," I say. "I'll sleep on the camp bed. You have my room. I'll be away for a few nights anyway, unless you want me to stay?"

"She's getting worse," Greg says, the words spilling out of him before any of us are quite ready to hear them, even him. "I didn't expect it to be this quick. I mean, I know they talked about the blood clots, but I thought . . . I'd hoped we'd have some time together, to say goodbye. I thought she'd come back and say goodbye."

Finally, Gran climbs the last stair, and puts a hand on Greg's shoulder. "Everything that's happening now, the things she says and thinks, the way she feels . . . it doesn't mean she hasn't loved you, more than any other person in her life. It doesn't mean that, Greg. This isn't her, it's the disease."

"I know, it's just . . ." Greg's shoulders descend, and, suddenly, it's as though the air is let out of him. He fades to half his size in front of our eyes. "I'll get the camp bed out of the garage."

Neither of us moves to follow him out of the front door, knowing he needs some time alone to mourn.

"Mum!" Mum comes to the foot of the stairs, calling up as if nothing has happened. "How do I get into this beans container, again?"

"You go," I say. "I'll try to mop up some of this."

"Are you all right?" Gran asks me.

"Are any of us?" I ask her.

"Mum!" I hear my mum shout again. "Can I do it with a knife?"

monday, february 2, 2009

greg

This is the first photo I took of Claire and Esther.

Esther is wrapped in a towel, and Claire's got that annoyed look on her face because she strictly forbade me to take any photos until she had brushed her hair and put on mascara. But I couldn't help it. I couldn't believe what had just happened.

I suppose most men think their pregnant partner is beautiful, and I was no exception. I loved the way she looked—the swell of her belly carrying our baby. And she was happy, then. Claire liked to bitch and complain about her ankles getting fat, her skin stretching, and about how she was far too old to be doing this, but I could see she loved it too, most of the time. She had this energy about her—this sort of vibration of life. And I would look at her and be amazed. You know, my baby was in there.

* * *

Esther came a little early, and even though Caitlin had been born early too, it took us all by surprise. As it had been such a long time since Caitlin, everyone thought Claire would most likely go overdue, because her body had forgotten that it had ever been pregnant before. Claire hadn't stopped doing anything while she was pregnant—not going for walks, or working—she even went out dancing with Julia, on Julia's birthday, even though she was as round as a ripe pomegranate. I hadn't wanted her to go, but I couldn't stop her, so I sent Caitlin out with them to keep an eye on her. Caitlin wasn't impressed.

When Esther was born, it was the middle of the night and Claire got up, suddenly—especially considering she was so big, by then. She was at the stage when she didn't do anything quickly. Like a supertanker—that's what she said she was like, it took her at least a week to turn around. But on this night, she got up like a rocket and went to the bathroom. I went back to sleep again, almost straightaway, but it could only have been for a few seconds because I woke to the sound of her calling. Not shouting my name at the top of her voice, but one quiet little call after the other, more like whimpers, I suppose. I went to the bathroom, and Claire was sitting on the tiled floor.

"He's coming." She breathed the words out.

It took me a second to get what she was on about, then I noticed there was a puddle of fluid between her legs, and I realized she was in labor. "Right, I'll call the hospital, tell them we are coming," I said. "And get your bag . . ."

"No, I mean he's coming *now*," Claire said, and then this wave of pain hit her.

"But that's impossible," I said, and I realized I was still standing in the doorway, so I crouched down. She wasn't screaming, or making any of the noise I was expecting. She almost wasn't there: her eyes were closed and she looked like she was concentrating hard on the world inside her. The next wave of pain passed.

"Tell that to the baby, and call 999!"

The call handler stayed on the phone and told me to look between Claire's legs, and basically use my fingers to measure how dilated she was. I did try, but Claire growled at me, like she was possessed by a devil. So I knocked on Caitlin's door, and although she could usually sleep through an earthquake, she got up immediately.

The woman on the phone said the ambulance was five minutes away, which seemed like a lifetime.

"Check how dilated your mum is," I said to Caitlin.

"What? No way!" Caitlin looked horrified.

"Oh, for chrissake, give me a bloody, mirror," Claire said, and I thought about it and remembered that this was my woman, and my baby, and I am six foot two and like to think of myself as pretty manly.

"I'm looking," I told Claire. "So just get over it."

Claire told me that she hated me, and used some choice swear words, too, but she still seemed quite in control, groaning a bit, closing her eyes, bracing herself with her back against the bath, her feet planted wide on the tiles. I felt sure that if it were really close, she'd be making more of a fuss. I got a towel and mopped up the fluid on the floor, and then looked.

The woman on the phone asked me again if I could estimate how far dilated she was. I said, "I don't know, but I can see the top of the baby's head."

The woman on the phone started to say that I should tell her not to push, but before she'd finished the sentence, Claire pushed—and there was a rush of life, and water and blood, and

I caught her, the baby. This mucky little pink and gray thing covered in crap. She shot into my arms! It still makes me laugh when I think about it.

"She's out!" I yelled at my phone, which I'd dropped when I went to catch the baby. Ever since then, Claire has said that this was the time all those Sundays playing bloody cricket finally paid off. Caitlin picked up the phone, and I laid the baby on Claire's chest. Her eyes were wide as she watched me do it— wide and full of wonder.

"She's asking if it's breathing?" Caitlin said, looking worried. But before I could check, this cry, a howl of intent, cut through the air, and I burst into tears—proper stupid woman tears, running down my face. I couldn't stop. Caitlin got a clean towel from the airing cupboard and we wrapped it around the baby, and then the doorbell rang. The ambulance had arrived. That was when I grabbed my phone and took this picture, even though Claire threatened to kill me. I wanted to remember that moment, exactly.

"He's so lovely," Claire said, oblivious to the two huge paramedic guys that had walked into our bathroom.

"She's a girl," I told her, and she looked even happier.

"Excellent," she said. "Another Armstrong woman to conquer the world."

II

claire

"Have you got enough money?" I ask Caitlin, who nods.

"Well, I've got your credit card and the PIN, so yes," she says.

"And you will look after my car?" I run my palm over the surface of the vehicle, which is painted my favorite color. It's hot and strong and bold. I can't remember what the name for it is, though. Something happened last night that changed things. I don't know exactly what it was, but I felt it when I woke up this morning: the blankness pressing down into my head. Perhaps it's the fog; perhaps it's the emboli. I picture them like bright little sparks, fireworks whizzing and banging. That would be a good name for the color of my car: emboli.

"I will try to look after your car," Caitlin says. She looks uncertain—of course she does.

Earlier today I waited in, being guarded by Greg while

my mum took Caitlin to the hospital. I waited, looking out of
the window, pinning myself to the moment when she would
come back and tell me how things were. The only way I knew
how to do it was to stay there, in exactly the same place, from
the moment they left until the moment they got back—certain
that if I moved, I'd lose the present moment. Greg kept trying
to make me do stuff—drink tea or eat toast or go and sit with
him in the kitchen—but that is because he doesn't know I have
to pin myself to a point in time and make my mind stay there. I
don't know how long it took, but I tried to open the front door
the second I saw the car pull in. Only they do something to the
door to stop me going out of it, so I can't open it anymore from
the inside. I waited on the other side for them to open it, still
making myself stay in that moment: making myself know what
had happened.

Caitlin has always been such an open book—I have always
known what she is thinking or feeling—but suddenly I couldn't
tell. I couldn't tell as she walked past me and flopped onto the
sofa in the living room. I looked at Mum.

"Eighteen weeks," she said. "Mother and baby doing well."

I don't know exactly what I felt so frightened of when I
walked into that room; I only know I had the sense that whatever she was going to say was likely to terrify me.

"Caitlin?" I asked her, sitting down on the chair opposite.

"I love my baby," she said, quite simply. "Like, with this
force I had no idea was possible. It's almost like I want to fight
someone, even though there is no one to fight. Oh, Mum.
There's a picture. Do you want to see?"

She handed me a photo. They're much clearer now than
they used to be, and I could see little arms and legs, and a profile
that looks just like Caitlin's.

"Oh, Caitlin." I wanted to hold her and hug her. "I'm so pleased."

"Me too," she said simply. "I'm pleased too, I think. But scared too."

"You will be a wonderful mother."

"Will you keep telling me that?" she said.

"If you keep telling me that you are pregnant," I said, and she smiled.

It seemed wrong, then, to dispatch her back out into the world, on her own, to go and find her father. And yet she is going. I can't stop her now, even if I wanted to. Ever since whatever happened yesterday happened, she has had this sort of quiet determination about her—this kind of resolution. For the first time, I notice that she is being careful with me, treating me like I am ill. Yes, something changed last night. But if it was something that has helped Caitlin be this stronger, more certain and purposeful person, then I hope it can't have been that bad a thing.

"Call me when you get there," I say. "And before you see him—and straight afterwards. Don't forget to tell him what I told you, okay? He'll be shocked at first, probably. . . . Perhaps we should write him a letter. . . ."

"No," Caitlin says. "This is the way it's happening. I'm going. And I will be back really soon, okay?"

I nod and kiss her—and then my mum, who has been watching us both, presses a wad of money into Caitlin's hand exactly the way she always used to do with a packet of sweets.

"Take care, poppet," she says, and Caitlin bears the childish nickname sweetly, kissing my mother on the cheek. Esther cries as the car pulls out, and I want to cry too. Not just because Caitlin is going, but also because now I am alone, with my mother in charge.

"She'll be fine," Mum says, as she guides me back into the house, her hands on my shoulders, as though I have forgotten how to walk in a straight line—which hasn't happened yet, I don't think. "She's stronger than she looks, that girl. I'm so proud of her."

"Me too," I say. "And of you—a great-grandma!"

"That's quite enough of that, my girl," Mum says, and after we've walked back into the house, she locks the door behind me. "Or should I call you Granny now?"

I'm writing in the book when Esther brings me a storybook to read to her. I've read this book to her about a thousand times at least, and I was just writing in the memory book, the tip of the pen obediently following my thoughts—or at least I think it is. I believe it is. I think words and the pen moves, and produces patterns and swirls on the page that look familiar, and it's comforting to assume that they mean something. Caitlin is driving to meet her father—no doubt with that little crease between her brows that she always has when she is driving on the motorway—and I am trying not to think of her weaving in and out of the big trucks in my flimsy little heart-colored car. Esther's book is full of animal drawings—a big rabbit and a little rabbit. Or possibly hare, I'm not sure. But it doesn't matter, and I don't mind, as I haven't lost the name for either long-eared animal, and that is a small victory. Only there are words, too, and it's the words that I cannot decipher anymore. Decipher. That's a good word. I have the word "decipher" in my head, which is a long and complicated word that I know the meaning of, but this children's book, with its large, simple symbols printed underneath the picture of Hare or Rabbit, might as well be written in Greek.

I know the words are there, and I know what they do. I've

read this book a thousand times or more to Esther, but I cannot remember what takes place between the big rabbit (or possibly hare) and the little rabbit (possibly hare).

I panic, anxious that this will be the moment Esther finds me out: the moment when she looks at me anew, withdraws from me, and joins the ranks of people who prefer not to engage me in conversation anymore.

"Come on, Mummy," Esther says, wriggling impatiently. "Do the voices, like you usually do. The really high one and the low one, 'member?"

The pitch of her voice soars and then falls; she knows exactly how it should sound.

I look at the picture of the big rabbit and the little hare, and I try to invent something about a magical rabbit who turned his best friend into a midget, and then . . . threw him at a plate in the sky. Esther laughs, but she is not satisfied; she is even a little bit cross.

"That is not the story, is it, Mummy?" she admonishes me. "Read me the proper story, with the voices, like normal! I like things to be like normal, Mummy."

It's those last words that crush me: Esther craving normal. Until now, Esther has been the only one who's assumed that everything is like normal, that I am just like I've always been, but for the first time she is seeing that it's not. I am failing her.

"Will you read it to me?" I ask her, even though she is only three and a half, and she doesn't know how to read beyond sounding out a few letters. This is one thing we have in common.

"Of course I will," Esther says confidently. "There is Big Rabbit and Little One . . . the mummy and the baby . . . and the baby wants some new Lego, the Doctor Who kind, so when

Mummy Rabbit says, 'Ooh, I love you, Little Rabbit,' the baby rabbit says can I have some Doctor Who Lego, please, specially with a TARDIS . . ."

As she goes on, seemingly happy to turn the story into a shopping list, I rest my chin on the top of her head and think about the things that we won't be able to do soon, or will never do. Will I be with Esther on her first day of school? Probably not. Or if I am, I might think she is Caitlin, and wonder why her black hair is yellow, now. I won't see her in her first school play, or take her shopping when she becomes more interested in clothes than toys—during those rare few years when she might have listened to my opinion on what she wears and how she does her hair. I won't see her pass her exams, or get into uni; I won't see her wear a cap and gown, become a fighter pilot, or a ninja, or Doctor Who, which is her ultimate ambition. Not a companion—she doesn't want to be a companion—she wants to be the Doctor. All of these things will be lost to me. Lives will play out behind my back, and I won't know a thing about them—that's assuming my brain hasn't forgotten to tell my lungs to breathe by then, and I'm not already dead. Dead might be preferable: if there is heaven, and ghosts, I could watch over her, watch over all of them. I could be a guardian angel, except I still know that guardian angels are party poopers. And anyway, I don't believe in God, which I think would stop me even getting through the application process, although I am fairly sure I could talk him round in the interview. "What about equal ops, God?" I'd say.

Stop thinking. Stop this crazy roller coaster of thinking and listen; listen to Esther telling you that she wants the Hot Wheels Super Racer Shooter track, and make yourself be here in this moment, with your daughter, breathing in the milky scent of her hair, feeling her body so relaxed against you. Be in this moment.

"We should bake a cake," I say. Esther stops talking and twists around in her chair, the book sliding to the floor with a plop.

"Ooh, yes," she says excitedly. "Let's bake a cake! What do we need? We need flour!" She hops off my knee, dragging a chair over to the cupboards, and climbs up onto the worktop without hesitation in a bid to find flour. I go to the kitchen door and listen. Mum is Hoovering again. Mum decided that I can't be trusted with cookers, flames, or gas, so if she knew we were making a cake, she'd come in here and supervise me, and then it wouldn't be me making a cake with Esther, it would be Mum.

Closing the door softly, I think perhaps we have long enough to at least put some things in a bowl and mix them around before Mum discovers us.

"Is this flour?" Esther asks me, producing a pink packet of something powdery, thrusting it under my nose for inspection. I inhale, and it reminds me of fairgrounds.

"Yes," I say, although I am not certain. "It might be."

"Do we weigh it?" she says happily. "On the scales?"

Climbing down from the chair, she fetches a small bowl from the cupboard.

"No," I say. "Weighing is for losers. We are going to live life on the edge."

"You fire the oven," she tells me. "You have to do that because you are a grown-up and ovens get hot, hot, hot!"

I turn around and stare at the appliance. I remember choosing it because it was big and showy, and looked like it belonged to a woman who knew how to cook, but I never knew how to cook, not even when I knew about flour. I have only ever cooked Esther's lasagna, which requires very little skill, and now even that has gone. So I look at the cooker, and while I remember that I picked it out because it looked like a cook's cooker,

I now wonder what all of the things do. I reach for something protruding out of the front and turn it around. Nothing happens, so I assume that I haven't done any damage, and at least Esther thinks I've done something.

"We need eggies," Esther says, going to the fridge and pulling out an array of things onto the floor, with a variety of splats and plops, until she finds a soggy cardboard box, right at the back, that is egg-shaped. She puts it on the table. It is full of smooth, beautiful-looking objects that look like they fit just perfectly in the palm of my hand. I love the eggs, because I know what they are, and because I have not forgotten them, and now they seem more perfect and more beautiful to me than they ever have before.

"How many?" Esther asks me.

"All of 'em," I say, because although I know they are eggs, I don't know how many there are.

"Can I do the smashing?"

I nod, even though I don't want to break the beautiful, round, friendly eggs. But Esther does, slamming the first one whole into what might be flour, so that the shell explodes, the clear insides oozing out between her fingers, puffs of powder rising up to greet our noses.

"This is fun," she says, her fingers dripping as she reaches for the second egg, and, smash, in it goes. Esther's laughter is raucous, like an old man's who smokes forty a day, rather than a little girl's, which makes me laugh all the harder, setting her off again. Her eyes sparkle as she looks at me.

"Again? Yes?" Her face is a picture of such joy.

"Yes," I say, gulping in air between giggles.

She reaches for the third egg, then climbs up onto the worktop, clearly with a plan in mind that she finds hilarious.

Her shoulders shudder with giggles. And then she drops it from standing height into the bowl. There is a dull thud as the egg meets it fate, and a puff of white in the air, and Esther does a little dance of joy. This is a perfect moment, and I do my best to cling on to it.

"What the . . ." Mum walks into the room. "That's gas," she says. "Oh my God, you're filling the room with gas!"

She goes to the back door and throws it open, letting a rush of cold wet air fill the kitchen, drenching mine and Esther's fun in health and safety. Going over to the cooker, she twists the knob I'd turned in the other direction.

"Get off there at once, young lady," Mum says, not giving Esther a chance to climb down, lifting her up by hooking her hands under her armpits. "Outside, now, the pair of you!" She looks at the mess on the table. "Outside now, until it's clear!"

She orders us out into the wet and cold, like we are a couple of errant dogs who've been caught chewing a favorite table leg, or something. Holding her breath, Mum goes back inside while Esther and I stand on the patio. Esther's hands are still sticky with the innards of the eggs.

"Is baking finished?" Esther asks me, miserably. "I want it to be baking again."

"You mustn't touch the cooker!" Mum says to me when she returns with warm stuff. She hands me a jacket as she slips Esther's on for her, holding it out so Esther can put her arms in. I stare at the garment she's brought me. It's not the jacket I want, and she knows that. I think she's brought this contraption as a punishment. I like to wear a hoody now, because it is simple: I know where my head goes, and can work out where the arms go from there. And there aren't any things to fix together, which I hate doing. I am still chasing it round and round, trying to get an arm in a hole, like a dog after its tail, when Mum steps in. She puts it on me like I am a little child, just like she did for Esther. I pout just like Esther.

"How many times have we told you? You just can't do things like that anymore!" Mum admonishes me.

"I don't know," I say, sullen. "I've got this short-term memory thing. . . ."

Mum's eyes narrow, and I can see that, this time, she is angry, really angry with me. Like the time I got very drunk in the Fifth Year, and came home from school and threw up on her bed, which she was asleep in.

"Why not?" Esther asks her, as Mum furiously wipes at her hands with an antibacterial hand wipe. "Why can't me and Mummy do fun things?"

"I mean," Mum says, "what if you'd lit something, or the pilot light on the boiler went on, or there was a spark from the light switch? We all could have been killed!"

"Killed!" Esther looks alarmed. "Like deads?"

"I didn't do it on purpose," I say unhappily, as Mum puts a scarf around my neck. "It was fine. It was . . . a mistake. We were having a lovely time. I didn't do it on purpose."

"No, you never do," Mum says. It's her stock response, one she's been giving me since the very first time I said I didn't mean to spray her entire bottle of perfume on the dog, drink all of her Christmas sherry and then need two days off school, have sex with the builder and then marry him. Only this time, I actually mean that I didn't mean it.

She finishes buttoning up my coat. "Wait there," she says. "I'm going back in to make sure it's safe."

Esther tugs at my hand in a gesture of solidarity. "We were only making a cake."

I look around for something for us to do while we are

waiting—a ball, perhaps, or Esther's little wheelie thing that she likes to whiz around on, especially downhill—and I see the back gate is slightly ajar. I'd imagined that it would be double-locked and bolted, but it isn't: it's actually open, revealing a slash of freedom beyond.

"Shall we go to the park?" I ask Esther.

"I should think so," Esther says, and leads me out of the gate.

12

claire

Esther knows the way to the park, even in the near dark, which it suddenly becomes, quite soon after we begin our expedition. That's winter afternoons for you: they are over before they have begun, and suddenly the night is rolling in, pressing down. I hold her hand and let her lead me, chatting away happily as she skips along, not remotely daunted by the fact that the sun has sunk almost all the way behind the black, tightly laced horizon of trees—or that the lights of the cars whiz toward us, a procession of eyes.

Esther is excited when we stop at a crossing, and she pushes the button. "We wait for the green man," she tells me with authority.

Across the street I see a telephone box, and it seems to shine out to me like a beacon. It reminds me of a warm summer's evening. Of going out of the house with a pocketful of twenty-pence pieces to talk to this boy I was seeing when I was a girl. We only had one phone in the house and it was in the hallway, so if I wanted to talk in private, I had to go to the bottom of the road and make a call from the box. It became a sort of a haven for me, that little box, with the graffiti etched into the glass and the cards offering sexual favors Blu-Tacked to the sides. It was where I organized my life, whispered sweet nothings and had them whispered in return into my ear, pressed against that receiver like it was a seashell and I was listening for the sea.

A while back, I stopped noticing telephone boxes—they are surplus to requirements these days—but now here is one. A thought comes to me from nowhere: it just materializes into an empty space, and underneath my tightly buttoned coat I reach into my cardigan pocket and pull out a piece of paper. Seeing it makes me remember the man in the café. The stubby pencil. The walk. Ryan. This is the piece of paper he gave to me in the café; this is the cardigan I was wearing that day, and somehow the slip of paper is still there.

"Esther, what's this?" I say, handing the piece of paper to her. She squints at it under a streetlight that flickers on above our heads.

"Numbers," Esther says. "Lot of them in a row. There is zero and seven and four and nine and . . ." In my jeans pocket, there are still a few types of money. Hard, shiny, silver money—remnants of independence.

"Shall we try this box out? It looks like a TARDIS, doesn't it?"

"A bit!" she says. I open the door and we squeeze inside. "Sames," she says, looking around, and I realize she is disappointed that it is not bigger on the inside. I lift her onto my hip and push the money into the hole, remembering exactly what I used to do when I was a girl. I lift the receiver and I can hear the comforting familiarity of a dial tone. Funny how the little thing that I used to carry around with me all day every day is now a mystery to me, but this . . . this all makes perfect sense, apart from the numbers.

"Now, Esther," I say, carefully laying out the scrap of paper across the top of the fixture. "Can you press the number buttons here, just like they are on the paper, in the same order? Yes? It's very important that you press them all in a row, just like they are on the paper, yes?"

Esther nods, and carefully presses the keys. I have no idea if she is doing it right, or how long my money will last, or even whether anyone will answer, but as I stand there with Esther on my hip, I feel excited and full of possibility, just like I did all those years ago when boys I liked whispered sweet nothings down the line into my ear.

There is a ringing tone, but only twice, and then I hear his voice.

"Hello?" That's all he says, but I know it is him.

"It's me," I say. "From the café, and the road."

I know they are foolish things to say, but I say them anyway.

"Claire, you rang," he says, and he sounds glad. "I'd given up hoping that you would. It's been a while."

"Has it?" I say. "I don't know when my money will run out."

"Who is it, Mummy, can I say hello?" Esther asks me. "Is it The Doctor?"

He laughs. "You're not alone."

"No, that's my little girl. Esther. We are going to the park."

"The park? Bit late, isn't it?"

"No, we like having adventures, Esther and me," I say. "Will you meet me tomorrow and we can have another talk?" I say it all at once, before I lose courage.

He hesitates. I wait, agonized.

"Yes," he says eventually. "Where? When?"

The only location and time that I can think are the ones that I say. "I'll meet you in the town library, at midday."

"I'll be there and . . ." The line goes dead.

"I wanted to say hello!" Esther says "Was that The Doctor?"

"How about we go on a really fast roundabout instead," I say, feeling elated by the prospect of my meeting. How I am going to get there, of course, is another matter entirely.

Esther starts trotting as she leads me off the main road and into the dark of the park, behind the railings that edge the large expanse of grass. The children's play park is ensconced deep in the shadows. We follow a barely lit path into dense nothing, and I can hear calling, kids shouting at one another, their voices echoing in the cold air. And yet I don't feel afraid, and neither does Esther when the swings and slide come into view.

"Oh, there are big kids on the swings," she announces loudly, as she pushes open the heavy gate that breaks the thick steel fence surrounding the park. "Mummy! I want the swings!"

I approach the girls, who glance our way and then ignore us, going back to their conversation, smoking in earnest. "Excuse me," I say. They look cold and bored, like they'd be far better off at home with their parents than out here, probably waiting for five minutes of attention from the boys we can still hear shouting in the dark. "Can my little girl have a go on the swings?"

"Bit late," one girl says, her face full of resentment, even though she promptly gets off the swing.

"It is—you should go home," I say. "And stop smoking, it will make you old and dead before you know it. We're okay to play out late. We're ghosts."

The girls look at us like we are mad, which obviously helps

our cause because they make their way quickly out of the park, muttering to one another under their breath about the crazy bitch.

"It's all yours," I say to Esther.

Esther is thrilled by the park in the dark. She whizzes and spins around and around on the roundabout, her little face glistening in the dark, illuminated with joy. Her teeth catch the streetlights as she laughs; round and round, she sparkles. I push her faster, as fast as I can, and then I jump on and hold on tight, flinging my head back so that the dark world of the park wraps around us—brake lights in the distance, the streetlights, the white shining circle in the sky ... each stretching out and turning to bright ribbons whipping around us, surrounding us as we laugh and laugh. I feel like the world is turning faster, just for us.

"Are you okay, miss?" A voice anchors our orbit, and I feel something, slow and steady, weighing me down, pulling us back to earth. The roundabout slows, and for a moment the world spins on without me. Esther falls onto her back on the ground and groans.

"I feel dizzy in the head," she says. "Ugh, I feel poorly in the tummy."

"Claire?"

I blink. The voice is heavy and unfamiliar. It belongs to a man, a youngish man, in a suit. How does he know my name? I don't have a son, do I?

"Are you Claire and Esther?" the man asks us in a friendly tone, and I realize it's not a suit he's wearing: it's a uniform. He's a policeman. For a second, I wonder what I have done, and then I realize. I committed the cardinal sin: I escaped.

"I'm Esther." Esther clambers unsteadily to her feet. "That's Mummy, not Claire!"

"Your mum and husband were worried about you," the policeman says. "They called us. We've been looking for you."

"Why?" I ask him. "Why are you looking for us? I took my daughter to the park, that's all!" I'm defensive, angry. We are fine. Completely fine. This is a step too far.

"It's quite late for a little girl to be out, and they were worried about you, Claire."

I do not look at him. I do not want to go. I want to be lost again with Esther in the ribbons of color, the whole world standing still because we are the ones who are turning.

"Esther," he says. "Would you like a ride in a police car?"

"Will there be a nee-naw?" Esther asks him, very seriously.

"No, sorry," he tells her.

"No thanks, then," Esther says.

"Well, maybe one or two nee-naws," he says. "Just very quickly. Come on, Esther. Let's get your mum and take you home. It's time for bed."

"It can't be," Esther tells him confidently. "I haven't even had tea yet."

saturday, june 5, 1976

claire

This is a button from my mother's favorite dress when I was a very little girl—almost five years old, to be precise, which is when she lost this button. I remember the date because it is her birthday, and that year we spent it alone, just the two of us.

That was the day it got caught on something and pinged off, never to be seen again—or so my mother thought. But I saw where it landed, and I secretly picked it up when she wasn't looking, and hoarded it away like it was treasure. Mum thought the button had just done that thing that things sometimes do when they just vanish into the fabric of the universe, and there is no chance of retrieving them—but that wasn't the case. I saw where it went, and I quickly picked it up and held it secretly in my fist. It was mine.

See how it is coral-colored and sort of carved, with a pattern, which I used to think was a face, but now I think it is just a pattern. I loved those buttons; I loved the dress they came off, blue as a cold sky. I think the glow of those buttons against the cool of the blue might be the first thing I remember about my mum. That and her toes.

Before Dad died, Mum did not wear shoes—never in the summer or inside the house, and quite a lot of the time not outside of it, either. I became very familiar with her feet, the shape of them, the particular bend on her right foot that was not mirrored on the left, the blond hairs on her toes and the blush of rough skin on the soles of her feet. We spent a lot of time together, when I was very little, me and Mum. Dad went to work, but Mum and I were always together. Mum wrote plays, back then, before Dad died and she had to get a job that would pay us money. Now I know that, but I didn't know it then. I remember her sitting at the kitchen table, her feet bare, her golden hair flowing over her shoulders, writing out a script by hand, and sometimes she read lines out to me and asked me what I thought, and sometimes I'd have an opinion. Mum had two plays put on in fringe theater in London; she still has the programs in a box. When she wasn't writing, we would play, and those were the times I lived for, because Mum was an expert at playing.

On the morning of her birthday, she'd filled the house with music and we'd danced, all over the house, up and down the stairs, in and out of the bathroom; we turned on the taps and the shower, opened all the windows and danced in the garden, round and round, hollering and singing. Mum was wearing her blue dress, and whatever she did I followed her, never taking my eyes off her, not for a second. She was like the flame and I was the moth, constantly fluttering around her, desperate to always be bathed in her warmth. I don't know where Dad was. I suppose he was away working, or something, but it didn't matter because afterwards, after we had danced, she cut me a huge slice of birthday cake and I sang to her. Then we fell asleep, lying on the living room carpet in a patch of sunlight, my head on Mum's tummy while she told me tales that came out of her head. It was when she got up that the button came off; it was then that I claimed it as my own. My piece of her to keep.

After Dad died, five years later, Mum changed, and I suppose that is not very surprising to anyone. Except it was to me. I grieved for him, but also for Mum and me. I missed that mother, the one who walked barefoot to the park, and made up stories in the long grass that, in my imagination, always grew right over our heads. There can't have been anything like life insurance, or an inheritance, to help financially. There was a widow's pension, left over from the army, but it wasn't enough, I don't think, and so Mum had to put on shoes and get a job, which meant tying up and eventually cutting short her mane of yellow hair. There was no time for stories, or dancing, anymore, and although Mum still wore the dress with the buttons sometimes, because we were too poor for her to get anything new, she didn't glow anymore. She stopped being special. After school, I went back to this other girl's house, and I hated her. I hated her stupid pink cheeks, and her mother who made me drink squash.

I missed my dad, although I don't think I really knew him, but I missed my mum more. My mum, who was tired, sad, and lonely, and couldn't seem to get better, not even for me. Which was why I held on to the button. It was a sort of talisman: I had an idea that if I kept it, then things might go back to the way they were once. That never happens, of course. Things never go back to the way they were once. I think I've been cross with my mum for a long time—not for being an imperfect mother, but for being a perfect one, for those happy years that I lived through and that then were suddenly gone.

I'm not a perfect mother: I am the opposite. I had Caitlin

because I wanted her. I never thought about what life with a single mum would be like for her, without a father to protect her, even from a distance. I never thought about the day that is coming soon, the day when she has to explain who she is to a man she has never met. I took Esther out in the dark, to a place full of danger, when I knew that I didn't know the way home. I can't read her stories from her favorite books anymore, and soon, too soon, I may even forget who she is. I want Esther to have this button, and the shoes in the cupboard that are covered in crystals—the ones I wore with the very hot-colored dress on the very happy day. I want her to have those shoes, and I hope she will think of me and remember that I tried hard to be a perfect mother for her, and that I'm sorry I failed.

13

caitlin

Whenever I think about what I am doing in a hotel room in Manchester, I freak out. So I write myself a list on the hotel notepaper. It makes me feel like I should be in a film: writing myself notes on hotel notepaper . . . it feels awfully dramatic. It feels like some kind of dream. I've never checked into a hotel room by myself before, and this is a nice hotel. Malmaison, right in the heart of the city. Greg booked it for me with his credit card. He said he wanted me to be safe and comfortable. Well, I am safe, but I wouldn't say I am comfortable. When I don't think about the reason I am here, I feel excited and grown up. And then I freak out again.

Before I got chucked off my course, I had a creative writing lecturer whose catchphrase was: push yourself out of your comfort zone and see what you are really capable of. For the first time, I feel like I am doing that. I feel like I am completely out of my comfort zone, and it is sort of exhilarating as well as awful.

My list is sort of like a to-do list, and sort of like an aide-mémoire, because it's not like I can change my mind about anything on it, even if I want to, not now. It's a short list. It reads:

> I am going to have a baby.
> I am going to meet my father.
> And he doesn't even know it yet.

I tucked the list into my pocket and came here, and now I'm holding it, the tiny little square of folded hotel paper, in the palm of my hand, imagining that I can feel the words with the tips of my fingers. The words are all that is stopping me from running away.

I wait outside the lecture theater, catching my breath, and just try to focus on this one thing: on going in there and seeing him. I try to forget everything else—Mum, her illness, the baby, everything—and just be here now, doing this. It's hard; I'm scared. It doesn't feel real, me here, about to go in there, walking toward the moment when I will be in the same room as my father. I can't picture it, even though it is now only seconds away.

I join the back of a group of girls, and slip into the lecture hall along with them. No one gives me a second glance. I still look like a student in my black, low-rise jeans and long black shirt. I brushed my hair into a storm before I came, and put on as much eyeliner as I could, cramming layer after layer of black around my eyes. The only color I'm wearing is the red lipstick that I put on for Mum: when I'm wearing it, I feel a little like she is with me.

My initial instinct is to sit at the back of the lecture hall, but it is solidly occupied, and by people who will know I am an unfamiliar face. So I go to the front row, which is empty, and all at once I can see him. My father. He is right there.

There is a dizzying moment, and I am tempted to laugh out loud, laugh and point, and maybe scream a bit. Fortunately, I don't do any of those things. Instead I sink lower into my seat, pulling up the collar of my shirt. It helps a bit if I think of myself as an undercover private investigator.

He's unpacking his briefcase, staring up at the screen and swearing under his breath at his Mac. He's obviously not got to grips with PowerPoint. I could help him with that; I am really good at presentations. He looks older than I thought he would. For some reason, I pictured him as still being the young man in the photo Mum gave me the day I decided to come here, thick black hair, tall, and ungainly in a sort of graceful way. But he is not as tall as I imagined, and there is an almost-bald patch on the back of his head that reflects the spotlights. He dresses quite well, though, for an older man, wearing what look like Diesel jeans, and a nice shirt . . . well, it would be nice if he didn't tuck it in and do it up all the way to the top.

Watching him arrange his notes, I see him glance up at the room, which is simmering with noise, perhaps trying to get a sense of what his audience is like today. The room can't quite be full enough yet, though, because he picks up his phone and checks it, maybe for a text from his wife, and then . . . I freeze.

He catches my eye and smiles at me. Instinctively I smile back in recognition, because I've seen that smile a hundred times before, in my bedroom mirror, or in photos my friends have taken of me that I used to stick to the wall above my bed. He looks like me! I expect him to gasp with the same sensation of recognition, and realize at once exactly who I am, this person who has been missing for so long. But he doesn't.

"Don't normally get punters in the front row." He actually speaks to me.

He's well-spoken, his voice is deep, rich. Yes, I think, it's rich. He's confident, sure of himself. He is speaking to me.

"I'm not a student here," I say, with ridiculous honesty, because I don't want the first thing I say to him to be a lie. "I just heard about the lecture, and how good it is, and I wanted to attend."

He looks pleased, really pleased—stupidly pleased, actually, like a man who doesn't get enough reassurance. I notice the thick gold wedding band on his left hand. I knew he was married, but I wonder what his wife is like, and whether she will like me. I wonder about my half sisters, and whether they look like me too. It's funny, I never think of Esther as my half anything: she was always wholly my sister from the moment she arrived. But these strange creatures that I don't know and can't even picture . . . I can't imagine them even being halves. Add us all up together and we might manage a quarter, perhaps.

"Well," he says, actually winking at me. "I hope you enjoy it."

I spend the next few seconds adjusting to the idea that my father is a man that winks at total strangers.

Of course, I don't listen to anything he is saying. I just watch him, and readjust my thoughts every few seconds into remembering what I am doing, and why. What I am doing is looking at the man who donated the sperm that created me. And even if one moment is all that it took, he is still half of me—of the way I look, the way I talk, the way I am. Maybe he is even half of the reason why, when everything went a little bit wrong for me, I went off down a dark and dangerous path determined to make it worse—a path I might still be on if it weren't for Mum and Gran charging to the rescue.

So he's talking and I'm just staring at him, and he glances at me from time to time, with a sort of frown, like maybe he's seen me around somewhere, or we have met before. And as the lecture is coming to an end, I know he is going to talk to me again, and ask me what I thought of it, or maybe even ask me where he's seen me before. And suddenly, I have the feeling that he knows, he knows who I am, and I panic. I get up, even though he is still talking, and I make my way along the row and then toward the exit, keeping my head down.

"Tough crowd," I hear him say, just as I go through the door. The students laugh, and I realize I didn't do a very good job of keeping a low profile.

Freezing cold air immediately bites at my cheeks, and I shudder. I don't know what to do next. I feel like if I just go back to the hotel, then it's over, and really nothing will have changed, so I follow the signs to the student union building, hoping to find a warm place to think. I flash my out-of-date card at a bored-looking guy on security, and he lets me in with barely a glance, not even at my red lipstick.

It's the middle of the afternoon, and the bar is mostly empty, except for a few students playing pool and watching some sort of American sport on TV. There's one guy behind the bar, leaning on it, his eyes fixed on the TV too.

"Do you do coffee?" I ask him, making him start. He looks at me, and then looks at me again, which makes me feel uncomfortable. I touch my hand to my face, wondering if I've got Biro on my cheek again, or rubbed my mouth without thinking about it, so that now I have a clown's mouth rather than a femme fatale pout.

"Coffee?" He says the word like he's never heard of the concept. His accent sounds local, but he doesn't look like working in a student bar would be his first choice of job. He looks like fronting a manufactured boy band would be his first choice of job. He's smartly dressed, wearing an ironed shirt tucked into skinny jeans, and a waistcoat, of all things, topped off with a thin black tie. He's got fairish brownish hair that's obviously been styled with the sort of care that only a girl should take—and is that a hint of mascara under those green eyes, or has he just got *really* thick lashes? I am looking so hard, I miss him repeating the question.

"Um, yes, coffee," I say. "You know, became popular in the sixteenth century, black in color, unless you add milk. I like it with milk. And sugar. Are you familiar with the concept of sugar?"

"You are funny," he says, lifting his chin a little and scrutinizing me by looking down an improbably straight nose. "I like that."

"I'd like a decaf coffee," I say sharply.

"Of course. A latte?" He smiles at me, and instantly I feel stupid for being sarcastic, because he has got this incredibly charming smile. I mean, it's ridiculous; it's like being thirteen again and having the stupidest instant crush on a boy in the Sixth Form. He smiles and he's all sparkly and pretty, and makes me want to squeal, like an actual girl. It feels like such a long time since I looked at a boy and thought about kissing him— weeks since anything like that has come into my head—but, oh my God, that smile! That smile is gold. Someone needs to get hold of that smile and exploit it to extort pocket money from thirteen-year-old girls the world over.

I dip my face away from him, and wonder about leaving before I try to flirt with the worst-dressed boy I've ever met, and then I remember what I am doing here, and why. I remember the baby, my mother, my father. All these reasons mean I can't run away from a boy with a sweet smile anymore. Life is no longer about hiding—and it's not about flirting, that's for sure. He probably likes music with tunes, I tell myself. And stupid sappy words. I bet he likes Coldplay.

"To be honest," he says, noticing that I have failed to reply, and kindly stepping in to save me, "all of the coffees come out of that machine, and they all taste more or less the same. Unless someone has hot chocolate, and then they taste of that."

"The cheapest one, then," I say, and I watch him grab a mug, stick it under a stainless steel machine and press a button. A few seconds later, a steaming cup of milky coffee is set before me.

"I haven't seen you round here before," he observes.

I roll my eyes, wondering if I can make a break for a table, where I might be safe. "I come in here every Friday. You don't remember me?"

"Nice try." He laughs, and wields that smile again. Stupid smile. "I wasn't trying out a line on you. I'd remember you, if we'd met before. I've got a thing for faces, and your eyes are the blackest I have ever seen."

"Oh," I say. I'm not sure how to take that.

"I'm a photographer," he tells me. "I'm always looking for interesting faces." He stares at me for one long intense moment, during which I think I might melt into a pool of my own hormones. "Yep, blackest eyes I've ever seen . . ." I sit transfixed, like a mouse about to be gobbled up by a snake, as he leans across the bar. "You can barely see the difference between the iris and the pupil. Can I photograph you?" He pulls back suddenly, and I blink as the spell is broken.

"No," I say, firmly, winding my fingers around the cup. "No, I'm not from round here. I'm just here for a day or two, maybe less, even."

My first encounter with my father has not made me want to introduce myself to him. If anything, it makes me want to know him even less—the way he looked at me, the curiosity in his returning gaze. I can imagine it. I know exactly how it will pan out. "Hello, I am your long-lost daughter, the one you never knew about or wanted. No, I don't have a career. I failed my second-year exams because of a boy who got me pregnant and then dumped me, and I went to pieces because I'm a sap, and it didn't help that I found out that my mum—remember her, the one you knocked up?—is seriously ill. And then I ran away from my seriously ill mother, and got a job in a strip bar. I've bounced around from stupid to stupid for months, and I thought I'd round it off nicely by coming to see you. Oh, what's that? You'd like me to leave now? Thought so. See you in another life."

"What you doing here, then?" the boy asks me, leaning his elbows on the bar.

Boys shouldn't have such nicely proportioned noses; they should have noses that are either too big or too thin, but his is perfect. It's hard to concentrate while looking at it, but marginally easier than trying to engage in conversation while looking at those green eyes fringed with thick lashes. He looks like he should star in a musical, for Christ's sake.

"I'm visiting someone," I say to the tip of his nose. "A friend, sort of."

"Boyfriend?" he asks, just like that, and for a second I think he might be interested. And then I decide it's probably just that he's northern, and northern people are always very frank and nosy, at least according to Gran, who thinks she knows everything because she retired to the Pennines. Not anymore, though. Now she is out of retirement, for one last job.

"No," I say, as if the very idea of such a thing appalls me. I feel myself color, which he notices, and that makes him smile, which makes me want to give him a dead arm. "My boyfriend's in London."

His smile wavers—maybe—just a little bit, perhaps? At any rate, he's not so cocky now. I've met boys like him before—fashionable boys who dress like they are in a band, and who own more pairs of shoes than I do. They usually turn out to be dicks. Well, Sebastian did, anyway. Sebastian, who I will quite soon have to talk to again; I'll have to explain to him that he is actually going to be a father, because I never want my child to be sitting in some bar twenty years from now working up the courage to explain to him who they are.

"So, what's your name, then?" he asks me. "I can ask you that, right?"

"Caitlin," I say.

"Zach." He holds out a hand with a wide silver ring on the forefinger, and I take it and shake it. He looks into my eyes, just for an extra moment longer than maybe he should, and once again I have to remember who I am, why I am here. I am not here to flirt with pretty barmen. My days of flirting with boys are over.

"Zach is perfect for you," I tell him.

He laughs. "Why's that?" he asks me.

"Because it's all cheerful and zipp-a-dee-doo-dah," I say, which makes him laugh again. He laughs a lot. He must be awfully happy.

"Caitlin." He says my name again, and it sounds familiar on his lips. "Your boyfriend is a very lucky man."

Whoa. Again he just says it, just like that. Like he's not a pretty boy in a tie, and I'm not a girl dressed entirely in black with the sort of makeup that makes me look like I might want to take a chunk out of his neck. I am not his type, and he is not mine, and we both know it.

"You think you're such a smooth operator, don't you?" I say.

"Nope." He shrugs. "Nope, I just say what I'm thinking. It's a curse and probably the reason I don't have a girlfriend at the moment. And I meant it. Your boyfriend is a lucky man. You're extremely interesting. . . ."

The moment is broken by voices, and I recognize one of them. It's my father's. My shoulders hunch up around my ears as Paul Sumner walks in with a group of three students, two girls and a boy. I can't stop myself staring at him in the mirror behind the bar while Zach leaves me and goes to take orders from one of the girl students. I watch my dad, half conscious that the girl is giggling like a loon as Zach serves her. He must have smiled at her. Paul sits at a table opposite the bar, locked in animated conversation with the other two students, and then he must feel my gaze because suddenly he looks up and sees me watching him. It's all I can do to tear my eyes away from his face. And I know he is getting up and coming over.

"You left before the end," he says.

"I . . . I had to go somewhere," I stutter. I am sitting at the bar, with an almost finished cup of machine coffee. We both know that was a lie.

"It's fine," he says. "I can't get rave reviews all the time."

His smile is cool and short, over in a flash. He nods, picks up the tray of drinks that the girl student ordered, and prepares to go back to his table.

"Wait," I say, standing up abruptly. A drink sloshes over his hands. He sighs and puts the tray down. "What?"

"I . . ." I wait for him to look at me and notice my black eyes, which are just like his, and for him just to *know*. But he doesn't. He just stands there for what seems like eons, his irritation growing. "I'm sorry," I say. "I'm really sorry I left early."

"It's fine." He smiles, and again it's gone in a flash. I watch him walk away.

"Are you okay?" Zach asks me. He looks concerned.

"No," I say. I realize I am shaking, and I feel like I want to be sick. I stumble out of the bar to where there is a flight of steps rising upwards. I sit on the bottom stair, rubbing my hands across my face. I just want to go home.

"What happened?" Zach is suddenly in front of me, crouching down so that his eyes are level with mine. "You look terrible, and you're shaking. What can I do?"

"I'm fine, just go away," I say. "I'm fine."

"No, you are not." He is adamant. "And no, I am not going to go away and leave you sitting here, looking so frightened. Was it him? That lecturer guy? Has he done something to you?"

"No!" I say, appalled. "No, he has no idea who I am. Please, go away."

But Zach doesn't move. He sits on his heels looking at me, his hands resting on the same step as my feet.

"I can't," he said. "I'm sorry, I just . . . I can't leave you looking so unhappy. My mum would kill me."

"What? What has this got to do with your mum?" I ask him.

"She brought me up to be chivalrous," Zach says seriously. "It's hard when you're living on a council estate in Leeds, but my mum had a lot of ideas about the way a person should behave toward other people, even ones they've only just met. Especially women."

"Yeah, well," I say. "I'm a feminist, so . . . go away."

"I'm a feminist too," Zach says, quite seriously, the hint of a smile playing around his lips. "I really am. That was another thing my mum was keen on: me learning to respect and admire women."

"What the hell are you going on about?" I ask him, though I have to admit I am distracted.

"You've stopped shaking," he says, and he lifts one hand from the bottom step and touches my knee, just briefly. "Maybe you need to eat something."

"Maybe," I say. "I am four months pregnant, after all."

It's the killer blow—the one that is guaranteed to stop his juggernaut of charm in its tracks. His hands fall to his sides, and he is visibly shocked.

"Whoa," he says, sitting back on the ground. "I did not see that coming."

"So, anyway." I get up, and my legs are still a little bit unsteady. "I need to get going." I carefully walk around him.

"Caitlin." He calls my name and I stop and turn around.

"What?" I ask him. "What can you possibly want from me now?"

He's still sitting on the ground, looking at me.

"Nothing," he says, and it sounds like an apology. "Just, take care, okay?"

friday, may 22, 1987

ruth

This is a photograph of Claire in her favorite dress when she was coming up to sixteen. It's funny, when I got the call, and I knew that I had to come back down here, I was getting ready to pack a bag and as I pulled my bag down out of the wardrobe, this photo came with it, or rather just before, fluttering down onto the carpet like a sycamore seed. I don't know how it got there, of all places, tucked under my overnight bag, in the top of my wardrobe, but I put it into my pocket and brought it down with me. It's only now when I look at it that I can see this dress, although it's made of cotton and not silk, is almost the same cut and style as Claire's wedding dress. She's always loved red from the moment I told her, when she was a very tiny little girl, that redheads don't normally wear red. From that moment on, she always insisted on wearing it as much as possible.

Here she is, standing next to Rob Richards, her first ever

boyfriend, on their way to the Fifth Years' Leavers' Party. I took this photo, and as I stood on the other side of the camera, looking at Rob's arm around her neck, I thought he looked like he was going to strangle her.

I didn't like Rob Richards, and that was no secret. First of all, I don't like people whose names are alliterative. But that's just me. I think it's needlessly showy, that's all. Second of all, he was totally charmless. Claire liked him, though; she liked him for a long time. He used to walk past the front of our house on the way to school, and she'd be there in the hallway, peering out of the window, waiting for the top of his head to go bobbing by just above the privet hedge, and then she would go out. One day, I said to her, "You're better off going out a few seconds before he passes. Better that he's following you, rather than the other way round."

Claire was furious with me for noticing her ploy, but the next morning, she left for school precisely twenty-four seconds earlier, before Rob's very high quiff passed the top of the hedge. Claire has always been many things: headstrong and stubborn, yes, but also determined. She got that from her father. Simon was a man who never, ever backed down. A quiet man, and a gentle one, even despite everything he'd seen in the war. But once he had a cause, a fight, he would battle until the very last. I met him—wearing his three-piece suit, with his coat tucked over his arm—on an anti-nuclear-weapons march. No one knew why the hippie girl, with her bare feet and flowers in her hair, fell for a man so much older than her and who looked like an accountant. But that was because no one else bothered to talk to Simon, to listen to the stories he had to tell about war, and why he battled so hard for peace. And I never guessed, not in a million years, that the quiet middle-aged veteran that used to come and take me out for tea was in love with me, until the moment when, one afternoon, he asked me very politely if he could kiss me, and I let him; and from that moment on I never wanted not to be near him. He was a determined man, and Claire was a determined girl. It was what I loved about them both.

I don't know how many weeks Claire walked to school just ahead of, or just behind, Rob Richards, or how she'd initiated a friendship with a boy in the Upper Sixth in the first place, but one afternoon she brought him home from school with her.

"All right, Mrs. Armstrong?" he said, as he came in through the back door, his ridiculous hair bobbing like a separate entity all of its own.

"This is Rob." Claire was trying really hard not to look like the cat that had got the cream. "He's my boyfriend now."

"Well ..." Rob Richards said, and then clearly thought better of protesting anymore, because from that moment on, he *was* her boyfriend, at least in Claire's eyes. When I say boyfriend, I think they enthusiastically exchanged a good deal of saliva, but I don't think they talked to each other, or even spent much time together, apart from standing on my doorstep engaged in public displays of affection that were mainly designed to annoy Claire's friends, who also liked Rob Richards.

Claire had it all arranged. She saw the dress in Miss Selfridge in town, and begged me to buy it for her for the leavers' party. I tried to tell her that most of the other girls wouldn't be going in massive fifties-style dresses, and that it wasn't like an American prom, it was a party. But Claire knew exactly what she wanted to look like, and when she put on the dress, she looked amazing, there was no denying it—like Rita Hayworth, only with big hoop earrings. The big night came, and Rob arrived to pick Claire up ... dressed in jeans and a shirt. As I'd suspected, Claire was very overdressed; still, she swept down the stairs like she was Scarlett O'Hara. But instead of telling her how beautiful she was, Rob Richards just look surprised and embarrassed. I wanted to punch him, but I didn't. I just stood there with my camera, as instructed, while Claire draped herself over Rob Richards' stonewashed denim shirt, and he reluctantly put his arm around her neck. I took the photo—I took three or four, and waited for them to leave—but Rob Richards looked sheepish, and asked if he could have a word with Claire alone. I went into the kitchen and listened at the door. Rob told Claire that he was finishing with her, and that he was taking her friend, Amy Castle, to the dance, and so probably it would be best if she didn't go. And no hard feelings. I waited for a moment until I heard the front door shut, and then I went into the hallway, where Claire was standing alone, looking into the mirror.

"Claire, I'm so sorry," I said. "How about we rent a video, and eat ice cream?"

Claire looked me up and down like I was delusional. When she turned around, I realized she'd been applying lipstick, in exactly the same shade as her dress.

"Are you nuts? I'm not wasting this dress. I'm bloody going," she said.

"Are you sure?" I asked her, thinking how beautiful she was, and how I didn't want her to walk into the bloody school disco in her ball gown and for everyone to laugh at her. "Shall I come with you?"

"Mother!" She planted a big lipstick-kiss on my cheek. "Don't be mental. Who cares about Rob Richards, anyway? I've had more interesting conversations with a pot plant."

And off she went, putting on a brave face, determined to have a good time, or at least look like it. And I'm sure that she did; I'm sure of it. But that night when Claire got in, she cried in her bedroom for hours. I waited until it was almost two in the morning to go in, expecting her to order me out of the room right away, but she didn't.

"It's okay to cry," I told her.

"It's all right—none of them saw me cry," she said. "I never let any one of them know that I cared even one little bit."

14

claire

Mum cannot see an alternative to taking Esther and me with her when she goes to the supermarket. So we wait by the door, hand in hand, ready for our coats to be zipped up against the cold. While we wait, I ponder how very mysterious zips are. For so many years, they seemed like such a simple invention: fast, convenient—zippy, even. And then, sometime recently, they became a mechanical wonder that I find impossible to fathom, or interpret. I feel the same way about the gate that has appeared at the bottom of the stairs, presumably to contain me on one floor only. Esther and I cannot make it undo, and we have tried extensively under the cover of watching *Peppa Pig* very loudly while Mum does things in the kitchen. At first it annoyed us, this newfound imposition on our civil liberties, but then Esther and I worked out that we do not have to undo the stair gate. We can simply climb over it. One nil to Esther and me.

I have been retelling myself the story of my phone call over and over again since the policeman brought us home, determined not to lose it. I'm not completely sure that it isn't just that—just a story I've told myself—but even if it is, I've repeated it so many times now, I have to try and go. To the library, at midday, to meet the man from the café and the road who is so ... I don't know why my urge to see him again is so strong, except that I remember him; I remember him enough to think about him. I think about Ryan who talks to me like I am *me*.

Mum is very irritated about having to go to the supermarket and take us with her.

The supermarket used to be my job. I used to like it, spending Saturday mornings alone while Greg and Esther watched TV in bed. I found it restful, floating around with the thing with the wheels, thinking and choosing. I'm not sure when it stopped being my job exactly, but I do know that the last time I went on my own, I came home with fourteen bottles of wine and the notion that we should have a party. Greg laughed. He used to think I was so funny and spontaneous. I used to think I was so funny and spontaneous, but I am not sure anymore if that was ever what I was, or whether it was just the disease disjointing me by slight degrees.

So now Greg arranges for the food to come to the house in a van. And yet despite his care in ordering in advance, we have run out of milk, mostly because I tipped it all down the hole in the kitchen this morning, while Esther demanded that Gran take her to the loo and talk to her while she had a poo, because pooing is so boring unless there is someone to chat to. Esther is a great accomplice. Ever since our late-night trip to the park, we are far more than mother and daughter: we are coconspirators and joint keepers of secrets.

We have also run out of bread, which I threw from the upstairs window (after climbing over the stair gate), over the fence into the garden of the people in the next house along. They've got a lot of birds now. On my way back, creeping past the bathroom, I winked at Esther—who was regaling Mum with stories of her top ten best ever poos to let her know the coast was clear.

Mum was outraged about the demise of the milk and bread, and said if she had to go out with all of us, then it might as well be to the town, since the prices at the corner shop were daylight robbery. And so we are all going to town. My carefully constructed escape plan is going incredibly smoothly so far, which makes me wonder if the disease is actually making me more brilliant, in ways I would never have imagined before. Perhaps this is like a flame, flaring briefly, burning brighter and more intensely than it ever has in the moments before it is finally snuffed out.

Mum shepherds us to the car. I'm half expecting her to attempt to strap me into a car seat too, but she doesn't.

I can't read the time on my watch anymore, although I still wear it, because I am used to the feel of it on my skin, like I am used to the feel of my wedding ring on my finger. So I listen to the radio, which Mum has tuned to Radio Four, and I know that it's eleven-thirty when we go out, and I know where the library is, and I feel exactly like I used to, before parts of my brain started filming up. I am in total control of my destiny. Today I'm doing something a married mother of two, and grandma-to-be, should absolutely not do . . . but can. I'm going to meet a man in secret. Alzheimer's me can do this—Alzheimer's me can have a clandestine liaison in a library with the man from the café—because it's only with him, and with Esther, that I am not debilitated by my disease: I am freed by it.

There was guilt when Greg went to work this morning. He seemed tense and upset, which isn't surprising because the police brought his daughter and me home last night in a car with the lights flashing. Mum just shouted at me a lot, wanting to know why I didn't understand, which I thought should have been obvious, I have a degenerative brain disease, but he just stood there, with arms crossed and looking so downtrodden, and so depressed, so defeated. Esther had had the time of her life, especially the part when she rode in a police car. But it wasn't the things that had happened that mattered: it was the things that could have happened. And I felt sorry that I had made him feel that way. Esther loves him very much, and he loves her, and me. . . .

I think he still loves me too, which is why he didn't shout at me. I wish I knew who he was.

He knocked on my bedroom door, just as I was about to go to sleep. He opened it and stuck his head through the gap. "Claire, are you okay?" he asked. I shrugged. "I just want you to know that I understand why you did what you did. You just wanted to take Esther to the park. I get that. It's just that, next time, will you tell one of us? So we can remind you about it being wet or cold, or dark?"

I rolled over and turned my back on him, and I said, "This is hell. This is hell. This life, where I can't even decide to take my daughter to the park for reasons that are entirely sensible, is hell on earth." I heard him close the door and walk away.

The first thing I did this morning was to pour the milk down the hole in the kitchen.

"Do you want to sit in the trolley?" Mum asks.

"I don't think I'll fit," I say, which makes Esther laugh and Mum purse her lips.

She lectures us both before we enter the maze of food. "Stay with me. Don't wander off, okay?"

Esther and I nod in unison, and Esther takes my hand, squeezing my fingers as if she already knows a secret. For a few minutes, we trail around after my mother, who loads up the trolley with milk and fruit that no one will eat, and I tell myself over and over again what I am doing, where I am going. What my secret plan is. I don't know if now is any time near midday or past it, but I do know it will have to be now or never. I pick Esther up and, kissing her, slot her into the wheelie thing seat. She protests for a little while, but only until I take a packet of crisps off the shelf and hand it to her. I trail behind, studiously looking at labels that I cannot read anymore, up and down the lines of food, and then up and down the next one until I am as near to where the outside door is as I can be. While Mum and Esther head up the next aisle, I continue down and out of the outside door, and into the world. I am becoming quite an expert at this.

The world is large, noisy, and different from how I remember it. The town I'm walking through today is different from the one I remember. I don't know which version it is I am remembering, whether it is one from last week, last year, or last decade: I don't know. But it's different from this version I am walking in now. It's rather like walking in a dream, where everything isn't quite right. It could be frightening to be out here, but I am not frightened: I am free.

The library hasn't changed, though. It's a great big old building with spires and turrets, and looks like it should feature in a book of its own. I can see it, at least its tower with the time on it, over the roofs of the buildings in between, and so I just keep heading toward it, my eyes fixed constantly up, wondering what the time is. I am forced to divert, turn down streets I don't remember being there, but I am not worried, because when I look up I can still see the tower, getting closer. I just think about getting to the library and nothing else, and it works. Eventually, I come into a part of the town that has no cars, like a square, and I have reached the library. I did it!

I look up at the stone steps that lead to a room full of books, and to Ryan, and it occurs to me what I am doing. I'm throwing myself off a precipice from which there is no way back. I am a married woman, married to a man who could not have loved me more, and who does his best every day to try and show me that this hasn't changed, even though I'm slowly ebbing away. I should take comfort in his steadfast love; it should make me feel better, but it doesn't, because I do not know him. He is nothing to me, and all his words and kindness feel like lies, because I do not know him. Even his face is becoming a meaningless blur whenever I try to recall him. And as for the precipice, soon I will be falling from it, anyway. Maybe it's better to jump rather than be pushed. I want to see this man, who wants to see me. That's all. Not to have an affair or hurt anyone, or try to run away. I just want to see this man who wants to see me. Me and not the disease.

It's cold and the inside of my neck hurts when I go from the cold air into the hot air of the library. He said he'd meet me in the reading room, and for a while I am afraid that I won't know what he looks like now. But then he is there. He turns around when I come in and smiles. It's the eyes I don't forget— the eyes that are so full of words.

"Hello," he says.

"Hello," I say.

"I'm so pleased to see you. I thought you might not come," he says all at once in a rush, as though there is more to say, but then no more words come.

"I'm pleased to see you too," I say. "I have thought about nothing else but coming."

We stand there looking at each other for a long time, and it's not about who looks like what, I just know that. It's not about the color of eyes, or hair, or the angle of a chin or the set of a mouth. It's just about looking, being there with another person who somehow knows you, and sees you. We just look at each other, and it's the strangest feeling to look at a person I barely know and feel that somehow I'm looking at a reflection.

"Shall we walk?" he says, and he takes my fingers and leads me deep into the walls of books. I breathe in the scent of dusty paper and, as I follow him, the pulse in the tips of my fingers ticks against the palm of his hand. For a moment, I am a little girl, a very little girl following my father to the romance section, where he secretly picks out romantic novels to read. I had forgotten that, until this very moment. My dad used to love to read romance. Sitting on a Sunday morning in the sunshine in the living room, he'd read a book cover to cover. I gasp in a quiet breath of warm air and close my eyes. For a second it feels like he is here with me again, and I am choosing books for him based on how pretty the lady on the cover is.

We stop in the darkest corner of the walls of books, our backs against a mosaic of spines.

"How are you?" he asks me in a whisper, even though there is no one else here and we are far from the front desk.

"I am complicated," I say out loud, because I don't know how to lie to him or how to whisper.

"Was it hard to get away?" he asks, smiling at me as if I am very marvelous. I like the idea that he thinks I am very marvelous.

"No, I hatched a brilliant escape plan," I tell him, and he laughs. When he looks at me, there is this light in his eyes: it is pure joy. I never expected to give anyone that intensity of happiness ever again. I can't resist it.

"I've been thinking about you a lot," he says. "The whole time, wondering how I could see you again."

"Why?" I ask him. "Why have you been thinking about me?"

"Who knows why?" His fingers trace along the ledge toward mine. Our hands touch, fingertip to fingertip. "Does it matter why? Isn't it enough just that I do think about you? All the time. Do you think about me?"

"When I remember to," I say.

I look at him, and try to make sense of what I see in his face, but it overwhelms me. I put my palm against his cheek to still us both.

"I'm married," I tell him. "And I have two daughters, and one is having a baby. I'm going to be a grandmother." I say the last few words in a tone of wonder, because the information has just come back to me in that second.

"And I'm married too." He covers my hand with his, keeping it in place. "I'm still very much in love with my wife. I really am."

"So we can't . . . this can't be an affair," I say. "I can't run away with you. We aren't the sort of people who would do that, are we?"

I wonder if I should tell him about the nature of my illness, but I can't. I'm perfect to him at the moment. I want to be perfect to him, for as many moments as I can be.

"No," he says. "You don't have to run away with me. You just have to be here with me now. That's all I wan

t. I just want now. Nothing else has to happen."

It's not until he says the words that I realize that is all I want too. I just want now. I am not sure which of us draws closer to the other, or when I know that we are going to kiss, here in the library among the racks of sedate hardbacks, but it happens effortlessly, beautifully. All I want is now, this warmth, the closeness, his smell, his lips, his touch, all I want is now, until it is not now anymore. This kiss isn't about sex, desire, or passion, or anything other than just knowing each other, just being close to each other: it's a kiss made only of love.

There's a cough from the other side of the wall of books, and we break apart. I lean my face against his, and we stand cheek to cheek, our heads slightly bowed, breathing each other in, the toes of our feet interlocked.

"I have to go," I say. "Mum must be tired of losing me by now."

"Don't go yet," he says. "Stay here a little longer."

"My mum will kill me," I say, and that makes him laugh, too loudly.

"Excuse me." A voice comes from behind the book wall. "If you want to talk, go outside."

There's a noise, a loud screeching, and I think it might be a fire alarm, but then I realize it's the thing in my pocket that my mother gave me. I take it out and look at it. He takes it from me and finds a way to make it quiet, so that it just chirrups silently in my hand. It doesn't stop, though.

"Quick, answer it!" he says, stifling a giggle, as the person on the other side of the books marches off, probably to get reinforcements.

"I don't know how to," I say, shrugging. "It's new."

He takes it, presses something and hands it back to me. I hear a tiny, tinny voice repeating my name over and over again. Slowly, uncertainly, I bring the thing to my ear as if it is a seashell. I hear Mum's voice.

"Where are you?"

"The library," I say.

"Why?" is all she says.

"I wanted to come to the library," I say, looking at him, smiling. "So I did."

Then the sound of my mother sighing, crying, growling . . . or something.

"Claire, will you wait there until Esther and I come to get you?"

"Yes." My smile falters when I hear the sadness in her voice, and so does his as he watches my face. "I'll wait here."

"Promise me," she says. "Wait on the steps. Don't go anywhere. Remember it, Claire. Pin it down. Wait on the front steps."

"I'll wait," I say. There is quiet and I don't know what to do with the thing so I put it back in my pocket.

"Excuse me." A cross-looking woman is marching toward us. "We've had complaints."

Ryan takes my hand and we walk quickly through the books, our footsteps echoing off them, right into the hall to the great big giants' door. Cold air gushes in and out as people come and go.

"I have to wait on the steps to meet my mum," I say, and then, "You must think I am very stupid to have to wait to be collected by my mum, but she's old, she's very needy."

"Not at all." We stand for a moment longer. It's like the lengths of our bodies are bonded together by some kind of magnetic force: we are simply drawn to each other, as though we're meant to be connected. "It's nice."

"I wonder how I will see you again," I say, knowing that the second I step outside, this moment will be over forever, and that in any one of the seconds that follow, I might forget him.

"There will be a time," he says. "I know it."

"I have to wait on the steps," I say.

"I'll wait here. I'll watch you until she comes."

"Will you?" I ask him. He squeezes my fingers one last time, and I walk out into the cold and stand on the steps, and breathe in the color and the life, and the rush of the traffic, and the smell of the air, full of dirt. I like now.

"Mummy!" Esther hops up the steps, two at a time. "Is it story time?"

"You can't go out anymore," Mum says. She takes my arm and tries to drag me away.

"Get off me!" I shout, and people turn and look. "Get off me!"

Mum lets go. Her face is white, and her eyes are red and swollen. She's been crying, and suddenly I feel her pain, like a hammer blow in the center of my chest. I shouldn't have done this.

"I'm sorry, Mum," I say.

"You can't go anywhere anymore," she says, standing there quaking, shaking, on the library steps. "I can't do it. I thought I could, but I can't. I can't take care of you anymore. I've let you down."

Mum is crying, her whole body trembling, the tears running and running. I put my arms around her, and Esther too, and I hold her while she cries. We stand like that for a long time, while the people of the town walk up and down the library steps around us. And then Mum breaks the embrace and wipes her face with a hanky.

"If we don't get the freezer stuff packed away soon it will defrost."

tuesday, july 11, 1978

claire

This is a photo of my dad and me on the beach in St Ives, Cornwall. It was blazing hot, but Dad still has full-length trousers on, and his shirtsleeves buttoned at his wrists. He's sitting awkwardly in the deck chair, as though it were the enemy, with me at his feet. I remember Mum squinting through the camera lens, her feet buried in the sand, the wind coming off the water, blowing her cotton skirt up around her knees, while I kneeled at Dad's feet, my hands buried in the hot, dry sand. I'm scowling in the photo, wishing she'd hurry up and get on with it, because I didn't want to be still for a moment longer. I look at it now, and I see that my dad and I have exactly the same scowl.

Dad hated being on holiday; he hated leisure time, I think. He was a man who always liked to have a purpose. Nothing he did was ever just to pass the time, or designed to be recreational, except for reading his books, and even then he only allowed himself that pleasure when there was absolutely nothing else that could be done with that time. How my mother got him to accompany us on this, our one and only family holiday, I do not know. I imagine a conversation about being part of the family, building a relationship with his daughter, taking part in life. My mum, with her bare feet and long hair, the freckles on her nose, and nails that were never painted, and my dad, standing in the heat of the day in a suit and tie, eyeing her as if she were a creature from another planet, not merely another generation, arguing about going on holiday. I wonder, sometimes, how they fell in love. I tried to ask Mum once, a few years ago, just as I was getting together with Greg. But she turned my question away with a simple shake of her head, and I never asked again. She did love him, though. I don't doubt that. I don't doubt that he loved her too—the way he used to watch her, as though she were miraculous.

That day, just after the photo was taken, Mum went off in search of ice cream and left us alone, Dad sitting uncomfortably in his rented chair, watching me aimlessly shift the sand around. "Shall we build something?" he said. I paused and looked over my shoulder, uncertain whether he was talking to me—he rarely talked to me directly. "A sandcastle," he clarified. "We'll need to dig down deeper, or go nearer to the water, to reach firmer sand."

I stood up and followed him as he walked, shoes and socks still on, down toward the shoreline, me trailing after him in my swimming costume. He picked his way in and out of the holidaymakers, through a patchwork of brightly colored towels occupied by people who seemed at ease with their near nakedness, whatever their size and shape. It was my father, a dark patch of sweat flowering between his shoulder blades, who looked incongruous and out of place. When we were a few feet from the gentle rush of the tide, he kneeled down on the damp sand and began to dig. I watched him for a while, and then I began to dig too, copying him as—without a bucket—he built a trench, a moat, and then from the excavated sand began to mold an incredibly intricate building, so delicate, so carefully constructed, that after a while I stopped trying to join in and simply sat on my heels and watched while he worked. Every now and then he'd glance up, as though he'd remembered I was there, but we didn't talk. Mum must have come back from her ice-cream hunt and spotted us there, playing together at the water's edge, and decided not to interrupt us, because I never did get that ice cream. We weren't playing, either: nothing about the process of creating that castle, with its fanciful turrets and ramparts, was about play. It was about making the best possible sandcastle. And even then, even at six years old, I understood that: I understood my dad, and I wanted to be like him.

When it was done, he rubbed the palms of his hands together, and climbed to his feet. I stood up and took up my position next to him, feeling awfully privileged to be there in that moment.

"The secret," he told me, taking my hand, "is to know when to stop. And now, I think, is the right time to stop." And as if he had commanded it, which when I was six years old I believed that he had, the sea rushed in, filling the moat with water. We stood, side by side, hand in hand, and watched the rushing water gradually rise over our toes and ankles, taking a little piece of the castle each time it went back out, until finally the foundations were washed away and it crumbled into nothing.

And then, without another word, we walked back to where Mum was sitting, and nothing more was said about ice cream. Later that night, in our little B&B, when Dad tucked me into the camp bed that had been put up at the bottom of their bed, I pretended to be asleep so I could listen to them talking about me.

"It looked like you really connected with her today," Mum said, using a word that my father would have disparagingly described as "Californian." "She's a great girl, you know, full of ideas and thoughts, so creative. You should get her to tell you a story sometime. I don't know where she gets that imagination from. I know it's not me."

"She is a very nice child," my dad had said, climbing into bed and switching off the light, although it couldn't have been later than nine. And then, a long time later (I can't be sure whether it was hours or minutes), I heard him say—although I've never been sure if it was a dream or real, but I think I heard him say, "She gets her imagination from me."

And when I think of that castle, with its asymmetrical spires and arches, doorways and steps, all created for just a few moments of beauty, I think perhaps I did.

15

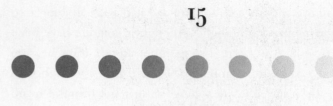

caitlin

Gran sounds strained on the other end of the phone. Mum went AWOL again for the second time in two days, and Gran is shaken, frightened. I need to go home. I try to insist on coming home right then, but Gran won't let me.

"What difference will it make if you come home now?" she says. "I've got Greg and Esther, who is such a little ray of sunshine in the middle of all of this. And since the last 'escapade' at the library, she's been calmer, more peaceful. Happy to be at home."

"Maybe we could take her to the library, now and then," I say. "Remember how she used to take me there three or four times a week when I was a little girl? Remember that time we went after school, and she started reading *A Christmas Carol* out loud to me, doing all the voices, scaring the crap out of me?

Other people started to listen too. They all thought it was some sort of event. And then the librarian threw us out for being disruptive. It's a special place for her, and maybe it will help if we take her there."

"Yes," Gran said. "Although I wouldn't put it past her to give me the slip in True Crime. You know, part of me is glad she's fighting everything around her, even me. If she wasn't fighting until the bitter end, she wouldn't be my Claire. And she's been writing in the memory book a lot. Page after page, like she's on a deadline."

"When I get home, I'm going to get her novel out of the drawer and read it," I say. "Maybe it's really good, Gran. Maybe we could get it published before she . . . Imagine how much she would love that!"

"I don't know, darling." Gran pauses. She only ever uses terms of endearment when she is about to say something sad. "If your mum had ever wanted it to be read, it would have been. The memory book, that's the book that matters—that's her life's work."

"I'm glad it helps her," I say.

"Her handwriting is unraveling, and it's not always easy to tell what she is writing, but perhaps that doesn't matter as long as she knows," Gran says.

"And Greg, how is he?" I ask.

"Coping, working a lot, staying out of the house, because Claire is calmer when he's not there."

Before I spoke to Gran, I tried his mobile phone, but he didn't answer. Sometimes I wish I had taken the trouble to make better friends with him, more quickly, so that now it would be easier to talk to him. I thought I had all the time in the world— everyone always does. It's a cliché, isn't it, to suddenly become aware of your own mortality. I look out of the hotel window, and the life passing below me on the street. I feel very far away from home.

"So, do you know what you are going to say?" Gran asks me.

I haven't told her about my failed first attempt, or about Zach from the bar sitting at my feet, apologizing for something he has got nothing to do with. I'm embarrassed at how inept I am at this, even though this is a unique situation. All I can think about is that I am going to be a mother myself, and a really important big sister: a lynchpin. I have to go through with this, be that person, the person I need to be, whatever the outcome. Not some crappy girl who can't string two sentences together. If I were my long-lost daughter, I'd tell myself to get lost.

"You'll be fine," Gran says, answering her own question when I don't respond. "I bet the words will just come to you. Look at how clever you are."

"Gran, I'm an accidentally pregnant college dropout," I tell her.

"Well, yes," she says. "Maybe, but an awfully clever one."

When Gran has hung up, I finish breakfast in my room. I decided as soon as I arrived that I didn't want to go down to breakfast and be the person sitting on her own in a corner of the restaurant. I don't want to go out at all, really—not back to the campus, or back to Paul Sumner. Today I know that he is taking tutorials in his office in the English Department. I'm not sure where his office is, but I am sure that I will more than likely be able to find it easily, and then it is just a matter of biding my time. I take care with how I look. After a shower, I dry my hair ever so slowly with the hotel dryer, so that it falls in smooth waves. Putting on just a little makeup, I leave my eyeliner untouched on the glass shelf in the bathroom. I look into my own eyes, for once bare of the outline I have painted on them for the last five years at least. I used to look in the mirror and wonder who I looked like—what mystery person made this face—but I see it now as clear as day. Her nose, her chin, her mouth. And even though her eyes are blue, and mine are almost black, I have her eyes too. It's got nothing to do with the pigment, only what's behind them. It's thanks to her I know I can do what seems impossible.

I smile as the lift takes me down, imagining Mum breaking out and running away to the library. I know it's been hard on Gran, what with Mum scaling fences and sneaking under trip-wires and laser beams. But somehow it makes me feel invincible too.

As the doors slide open I see Zach sitting opposite the lift, reading a paper. I press the CLOSE DOORS button again several times, and the person who is standing outside waiting to go up in the lift repeatedly presses the CALL LIFT button. As our thumbs battle it out for maybe fifteen seconds, Zach looks up and sees me.

"Caitlin!" He calls out my name as though we are old friends. Short of going back upstairs with the man I have already annoyed, there is nothing I can do to avoid him.

Reluctantly, I concede defeat, stepping out of the lift as the victor barges past me, muttering under his breath. I stay where I am and let Zach, if that is even really his name, come to me, because there is a CCTV camera pointing right at the lift doors.

"Are you stalking me?" I ask him, although admittedly it does seem preposterous that a man wearing black-and-white-checked skinny jeans, a wine-colored shirt and yet another waistcoat would try to stalk anyone, apart from maybe the person who told him those trousers were a good idea. All he's missing is an ill-advised trilby.

"No! Well, a bit." He offers me a small folded-up square of paper. "I found this. You left it on the bar. I'm sorry, but I read it."

I take the piece of paper. I don't need to look at it to know that it is my list.

"So, now you know a little more about a complete stranger who means nothing to you, so what?" I say. "You just turn up at my hotel, in a textbook example of extreme weirdness?"

"I wanted to make sure you are okay," Zach says. "I mean, yesterday, it must have been hard for you, to see your father that way, without him knowing about you. Especially . . . you know, in . . . um . . ."

"In my condition? Why is it that men just can't say the word 'pregnant'?" I raise an eyebrow. I cannot work him out. What is he doing here? What on earth is in it for him? "Look, are you some sort of religious nutter?" I ask him. "Is this about getting me into a cult, or something? Because I've read about it, how they get good-looking people to go and flirt with the vulnerable, and the next thing you know you're living in the middle of Kansas married to a man with a beard and sixteen sister-wives."

"So, you think I'm good-looking, then?" Zach grins and I blush at once, which infuriates me, because despite the fact that he dresses like a popstar who shops at Topman, he is undeniably attractive—which makes me even more cross, because I am quite obviously not in any position to be finding boys attractive, especially strange boys who turn up unannounced, for no apparent reason.

"Oh my God, what are you doing here?" I ask him again, exasperated with myself as much as with him. "What business of yours can it possibly be?"

"It's not, I suppose," Zach says. He looks awkward and embarrassed. "I thought . . . you know, you're far away from home and pregnant, and you've never met your dad. I just thought that . . . you maybe could use a friend."

"You're a pervert," I say. "You are one of those perverts that fancies pregnant women. You're a cult-joining, pregnant-woman-fancying pervert."

"You don't meet a lot of nice people, do you?" Zach frowns and smiles at the same time.

"Don't feel sorry for me!" I order him, with one out-stretched finger, raising my voice so that the people on the front desk look up.

"Look, why don't we have a coffee, in there." He nods toward the bar. "And, as an ice-breaker, you can tell me your other theories on my psychosis, and maybe neither of us will get arrested or thrown out for causing a commotion, and you'll see I'm just a bloke who is, oddly, pretty decent."

He seems so easy, so happy in his own skin, as though turning up unannounced at the hotel of a person you have only met fleetingly, with some unasked-for offer of solidarity, is the most normal thing in the whole wide world. I can't make sense of his being here, apparently just for me.

"You don't understand it, do you?" he says, thinking for a moment. "Look, I'm not from a cult, I'm not a pervert who's only into pregnant women—although I would say that finding pregnant women attractive isn't necessarily intrinsically wrong. But my mum brought me up to be really, really nice. She had this crazy obsession with turning me into a decent sort of person, one who gives a damn about the world and the people in it. I went through a rebellious phase when I was fifteen, and for about four years did exactly the opposite of everything she'd taught me to, and lost a lot of people who cared about me, did some stuff I shouldn't have, and then I realized that life was miserable—that it sucked. I finally got that my mum was right. The world is a nicer place when you care about people. Which is kind of sappy, but there you go. I'm a sappy bloke."

"Is your mum Mother Teresa?" I ask him.

"No." He smiles. "She died, actually. When I was fifteen. Lung cancer. She never smoked, but she worked in pubs most of her life, so ..."

"My mum is dying," I say. "Well, not dying, exactly. She has early-onset familial Alzheimer's, and there's a fifty percent chance that one day I might get it too."

There's silence—just a beat when nothing happens, except the chatter in the hotel lobby and the dim rush of traffic outside the building.

"You're having a really stressful time," he says. And it's not a question, or a platitude: it's just a statement of fact and, for some reason, hearing someone else say the words out loud is quite calming. Yes, it helps: to acknowledge that I am having a really stressful time. I feel better.

"So, do you want a coffee?" I ask him. "You can help me plan how I introduce myself to my dad."

"Does this mean you've stopped thinking I am either going to induct you into a cult or try to abduct you?" Zach asks me cheerfully.

"No," I say. "But I've got no one else to talk to, so I'll chance it."

It was not as easy as I first assumed it was going to be to get into the English Department building. You needed to scan your ID card electronically, or have a staff ID pass.

"Well," I say to Zach, "give me yours, and I'll use that to whiz in before anyone notices I'm not in a boy band."

Zach grins. "My card won't work in there. I'm only in catering."

"Your student card, then?" I demand, holding the palm of my hand out flat.

"I'm not a student," he says.

"Yes, you are!" I'm brought up short by this. I mean, why would anyone my age be hanging around a university campus, working in a university bar, if he's not a student? "You said you were a photography student?"

"A photographer, not a student of photography. And I'm a skint one, so I work in the bar to help me pay the bills. I'm not ready to do weddings yet. Not quite yet. Maybe this time next year, if I haven't had my big break."

"Where do photographers get big breaks?" I ask him, diverted from my real purpose.

"Well, I've yet to quite work that out," he says. "But I'm sure there are big breaks for photographers. Somewhere out there."

"And if that fails, you've got the right haircut for *The X Factor,*" I say.

I like the fact that he is not a student, and that he doesn't seem to have much of a life plan apart from avoiding wedding photography and being a decent person. I like his lack of a life plan.

"So," he says. "We'll have to bluff our way in."

"What?" I question him in an unfeasibly high voice.

"Yep, I've seen it in the movies all the time. Come on."

A little dumbfounded, I follow him into the faculty block's reception, where he leans across the desk and twinkles at the woman—and I mean twinkles. One look at him and she is more or less melting over the desk. It's ridiculous.

"Hey," he says, and she giggles. I almost want to reach over and shake her, and tell her to stop it, but then I remember that he is using his superpowers for good—for my good, anyway—and I restrain myself.

"We've got an appointment with Paul."

"Sumner or Ridgeway?" the girl simpers.

"Sumner," he says. "Sorry, to me, he's always just Paul."

"And how do you know him?" she asks, completely inappropriately in my view, and obviously in a desperate bid to strike up a conversation with a man who could easily be my boyfriend, as far as she knows. It's women like her that hold back the march of feminism.

"He's her dad," he says, nodding at me. "This is Caitlin."

"Oh!" The girl looks at me in genuine surprise. She has only just noticed that I am there. "I didn't know he had older kids."

"From a previous relationship," I say, wondering exactly how come I am revealing my secret past to this woman and not my father.

"Oh, well, you'd better go up, then. Just push on the gate when I press the buzzer, and go through." She beams at Zach again, and lets us into the faculty building.

"Shall I call up, let him know you are on your way?"

"Oh no, thanks," Zach says. "We want to surprise him."

"How can we surprise him if we have an appointment with him?" I hiss, as we make our way up the stairs to the third floor, where he has an office.

"Luckily, we weren't trying to get past your steel trap of a mind," Zach says, clearly enjoying himself far too much. "We're in, aren't we? And we didn't lie very much, so that's a good thing."

"You are so strange," I say, as we stop outside Paul Sumner's office. I can hear his voice on the other side of the door. "There's someone in there. We'll wait for them to come out, and then I'll knock."

"Yep," Zach agrees. "And what are you going to say?"

"I have no idea," I say. "I'll just explain that . . . I'll apologize for being weird, and then I'll tell him who I am. And then . . ."

The office door opens, and a pretty young girl walks out, clutching folders to her chest, her cheeks two bright-pink full stops.

"He's a fucking bastard," she tells me, then marches off down the corridor.

"Oh, good," I say.

"I'll wait out here," Zach says. "I'll be here when you come out."

I pause. Somehow I expected him to come with me. But of course he wouldn't—that would be weird. Weirder. Another student, a boy this time, lumbers up the corridor looking half asleep.

"Quickly," Zach says, "or you might miss your chance."

And before I know what's happening, I open the door. Paul looks up from some papers he is reading, and recognizes me. I'm the crazy girl from his lecture—the strange girl from the bar.

"Can I help you?" he asks me, looking puzzled.

And there really is nothing else to do but to say it.

"Do you remember my mum, Claire Armstrong?" I ask him, as I close the door behind me.

He smiles. "Claire, yes, I remember Claire. Claire is your mum? Why didn't you say so? Of course I remember Claire. My first love, how could I forget?"

He is beaming. He looks so happy to hear her name that I smile too, and then the tears come, filling my eyes, and I can't stop them.

"Oh, look . . ." He passes me a box of tissues. "I'm sorry. I don't even know your name."

"I'm Caitlin," I say. "Caitlin Armstrong. I'm twenty."

"So nice to meet you, Caitlin," he says. "You look like her, you know. I knew there was something about you, when you sat in the lecture yesterday, something I recognized, but I just couldn't place it. But, yes. Different coloring, of course, but other than that . . . You look just like her."

I just sit and stare at him, taking him in. He has kind eyes, and his smile when he heard Mum's name was warm and friendly.

"So are you studying in Manchester? How is Claire? I've often wondered what happened to her. I always thought I'd see her name up in lights somewhere. She had something about her. Something that set her apart."

"Um . . ." I take a breath. "I don't study in Manchester. I came here to see you. Mum told me to come, because she is ill and she thought it was time that I met you."

"Met me?" Paul asks, looking confused. "I mean, if there is anything I can do to help . . ."

"I don't know if there is," I say. "But, um, the thing is . . . Paul, I'm sorry because I know this is going to be a shock to you, but you are my father."

Paul stares at me for the longest time, and I'm wondering if he is noticing that my eyes are as black as his, and that our hair has exactly the same kink in it. Or that the tops of our thumbs are square. I wonder if he is noticing these things.

"Look, young lady," he says, standing up abruptly, "you don't turn up at someone's place of work and come out with rubbish like that, okay? I am not your father, and I'm sorry that you have got it into your head that I am, but I am not. Your mum and I split up a long time ago, and there was no pregnancy. She would have told me. She would have let me know. And I don't know if this is because your mother is ill—which I am very sorry to hear, by the way—and you've been rooting around in her past and trying to make sense of things . . . I am sympathetic, I am. But I am not your father, and you need to go now."

He stands up and goes to the door, opening it.

"She never told you about me," I say, not budging an inch toward the door. "Or me about you. I always pretended I was made in a test tube."

"Oh God." Paul looks horrified, frightened, sick. "Look, you must be going through a terrible time, but I am not your father."

"Yes, you are. Mum told me you were, right after they diagnosed her with Alzheimer's, and she wouldn't lie."

"Alzheimer's?" Paul repeats the word. "Oh, Caitlin, the same disease as her dad?"

"Yes," I say. "Yes, it runs in the family. And that's why she told me about you. She wants me to have a family."

"Oh, Caitlin," he says again. "I'm not your father. I can't be. Look, if it's Alzheimer's, well, haven't you ever thought that maybe Claire is remembering it wrong? Maybe it's all in her head?"

"No," I say. "Mum wouldn't lie about this."

thursday, july 26, 2001

claire

This is the daisy chain that Caitlin made the summer she was nine, and this is the cover of the copy of *Jane Eyre* that it has been pressed in up until now. My copy of this novel has been so well read, so many times, that the cover all but fell off when I was looking for the daisy chain, and I think it's right that the two things stay together. Two things that represent such a wonderful time in my life.

I was out of a job that summer—between jobs, if you like. I was still looking for my first proper teaching job, and we didn't have very much money at all. We lived in this little two-bedroom Victorian terrace that I rented. It was a pretty little house, but it was a winter house, meant for cozy evenings in front of the fire. Even though that summer was blazing hot, the house remained cool and dark inside, like another world altogether, and so I would take Caitlin out as much as possible. I had this old picnic basket that used to be Mum's, and that I had rescued when she wanted to throw it out, because I'd always loved to play with it as a little girl. It was a proper, woven basket, with a red gingham lining. Once, it came with a full set of white china plates and proper metal cutlery, but by the time I had full ownership of it, all of the plates and most of the cutlery had gone. I still loved it, though. I packed it up with sandwiches and bottles of pop, and with the sun beating down on our heads as we went to the park, I felt like I was leading a perfect life. A perfect mother, with a perfect daughter, and my not-so-perfect picnic basket.

We took books to the park. I was lucky that Caitlin loved to read as much as I did. Often, she'd be off, chasing ducks or imagining some game, usually on her own but sometimes with school friends she'd bump into. But most of the time she liked to sit next to me, and we'd read. She had a copy of *Harry Potter and the Philosopher's Stone.* I was reading *Jane Eyre* again.

One sleepy afternoon, lying under the branches of a cedar tree, she put her book down and rolled onto her side. "What's it about, Mum?" she asked me.

"It's about a young woman, an orphan, who is left to fend for herself in the world. When she is about your age, she is sent to a horrible, horrible school, and when she is older she becomes a governess at this big old scary house, which is full of dark secrets."

"Is there magic?" she asked me.

"Not the wand-waving sort," I said. "But I think it's magical. I always have."

"Will you read it to me?" she asked me, lying on her back and looking up at the branches of the trees. I felt sure that she would get bored before I'd even read a chapter, and go back to *Harry Potter,* or spot a friend on the other side of the park and run off to play. But she didn't. She listened, her eyes open, gazing up at the dark, cathedral branches of the trees, as though she could see the book playing out among them.

Every day we'd come out into the blazing July sun, and I'd read to her, for almost a week. And she'd listen, sometimes sitting up, and once making this daisy chain, which for a few short hours she wore on her head like a crown. They were some of the happiest days I can remember, those moments when something that I have loved since I was a child became something that she loved too. And all of the darkness and chaos of Rochester and Jane's romance became entwined with the light and joy of that summer. I picked her daisy chain up off the grass at the end of one day, and pressed it in the back of the book.

When we finished it, the middle of one Thursday afternoon, Caitlin scrambled to her feet and brushed grass and pine needles off her shorts and said, "That was cool, Mum, thanks."

I watched her for the rest of the afternoon, playing by the lake with some friends, and I realized then what I had done. I had made this person. I had helped create this little being who didn't mind singing in front of an audience, who felt happy to join in with her friends' games, even when she wasn't strictly invited, and who would put down a book full of magic and excitement to listen to me read to her the story of a little governess, and have all the imagination to let herself surrender to it. And I felt incredibly proud. Caitlin's confidence gave me the confidence to go on and do the things I have—to lead the life I have. And I wonder if she realizes that. I might have made Caitlin, but she made me too.

16

claire

"I was thinking." Greg sits down on the sofa next to me. "Maybe we should book an appointment to see your counselor, together?"

"My counselor." I say the word slowly, carefully. I had forgotten that I had a counselor, which is interesting to me. So far, of all the things I have forgotten, I have not even for one second forgotten that I have the disease. Even when I forget that now is now, and I'm somewhere else, the disease is still here, lingering, like the background hum of a fluorescent light. But if I forgot Diane, right up until he mentioned her—Diane, my well-meaning, stupidly well-read, and infuriating counselor—then maybe that means something. Maybe it means I have been traveling, without even knowing it, further into the dark.

"I'm not ready," I say, out loud.

"I don't mean right now," Greg says. His hand hovers over

mine for a moment, and then retracts. "I just mean that I could call and make an appointment. To be honest, Claire, I thought I would be able to handle this much better than I am. I thought it would be all about me being brave and stoical, and strong, holding it all together. I didn't realize that it would have this impact on us. I miss you, and I don't know how to deal with the way things have changed."

I don't say anything for a moment. I am trying to understand the reason some things stick, and some things don't—the reason Diane totally slipped my mind and yet I remember every single detail of my twenty minutes in the library with Ryan. Why is my brain giving me that to hold on to, when it will not let me know how much I have loved Greg? I look at him. He is such a good man. Knowing him has been a good thing for me— and he has given me Esther—but why won't my brain let me feel that now, when I would most like to be able to?

"I am sorry," I say, and he looks up at me, scrutinizing my face as though he's trying to check it's really me. "I don't want to hurt you. The last thing I want is to hurt you. You are such a nice person, and a great father. And you are really very kind to me. If I were you, I'd have packed my bags and legged it by now."

"That's the one thing that I can't do," Greg says. "I can't ever leave you, Claire."

"Thank you," I say, and I smile, for him. The disease cuts bits of me off, or suffocates them, but I am still me. I still know what is right and what should be done. I want to be the best wife I can be before I go, even if that means learning to be polite again.

"Yes," I say. "Yes. Book the appointment and we will go together. You never know, it might help."

"Thank you." He is careful to be calm, to keep his emotions in check. "Thank you. Well, I'd better get off to work. What will you do today?"

"Well, my jailor has got me on full lockdown, so I'll probably hang out with Esther and write in my book a bit more. I'm hoping Caitlin will be in touch on the talker, and tell me how she is. I'm sure she will when she is ready."

"I'm sure she will too," Greg says. "Right, then. I'll see you tonight."

"I will almost certainly be here," I say.

A few moments, or a few hours, after he has gone, Esther brings me a book.

"Read to me," she says, and I open the pages as she climbs onto my lap. But the words still aren't coming, and this time the pictures don't mean anything, either. I close my eyes and try to make up a story, but Esther knows this book off by heart, it seems, and she won't put up with my efforts to make something up. Nor will she tell me the story herself. She is angry and disappointed with me.

"I want you to read to me, Mummy, like you used to! What wrongs with you?"

"This book," I say, throwing it hard across the room. It pounds into the wall with a loud bang, and Esther cries. I try to put my arms around her, but she fights me off, running upstairs, sobbing her heart out. Esther hardly ever cries like that, those awful shoulder-shaking sobs punctuated by long drawn-in breaths of silence. Esther is such a sunny child, and I have made her cry.

"What on earth is going on?" Mum comes into the room. She has been somewhere deep in the house, cleaning something that she invariably cleaned yesterday, and the day before. I have come to realize this is a way for her to be with me and yet not be with me at the same time. She hides away, scrubbing at something that is already spotless, so she doesn't have to look at me failing.

"I can't read to Esther," I say. "She is angry with me, and I am angry with me. I threw a book."

Mum looks sad. She sits down on the edge of the sofa, holding a duster.

"I'm not very good at this, am I?" I ask her. "It would have been far better if I'd have got cancer, then at least I could have read to Esther, been in love with my husband. Been allowed out on my own."

"You don't have to be good at it," she says, smiling. "It's so like my overachieving daughter to want to be good at having Alzheimer's."

"Well, I blame you for that," I say. "You always told me the key to success is being happy, and I decided quite early on that it was actually the other way round. And now . . ."

I stop, because I get the feeling that the thought that's popped into my head isn't one that anyone else will like.

"And now?" Mum prompts me anyway.

"Now I wonder what happiness is anyway," I say. "I wonder what emotions *are,* really, if they can be so altered and changed by plaque in my brain or the little emboli. Are they even real?"

"I think they are real," Mum says. "I love you more than I have ever loved anyone—even your father, and I loved him very much. And Greg loves you, and that is real, much more real than I thought, I'll admit. Esther and Caitlin love you. A lot of people love you. And all of the feelings they have for you are real. I think it's love that lasts. It's love that remembers us. It's love that is left, when we are gone. I think those feelings are more real than our bodies and all the things that can go wrong with them. This"— she pinches her forearm—"is just the packaging."

Her words move me in a way I didn't expect: somehow, she has made me feel hopeful, not for a cure, but for some sort of peace in my head. My poor, busy, never restful, dying brain.

"You'd better go and see Esther," Mum says. "There are other things you can do together, apart from read. Get her paints out, or play in the garden?"

I nod and trudge up the stairs to find Esther sitting on her bedroom floor, looking out of the window. It's a blustery, cold day outside, but at least it's not raining, for once.

"I'm sorry I threw the pages," I say.

"It's a book," Esther says.

"I'm sorry I threw it," I say again. "I got cross. I've forgotten how to read the words."

"I forget sometimes which is my letter," Esther says. "I know it is an 'Eh' but I'd like it to be a 'Ja.' They look much nicer, and I want to be called Jennifer."

"Jennifer is a very pretty name," I say, venturing on to the floor next to her. "But you are much prettier than that."

"Don't worry, Mummy," Esther says. "We can learn to read together at the same time. Sames."

"What else would you like to do, instead?"

"Chocolate fountain and marshmallows?" Esther says with a big smile.

"Or painting?"

"Or park?"

"Or garden?"

"Okay," Esther concedes. "The garden, then. What shall we do in the garden?"

I can't think of anything that can be done in our very small, square garden, so I say the only thing that comes to mind.

"We're going to dig an enormous hole."

*   *   *

We haven't been digging for very long when Esther gets bored and puts down her trowel and goes to the gate. She rattles at the latch, and I realize that the poor child is sharing much of my confinement.

"Shall we go to the shop and get buttons?" she asks me hopefully.

"We could ask Granny if she's got some," I say. I can see Mum in the kitchen, washing up, even though we have a contraption that does it, as an excuse to keep an eye on us.

"No, I want to walk to the shop, and see the trees," Esther says so plaintively that I also miss the trees on her behalf.

"I have to ask Granny," I say. "See if she can come with us."

"Granny makes me eat apples," Esther says darkly. "And I want a magazine with a thingy on."

Esther means any type of comic or magazine aimed at children with any sort of free gift attached to the front. There is something about the joy of getting something free on the front of something else that cannot be rivaled, in her book. She does not care what the object is, and it's usually broken or forgotten by the next day, but the thrill of acquiring it is often enough for her. Greg and I joked once that her next Christmas stocking should be made up of freebies from magazines. I start as I remember the moment. . . . Standing in the newsagent's while Esther hopefully brought us a pile of six or so magazines . . . He put his arm around me, and kissed me on the cheek. I remember how it felt. I was happy. I'm happy now thinking about it.

"The shop is at the end of the road, isn't it?" I say to Esther, wondering if I am remembering a real shop, or the shop of my childhood where Mum used to send me to buy pints of milk in glass bottles when I was about seven years old.

"Yes," Esther says confidently, although I am sure she would answer the same way, even if I were asking for directions to Disney World.

"This is what we will do," I say, feeling emboldened by my memory of feelings. I sense that I am in a moment that is free from symptoms, and that I should do something with it. "We will walk to the end of the street, but if it's not there, then we will have to turn around and come right back, okay? Because we can't worry Granny again. It isn't fair."

"Okay!" Esther jumps up and down excitedly. "Let's take a biscuit!"

"A biscuit?" I say.

"Like Hansel and Gretel," she says. "So we will find our way back."

"We won't need a biscuit," I tell her. "I've got a good feeling."

I can't see Esther, and the panic rises and rises in my chest. How many minutes has it been since I last saw her? How many hours? I walk outside the shop and look around. This is not the end of my road, or at least not the road I last remember living on. I am sure I came out with Esther, and now I can't see her. The traffic goes by very quickly. It's almost dark. I go back into the shop.

"Did I come in with a little girl?" I ask the man behind the counter. He ignores me.

"Did I come in with a little girl?" I repeat. He shrugs and reads his paper. "Esther!" I shout her name very loudly. "Esther!"

But she is not in the shop. Oh God, oh God. We left the house, out of the back gate, we turned right, and we were just going to walk to the end of the street. What happened? Where is Esther? Oh God, oh God. I take the calling thing and look at it. I don't know how it works. I don't know how to make it connect with someone. I stumble out into the street and see a woman walking toward me, her head down because of the cold, and I grab her, making her start and pull away.

"Please, help me," I say. "I've lost my little girl and I don't know how to make this work!" I'm shouting. I'm scared and confused. She shakes her head and marches on.

"Someone help me!" I shout at the top of my voice, in the middle of the street, as the sunlight dies and the headlights glare. "Someone help me. I've lost my little girl! I've lost my Esther. Where is she?"

"Don't worry." The shopkeeper appears in the doorway, and beckons me over. "Come inside, madam, come inside. I'll phone people for you."

"My little girl." I cling on to him. "I should never have taken her out. I'm not capable of looking after her on my own anymore. I can't even read, and I've lost her, I've lost her. She is all alone."

The man takes my phone. "Tell me a name," he says.

"Mum." I sob the word as I look around for any sign of her. "Esther, Esther."

"Hello?" The man speaks. "I think I have your daughter with me. She is very upset. She says she has lost her little girl? Okay, okay. Yes. One moment, please. Madam?" I cling on to the counter. "It's okay, your little girl is safe. She is at home with her grandmother. Here, here. Talk to her."

"Mum?" I press it against my ear. "What have I done? I've lost Esther! I took her out, even though I knew that I mustn't, and now she's gone, Mum. She's gone."

"She's not." I hear Mum's voice. "Esther is here with me, darling. Mrs. Harrison from three doors up found her in her garden talking to the cat. She's here, and she's safe. Esther said you were going to the shop, but that she stopped to talk to the cat and you didn't. Mrs. Harrison went to the shop to look, but you weren't there. Do you know where you are?"

"No," I say. "No."

"Let me talk to that man again."

Numb, frightened, and still shaking, I hand the thing back to the shopkeeper.

"I told your mum where we are," he says. "So no need to worry. She's coming to get you. Would you like a cup of tea?"

I nod, and seeing a magazine covered in cellophane with some bright-yellow-and-pink plastic toy behind it, I pick it up. But as I pat my coat pockets, I realize that I don't have any way of paying for it.

"For your daughter?" he asks me. I nod, mutely.

"It's okay, you can keep it," he says. "On me. Now, you sit down here on this stool, and I'll bring you a cup of tea. You'll be home soon, no need to be afraid."

"It's okay." Mum helps me into the warm water in the bath, and holds my hand as I sit down. "It's okay."

I ask her to leave the door open, because downstairs I can hear Esther singing and talking with Greg.

"It's not," I say. "It's not okay anymore. I'm not her mummy anymore. I've stopped knowing how to read to her, how to keep her safe. I had no idea where I was, Mum, or how I even got there. I can't be trusted anymore, not even with my own little girl."

"It was my fault," Mum says. "I just nipped to the loo, and when I came back . . ."

"I'm not a toddler," I say. "And you are in your sixties. You shouldn't have to be checking whether or not I've drowned myself in a puddle. You shouldn't have to go through this, Mum. I need to go back to see the doctor. We need a better plan. A care plan."

"Lean forward."

I hug my knees and Mum squeezes hot water from the sponge over my back, gently rubbing it.

"Lie back."

I lie very still and let her wash me—my arms, my breasts, my stomach, my legs.

"We can manage," she says after a while. The steam from the bath is making her cheeks damp.

"I don't want you to manage," I say to her. "I don't want you to. This is your life, and you were happy, with your friends and the singing and the *Daily Mail*. You were happy, Mum. You'd done the hard stuff, and now you were getting to have contentment. I don't want you here, wondering what terrible, dreadful, stupid thing I'm going to do next. I want you to be free of me. Not washing me like I am a baby."

Mum bows her head as she kneels by the side of the bath. "Don't you see?" she says, without looking up. "I could no more go back to the house and the things I do back there than I could cut off my arm. You *are* my baby, my daughter, my little girl. No matter how big or old you get, you are mine, my precious child. I won't ever leave you, Claire. Not while there is a breath in my body."

"Mum." I reach out and touch her cheek, and she covers her face with her hands. I lean over the edge of the bath and put my arms around her.

"You are the best mum," I say. "The most amazingly wonderful mum that there is."

"I'm not," she says. "You are, and I'm going to help you to keep being that for as long as I possibly can. We're not there yet,

Claire. We are not at the end yet. There's so much more to do—psychotherapy maybe. Your counselor—you've not really taken her seriously yet, except for keeping up with your book. And we'll go back to that Mr. Rajapaske and talk about drugs. And I won't try to keep you in so much. We'll arrange things for you to do, safe things. It's my fault. I want to wrap you up, and protect you. I want to stop this awful thing from happening to you. I think . . . I think maybe I thought I could keep you in the house like Sleeping Beauty, then nothing would ever change."

"I don't want to go out anymore," I say, and I mean it. For weeks, the outside world has been the place I've longed to escape to, a place where I can be me. I always thought that when the time came to give up, to stay indoors, I would already have fallen off the precipice, or be lost in the fog. I thought I wouldn't know when the time came to admit defeat, but I do know. The time is now. "I never want to go anywhere again. I never want to feel that frightened again. I never ever want to put Esther in any sort of danger again. I'm sorry, Mum. Please, just lock me up and throw away the key, now."

There's a cough outside the door: it's Greg. "Caitlin is on my phone. She wants to talk to you, Claire."

Mum reaches through a gap in the door for the thing, the phone, as Greg calls it, and I take it. "Caitlin," I say. "Where are you?" Because for a second I cannot remember, and I'm frightened that she is lost too.

"I'm in Manchester, Mum," she says. Her voice seems so small and far away. I look around, trying to see her, and then remember that she is not here. "I spoke to Paul today."

Paul, Paul, my Paul, her father Paul. She went to Manchester to see her father. "How was it?" I ask her.

"Not good." I strain to listen for clues in her voice. She sounds oddly calm; her voice seems light, peaceful. Is that how it really is, or how I want to hear it? "Paul says that he isn't my father. He said . . ." She draws in a deep breath. "He says that maybe it's all in your head, because of the AD, and that. I mean, I know that it's not. I just have to look at him and I know that he's contributed to my gene pool—and he's not blind, he must see that too. But he doesn't want to face up to it, and I don't really blame him. Shall I come home?"

I find myself standing up, water pouring off me, running down my body in rivulets. Mum grabs a large soft wrap, still warm from the radiator, and winds it around me.

"Paul Sumner says you are not his?" I ask. Of all the things I'd expected, it wasn't that. I didn't expect him to deny what is written all over Caitlin's face.

"He says that he isn't my father, and that maybe you got muddled up, because you were ill? He was so sure, Mum. And he was so sure that I stopped being sure. And now I don't know what to do, and I'm not sure I even care. Shall I just come home? It seems pointless being this far away from you now. Greg told me about today. It sounded so horrible. I want to be at home with you all."

"No," I say. Stepping out of the bath, I walk into the hallway and find Greg standing there, looking uncertain and wary. He sees me and averts his eyes. "No. You stay there. I'm coming. I'll talk to Paul Bloody Sumner."

"But Mum, are you sure? After today?"

"I'm coming," I say, meeting Greg's eyes, and he nods.

"Claire." Mum is leaning in the bathroom doorway. "A few moments ago you said you didn't want to ever leave home again, and now Manchester? Are you sure?"

"I am not leaving things like this," I say, determined. "This isn't about me: it's about Caitlin. I need to fix this. I have to go.

You will come with me, and we'll take Esther. It will be a girls' road trip. You'll make sure that nothing bad happens. . . ."

"Will Greg come too?" Caitlin asks hopefully, listening in to our conversation. It's touching that she wants him there as part of the family, but he's part of her family now, and not mine.

"Greg's got work to do," I say.

He stands on the landing for a second longer, his arms wrapped protectively around his body, and then he walks into Esther's room and closes the door.

"We'll come up first thing," I say, looking at Mum, who simply nods. "Caitlin, are you okay? Are you very sad?"

There is a pause on the end of the line.

"Actually, funnily enough, I am not sad at all," Caitlin says, sounding rather bewildered. "I think I might be sort of happy."

A little while later, after Mum has dried and brushed my hair and the house is full of sleep, I get up to go to the bathroom. Hearing a noise, I pause outside Esther's room, and I worry that she might be having a nightmare about being left in a street by a woman who forgot she existed. I stand there, and listen, and very slowly I realize it's not Esther, but Greg—and he's crying. My hand goes to the doorknob and floats over it for a moment or two, and then I turn around and go back to bed.

I don't know what I would say to him.

friday, july 24, 1982

ruth

This is a postcard from St Ives, my first ever holiday with Claire on our own after her father died. And it was also the place that I lost her.

I didn't want to go on holiday without him. Even though we had only ever been on one family holiday before, it felt wrong to carry on. Looking back, I think I felt that it shouldn't be allowed—Claire and I carrying on living our lives almost exactly as we had before. I thought that we should mourn his passing forever. But that wasn't fair. Claire loved him, but she never knew him the way I did, he never let her. For her, his death was sad, but understandable. For me, it was losing the love of my life: the one person in the world I respected and adored above all others. I didn't want life to ever get back to normal.

Claire needed a break, though. My mum said so, and for once I listened to her. It's funny, now I think about the way we went about having that holiday. Even then, in the eighties, you only flew abroad if you were rich, and I hadn't learned to drive. I was to pass my driving test later that year. So we got a coach from Victoria, like a package holiday. Me and Claire and a lot of much older people, pensioners, wondering what on earth we were doing there—and the truth was, I didn't really know, except I knew I had to take Claire on a holiday, and I didn't want to have to think about it.

It must have been hard for her. I'm not even sure I told her we were going until the day I packed the bags. We sat on the coach for six hours, and we barely spoke to each other. She sat in the aisle and read *Jane Eyre*. I stared out of the window and thought about him, about how sweet and gentle he could be when no one was looking. How he'd loved me, and I'd loved him. How I'd lost him, the man who made my knees wobble when he kissed me; and he'd lost me, toward the end thinking I was his mother. We hadn't lost our love, though, not at all. It was there, still there between us. The love was still there.

Our hotel was a pretty awful one. I don't remember much about it, except that it was barely clean. None of it mattered to me really, although I do remember Claire being disappointed because she thought she'd be able to see the sea out of the window, and all she could see was the air conditioning unit screwed onto the brick wall opposite.

We were there for a week, come rain or shine, and I hardly remember any of it. It was before St Ives became packed with trendy shops and cafés, I know that much. It was sunny, but not warm, and a lot of our time was spent at the beach, me sitting in a deck chair behind sunglasses, while Claire paddled in the water, kicking listlessly at the waves. She got sunburned because I forgot to put sun cream on her. I was miserable. So sad. So lonely. I didn't want to be there, and I didn't want to be at home.

The only place I wanted to be was three or four years earlier, before we knew about the dementia. I could never imagine being happy again.

One evening, we walked through the town, because Claire was so sick of the hotel food that she nagged and nagged me to take her out for dinner. There was a fish and chips place in the town, where you could eat in. So we walked through the town, and it was very busy, full of people, all with the same idea, it seemed, and then suddenly I caught a glimpse of the back of a head, and I was sure it was him. I was just sure it was. I thought somehow he had followed us here. Who else would it be wearing a gray suit jacket on this summer's evening, his red hair shining? I followed him, my eyes glued to that glimpse of red, ducking down streets, pushing through the crowds, until I was almost running, desperate to catch up with him, right up until I turned a corner and bumped into the red-headed gentleman in the gray suit. I grasped at his shoulders, flung my arms around him and wept with relief, until the gentleman in question pushed me off him and told me to sober up. I looked into his face—a face that meant nothing to me. He wasn't a ghost and he wasn't a miracle: it was my mind playing tricks on me. I even got the hair color wrong. He wasn't a redhead—he was blond.

It was then I realized that Claire wasn't with me, and it took seconds, several of them, for the arrowhead of fear to pierce through the muffled miasma of grief; and then it struck me in the heart, which suddenly began to beat fast and I was alive again. They were a terrible, terrifying ten minutes, maybe even less, as I ran back the way I came, shouting out her name, people looking at me, the mad woman in the street screaming. But in those few minutes, however many of them there were, the blood rushed in my veins, life shot through me: longing, fear, anxicty like I have never known since, not until recently, spreading through every vein, with every beat of my heart.

Then there she was, looking in a shop window, like she hadn't even noticed I was gone. I picked her up—much to her horror—and held her tightly, until she began to fight me.

I'd lost her, and then I found her again, and I found myself at the same time.

17

claire

I am not sure what wakes me, but as I lie alone in bed, I get the feeling that I have forgotten something really important—which is ironic, because obviously I've forgotten a lot of really important things, recently. But this feels more urgent, more worrying. I sit up and push my fingers through my tangled hair, and take a breath and consider.

Esther is sleeping at my side, her face hidden by her mass of blond curls, her fingers folded inward into the palm of her hand, which rests on the pillow next to her ear. The sound of her breathing comes in regular rhythmic waves. I'm grateful that it is not Esther I have forgotten—Esther who has become my best friend and guardian in recent weeks. She always wanted to be an angel, and now, short of wings, she sort of is. I smile at her, but still the nagging loss is dragging at my chest. Caitlin is alone in Manchester, I remember, and today I am going to her.

Mum is taking me and Esther. Mum is driving us in her Nissan Micra. We are going to see Paul, my boyfriend. No, wait, Paul is not my boyfriend anymore, and he hasn't been for a long time. Is that what I've forgotten, what I've lost? Paul. Paul, who wrote me poems about sunshine in my hair and didn't wear underwear. Not ever. No, it's not that.

I get up, and look at the woman in the glass for a while, trying to reconcile myself with her reflection. Recently, I find it harder and harder to remember my age. I don't feel it, whatever it is. I feel seventeen, full of promise and life. I have this crazy sense of expectation about the future and what it still holds for me: dreams and daydreams of what might come. I am not so sure if it is the disease or me who feels so stupidly optimistic. Part of me feels like I should have stopped hoping or caring by now. It's not fair, to feel hopeful. Not when there is no hope.

What is it that I have lost in the night? What have I forgotten?

It's very early. The house is quiet and still, the sky just lightening into a bruised shade of purple. I pull back the curtain and look out, and he is there, and I know at once who it is. My memory doesn't hesitate for a moment. It's Ryan.

I catch my breath. What is he doing there in my garden? Just standing there on the ice-encrusted grass, staring at the ground, his hands in his pockets. My heart is pounding, and again I am overwhelmed by expectation: he is there and it is proof that life still holds surprises for me. I never expected to see him again after the library incident, and yet he's here, and he's waiting for me.

In too much of a hurry to bother dressing, I tiptoe quickly down the stairs in my bare feet, careful not to wake anyone up, especially not my husband, who is sleeping in Esther's room. I climb over the stair gate, slip my coat on over my nightshirt, and run over the smooth tiles in the kitchen. I feel a little as if I might be able to float, like Peter Pan on a wire. And then I remember: the door will be fixed shut and I will not be able to open it. I stand there for a second, looking at his back, shrouded in the dawn, through the pane of glass in the kitchen door. I reach out. Magically the handle melts under my fingers and a cold blast of air greets me, the door opens easily. Is this a dream? I wonder, as the world changes around me, bowing to my bidding, and allows me to go to him. It might be a dream, or a hallucination. Mr. Doctor Long Name said something about hallucinations toward the end. Is seeing him there in the garden a sign that I am almost there? The grass feels freezing, crunching under my bare toes, and the cold quickly finds its way under my coat and nightshirt. I begin to shiver, my iced breath billowing into the air. This is real. I believe it. I really am standing in my garden at dawn, looking at Ryan's back, and he really is waiting for me. After all, it sounds like something someone like me would do, doesn't it?

I pad across the grass, a drizzle of pink bleeding into the sky as the sun struggles to be born.

"You're here," I whisper, and he jumps, turning to see me. He smiles. He looks happy to see me, but surprised too, I think. "What are you doing here?" I ask him. "What if someone sees you?"

"You've got nothing on your feet," he says. "You'll freeze to death."

"I won't." I smile. I laugh. Actually, I sort of like the cold. I like feeling something this much. "What are you doing here? Why didn't you throw stones up at my window? I might have missed you!"

"I couldn't sleep," he says. "I wasn't thinking of getting you up. I just wanted to be near you. Which makes me sound mental."

"Not at all." I step toward him, and he puts his arms around me, all of me, pinning my arms to my sides, and lifts me up two or three inches into the air, to rest my toes on the tops of his boots. I put my arms around his neck and we stand nose to nose, warming each other. "Romeo crept up on Juliet at dawn, or sunset—one or the other—but there was something about a light breaking, yonder," I tell him. "And besides, I don't think I mind if you are mad, because that just means we match. I wouldn't want you to be a figment of my imagination, though. That would make me sad—if you weren't real."

"I'm real," he murmurs into my hair. "And so are you. God, I've missed you, Claire." His hands find their way under my coat, and I feel his fingers roam down my back and over my bottom, the thin cotton of my nightshirt hiding nothing from him. This is new—this heat between us—it's new and wrong. We are two people who cannot feel this way about each other, and yet it doesn't feel wrong to be touched by him like this. It feels wonderful, welcoming. I press myself even closer into his body, bury my face in his neck and lose myself in his touch. For now I am more than the disease: I am a woman—a desirable, lovable woman. I am me again. For just these few moments, I am purely me, and it's only him that can give me this gift.

"Claire, I need to tell you something," he whispers.

"I need to tell *you* something," I say, because now is the time for the truth. Now before this happiness turns to hurt.

"Me first," he says.

"Please, don't tell me that you aren't real," I caution him.

"Claire, I love you," he says into my hair. "I love you so." I pull back and look into his face. I barely know this man, and yet everything about him seems so true.

"You can't love me," I tell him gently. "You mustn't. I'm not here. Or I won't be soon. I'm sick, and I'm disappearing. And

I'm married. And I have my daughters. And I don't know how much time I have left knowing them. I can't leave them, don't you see? Not the girls, or Greg. I have to stay with him for as long as I can. Because they love me too, and they loved me first."

As I speak, his eyes fill with tears. He blinks and they roll down his cheeks. I smooth them away with the palms of my hands.

"I don't want to take you away from your family," he tells me. "I don't want to do that. I just had to tell you how I feel, that's all. And I hoped you'd listen and understand that when you are gone, I will be heartbroken. I will be bereft, and lost and alone. And I just need you to know that. That is all."

"Oh, my love." I kiss him then, suddenly gripped by a passionate urgency I haven't felt in months. I've been so insulated by uncertainty and loss. Just for now, though, my body takes over and I want to fold him into me; I want to be absorbed by him. As the day begins, and I feel the first touch of the warmth of the sun on my face, I know that I only have now, these last few minutes before the world wakes up and being here in his arms isn't possible anymore.

"I do know," I tell him, breaking the kiss, holding his face in my hands. "I do know, and it means so much to me. I love you too, somehow. I don't know how. And I'm sorry we met now, at exactly the wrong time."

"It's not the wrong time," he says. "It's exactly the right time."

We hold each other, our arms entwined, until the bruised sky fades to a pale cool blue and the ghostly shadows of the bare tree branches are imprinted in what is left of the frost on the grass.

"I have to go in," I say, glancing up at the house. "They will be up soon. They will think I've run away again." I pause, reluctant to step off his feet and away from him, because it might be the last time I ever feel alive like this. Human like this. "I don't know where you came from, or why you came now, but I am glad we found each other, even if it's just for now." I touch his lips with the tips of my fingers. "And if you are a dream, you're the best one I have ever had. Goodbye, my love."

I step back onto the wet grass, and I walk backwards, reluctant to take my eyes off him, in case he disappears along with the mist of dew being burned up by the strengthening heat of the day.

"I might not see you again," I say. "Or if I do, I might not know who you are. My illness, it's Alzheimer's Disease. It's eating me away, bit by bit, taking everything I love away from me. Even you."

He reaches out a hand to me. "Come back, just for a little longer."

I shake my head. "I know you love me. I can feel that you mean it. But you mustn't, you mustn't love me, because I will hurt you, and there is nothing I can do to stop it. You . . . you still love your wife. You're not the sort of man who just stops loving someone. I know you aren't. That's what makes you so incredible. So go and find her, and win her back, and forget about me. Because . . . I will forget about you."

"Claire, please. I'm not ready to say goodbye." His hand still hovers in the air, looking so strong and safe. I long to take it, but I know I can't.

"Me neither," I say, but the words catch in my throat. Slowly I turn around, and begin to walk away.

"You'll see me again," he promises. "And you will always know who I am, even if you don't always know it. You will feel it." I turn my back on him, and let myself back into the kitchen, where the onslaught of artificial warmth stings my numb cheeks and toes. When I turn back to close the door, he is gone.

"What are you doing?" Mum comes into the kitchen, her dressing gown knotted tightly around her. She sees me, and her exhaustion turns to fear. "Why have you got a coat on? Were you going somewhere?"

I shake my head and hold my hands out to her. "I was just in the garden," I say. "Come and look at it." She comes over just as the last of my footprints in the frost have melted away. "Look," I say. "The sun is up and, for once, it isn't raining. It's going to be a beautiful day."

18

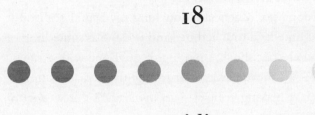

caitlin

I wake up with a start, and sit up, not sure where I am, and then gradually it comes back to me. I am still in Manchester. The filmy light of morning seeps through the thick net curtains against the window. And I am not alone.

Very quietly, very slowly, I turn my head and see Zach, still slumbering next to me, lying on his stomach, his blondish hair messed up, which he would hate, and his lips slightly parted as he sleeps. Carefully, I climb out of bed and go and lock myself in the bathroom.

I didn't react in quite the way I thought I would when Paul Sumner more or less told me to get lost. I was certain that I would feel rejected, and cry—feel hurt, despair, and confusion, all of the things that I have been feeling on a loop for the last few months—but I didn't. I had a weird surge of feeling strong, and happy, and sort of relieved. I walked out of his office and the faculty building with Zach behind me, asking me what had happened. I didn't tell him until we were outside.

"He didn't believe me," I said. "He thinks my mum's made it up because of the AD."

"Shit," Zach said, looking stricken on my behalf.

"Well, look, it's fine," I told him brightly. "I gave it my best shot, and I'm grateful for your help, so thanks. What I'll probably do now is just . . . go home, I guess."

"No, don't go," Zach said, touching my arm. I realized it was the first time he'd touched me, and it came as something of a jolt, like an electric shock, shooting through me with a *zap!*

"Well . . ." I moved away, ever so slightly, so that his fingers were no longer making contact with my arm. "I think I sort of have to. I mean, I can't think of a reason to stay here."

"Do *you* think Paul Sumner is your father?" Zach asked me.

"Yes," I said. "Yes, because Mum doesn't lie, and anyway, have you seen him? I look like him, a lot like him. It's weird, actually, how much like him I look. But it doesn't matter. He doesn't want to know, and I get that. So . . . I've come this far without a dad, but I do have a mum, and she needs me, so I'm going home."

"You've got to give him another chance," Zach said, stepping to his right to block me from leaving. "This is too important not to."

"He doesn't want another chance," I pointed out. "And who can blame him?"

"But he needs it," Zach said. "He might not know yet that he needs it, but he does, and one day he will wake up and realize what he's done. So you need to stay and give him another chance to be your father."

"Are you Jesus?" I asked him. "I can't think of a reason why you would care, if you are not Jesus."

"No!" He laughed. "Jesus wouldn't wear this shirt."

"That's because Jesus has taste," I said.

"Phone home, talk to your mum. I bet she won't want you to just give up."

"Do you drink?" I asked him.

"Yes, a bit," he said.

"Well, I can't, so shall we go to a pub and I'll watch you get drunk?"

Zach shook his head and laughed. "Let's go and have lunch. I know a nice place. And then you can go and phone your mum, okay?"

"Maybe *you* should be my dad," I said.

And that's the thing about Zach that I don't understand: he is so funny and kind and *nice*. And I wonder why I find it hard to believe that a person can be so funny and so kind and so nice to another person, one they hardly know, for no apparent reason. I wonder if it was because of Zach that I didn't curl up in a corner after Paul told me to go away. Or if it's because of me. I think mainly it's because of me, because when I decided that I love my baby, I also decided to be the sort of person who isn't defeated by setbacks, because if my mum has taught me anything, it's that mums are warriors: they might be knocked down, but they always get back up. It had helped that I knew Zach was there outside the door, though, waiting for me.

That must be what it's like having someone in your life, knowing that there is someone there who's got your back. That must have been what it was like for Mum and Greg. It was a nice feeling, and it made me feel better, like I was somehow bigger and more grown-up than I feel most of the time.

We spent the afternoon together, and it was just nice. There was no agenda, or tension, or mind games, like there always seemed to be with Seb. Zach is just very good at being a man; he doesn't seem to need to keep proving to everyone around him that that is what he is. I was sleepy after lunch so we went to see a film, something Zach wanted to see—a ridiculous heist movie with lots of car chases. I fell asleep after maybe twenty minutes, and woke up with my head on his shoulder as the credits rolled. He kissed me on the forehead and told me that he had to go to work. I didn't want him to, but it didn't really seem fair to ask him to quit a shift based on our short friendship.

He walked me back to the hotel, and it was a strange walk, one full of meaning when there wasn't any, really. I am a pregnant girl with a sick mother. I have much more to think about than nice-looking blondish boys with terrible taste in clothes and music. If things had been different, if I'd simply split up with Sebastian, or if Mum had carried on simply being Mum, then maybe I could have got excited about the way Zach made me feel when he looked at me, as he walked me through the busy streets of Manchester yesterday afternoon. I still remember the way he watched me, and then looked away when my eyes met his. How he punched his number into my phone in the hotel lobby, and told me to call him if I needed anything, and then called his own number before giving my phone back to me, so he'd have my number too. And how he waited with me until the lift came, and then, just before I got in, kissed me on the cheek when he said goodbye. In another life, I could have been excited about all of those things, and the possibility that something new was just beginning. But not in this life. And anyway, if it wasn't for Mum and Paul Sumner, I never would have come to this city, at this time, and met Zach working a shift in a bar on the university campus. Which is why I need to keep telling myself that this is not meant to be. This is not something special that has happened just at the time in my life I most need it. It's a series of coincidences that I will have to let go of—today, or tomorrow at the very latest.

I was trying to fall asleep in front of the TV, and trying not to think about what will happen when Mum, Gran, and Esther get here, when my phone rang, making me jump. My first thought was that something terrible must have happened, but then I saw Zach's name. It was just after midnight.

"Hello?"

"It's me," he said.

"I know," I said.

"Just thought I'd check and see if you were okay," he said. "To be honest, I've been thinking about you all night. Not in an inappropriate way," he added hurriedly. "Just thinking about all the stuff you've got going on."

I had to admit I was disappointed: I kind of liked the idea of him thinking about me in an inappropriate way. I put my hand flat on my belly, which was just beginning to curve with the baby inside, and smiled to myself. Maybe one day I'll be lucky like Mum, and meet the right person, who'll always have my back. But not now. Now I just need to focus on my family. I need to have *their* backs.

"I'm surprisingly okay," I told him. "It's odd, actually, because I've been an incredible mess for ages, and now suddenly everything seems really clear. And I am going to give Paul Sumner another chance. Well, I'm not sure if another chance is the right phrase. Another attempt, maybe. My mum, my gran, and my little sister are all coming up tomorrow to sort him out, so maybe it's more like a vendetta."

"Shall I come over?" he said suddenly. "Now?"

"To my hotel room?" I said. "Sounds inappropriate."

"No, I mean not to . . . just to see you, to hang out and talk? I like hanging out and talking to you."

"I don't mean to be funny," I said, "but don't you have your own mates?"

"Yeah." He laughs. "I've got loads of my own mates, and one new one, who I probably won't see again after tomorrow. So can I come over? Just to hang out. Watch a film or something? Your choice, this time. No car chases, promise."

And I realized, all of a sudden, that having him with me would make me really happy, and yet sort of sad all at once. And so I said yes.

We were halfway into the film when I turned to him and asked him a question that had been bouncing around in my head since he'd first mentioned her. "Tell me about your mother," I said. "Tell me what she was like?"

He turned to look at me, and then shook his head. "She was a really great woman, funny and strong and kind. My dad adored her, we all did. She was glam too, you know? Hair and makeup always done for work behind the bar, and for church every Sunday."

"So you *are* a religious nutter!" I said, nudging him in the ribs.

"Not exactly." He grinned. "Mum's faith meant a lot to her, and some of it's rubbed off on me. I mean, I prefer to think that there is something out there rather than nothing, don't you?"

"No," I said simply. "I don't want there to be something that decided to make my mum, or yours, so sick just on a whim. I'd rather it was all random, horrible chance. Otherwise it's impossible to understand."

"Yeah." He nodded. "I felt like that when she died. We all felt like that. We didn't know how much she held the three of us together until she was gone. Dad was so angry; I was so angry. I lost him too, for a while. We went our separate ways for almost four years. I'd hear about him getting thrown out of the pub that

Mum used to work in, spending the night in the cells. He'd hear about me bouncing from one hovel to the next, waking up tired and confused."

"And then you found Jesus?" I asked him a little mischievously.

"And then I gave my dad a second chance, and he gave me one too, because we both worked out, before it was too late, that Mum would be so upset to see how we'd reacted to losing her. It would be like everything she'd done when she was alive was for nothing. So me and my dad made friends again. It was a slow business—it took a long time—but we needed each other. We sorted each other out. He's my family, and I love him."

"And that's why you think I need to give Paul another chance?" I asked him.

"I think so," Zach said. "I don't think you should ever turn your back on any human relationship when there is still even a shred of hope."

"I have a family already, though," I said. "Most of them will be heading this way first thing in the morning. And I don't want to force my way into someone's life. Not even if he is my biological dad."

"You," Zach said quietly, looking right into my eyes in that popstar way of his, "you will never have to force yourself into anyone's life. Anyone with half a brain can see that you are . . . something wonderful."

"I must have met a lot of people who are brainless, then," I said to deflect the moment, which seemed like too much for two people who were just hanging out.

"That," Zach said, leaning back against the headboard and crossing his arms, "is entirely possible."

A little while later, when I was almost asleep, his voice woke me. "What are you going to call your baby?" he asked me.

It was the first time since I'd told him I was pregnant that he'd asked me any direct questions about it.

"I have no idea," I said sleepily. "Maybe Moon Unit, or Satchel. Maybe Apple, if it's a girl."

"And what about the father, what does he think?" He asked me ever so carefully, and it occurred to me that I hadn't mentioned him yet. For all Zach knew, he could be waiting at home for me now.

"He doesn't know yet," I say. "We split up, and then he thought I'd got rid of it. But I will tell him. I have to because, well, look at me. A textbook case of history repeating itself. I have to make sure this little one doesn't do that."

"Good," he said simply. "You should tell him."

I don't know when we fell asleep, or who fell asleep first, but it was probably me. All I remember was that one moment we were talking about the true meaning of *The Shining,* and the next I woke up with my back pressed against his, and we were the opposite of spooning, curled away from each other . . . and yet I felt somehow fully embraced.

I do wish I hadn't fallen asleep in my clothes, although I suppose it is marginally better than falling asleep without them.

Now I wonder about having a shower, but it feels wrong, being naked with him next door, and so instead I brush my teeth, take off my makeup and wash my hair, leaning over the bath so that the rivulets of warm soapy water defy gravity to run up my elbows, soaking my shirt. I wrap a towel around my head and look in the mirror. I look stupid, so I take it off again and attempt to towel-dry my hair as much as I can, until it is hanging in damp ringlets. I look slightly less ridiculous. I walk back into the bedroom, and he is still asleep, still curled up on his side. He looks so . . . ridiculously beautiful that I have to remind myself that beautiful boys with lots of friends don't fall for pregnant girls with stupid hair and very sick mothers. Oh, but how wonderful it would be to think that they might.

I sit on the edge of the bed and touch his arm. He really is flat out—clearly a very deep sleeper. Shaking him gently, I watch as his eyes finally flutter open and focus on me. He smiles. It's such a sweet, happy, sleepy smile that I want to kiss him. But I don't.

"It's morning," I say. "Just gone eight."

"I stayed the night!" He sits up and stretches. "I'd better go home and get changed—I've got work."

We sit looking at each other for another moment.

"I don't want you to leave Manchester without saying goodbye to me," he says.

"Okay, I won't," I promise. "I don't want to leave without saying goodbye to you, either."

I watch him get out of bed, pick up his things, run his fingers through his hair until it's slightly less crazy, and then I stand up as he walks to the door.

"I'm going to hug you," he warns me. I nod my assent, and we embrace, my arms around his neck, his arms around my waist. We stand chest to chest, and I rest my head in the curve of his neck. He squeezes me ever so gently.

"Take care, both of you," he says, as he lets himself out of the door.

And I realize that, apart from Mum, he is the first person to talk to my baby like it's a person in its own right. And that makes me happy.

"Rosie!" Mum squeals when she sees me, running over to me with her arms outstretched. "Rosie McMosie! We are going to have a blast!"

She kisses me on the cheek and rocks me from side to side as we hug.

"The first thing we need to do is to give the oldies the slip, and then we'll hit the town, yeah? Know any good bars round here?" Mum looks expectantly at me.

"Um . . ." Esther, who looks sleepy and confused after the long drive, screws her fists into her eyes and blinks, scrambling down from Gran's arms as I come into focus. "Caitlin!" She shouts my name with about the same level of enthusiasm as Mum had called out this Rosie's. "Yay!"

I pick her up and kiss her.

"This is my kid sister," Mum tells me. "She's not too annoying most of the time."

"Mummy's playing pretend," Esther tells me sagely.

"Hello, darling." Gran kisses me on the cheek, and Mum rolls her eyes at me, waggling her eyebrows like we have some sort of shared joke about mums, which makes me laugh—my mum, joking with me about mums. "Claire," Gran says. "We are in Manchester. We've come to see Caitlin, to help her talk to Paul Sumner?"

"Oh, him." Mum grins like . . . well, like me, I suppose, this morning. "I think he fancies me." She winks at me. "Is he here? Oh my God, what am I going to wear?"

"Claire," Gran says again, taking Mum's hand and looking her in the eye. "This is Caitlin, your daughter. She's twenty years old, remember? And having a baby, just like you did at her age."

"I'm not getting pregnant at twenty," Mum says, appalled. "Who would be stupid enough to get knocked up at twenty?"

"You, dear," Gran says. "And Caitlin is about to make you a granny."

Mum looks at me. "Oh," she says. "You aren't Rosie at all, are you?"

"No, Mum," I say, holding out my arms to her.

"Oh, hello, darling." She kisses me on the cheek and holds me again, differently this time, like a mother should. "I've missed you. Now, let's hatch a plan to make your father see sense."

wednesday, july 3, 1991

claire

Dear Paul,

I'm sorry that I am not there, that I just went the way I did, without leaving you a note or telling you where I was going, or why. It must seem like I had a very big secret, running away like that. But it's not about you, or anything you've done wrong.

I suppose you guessed that I came back to my mum's. You call every evening, and she says I am not here, because I've begged her to. But she thinks I am wrong. She thinks I should talk to you. I think you will stop calling soon. I think you are probably most annoyed that I just went without telling you why, not that I have gone. You might not think that is the way you feel, but if you concentrate really hard on why you want to talk to me, I bet that's it, isn't it?

Is that wrong? We talked a lot about being in love, didn't we? About being together, but ... something happened, something that means we have to be serious about all the things we said. We have to really mean them. And how can we really mean anything when we haven't finished growing up yet? I still don't eat broccoli, and you have to listen to a radio at night to be able to sleep. I thought about it, and decided it was just better to take the worry away, to separate us now, when it will be clean and certain.

I keep saying to Mum: this is the nineties, and a woman doesn't have to be defined by the man she is with, or the choices she makes. A woman can do things her way. There aren't any pigeonholes anymore: we can do anything. Mum looks at me, and I know she used to believe that, but she doesn't anymore.

I'm trying to tell you that ... It seems so strange, so funny. To write it—to say it out loud. To know that it is true. But it really is, and I am smiling when I write this.

Paul, I'm pregnant. I know that logic says I shouldn't have the baby—that I should "take care" of it, and go back to college, and start again, and pretend that this hasn't happened. But I can't do that. I love this child already, from the instant I knew it was there, more than anything I've ever loved. The way I feel about this baby, the love I'm feeling, is how I know that I don't really love you. I mean, I do love you, but not enough to make us being together right.

And I know that if you read this, you will come and find me, and you will try to make us work, because you want to be that kind of person, and that is the thing about you I will always love. But it wouldn't make it right, Paul. So I am sorry. I'm not going to send you this letter.

I'm sorry,
Claire

19

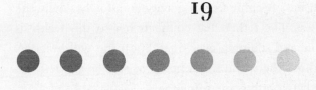

caitlin

Not for the first time since we set off from my hotel, leaving
Gran and Esther planning a trip to the cinema, I have serious
second thoughts. It's hard to know why we are doing this. I
mean, I know the practical reasons, and I even know the emo-
tional reasons, I suppose. Yet still, even knowing all of that, it's
hard to feel that it makes sense to go and turn my life, and Paul's
and his family's life, upside down. And for what? We know nothing of each other, we're strangers. Zach says I owe Paul a chance
to get to know me, and Mum has an idea that having Paul in
my life will replace what I am losing in losing her. And I can see
why she would think that, but the truth is that nothing can ever
replace my mother. Not anything. Especially not a man who,
until recently, I thought had rejected me, and for whom I have
not even been a nebulous idea.

And yet Mum and I are going to Paul's house to tell him the truth, whether he likes it or not.

This wasn't how I planned it, but when I saw Mum, and saw that somehow, in the very short time since I last saw her, she has faded a little more, I knew I didn't want to take her onto campus, where it would be crowded and confusing. I have to protect her as much as I can from the world outside her head.

Watching her float between this world and hers, I realize it's as though she's become free of gravity, and slowly, slowly, she is floating away. The tether that connects her to this reality is gossamer thin, and spinning ever finer. Soon she will be gone, but I don't think the world she is going to will be any less real for her, and that comforts me somehow.

So as Mum, Gran, and Esther checked into their room, I called Zach and asked him if there was a way of finding out where Paul lives. He called me back within half an hour, and it turns out that he knew someone who knew someone who was studying under Paul. As fate would have it, my father has a barbeque at his home every summer for his students, so this girl knew exactly where he lives. Strange how easy it is to find the home of my father, and now the man who has been worlds away from me for my whole life is just minutes away. And all the way over there, I keep having second thoughts . . . third and fourth ones too.

Turning up at his home, where his wife and children will be, doesn't seem fair, and I worry about him, and his family. Gran said it didn't have to be dramatic, though. She said there doesn't have to be a scene. All we have to do is ask for a quiet word, and when he sees Mum, he will agree to a meeting somewhere else, maybe at the hotel, to talk things through.

That's all this is: an introduction of sorts. So I put away all my doubts and take a breath, glancing at Mum, wondering where in time she is at the moment. She was with me when we got in the car, but we both stopped talking as we neared Paul's house. There's a new dreamy quality to her now, a little like when she first met Greg and I'd find her standing perfectly still, gazing out of a window daydreaming about him.

We pull up outside Paul's house. It's a nice detached Victorian house, maybe three stories, with a gravel drive and a garden. There are small conical trees in pots standing either side of the door, and the grass is very green and very neatly trimmed, just like the privet hedge. The light from the front room shines out into the world, and as we go to the front door, up three stone steps, I can just about see into the basement kitchen where Paul's young children are eating their dinner.

"We don't have to do this." I stop Mum, who smooths down her hair. She is holding her memory book, in which the letter that she showed me for the first time this morning is neatly stuck. The letter, written in her own hand, so familiar—always disorganized, looping madly, leaning forward and then backwards again, as if she's never really decided who she is. There is something more careful than usual about the way this letter is written, though—as if it had been rehearsed—and when I read it, I realized that must have been true. The letter that she folded inside the memory book is probably a much-honed version, and I understand finally what she was trying to tell him and me. Mum always knew that Paul wasn't the love of her life, and she knew that to try to make their relationship something it wasn't, purely because of me, would be a mistake. Twenty-one years ago, when Mum discovered she was pregnant by her first proper boyfriend, she decided that she wanted me more than she wanted him: she chose me. And not everything she decided since then has been perfect, but neither has she once wavered from that first decision. Even in deciding not to tell him about me, even then, Mum chose me; and now I am choosing *my* baby, and our future together.

Mum holds the book to her chest, cradling it across her heart like a shield. If everything were okay, if she were well, even then this would be an almost impossible thing to do. But as it is, with her life, her mind in such chaos, it seems an incredible notion that she should turn up here and do this. But even now she is choosing me, putting me first.

The door opens, but it isn't Paul who appears: it's his wife. She is small and neat, her blond hair tied back from her face, and she's dressed in a jacket with a scarf wrapped round her neck, looking as though she is about to go out.

At the sight of us, she stops abruptly, and raises her eyebrows questioningly. "Hello," she says pleasantly. "Can I help you?"

"We're here to see Paul." Mum grins at her. "Who are you?"

"Um, Mum," I say, stepping between the two women.

"I'm Alice." Alice is still smiling, but it's faltered a little, tinged with just a hint of concern. "I'm Paul's wife. Are you a student?"

"Yes," Mum says. "You're Paul's mum, you mean? He's not married. He better not be." Mum laughs. "Married, Paul!"

"Mum." I turn back to Alice. "I'm sorry. This is my mum. Her name is Claire Armstrong. She knew your husband—they were at university together."

"Oh." Alice does not look reassured, only more alarmed, and I realize she thinks Mum is on some midlife-crisis road trip to track down her lost first love.

"Is he in?" Mum asks. "What sort of party is this, anyway?"

"Mum," I say. "She's not well. She ... really needs to talk to Paul."

Alice still stands between us and the door to her home, and I see the conflict on her neat, pretty face. Blue eyes, small nose, pretty mouth, lovely hair, thick and blond and smooth. Short and tastefully dressed with understated chic. She is the opposite of my mother. And she isn't at all certain about us.

"My children are eating their dinner," she says, "Perhaps you could leave a number and I'll ask Paul to call you. . . ." Tutting and tossing her hair over her shoulder, Mum struts past Alice and into the hall. I follow her at speed. "Hello, Paul?" Mum calls out. "Hello, babe? Where are you?"

"Excuse me!" Alice raises her voice. "You don't just walk into my home. I want you to leave *now*, please."

"I'm sorry," I say again, holding out my hands to placate her. "We'll go. Mum . . ." I put my hand on her arm, but she doesn't move.

"Go?" She looks perplexed. "Don't be silly. We just got here. Where's the booze? Have you got a DJ? Not much of a party, is it?" she all but shouts. "Turn the music up!"

"Oh Christ." Paul blanches white as he appears from the basement and sees Mum, and then the look on Alice's face. "What's going on?"

"You tell me," Alice says to him. "They just turned up. This woman here knows you, apparently."

"I do know him." Mum smiles flirtatiously. "From top to bottom, hey, Paul?"

"Mum," I hiss at her, the excruciating awfulness of the situation making it almost impossible to see a good way of leaving. I only know that we must, before we cause more damage. "Mum, Claire, come on. We've come to the wrong place."

"No, we haven't, and we're not leaving. We came to see Paul," Mum says, breaking free of me, whirling round to fling her arms around Paul, and kissing him quite firmly on the lips. He resists her, watching his wife's eyes widen with horror as each millisecond ticks by.

"Alice, I'm so sorry," Paul says, prying himself out of Mum's arms. "This woman is sick."

"This woman?" I ask him. "She isn't just some random stranger, and you know it." I turn to Mum, saying her name. "Claire! I am your daughter, Caitlin, remember? And we came to see Paul today, to talk to him about the . . ." I glance at Alice. "About the past. When you were at university together, remember?"

"Oh." Claire blinks. "Oh. But . . ."

"I knew this was a bad idea," I say. I turn to Alice, whose expression is balanced finely between fury and upset. "I'm so sorry. We didn't mean to barge in like this. You must think we are awful. Please, let me explain. This is Claire Armstrong, and she's my mum. She has early-onset Alzheimer's, and it's quite advanced, so sometimes she gets in a muddle. Things happen in her head, and stuff just comes and goes. We never quite know which. But we certainly never meant to burst into your home and cause a scene, did we, Mum?"

Mum looks at her book, still in her arms, and I see some sort of remembrance pass over her face. "Oh shit," she says quietly. "Sorry, Paul. Sorry . . . er . . . Mrs. Sumner."

Alice stands stock-still for a moment as she takes in the chaotic scene unraveling in her hallway. "I don't want the children to be alarmed," she says.

"Of course not," Mum says. "Of course you don't. I'm so sorry. I'm only here for Caitlin, for *my* child." She turns to Paul, who is staring at her as though she has just materialized out of thin air.

"It's fine," Alice says eventually. She looks at me, and her smile, though faltering, isn't fake. "It's fine, come in. Come and have a cup of tea with us. I'm sure Paul would love to talk over the old days with you. You obviously have something important to say." Alice smiles at Mum.

"But you were going somewhere . . ." I say.

"Nowhere important, just the gym, it will still be there tomorrow. Come on, Paul. Claire must be feeling very disorientated, in unfamiliar surroundings. And she's come all the way to talk to you, so you will come and sit in the kitchen and talk to her, okay? You can take that stressy look off your face. I do know you had girlfriends before me. I had boyfriends before you, believe it or not. I'm not going to divorce you over past loves."

I watch Alice take Mum's coat and lead her into the kitchen. Paul and I exchange wary, uncertain glances. I shrug apologetically and follow them down the stairs.

"My gran had Alzheimer's," Alice tells us, pouring us cups of tea as we sit around a large table with her two daughters, who are staring at us like we just dropped in from outer space, which I guess we sort of did. "I remember thinking at the time it's almost like being a time traveler. What's to say that isn't exactly what it is—and it's just that the rest of us can't know it?"

"I always did want to time travel," Mum says, smiling at the girls. "I'd like to make friends with Anne Boleyn, or hang out with Cleopatra. I'm Claire, what are your names?" The girls respond to her smile, just like her pupils always did; and as they relax, so does Alice.

"I'm Vanessa, she's Sophie." The older one, who is dark like me, nods at her younger, fair-haired sister.

"I'm very pleased to meet you both, and thank you for not minding too much that we just turned up in the middle of your dinner."

"It's okay," Sophie says. "Dad made it, and it wasn't very nice."

"Why are you here?" Vanessa asks her. "Are you friends with Daddy?"

"I was once," Mum says, glancing at Paul, who is standing, his arms crossed protectively over his chest, leaning against the counter, unwilling to sit down with us. Mum ignores him, looking at Alice instead. "But for now I just want to see my daughter settled and sorted out, before ... well, before I zap off to see Cleopatra."

"Of course," Alice says. She sits down between her daughters. "That's fair enough."

I smile at the girls, and resist the urge to stare and try to find our similarities. But it seems I don't have to: Alice is looking hard at me, and then at Vanessa, and then at Mum.

"So, you came to talk about the past, and it's got something to do with your daughter?" She is talking to Mum, treating her like a whole person, even after everything, even after the way we turned up and barged in. And it's more than that. I can tell we aren't going to need to do the big reveal: Alice has worked out already what Paul didn't want to believe.

"Yes," Mum says, and perhaps seeing Alice's thought process as well, adds, "But maybe we shouldn't talk in front of your girls."

Paul begins to agree, but Alice stops him. "No, it's fine. We're a family. We deal with everything all together. I think that's what makes us stick together. I hope so, anyway." Alice nods for Mum to continue.

I take a breath, and Mum reaches out and takes my hand.

"The thing is, when I was going out with Paul, I got pregnant with Caitlin," my mum says bluntly. "And I wanted to keep the baby, but I didn't want to keep Paul. No, that's not quite right. I loved him, a lot. But I knew even then that we weren't for keeps. And so I wrote him this letter, this letter that I never sent. And I never told him about Caitlin, which was wrong of me."

"I see," Alice says very carefully, smiling reassuringly at her little girls, whose eyes are wide with shock. She looks intently at me and I hold her gaze, determined to take her scrutiny.

"And Caitlin came here to tell Paul ... well, just that she exists, I suppose. Because I asked her to. I wanted to put things right. She went to see him the other day and he, well, he didn't react as we hoped. Caitlin was ready to come home, but I persuaded her not to. And I came to be with her and to ... to tell him that it is true. I have proof."

"Oh, Paul," Alice says, her eyes filling with tears as she looks at me. "Look at her. She's the image of you. How could you even doubt that she is yours?"

It was the last thing I expected her to say—the last way I expected her to react—and yet there she was, just looking at me, and looking was enough. The sudden surge of relief at being seen, and being known as a whole person, almost knocks me to the floor. This is it—this is what it feels like to really know who you are—and it is Alice, not Paul, who has given it to me.

"It came out of the blue," Paul says. "I was thinking of you and the girls. I didn't handle it right." He looks at me. "I am sorry if I hurt your feelings. I'm so sorry. I got it all wrong. . . ."

Mum pushes the open book toward Paul, and Alice walks around to read the letter over his shoulder.

I smile at Vanessa, the dark one, and she smiles back at me, nudging her sister, who mirrors her expression. "This is crazy, batshit mad, isn't it?" I say, the swearword making them giggle. "Oops, sorry."

As they finish reading, Paul continues to stare at the book

for the longest time. And then he looks at Mum, and this look passes between them, this moment of recognition: a hello and a goodbye in a single moment. Mum nods, just slightly, and Paul looks at me.

The strangest thing happens as our eyes meet: I see the muscles of his face reform, and his eyes—that have been so closed off and embattled—really see me for the first time. For the first time, I am looking into the face of my father. The world shifts a little, and I realize that it will never be the same.

"I never knew a thing," he says. "All these years . . ."

"No, you didn't, and that was my fault," Mum says. "I thought I could do it all alone, and I could. But Caitlin couldn't. She shouldn't have had to. I was selfish."

"We don't want anything," I say to Alice, because she is easier to talk to than him. "Mum just wanted us to connect. We're not after money, or even contact, if that's not what you want."

"What do *you* want?" Alice asks me.

"I'd like to be your friend," I say, realizing all at once that this is true.

"So, that girl is, like, our sister?" Vanessa says. "From when Daddy went out with this lady, in the olden days?"

"That about sums it up." Alice smiles, and looks at Paul. "It's a lot to take in, isn't it, darling?"

"It's cool," Sophie says. "It's cool to just suddenly have a big sister! Daddy, isn't it cool?"

Paul nods, and for a minute he covers his eyes with his hands. "I couldn't understand how you could just leave the way you did," he tells Mum at last. "I tried for a few weeks to find you, to ask you why. It hurt me. It hurt me a lot—more than I expected. There wasn't anyone else as important to me again, not until Alice. If I'd have known about Caitlin . . ."

"I know," Mum says. "I know. I cheated you both of some

wonderful years of being together. And now here we are, strangers, sitting around a kitchen table. But hopefully we won't be strangers forever. Well, you two won't be, at least. Hopefully, you will try to get to know each other a little better. Build a friendship."

"Are you staying in Manchester?" Paul asks me.

"I don't know." I falter. "I'm not sure. I mean, Mum needs me at home, so . . ."

"I don't," Mum says. "I need you to be happy and living your life, and to pop in for visits, but I don't need you at home."

"Well," Alice says. "We want to get to know you, Caitlin. We'd love to. When you think about it, this is a wonderful thing. A miraculous thing." She laughs and claps her hands together. "I'm sure it will take time and lots of getting used to. And you don't have to stay here—we can come down to you. It will be easier, probably. We'll take it in turns. We're all going to be freaked out for a bit, but it's going to be just wonderful, I know it is."

"I like you," Mum says, smiling at Alice. "Yes, I like you a lot."

Alice gets up and comes over to my mum, stretching out her arms. After a moment or two, Mum gets up and hugs her. And it's so funny to see his face as he watches them, that Vanessa and Sophie and I burst into a fit of giggles as Paul—our father—turns the color of a beetroot.

thursday, march 10, 2005

caitlin

This is a copy of the cover of *Rhapsody in Blue* that my mum used to own on vinyl, and which used to belong to my grand-dad.

When I was about twelve, all the girls at school stopped talking to me, for reasons that I still don't really get. But there always used to be one person out of favor, and this time it was me. I arrived at school and gradually realized that I had been sent to Coventry. It made me miserable, so upset. I couldn't understand what I had done wrong. Mum had started working as a teacher at another school by then, and so I got home before her. She found me sitting on the stairs, sobbing my heart out.

"What's up?" she asked me.

I remember her dropping everything the moment she walked in the door, and putting her arms around me. When

Mum hugs you, there is always this cloud of coconut-scented red hair, the fragrance of a shampoo she has used since I was little. It's never changed. I told her about the girls leaving me out at school, and not knowing why they did it. Mum said they were jealous of me because I was beautiful, clever, and funny, and all the boys looked at me. I knew this wasn't true, but I liked that Mum thought it was. If Mum thought that way about me, then it helped me feel better. Everything was happening back then—hormones popping off in my body like fireworks. I felt like I'd changed completely from one day to the next. Not only the way I looked, but also the way I felt—the person I was.

Mum said that what I really needed to do was some inter-pretive dance.

I remember laughing, even though I was still crying, be-cause it was typical of Mum to say something so stupid, so out of the blue, just to make me smile.

"No, I'm serious," she said, kicking off her school shoes and unzipping her pencil skirt and dropping it to the floor, so that she was just in her tights.

"Mum!" I screeched. "What are you doing?"

"Getting ready for interpretive dance," she told me, going into the living room. "Come on, you."

In the living room she drew the curtains, which made the room glow a sort of pink. In the corner she kept her dad's an-cient record player, and underneath it a collection of LPs that sometimes she would take out and look at, although I never heard her play them.

"Now this," she said, carefully selecting one, "is what it's all about. George Gershwin, *Rhapsody in Blue*."

"You're crazy," I told her when she started up the turntable and then carefully lowered the needle to the record. How on earth could old-man music cheer me up? I heard a few crackles and bumps coming from the giant speakers that had been part of the furniture for so long I had forgotten they had a purpose.

And then there it was. That single, soaring, vibrating note of a clarinet, cutting through the air so sharply that it almost lifted me off my feet in shock. I stood there, completely still, and listened to the soft rhythm of the piano, the repeated motif of the clarinet, and then the wave of the orchestra joining in.

"Dance!" Mum ordered me, swaying and pirouetting around me, waving her arms above her head. "Let's dance to the music and pretend that we are in New York City, and there are people everywhere, traffic crowding the streets, steam coming up through the vents and lifting up our skirts, and we are movie stars."

I watched Mum jump and leap around the front room, while I was still riveted to the spot by the music. I'd never heard anything like it. I'd always thought that classical music, music with violins and stuff, had to be boring and dull. But this . . . this was thrilling. I closed my eyes and I could see the skyscrapers, the old-fashioned yellow taxis, and ladies in hats and gloves bustling along the street.

"Dance!" Mum grabbed my hand and dragged me after her. "Dance!"

I was twelve, and self-conscious, and still found my newly emerging body hard to understand, but the more I looked at her skipping around the living room in a whirl, the more I laughed and the more the music took over. And without really thinking about it, for the first time in ages I stopped worrying about how I looked, and I just joined in. We danced past the record player, making the needle skip a little, and Mum turned it up as loud as it would go.

Suddenly the house resounded with crashing music, filling

every corner with melody and noise and another world that I
was somehow part of. We ran up and down the hallway, up the
stairs; we skipped and pranced, twirled and wound our way in
and out of rooms. We jumped on beds, and Mum even turned
on the shower in the bathroom, sticking her head under the water and running away, screaming. So did I, the water running icy
cold down my back and shoulders. We marched and stomped,
leaped and ran. And then the crescendo came, and I felt almost
like I might fly when Mum threw open the living room curtains
and windows, and then the kitchen door, and we spilled out
into the garden. Grabbing my hands, she spun me around and
around, laughing as the world blended into a whirlpool of color,
and finally we collapsed onto the grass, laughing. We lay there,
then, in the spring sunshine, hand in hand, the grass prickling
beneath my neck, Mum still in her tights, and everything was so
perfect. So happy.

"The world is full of people who will try to bring you
down, Caitlin," Mum said, turning to look at me. "And full of
things that will make you sad and angry. But they are only people and things, and you, you are a dancer. Dancers are never
defeated."

It was such a silly thing to say, and it didn't really mean anything, and yet I still think of it, sometimes. That crazy half hour
of dancing round the house with my mum in her tights, listening
to *Rhapsody in Blue* back when she was just merely eccentric and
not ill. I think that, somehow, in some way, it taught me more
about being resilient than anything else ever has.

20

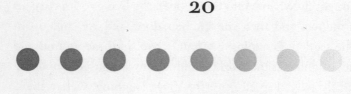

claire

It turns out that Esther loves staying in hotels. She's stayed in hotels before, of course, but she's probably been too little to remember them, or for them to matter to her in any real way. But for now, the idea of living in a big house full of bedrooms, where they bring you whatever food you like, and where there is a café for dinner and our very own bathroom, makes her very happy. She's sitting in the bathtub up to her ears in bubbles while Mum sings to her. Of course, it's ridiculous that she is still up at this hour, but she loved sitting in the restaurant so much, with her pretty dress on, sitting on a big girl's chair and all the waiting staff fussing over her, that I was glad I'd let her do it. I was glad to see the way her face shone in the candlelight, even when it was covered in a shiny slick of pasta sauce.

Today was good, I think. Long and odd. I haven't slept

since I woke up just before dawn and went into the garden. It seems like a dream now, like another world, another person. I am not actually sure that it happened, and yet the thought of it still makes me happy. Perhaps that will be what it's like when I meet the very edge of the cliff: perhaps it won't be frightening at all, but just like my meeting in the garden this morning. Reality doesn't always have to matter, does it? If it *feels* real, then that's all that matters.

I didn't even say goodbye to Greg when we left. He wasn't there. He'd gone to work while I was getting Esther ready. And it was so odd, because I felt like my leaving was a permanent thing. That somehow, when we drove away from the house, I wouldn't be coming back again. At least not in the same way.

Now, as I sit on the bed, I know and feel and see everything. Everything is completely clear. I know what the telephone next to the bed is for—I know its name, and I know how to use it. I know how to lock the door, which hotel I am staying in, on which floor, and why I am here. I know we went to see Paul and that, for a while, I lost it—though I can only remember that hazily, like meeting Ryan in the garden. Now I feel present and correct and whole. Healthy and hearty and righted. I don't know how long this will last, this random connection of synapses that make me *me* again, and so I get up and pick up my bag and gently let myself out of the room. I'm going to treat myself to a gin and tonic in the bar. After all, this might just be my one last stand. It deserves to be toasted with a drink.

I see Caitlin straight away sitting at the bar, wearing the pretty floral dress that I bought her, her black hair brushed out and shiny and rippling down her back. I stop and look at her. She looks so beautiful, like a butterfly that's shed her cocoon of black and decided to live. Her little bump rises expectantly

under her ribcage; her legs look long and pale in an unprecedented pair of high-heeled shoes. A pair of my red heels. She's
toying with an orange juice, trying very hard not to look like
she is waiting for someone. My heart leaps into my mouth as I
look at her. There's something about her that's so hopeful and
strong, and it terrifies me. Just like when she was a tiny girl and
I waved her off to her first day of school, into a world where
she would one day learn that not everyone loves her. I don't
want to leave my Caitlin, nor my Esther. I want to always be
here to tell them I love them, and that whatever happens, they
can get through it. And that's the cruelty, the unfairness. It's
not the disease that I'm scared of, or the strange, dark, wonderful world it's leading me into. It's knowing that I'm failing
the people I love, and that there is nothing I can do to change
that.

"Hello." I approach Caitlin cautiously.

"Mum!" She looks surprised to see me. "How did you get
out?"

I laugh and she blushes.

"You know what I mean."

"How did I escape my prison, you mean?" I slide onto the
seat next to her. "I let myself out of the door, of room 409, and
I came down in the lift for a G&T. And I found you, looking, I
might add, rather wonderful."

"Stupid dress." Caitlin looks embarrassed.

"You're waiting for someone, aren't you?" I say, tipping my
head to look at her. It's impossible to describe how I am feeling at this moment: so proud, so loving, so protective, so sad and
joyous, all at once. In this one second as I look at my daughter—
a young woman now, a strong woman who has overcome so
much to be sitting here wearing my red shoes, I feel it all. "Is the

person you're waiting for the reason you feel so happy, by any chance?" I add, remembering—miracle of miracles—our earlier conversation.

"It's stupid," Caitlin says, and she looks at me as if to gauge whether or not she can talk about it with me.

"It's okay," I say. "All of my marbles are present and correct for the moment. The fog has lifted, and I can see for miles and miles. Actually, just text your gran and tell her I'm with you, will you? I promised not to freak her out again."

"Oh, Mum." Caitlin blinks back tears, which collect in her long lashes, as she sends a message to her gran. Her phone buzzes seconds later.

"Gran says enjoy yourself," Caitlin tells me.

"Tell me about the boy!" I urge her, tickling her a little in the ribs to annoy her, to stop her from feeling sad.

"I just met him, completely randomly," she says. "He works in the student union bar, and takes photographs. I mean, I only met him two days ago, Mum. And he looks so stupid, like a flipping skinny Gary Barlow on speed. Stupid hair—and his dress sense, Mum! He wears ties, and hats for no reason. And ridiculous shoes. Like he really thinks about what he looks like. It's so dumb."

"So he's a bit vain?" I ask, uncertainly.

"No, not at all," Caitlin says, and the surprise is evident on her face. She looks up at me, earnestly. "Mum, he is *so* nice. I mean, I always thought nice was boring and easy, but it's like he decided to care about the world, and the people in it, and help them even when everything is quite clearly shit. I mean, who does that? Don't you think that's weird? Isn't that the sort of person you shouldn't get involved with?"

"A nice person who cares about the world and the people

in it?" I repeat. "No, you're right, you should totally stay away from him. Go out with a nice violent drug addict, or something."

"But Mum," Caitlin says, leaning forward. "I'm pregnant with another man's baby! What sort of man, even a nice one, wants a girl who is pregnant with another man's baby? I mean, who wants that world of complication in their lives? And can you even just go out with someone who's knocked up? I mean, can you just date? Without it having to end up in a relationship? And what about, you know . . ." She lowers her voice. "Sex. I mean, we haven't had any sex yet. We haven't even kissed, actually, and maybe, maybe this is all in my very confused and busy head, and maybe he just likes me as a friend, and has just been around helping me because he is nice, and . . . what am I doing in this dress?"

I reach out and put my hand on her head, just like I used to when she was a baby and getting in a state. I'd reach out and put my hand on the top of her head, and somehow it seemed to calm her, and eventually she'd stop crying and look up at my fingers, distracted. Caitlin does exactly the same thing now, probably wondering why my hand is on her head, and yet it works—it grounds her.

"Falling in love doesn't wait to happen at mutually convenient times," I say, removing my hand. "You can't think about it that way. Greg and I, we couldn't have met each other at any other time in our lives—any earlier just wouldn't have worked. And we aren't going to get enough time together, and it is really sad. But the years we've had—the times we've had together—that's the gift."

"You remember Greg?" Caitlin asks me softly.

"Of course I remember him," I say. "How could I forget the man I love?"

"Oh, Mum." She reaches in her bag for her phone. "Mum, call him. Call him now and tell him that you love him. Please."

I frown and take the phone, and dial his number without thinking. It rings for a long time and then goes to his voicemail, the same message as it has always been, even when I first called him to book a job. He's never changed it. I feel like I'm phoning him back then, on that fresh spring day when neither of us knew how important that first phone call would prove to be. I listen to the sound of his voice from back then, back before I knew him, and I leave a message. "Greg, it's me. It's Claire. I'm with Caitlin in Manchester. We went to see Paul and it went well, I think. It went as well as it could go. Look, I'm feeling good. I'm feeling normal and together. And I just want to tell you, while everything in the world is exactly as it should be, I just want to tell you, Greg, that you are the love of my life. I have loved you more than I ever thought it was possible. I love you, and I will always love you. Even when I don't remember it. I promise you. Goodbye, darling."

I hang up the phone, and it's only when I look at Caitlin's face that I get a sense of what I've missed while I've been away.

"Has it been very hard on him?" I ask her.

"Very hard," she says. "But he never stops loving you, Mum, not for a second."

I signal to the barman and order my drink.

"Caitlin," I say slowly, taking a sip and feeling it fizz through me. "Listen to me, darling, while I have something to say that makes sense. Okay?"

Caitlin nods.

"You have to decide to let yourself be happy. You have to decide it now, for me. If this boy, this nice boy, makes you happy, then let him. Don't question it. Don't push it away because it doesn't seem to fit with how things should be. Decide to be happy, Caitlin. Decide that for me, and for your baby, and for you. Don't spend a second worrying about what might have been, or what might be. Trust your heart to know what to do, because I promise you, the world might crumble away around you, your brain and body might betray you, but your heart, your spirit . . . that is what will stay true. That is what will define you. And when she is old enough to need to know this, explain it to Esther too. Tell her: What will be left of us all, is the love we have given and received."

"Like in the poem at your wedding," Caitlin says.

"Oh yes," I say, and something chimes in me, falling quietly into place. Just like the poem at my wedding.

Caitlin puts her arms around my neck, and slipping off her bar stool hugs me in a way that she hasn't since she was a child. She is holding on to me, anchoring me, tethering me, trying to make me stay. And I wish with all of my heart that I could stay here with her forever. She is hugging me, squeezing me tight, and we know, somehow we both know that whatever happens in the weeks and months and maybe years that will follow, for both of us, this moment . . . this is our goodbye.

"Hello." We pull apart and I see the boy, blond and clean-cut like Caitlin said, dressed to within an inch of his life, wearing the nicest smile I have ever seen. He doesn't look at me—he looks at Caitlin, and his eyes are shining. "You're here," he says. "I wasn't sure if you would be, so I just thought I'd pop in and . . . you are here. So . . . that's good."

"Um." Caitlin's porcelain skin flushes pink, and she self-consciously smooths down her skirt. "This is my mum," she says, gesturing stiffly at me.

"Oh! Hi, hello, Mrs., um, Caitlin," he says, and offers me his hand. He has a good handshake—firm, decisive. And the sweetest smile. And although he must know about the AD, he looks me in the eye. He doesn't look afraid of me.

"Hello, The Boy," I say, and he looks perplexed.

"Mum, this is Zach," Caitlin says. "He even has a name like a popstar."

Zach laughs, and shrugs.

"So, you just thought you'd pop by on the off-chance of bumping into my daughter, who was just sitting in the bar in her only dress on the off-chance that you might pop in?" I say, exercising my God-given right as a mother to embarrass them both.

"Mum!" Caitlin exclaims. "Oh my God!"

"Ha, yes," Zach admits ruefully, never taking his eyes off Caitlin. There's a part of me that feels like I should give him a speech, tell him how precious she is, and how he mustn't hurt her or mislead her, or let her down—because if he does, I will haunt him, even if I'm not dead. And yet I look at him, looking at her, and I am overwhelmed by the feeling that such a speech is simply not required. Both young people look at me sharply, and I realize I've let out an audible breath of relief that came with the sudden certain knowledge that Caitlin is going to be okay, with or without Zach—but, for the foreseeable future, with the boy that has made her "happy."

"I think I should leave you to it," I say, getting up. "It's about time I went back to room 409 anyway."

"No." Caitlin stands up too, and catches my hand. There is a tremor in her voice. "No, Mum, don't go. I'm not ready for you to go."

I reach out and touch her cheek. "I'll see you in the morning," I tell her.

She leans her face into the palm of my hand, and nods once.

"Goodnight, darling," I say. "Goodnight, Zach. You are a

very handsome young man. Caitlin is right: it really is quite ridiculous."

Zach closes his eyes, mortified, and I hear him burst into
laughter as I walk away from them both.

I'm waiting for the lift doors to slide open when I hear
his voice.

"Hello, Claire."

Turning slowly, I see him standing there, smiling at me.
The same look in his eyes as there was in the café, the library, the
garden this morning. A look that makes me want to sing to the
world about my happiness and good fortune.

"It's you," I say.

21

caitlin

Last night I sat and talked with Zach in the bar for a long time. I told him all about seeing my father again. About not knowing whether I should stay and try to get to know Paul better, or go home to be with Mum. I told him what she said to me before he came in, and that somehow I felt as though something had ended, as though we'd said goodbye.

"I don't know what to do," I said.

"Are you sure you don't know what to do?" Zach asked me. "Or is it that you don't know if what you want to do is the right thing?"

It took me by surprise, what he said, because I knew what I wanted to do when I looked at him.

"What do you want to do?" he asked me.

"I'm not sure I should say," I said. "I'm not sure. . . ."

"Be sure, Caitlin." He laughed. "Look at everything you've

done, everything you've come through already, and all the choices you've already made. Life-changing choices. If there is one person in the world who can be sure, it's you."

"I want to stay near you," I said. The words rushed out before I could censor them. "I want to get to know you more. It seems crazy to me, because of everything that is happening to my family and me, but I feel like . . . I feel like there is something here to find out about. I mean more than just getting to know Paul. I mean between us?" I paused, but Zach didn't respond. He just sat there, looking at his drink, which was a whisky and coke. Not a pint or a bottle of beer, even. A whisky and coke. A girl's drink.

"Oh, look, I'm sorry," I rushed on. "I'm such an idiot. Obviously, I am an idiot and you are nice, really nice. And for some reason there just aren't a lot of really nice boys around. It's like there's a rule that they have to be pricks until they hit at least thirty, or something, because I don't think I've met a nice boy before you in my entire life. Well, not one that I also fancied, anyway, because normally if a girl says a boy is nice, well then, that's the kiss of death, right? And why? Why would we prefer a person who is not nice over one who is nice, and what's wrong with nice anyway, and . . ."

"Caitlin." Zach put his hand on my wrist to stop me talking. "I'm sorry."

"It's fine," I said, feeling really like the most stupid person that has ever lived for putting myself out there like that to get knocked down again, but also at the same time sort of wonderful and brave and happy. "You've been so kind to me."

"I haven't," he said.

"No, you totally have," I said. "Unless . . . you are the sort of pervert who fancies pregnant girls and wants to get me in his cult?"

"No, I mean, yes, I have been kind to you. Yes, I have. But not because I'm better than any other bloke ..."

"You are, though," I said, stupidly, but sort of enjoying just liking someone, out loud, and not having to pretend like I didn't care either way.

"Okay, okay, fine, maybe I am nice and good, and hell yes, I suppose I do try to be those things, and they are partly the reason why I wanted to help you. But the other reason is because I really, really, really fancy you."

I snorted my orange juice all down the front of my floral print dress, and then laughed, and then snorted again. "Really?" I asked him.

"Yes, although I don't know why that surprises you," he said.

"Because I'm pregnant, and confused, and a dropout, with a really complicated and sad life that is about to get more complicated and more sad. I'm not the sort of girl who boys would normally fancy right now—not even nice ones."

"It seems to me that you can't decide to like a person based on their personal circumstances," Zach said. "It seems to me that sometimes you can like a person because of who they are, despite their personal circumstances."

And that was when I said, out of the blue, with no warning at all: "You would have made an excellent Knight in Shining Armor ... not that I need one."

Which was when he kissed me, and soon after that I kissed him back, and soon after that we realized that the kind of kissing we were doing probably wasn't appropriate in a public place. We walked to the lift, hand in hand, and when I pressed the button for my floor, we kissed again, right there in the foyer, and I realized I didn't care who was looking at us—I didn't care about anything but kissing him. I've never felt that unselfconscious before in my life, except for that one time when I was dancing with Mum.

The lift came, too soon.

"Goodnight, then," Zach said.

"I'm a dancer," I said.

"That's nice." He grinned at me.

"I don't want you to go," I said. "Come upstairs for a little while."

"I'm not sure," he said.

"About this?" I asked him.

"I'm not sure if I come upstairs it will be just for a little while," he said.

"Then come upstairs for all night. It's not like you haven't slept over before."

We kissed in the lift, me pressing him up against the wall, my hands running over his torso, up and under his shirt. I felt bold and brave and powerful with happiness. When we reached my floor and broke our kiss, he looked at me like I was something really special. I opened the door to my room and let him in, and he walked over to the window, far away from me.

"Caitlin," he said. "Think about this. About if you are ready—if this is the right time for you. Because you know I am happy to wait, to take things slow, to just get to know you at your own pace. This thing, between us, it isn't something that has to be rushed. This is something that will last."

And I don't think I have ever felt as clear, or as strong, or as certain about something before in my life. "I don't want to wait to feel this happy," I said. "Do you?"

"God, no," he said.

And then it was a long time before we talked again.

*   *   *

And now the sun is up, and his arms are wrapped around me, and I can feel the graze of his stubble against the back of my neck, and the warmth of his thighs against mine. And then suddenly there is a knocking at the door, urgent and low. I sit up, dragging a blanket around me, and open the door.

"Caitlin, is your mum with you?" Gran peers round the door, and sees a foot.

"Um, no," I say. "Why, has she gone out?"

"I don't think she ever came back," Gran says, too anxious to mention the foot. I step out into the corridor and see Esther, in her pajamas, raiding the chambermaid's trolley for biscuits.

"That's not possible," I say. "It's not. I texted you last night to tell you she was with me, and she was completely together, just like the old Mum—nothing missing, no gaps. She was wonderful, actually. She called Greg, left him a message, and then said she had to get back before you worried about her. She knew the room number and everything. I mean, she came back to the room last night, right?"

"I don't know," Gran says unhappily. "I fell asleep with Esther, and when I woke up this morning, she wasn't in the room with us. Her bed hadn't been slept in. I'm so stupid. I should have made myself wait up for her. I don't why I didn't! What if she's wandered off up here? She doesn't know anyone, or anything. She'll get lost or hurt or . . ."

"It's okay," I say, and I don't know why, but I know that's true. "It's fine. Hang on, I'll get dressed. She's probably just having breakfast."

I hurry back inside, the sick feeling tilting the room as I rush to get dressed.

"What's happened?" Zach sits up.

"Gran thinks Mum hasn't been in their room all night," I

say, dragging on leggings and last night's dress. "I knew I shouldn't have let her go off. I should have taken her upstairs. . . ."

"It's okay," Zach says, leaping out of bed and pulling on his clothes. "We'll find her." And I pause for a second, watching him get dressed to come and help without even a second thought. A few seconds later and he's buttoned up his shirt and slipped on his shoes. We go outside and Gran is there on the phone.

"I keep calling Greg," she says, eyeing Zach curiously. "But I just get his answer phone."

I make brief introductions before Zach takes charge. "Right, well, the first thing to do is to ask at reception," he says. "Your mum is really beautiful. . . . I mean, distinctive-looking, with her hair and everything. I'm sure they will have noticed her."

The four of us travel down in the lift, Esther staring at Zach from under Gran's arm, her eyes wide and round, probably because he looks like a Disney prince.

The second the lift door opens, I all but run to reception, my hand placed over my bump as I jog. Gran's not far behind me, with Esther a few steps ahead. But before I can ask anything, Zach calls my name. He's looking into the restaurant. He beckons me over.

"Your mum's in there," he says calmly. "With a man."

I gasp, horrified. Oh my God. Sometime between her leaving me last night and before she got to her room, someone spotted her and took advantage of her. I've heard about things like this happening, but she just seemed so happy last night, so normal and so *her*. I don't want to look. I don't want to know, but I have to.

I walk into the room, and it's easy to find Mum: her shock of hair burning like a beacon. She's leaning in to kiss someone over coffee. I feel sick. If Greg could see this now. If Greg ever found out, it would kill him. Steeling myself, I walk over to the table. And then I see him.

"Caitlin!" Mum looks so pleased to see me. "This is my lover," she tells me. "My hero. My library lover, my garden dancer, the one person who can see past everything and still see me. This is him, Caitlin. This is my dream man. He came to find me — he always comes to find me. I don't know how, but he does. I hope you like him. I want you to like him."

I look at the man holding Mum's hand across the table, and I know that I am crying, with happiness and relief.

"Hello, Greg," I say.

"Hello, Caitlin," he says. "Just taking some breakfast with Ms. Armstrong here."

"I don't think I want to be Ms. Armstrong anymore," Mum says. "I want to be Mrs. Ryan. Mrs. Greg Ryan."

Her fingers close around his, and they look like they will never part.

about a month ago

greg

This is the corner of the napkin I gave to Claire to dry her face with on that first night in the café. I think about it as the first night, because it was. It was the first night of Claire seeing me again, the way she used to, even though she thought I was someone else, someone new.

I didn't go there to try and trick her. I didn't know what would happen until it did. Ruth rang me to tell me that Claire had walked off after the hospital, and somehow I just knew where she would be.

At first it hurt me when she didn't recognize me, and then it hit me. It didn't matter who I was. It only mattered that she saw me—that she talked to me the way she used to. It was just a glimpse of how things used to be, can still be, from time to time, but it was enough to keep me going, to give me hope. And I still believe that it was me Claire was talking to, and that she always knew it, on some level. Because I believe that when two people are in love, the way that we are in love, the love lasts, whatever else happens. Perhaps for Claire everything about me was altered when we met in the café. But the love ... the love stayed the same.

I didn't plan to keep that meeting a secret, either, but it was just so special. So rare. I didn't want to scare Claire off by talking about it.

No one really noticed that when we were both in the house, her house, Claire was becoming ever more distant and cold to me—no one except me. In the house, I became a stranger, an invader. Claire tried to be kind to me. She did her best, but she couldn't hide how it felt to have me there.

Outside of the house, though, I was a different person entirely to her—different, but still the person she loved.

Claire used to say it took her a lifetime to fall in love with me, and it did. This second time, though, it took seconds. Because we were already in love.

The second time, when I came to bring her back from looking for Caitlin, I did hope that it might happen again. I wished for it. And when it did ... it felt miraculous. And that was when I realized, if I could just keep this connection with her— this bubble where we could love each other—then perhaps she would see me as her husband again. She might recognize me. It was selfish, it was unfair, especially when I met her in the library. It was wrong to put Ruth through that, but what else could I do? I had to be with her, whatever chance I got, and I had to hope that it would be enough to make her remember our marriage.

And then she found me in the garden. I hadn't been able to sleep, I was so unhappy, so confused by everything that was happening. I went outside because I wanted the cold to numb the pain out of me, and then suddenly she was there. I don't think I have ever felt so close to her as I did in those few minutes.

She said goodbye to me, for good. Left me and chose me, and our marriage, all at the same time. She told me she needed to be with her family, and that I should go and find my wife. And that is what I decided to do.

Then the most miraculous, wonderful thing happened. When I arrived in Manchester, my wife was waiting for me. Perhaps we didn't have very long to be together again like that. And perhaps it might never happen again.

But now I know that I can hope, and I know that I will go on hoping, always hoping, that she will come back to me, one last time.

tuesday, june 19, 2007

claire

This is the quote—handwritten on a piece of headed paper—
the quote Greg gave me on the day he came to the house for the
first time to look at my loft. Caitlin was away on a school trip
and I had just come off the phone to Mum, who'd called me to
discuss the article she'd cut out of the *Daily Mail* for me, about
how chocolate gives you cancer. Mum always liked to follow
through on her helpful handouts with a chat.

I wasn't ready for him arriving, and I didn't plan to be: I
didn't know I was about to meet the love of my life.

I didn't think I needed to worry about the hole in my
slightly too-tight jeans, the surge of flesh that burgeoned over
the top of the waistband, or that I was wearing one of Caitlin's
old T-shirts that had a picture of a skull on the front and a rip
along the neckline. Or that I was sweating from trying to clear
the attic of all the accumulated stuff that had built up over the

years I had owned the house. It was chock-full of memories, some of them important, some of them just moments in time that meant something to me and no one else. I think I even resented his arrival as I pushed boxes into corners, mentally making a note of all the things I would have to throw away just to have an extra room in my loft, which, on reflection, I didn't really need.

The doorbell sounded while I was still up the ladder, and it took me a few seconds to climb down, so while I was stumbling down the stairs, it sounded again. I was quite cross. My cheeks were shiny and red, and I smelled of dust and perspiration when I opened the door and first met Greg.

"Mrs.... Armstrong?" There was the faintest pause between the two words, as though, somehow, he sensed they didn't go together.

"Ms.," I said, the way I always do. "I don't feel the need to be defined by my marital status."

"Fair enough." He didn't seem to care one way or the other. I let him into the house, which was hot and full of sunlight, showing every streak of dust and carpet scuff.

"So, it's upstairs," I told him.

"Lofts generally are," he quipped, and I glared at him. I didn't need a funny builder.

I climbed the ladder into the loft first, and he followed me. I remember feeling excruciatingly aware that this man's nose was inches from my bottom, and wondering what my bottom looked like these days. It had been an awfully long time since I'd bothered to consider it.

We stood there for a moment, bathed in the light of a naked electric bulb, as he took a pencil out from behind his ear and noted a few things down. He wore a tape measure on his belt, like a Wild West gunslinger.

"Pretty straightforward job," he said. "I'll do the drawings, the calculations for you, and we'll get a structural engineer to sign off on it. You don't want stairs, just a better ladder and a couple of Velux, so it's going to be pretty quick. Need an extra bedroom, do you?"

"No," I said, my hands on my hips as I looked around, trying to imagine this room the way I wanted it: flooded with sunlight, the floorboards stripped and varnished, the walls white-washed. "I want to write a book, and it seems like all the rooms I have in the house already have a purpose that stops me from concentrating on it. So I thought a book-writing room would be the answer." I smiled at him. "I expect that seems like craziness to you."

"Not at all," he said. "It's your house, and writing a book seems like a better idea than some."

He smiled, not at me but at the space around us, and I could see him picturing it finished, too, and that the idea gave him pleasure. And that was the first time I noticed how broad his shoulders were, or how muscular his arms were, or the contour of his stomach muscles under his shirt. And then suddenly I did, and I registered too that my hair was screwed up into a Muppet knot on top of my head, and I was wearing my daughter's ripped T-shirt and a pair of jeans that technically didn't fit me anymore. Oh, and that I was certainly older than him, although I wasn't exactly sure by how much. I realized all of those things, and at the same time I was annoyed with myself for caring.

"So, shall we go downstairs, and I'll work out a quote for you—just a basic one at this stage, to give you a ballpark? Then if you decide to go with me, I'll do you an itemized quote and a contract, so you know exactly what you are paying for, okay?"

"Fine," I said, suddenly only able to utter words of one syllable.

He went down the ladder first, and then me. I was about halfway down when I lost grip in my stupid flip-flops and fell the rest of the way, stumbling back off the ladder and into his arms. There wasn't a moment—no lingering, no touching a fraction longer than needed. He just set me straight on my feet with workmanlike efficiency.

"Never did quite get the hang of that standing up on my own two feet thing," I said, blushing inexplicably.

"Well, we can't all be good at everything," he said. "I can't even imagine writing down anything longer than a quote."

I'm not sure precisely when I decided I was in love with him, but I think it might have been at that moment, the moment he went out of his way to put me at my ease. I followed him down the stairs and by the time we reached the bottom step, it was official. I was besotted, and that's the right word for it. Besotted. Because I knew right then it was a hopeless love, a love that could never come to anything, because I could never be that lucky.

We walked into the kitchen and he leaned against the counter and started to write. I spent the entire time looking at his bottom, smiling to myself about what an idiot I was being, and thinking about how Julia would laugh with me at school the next time I saw her. Just the thought of how mortified Caitlin would be, if she could see me, leaning up against the fridge, ogling this beautiful example of manhood like a crazy woman, made me giggle out loud.

Greg looked at me over his shoulder and then, seeing me smiling, turned around.

"What's so funny?" he asked me.

"Oh, I . . . oh, nothing." I giggled despite myself. I giggled like a teenager bumping into her crush. "Ignore me, I am just being really, really stupid, for no apparent reason."

His smile was so sweet, so slow, so full of humor. "I don't think so," he said. "I'm very good at first impressions, and you are certainly not stupid."

"Oh, really?" I asked him archly, knowing I was flirting fruitlessly, and deciding I didn't care. "What am I, then?"

"You are a woman who is going to write a book."

I look back on that time now and wonder if I was right and if I was wrong at the same time. I knew that Greg and I were too good to be true, that it couldn't last, and I was right but also wrong. It can't last, but not because we don't want it to—and it will last even when it's over. It will last within Greg and me, no matter what separates us. And it will last in Esther and Caitlin, and the baby. It will last and last, even when it's finished forever, because in my heart Greg and I will always be holding hands, like the husband and wife in "An Arundel Tomb."

And in the end, I did write a book. We all did. We wrote the story of our lives, and I am here, among these pages. This is where I will always be.

friday, august 27, 1971

claire is born

This is the first photo taken of you and me, Claire, in my hospital bed, sitting up with my bedcoat on, especially crocheted for me by my mum. Husbands didn't stay for the birth in those days: they visited, for an hour a day, and then got sent packing. And I was glad—I was glad to have that time alone with you, my new baby, my fresh little person. This tiny soul that I had made and brought into the world. I didn't want to share you with anyone.

Then, in your first few days, your hair was a jet-black down, with no hint of your father's red hair anywhere to be seen. Your face was scrunched up and closed, your eyes tightly shut against this bright and unfamiliar world. The midwife said I had to put you down at nap-time in the nursery with all the other babies; she said I had to get some sleep. They came round and collected all the babies at a certain time, wheeling them off down the corridor in a long procession. But I wouldn't let you go, Claire. She tried to take you, demanded it, but I said you were my baby and I wanted to hold you; and then, to be extra rebellious, I let the bottle of formula go cold on the bedside table and I breastfed you myself. They left us alone after that.

It was almost a full day before you really and truly opened your eyes and looked at me. They were the brightest blue, even then. Babies' eyes aren't supposed to be so blue, but they were. Luminous, even, and I thought it must be because this tiny little bundle I held in my arms was so full of life, so full of promise, and so full of future.

Before I met your father I thought that love and peace would change the whole world, but looking into your eyes, I knew that all I had to do was let you be whoever it was that you wanted to be, and to love you, and that would be the best and closest thing I could ever do to change the world for the better.

"You are going to be brilliant," I told you. "You are going to be clever, and funny. Brave and strong. You're going to be a feminist, and a peace campaigner and a dancer. And one day you are going to be a mother yourself. You are going to fall in love and have adventures and do things that I can't even imagine. You, little Claire Armstrong, you are going to be the most wonderful woman, and you are going to have the most amazing life: a life that no one will ever forget."

Those were the first words I said to you, Claire, that first time you opened your eyes and looked at me. I remember those words exactly as though I were in that room right now, holding you in my arms at this precise second. And Claire, my beautiful, brave, clever girl, I was right.

acknowledgments

Thanks so much to my lovely editor, Linda Marrow, Elana Seplow-Jolley, and all the fantastic team at Ballantine—I am so thrilled to be published by such a wonderful house. Also thanks so much to my U.S. agent, Jill Grinberg, whose faith in me and hard work on my behalf I have very much appreciated.

And huge thanks to my agent and friend, Lizzy Kremer, who is a constant source of strength and inspiration. Also the very lovely Laura West and Harriet Moore at David Higham Ltd, a true dream team and a writer's best friends.

Thanks to my friends, who put up with me during the writing of this book, especially Katy Regan, Kirstie Seaman, Catherine Ashley, and Margie Harris.

Special thanks to my husband, Adam, who does so much to help and support me, and to my beautiful, noisy, energetic, constantly busy children, who keep me on my toes.

And finally, a thank-you to my mum, Dawn, who this book is for. You taught me how to be a mum.

the day we met

Rowan Coleman

A Reader's Guide

a note from the author

About three years ago I was sitting at my desk in my office, looking out the window, thinking about a dream I'd had years ago. It's a very long story, but I first met my now husband, Adam, when we were both twelve, starting a new school at the same time. I fell in love with him at first sight, I actually did, just like they talk about in movies and books.

Years went by, years of nothing much happening between us (well, we were only twelve) and then around the age of sixteen there was a romance, and there continued to be on and off again for the next twenty-five years. But we never did quite get it together; something, maybe fate, would always conspire to keep us apart. Around fourteen years ago, after a really long time without seeing or hearing from Adam, and believing that that door was finally shut for good, I woke up from a dream so strong and so powerful that I had to check that it wasn't real. I'd dreamed that I'd married him. I dreamed that a few years earlier, when we had been together, we'd run away and gotten married. And then things fell apart again. My head knew that that had never happened, we had never gotten married, but my heart believed it. My heart remembered how I felt about him, and how I always have felt about him, and it wouldn't let that feeling go.

Another ten years would go by between that dream and finding him, quite by chance, again. This time we would not be parted, and four years ago we were married at last.

So as I sat in my office and thought about that dream, I thought about how even when life changes everything, everything around you, some things are so indelibly printed on your soul that they never go away. Love will always remain, whether you want it to or not. And that thought, that memory, was the very first inkling of the idea that would become *The Day We Met*.

There was another incident too: a few years earlier I almost lost my mother. My mum is an amazing woman; she was married in the fifties and was raised to be a wife and mother. For twenty-eight years that was what she did—until my dad left us. Mum had no choice but to change completely, change everything she knew. Battling grief and loss, she went out and got a job, supported my brother and me, and guided us single-handedly into adulthood. My mum brought me up to be strong and independent, to always try my best, to never give up, to believe that my gender would never prevent me from doing anything I chose to do. She encouraged me to take the chances that she never had, and she taught me how to be a mother. So when over a period of years she became increasingly ill, forgetful, and uncoordinated, with a severity that increased in slight but devastating increments, my brother and I feared the worst. She was diagnosed with high blood pressure, with having most likely suffered transient ischemic attacks (sometimes described as mini-strokes), but that never really felt right to me. I saw her change; I saw her personality descend into depression. There would be attacks when she didn't know us, when she forgot that a friend had died and would insist on ringing his wife at three in the morning to prove that I was an "evil liar." It was hard, and although she wasn't even seventy, I believed that the relentlessly cruel disease of dementia was taking a grip on her and taking her away from me. Then one Christmas she became so ill that she was rushed (against her will) to hospital. They were on the point of sending her home, deciding she had overeaten, when I insisted on a CT scan. They discovered that there was a large cyst in her brain, and she was at once rushed to another hospital, where the cyst that was putting enormous pressure on her brain was drained. I will never forget walking into her hospital room just hours after the operation: my mum, the woman I loved and admired, was sitting up in bed, talking and laughing. I had my mum back, and I thank God for it every day since. But it didn't stop me from thinking about dementia and Alzheimer's and how this devastating disease is so little understood, and I knew that one day I wanted to write a book about it as best as I could—a book that would somehow open up the mind of a sufferer and show it to the world.

Well, on that day that I remembered my dream about Adam, these two ideas collided, and Claire was born. Several months of research, writing, and rewriting followed, and I found myself pouring my own memories into *The Day We Met*. Claire's red wedding dress is my red wedding dress. Claire and Caitlin's dance to *Rhapsody in Blue* actually happened when I was a girl. My mum sends me newspaper clippings every week. (Even though I see her in person more than once a week!) I watched my little girl dance and sing solo in the school play full of fear and anxiety and then relief as she came into her own and showed me a strength I never knew she had. Those are some of my memories that are in the book, and there are others too.

So, sometimes when you are working on a novel, there occurs, so rarely, a kind of alchemy that produces from a jumble of words and ideas, thoughts and emotions, something precious. And that's how I feel about *The Day We Met*. I hope you do too.

—Rowan Coleman

questions and topics for discussion

1. A consistent thread throughout the novel is that of history repeating itself. Both Caitlin and Claire get pregnant young and without husbands, and Ruth must watch her husband and her daughter succumb to the same disease. What do you think Coleman suggests about fate? Do we have the ability to carve our own destiny? Can we be prevented from making the same mistakes that our parents and their parents made?

2. After watching Caitlin in a play, Claire realizes, "Being a mother is about protecting your children from every conceivable thing that might cause them hurt, but it's also about trusting them to live the best way for them, the best way they can; and trusting that even when you are not there to hold their hand, they can succeed." Do you agree? Was Claire right to shield Caitlin from the truth about her father? If you were Claire, what would you have done?

3. Why do you think Claire can confide in Ryan more easily than she can confide in the rest of her family? Why is an outsider more appealing to her at this time in her life?

4. At one point, Claire realizes that people have started seeing her as the crazy person, as "the one that no one looks in the eye anymore." How do you think it would feel to be aware of being a pariah? If you saw Claire in her altered state, what would you think/assume?

5. Do you agree with Caitlin's decision not to find out if she has the Alzheimer's gene? What would you have done in her situation?

6. If you and your loved ones were making a memory book of your life, what would you want to include?

7. How did you feel about Claire's relationship with Ryan before and after it was revealed that he was Greg? Were you surprised? Was Greg right to mislead her? Why is it important that she have this experience?

8. At the end, Claire says, "I did write a book. We all did. We wrote the story of our lives, and I am here, among these pages. This is where I will always be." Beyond an exercise assigned by her doctor, why do you think the book becomes so important to Claire?

9. If you knew you had early-onset Alzheimer's, would you change anything about your life?

10. As Claire starts to lose her memories, she worries that she's starting to lose hold of her identity. Do you believe identity and memory are intrinsically linked, or can they be separated?

about the author

ROWAN COLEMAN lives with her husband, and five children, in a very full house in Hertfordshire. She juggles writing novels with raising her family, which includes a very lively set of toddler twins whose main hobby is going in opposite directions. When she gets the chance, Rowan enjoys sleeping and sitting, and she loves watching films; she is also attempting to learn how to bake.

The Day We Met is Rowan's eleventh novel; others include *The Accidental Mother* and the award-winning *Dearest Rose,* which led her to become an active supporter of Refuge, the charity against domestic abuse.

Rowan does not have time for ironing.

www.rowancoleman.co.uk
@rowancoleman
Find Rowan Coleman on Facebook